SINGING INTO THE PIANO

SINGING INTO THE PIANO

—

TED MOONEY

ALFRED A. KNOPF   NEW YORK   1998

THIS IS A BORZOI BOOK
PUBLISHED BY ALFRED A. KNOPF, INC.

www.randomhouse.com

Library of Congress Cataloging-in-Publication Data

Mooney, Ted.
Singing into the piano / by Ted Mooney. — 1st ed.
p.   cm.
ISBN 0-679-41692-7
PS3563.O567S56   1998
813'.54—dc21   97-49467
CIP

Manufactured in the United States of America
First Edition

For Janet Hobhouse

SINGING INTO THE PIANO

*Le rêve de l'état est d'être seul, pendant que
le rêve de l'individu est d'être deux.*

The dream of the state is to be one, while
the dream of the individual is to be two.

JEAN-LUC GODARD

ONE EVENING, in a large city on the eastern coast of the United States, a Spanish-speaking man widely honored in both the Americas for his intelligence and probity stepped up to the dais from which he was about to address his audience and discovered that at the table nearest him—there were one hundred fifty tables in the room that had been rented for this occasion—a young woman had fallen ostentatiously asleep on the shoulder of her escort. Sleep, being as relative as most things in prosperous nations, did not seem to command her hand, however, which remained inserted well past the wrist in the opened fly of her companion's black wool trousers, where it was as calmly active as the heartbeat of an owl at dusk. This woman's escort (his name was Andrew) appeared nonplussed but attentive in equal measures to her and whatever was about to be said.

It should be mentioned at once that the speaker, Santiago Díaz, was possessed of both great delicacy and perfect teeth, so that a smile from him was a striking event. He shuffled the papers that he had brought with him and smiled.

"I was going to speak in Spanish," the distinguished man said in Spanish, "but perhaps," he went on, switching to English, "it was presumptuous of me to make a decision of that sort before joining you here."

As the man of honor spoke, Andrew became aware that a number of people seated at the tables surrounding his were half-rising from their chairs to ascertain the degree of his own exposure and the intent behind it. Only then did it occur to him to wonder why he had not put a stop to what was transpiring between him and the blond-haired woman beside him, but he saw at once that he loved her completely and that he drew pleasure recklessly from everything she did and was.

"Edie," he whispered into her ear.

She shifted so that her forehead lay flat against his shoulder and her hair hung down over his jacket's lapel like sentient drapery. Her fingertips tenderly but with increasing urgency traced the underseam of Andrew's cock. She began to snore audibly.

"When I decided to stand for the presidency of my country," the speaker went on, "it was in recognition that my people have come to a consciousness of needs—of our needs—that had till then eluded those who govern, those who have fled, and those who, like myself, were sent abroad by their parents to find answers to our country's problems. Those answers, I now see, have always lain before us in plain view."

This last phrase caused a titter of amusement in that part of the audience whose line of sight took in the spectacle Edith was creating. At her and Andrew's table, which, like all the others in the room, seated eight paying guests, a woman whose paintings were known throughout Europe and the Americas scribbled a note on her cocktail napkin and passed it to the man sitting next to her. He smiled, nodded, and passed it to the woman on his right. She collapsed in decorous giggles and handed it back.

"Edie, darling. Wake up. We're making a scene."

"I want to," she murmured in what still seemed to be sleep. "I mean I want to . . . you know."

He saw that her left nipple, as sweetly swollen as a new mushroom after rain, had come to push noticeably against the fine brown grain of her blouse.

"When I was making notes for this speech," continued Santiago Díaz, abandoning the notes before him and turning to address Edith and Andrew as if they were the only people in the room, "I sat alone at home in Mexico City, staring at my computer screen and trying, of all things, to decide the moral relationship between the words *derecho* and *obligación*."

Díaz, a tall man, paused, and after a small smirk of self-mockery repeated the two words slowly in English, looking first at Edith, then at Andrew. He seemed to be naming conditions that the two young people before him brought respectively to mind. " 'Right' and 'obligation.' "

Without moving her head, Edie whispered, "Andrew. I won't be able to stand up after." She squeezed his cock. "I'm so wet that I've made a spot." She sighed and seemed to fall back asleep. "On my skirt. People will"—she half-yawned—"*see.*"

In an attempt to calm her Andrew cupped the top of her thigh with one hand, but despite his best intentions this gesture became a caress. Fear, shame, and what might ordinarily be called judgment seemed to have left him summarily on the day he had met Edith.

"But I realized after a time that these two very abstract words had nothing to do with my country: philosophy is poor consolation to those struggling daily for their lives. So I turned off my computer and went out of my house for a walk."

Seated behind Díaz in a crescent formation that gave them no view of Andrew and Edith were nine men and women who this night made up the candidate's advance team—security specialists, campaign handlers, and, should it come to that, ministers of his cabinet. Luis Arévalo, Díaz's campaign manager and unofficially designated Minister of the Interior, began, at his superior's last words, to grow agitated. He crossed, then uncrossed, his somewhat spindly legs. A television crew had just entered the room from both of its far corners. This was in express violation of prior arrangements. *Bad enough*, thought Arévalo, *that Santiago has chosen this moment to become inspired and toss out the harmless speech I wrote for him.* Arévalo was not a calm man, but he had learned the look of calmness because he was a professional.

"Mexico and the United States have always had a troubled but dramatic relationship. I am sure I needn't remind you of our pre-revolutionary leader's proud lament for a Mexico 'so far from God, so near to the United States.' " Suddenly at a loss, Díaz looked down at his podium, where a glass of Chilean wine rested untouched, as motionless as a volcanic lake. "On my walk," he said after a moment, "I decided that perhaps the terms might now, with all due respect, be justly reversed: near to God, far from the U.S." He found himself staring at Edith and Andrew again. "That, of course, is why I am here."

To everyone's surprise and confusion, this comment produced a round of thunderous applause. Luis Arévalo, who had noticed that the television crew was attempting to set up floodlights, took advantage of the resulting pause to stand. Immediately he realized, from this new vantage point, exactly what was distracting his employer and friend. He sat back down and leaned forward to whisper into the ear of the security man on his left. He pointed discreetly at the TV crew in back.

"Andrew," Edith murmured, "Andrew, am I making you happy?"

"I don't know," Andrew answered, although he knew that she was. "Does James have a view of our table?"

Edith had come to this fund-raising event with James, Andrew's closest friend, but had contrived to switch the place cards during the cocktail hour so that she and Andrew might be seated together.

"James?" she said as if addressing a fact of life now beyond her. "No, Andrew, I need you to—"

There was now a faint but continuous hum of conversation coming from the tables behind them. Andrew did not need to turn his head to know that James could see neither him nor Edith.

"As of course you know," said Díaz, recovering his composure, "Mexico City is the largest city on the planet. But it is also one of the most intimate. Only a few minutes after I left my computer and its abstractions behind I was speaking with a woman of my country. She sat in the alley beside her home grinding cornmeal on a *metate*, a mortar and pestle no different from those used by her earliest, indeed prehistoric, ancestors. The pestle was of the kind we call *mano*—a wand of volcanic rock as long as her forearm. With what ferocious certainty she wielded it!"

Díaz broke off to gaze momentarily at the glass chandelier above him, and the hold he now had over his audience was such that most of the people present followed his glance. The chandelier was crookedly hung, its poignancy oddly increased by the layers of dust that had accumulated over recent years upon its less-than-crystalline facets.

"The true strength of Mexico, a perseverance that has sustained us for generations—I could see all that in her."

The security agent to whom Luis Arévalo had spoken gestured to another man, taller and younger than himself, his right arm in a bandage-wrapped cast that his suit jacket had been pinned back to accommodate. The pair left the stage unceremoniously to the left and right.

"She asked me," Díaz went on, "my name. She asked me whether I had any children in the *colonia*, the neighborhood, because she did not recognize me." It was well known that Díaz, though many years married, had no children—his career was said to have prohibited it—and he did not bother to recount his answer. "This woman might easily have been my grandmother, although she was not old. She did not cease working with the mortar and pestle as she spoke to me, and I realized"—he swallowed—"that she had hope of being able to place me. Of *seeing* me in some way."

Edith, with her free hand, took Andrew's nearer one and guided it up her skirt. She was wearing no underwear—she had used a garter belt for her stockings—and she was wet between her legs. Certainly she was in no normal way asleep, but—she was wearing her grandmother's necklace of silver and topaz—it occurred to her in her first reluctant lunge to consciousness that she had perhaps become dry in her assessment of herself.

"Andrew," she said, "do you remember that time in Texas I told you about? With the stop sign?"

As Andrew recalled, that time had to do with an instance of true love. "Hush, Edie," he answered, pressing his temple momentarily down upon hers, "I love you. Now hush." His finger made its way up into the humid warmth from which all that he seemed to care about now emanated. Possibly he himself was president of—or over—something not yet recognized by the world.

"I am not a lawyer," said Santiago Díaz.

Immediately, and with a satisfaction that surprised him, Andrew remembered that he himself *was* a lawyer—an attorney specializing in probate in the State of New York. Edith parted her thighs slightly. Andrew thought of the word "lava." It was superior to the word "lawyer."

"But," continued Díaz, "I saw that the law I was witness to—this woman's persistence in the face of her lot, our lot—had without my asking made me an *abogado* for the children she had already imagined me to have had." He paused to adjust the microphone but ended up only touching it. "I saw my *obligación.*"

"We can't do this without lights," the cameraman whispered to his assistant. They were standing at the back of the room. "Give me some idea of the time frame here, Valerie, okay? I mean I thought this place had already been checked out."

"The guys are on it," Valerie answered. "Any second now."

Valerie looked at the chandelier and shook her head disgustedly. The TV station had twice pulled them off this story before it had even happened, so nothing had been checked out. She saw one of the lighting crew run a cable hurriedly up a side aisle, and she set off in his direction.

"Fuck," said the cameraman, leaning back against the wall and folding his arms across his chest.

A droplet of first come broke over the head of Andrew's cock and met Edith's thumb. She rubbed this evidence of herself gently back into him—wetness for wetness—and the two lovers then relaxed for a moment. Together they owned a wave beyond the seventh one, some mass that would eventually crash upon this beach where they now found themselves. There was no point in worrying about anything until then.

Santiago Díaz gazed again down at Edith and Andrew. He understood that it would not be a useful political gesture to speak about God in front of the people assembled before him, but he was reminded of God, and of what the woman in Mexico City had spoken to him about, by—he groped through the languages he knew for the proper word—the "sheerness" of what he was witnessing. Had he already used that word, "witnessing"? Certainly the word "sheerness" was stupidity itself. He put his hand in the pocket of his suit pants, as he had been told by both his mother and his campaign manager never to do.

"But I am not telling you," he went on, "about 'Mother Mexico' or an imaginary thing like that. I am telling you that when this woman looked at me, trying to recognize me, while I tried to imagine my *obligación*, she brought the pestle down so hard upon the *metate* that it split in half."

Arévalo's men walked quietly up the side aisles. The object of their movement was a gray metal box suspended at shoulder height from the wall that separated the lecture hall from its offices.

"It was a stone *metate*," Díaz said. "A bowl made of volcanic stone."

In his seat, at the opposite side of the room from Andrew and Edie but considerably behind them so he had little view of anything, James drew a series of linked hexagons on the back of his place card. Edith's assigned place beside him had been taken by a woman whose hair was vaguely familiar to him—from Cable Network News, he decided. Smiling bemusedly to himself, James wrote the word "stop" in the last hexagon.

"When she saw that she had broken her mortar," Díaz continued, "this woman stood up to see how bad the damage was. She showed no irritation." Díaz resisted the impulse to touch his brilliantined hair, which he knew remained perfectly in place. "And I found myself wondering how often she had been witness to broken things."

"Goddamnit, Val," said the cameraman under his breath. "We're missing all the good shit. We got to *move.*"

But his assistant was right beside him. "Moving, boss, moving." She touched his shoulder.

"Edie," breathed Andrew. "You're going to make me come."

"Come with *me*," she whispered. "With *me.*" These words were an absentminded kind of song. Andrew already knew from the way she butted her head almost imperceptibly against his neck that she had by now begun to feel the last undertow that would feed the wave that together they had made and bought.

A gringo slut, thought Arévalo. *Santiago has been around the world but what is this way that he can forget our country's future at the sight of a spoiled* yanqui *whore?* The answer came to Arévalo immediately: Santiago Díaz was confident. At this recognition, confidence flowed into Arévalo as well, and he leaned back in his chair. As befitted his occupation, Arévalo was able, when he understood the reasons for events, to feel a great anticipatory affection for the future and everyone included in it.

"The cornmeal this woman had been grinding had spilled through the broken mortar into the dust of the street—lost and wasted. About this misfortune she said nothing. She stepped around the broken mortar, and came up to me, very close, with her hands on her hips. She looked at me." Díaz looked at Edith and Andrew, and he was momentarily overcome by a longing to be with—what? His wife? His country?

But he knew that what he wanted to be with was himself. No doubt this meant he really was about to become president of Mexico. But not before he had finished this story he had not meant to tell.

We really are going to come together, thought Andrew. *Right here.* He closed his eyes, then opened them again.

Edith tried to think about her purse, which she had unaccountably left upon the strings of the open piano which Díaz's advance team had rolled to the wall by the lecture hall's offices. *I mean, how come?* was as close as she could get to this thought. *It was a grand piano,* she remembered, letting it go at that.

Andrew knew that he was behaving weakly, but the sensation was one of having almost unlimited power. Unqualified power. He locked eyes with Díaz. Someone had to know what was going on around here, though it was hard to say exactly who that might be.

At that moment the television lights came grandly on. The TV news team moved with ducked heads past long-uncleaned, elaborately framed portraits of South American heroes and conquerors. And as if caught in the act of savoring an illicit pleasure—though no one present could have said what it was—more than half the audience made a show of staring distractedly at these paintings.

Díaz blinked in the sudden luminescence. He spoke. "This woman, the one I am describing to you, looked back over her shoulder at the ruined mortar, then she said, 'You must know my grandson, Zavalito. Maybe you have heard him on the radio. He sings like an angel.' "

Díaz paused to show he knew the name Zavalito, the personality represented by the name. If his listeners did not know the voice of Zavalito, Santiago Díaz's pause existed to suggest, they were not fully ready to accept what he wished to tell them.

What is this shit he is saying? thought Arévalo, fixing his eyes first on Díaz, then on a poorly painted portrait of Simón Bolívar in the room's middle distance. Perhaps, Arévalo considered, he had not been strong enough in advising his friend, the presidential candidate. To disguise this self-doubt from himself Arévalo touched his suit's breast pocket. He wanted to see if his passport was on his person.

Love is really a kind of come-on, thought Andrew. *Isn't it?*

I don't care what else, thought Edith. *I want to come with him.*

Arévalo's men had by now converged upon the gray metal box that had been the target of their movement. A loop of heavy-gauge wire, painted the same gray as the box, stood out from one side of it like the outline of an ear. Considering it, the men conferred.

James put away his pen, stood up, and, excusing himself, left the hall.

Santiago Díaz drew the kind of breath that a singer might take before a cherished but difficult passage.

Feeling Andrew come in her hand—a series of hot urgent jets that were accompanied by only the quietest of sighs on his part—Edith bit down hard on her lower lip and came as well.

"This woman turned on me with a rage that I understood at once," Díaz finished. "She approached me until her face was but a few centimeters from mine and said, 'Tell me this, you who have no children, where in all the world is the father that deserves a son like my Zavalito?' "

Then one of Arévalo's men pulled the switch on the fuse box and every light in the room went out.

Some minutes later, when the first of the flickering candelabra were hurried into the lecture hall, Santiago Díaz could see immediately—though he could think of no reason, decent or prurient, why he should notice—that the chairs where Edith and Andrew had moments earlier made love before his eyes were now empty.

Beneath his fingers, the paper on which his speech was written felt like dead palm fronds. He sighed and let his eyes rove the room. He had lost his real audience.

"That is why I am standing for the presidency of Mexico," said Díaz to no one in particular.

————

"TAXI!" called Andrew.

"No," said Edith. She was not quite falling from his arms.

"Yo!" shouted Andrew. "Taxi!"

A large, rat-trap-shaped vehicle veered with unlikely grace across the avenue, stopped in front of them, and popped loose its locks.

Andrew opened the cab's door. Edith, who Andrew could not help but notice did indeed have a wet spot, tadpole-shaped, on the back of her skirt, slid with perfect propriety into the offered seat. She had an affinity for taxis.

When Andrew was seated beside her, she turned to him as if she had not seen him for some time. She rearranged her necklace so that the clasp was lopsidedly visible near her right shoulder. A brief consultation with the cab's rearview mirror made it clear to her that she could not gracefully consider her makeup situation at the moment. "Where are we going?" she asked.

An immense current of tenderness passed between the two of them, causing each brief embarrassment.

"It's Kevin," said Andrew. "I forgot his baby-sitter had to leave at ten."

Edith saw from the LCD clock on the driver's sun visor that it was ten-fifteen.

Kevin was Andrew's son by his first marriage.

"Andrew," said Edith, resting her head again upon his shoulder, "we'll never be done with each other, will we? With loving each other, I mean." She sighed because she knew it was an inadequate thing to say. From several points of view they had just made the future of their love unbearable to anyone but themselves.

Putting an arm around her, Andrew drew Edith still closer to him. "Two bank robbers in bed," he whispered into her ear. "What could be safer?"

"Nothing," she answered.

"Marry me," he said. His own words astonished him enough that he pulled slightly away to look at her.

"Okay," Edith responded after a moment. She looked a little scared. "Yes. As soon as possible."

Another dozen blocks passed before Andrew looked up from her. It was hard to see exactly where they were. "Anywhere around here is fine," Andrew told the cabdriver, pushing some money through the plastic security window.

On the street, the wind had picked up very suddenly, and there were sheets of crumpled newspaper blowing around like oil-damaged seagulls. Andrew held the cab door open for Edith, but no sooner had she emerged from the vehicle than she lunged back in to grope fruitlessly about the floor and seat. When she got out again, she turned to Andrew, and, in a gesture he had not seen till then, pressed her forearms together before her, wrists beneath her chin, so that taking her into his arms he enfolded her completely.

"Oh, Andrew. I left my purse back there."

"We'll call," he said. "It'll be okay. Come upstairs."

And although she had had very little to drink at the banquet hall, her lively behavior notwithstanding, Edith now stumbled half a step away from Andrew, half a step back, took three shallow breaths, and fainted dead away in his arms.

This had never happened to Andrew before, but he had seen it in movies. He carried her into his building, a pre–World War I affair of dark stone, elderly Viennese women, and the hopeful children of well-educated men and women. Andrew's elevator man at that hour was a Pole who had seen many things and spoke about them with humor in five languages. Shyly, Andrew hoped that the two of them might make sense of the woman in his arms, but of course making sense of what he carried was his own responsibility. The elevator man said only, "You are always surprising, Andrew. I will see you tomorrow."

Andrew thanked him. "You're surprising, too."

He edged Edie out of the elevator and surprised himself by managing simultaneously to hold her, find his keys, and open the door. All the lights in his apartment were turned up, somewhat alarmingly, to their full brightness.

"Daddy!" said his son, running full tilt toward him. Kevin was three years old, but like many children of divorce he was precociously aware of time's passage and its possible meanings. So when he saw that his father was carrying an unconscious woman in his arms, he fell abruptly still to take in the spectacle.

Andrew put Edith gently down upon the once-cream-colored sofa, then bent to embrace his son, whom he loved thoroughly.

"Who's that, Daddy?"

"That's Edith. She's asleep now because it's late." From Andrew's bedroom came the sound of the TV, tuned down very low to gunfire and rock music that had already been stylishly muted by the producers. "You should be asleep too, bucko," Andrew continued, lifting his son up in his arms. "Where's your aunt Sarah?"

Toward the back of the apartment, the toilet flushed.

Kevin turned his face guiltily away from Andrew's. "Aunt Sarah wouldn't tickle me," he said.

There was a creak from the bathroom door as it opened, and at the sound Edith sat as suddenly and serenely upright as if she had been living in the apartment, which she had not till that moment seen, all her life. "Wouldn't tickle you?" she asked Kevin. "Well, maybe she didn't think you were ready for the extraspecial Indian tickle. You have to pass certain tests, you know."

As the child fell silent at this intimation of unsuspected bounty, Sarah, Andrew's younger sister, appeared in the hallway. She was a heavyset, dark-haired woman, whose prominent cheekbones did in fact give her the look of a Native American.

"Andrew," she said, taking in the sight of Edith as placidly as possible while stifling a yawn. "We were beginning to despair."

"Sorry," he answered. "Everything kept running over. I mean, I was going to call, but in the end it just seemed faster to get here."

Edith made a fluttery movement toward finding her lipstick,

but she then remembered it remained in her purse, somewhere back at the banquet hall. So she stood and addressed herself brightly to Sarah. "Hi, I'm Edith Emerson. You must be—"

"Sarah. Andrew's devoted sister. Nice to meet you."

"Indian tickle?" said Kevin warily.

"Lovely to meet *you*. I'm afraid it's my fault we were late."

"Oh, no big deal," said Sarah, "Really." Then turning fully toward Andrew and Kevin she drew a wide-toothed comb from the back pocket of her jeans and began sleepily combing her hair. "Listen, Andrew, I told Judith I'd be back home in time to take her to a club later. Everything okay?"

He held Kevin in his arms. "Yeah. Just fine, really. Thanks."

Sarah smiled, then walked over to Edith and shook her hand. "Good night," she said, then almost turned away before adding, "Oh, by the way. What's an Indian tickle? Andrew's going to be living with that one for at least twenty-four waking hours."

Edith laughed, put her hand to her mouth. "An Indian tickle? That's when you, the ticklee, have to keep your eyes open through the whole thing. And—this is supposed to be the hard part—you have to try not to laugh."

Suddenly the three adults were looking at Kevin as if he were a postcard they had just received from someone they used to know and had always wondered about. Kevin had fallen deeply asleep. He was snoring softly. The sound created a silence in which no one looked at anyone but him.

SANTIAGO DÍAZ had attained the celebrity that had placed him on the dais that night by the worldly disorder that is in public life called politics but that in private life has no simple name.

Although he had indeed been born in Mexico City and sent abroad for his secondary education (to England in fact), he had confounded both his parents and himself by failing to achieve the glittering academic success his Mexican teachers had predicted for him. At the same time, however, he became, almost without noticing it, the finest soccer player ever to attend this centuries-old institution. He was shortly made team captain, was admired by all, and when it became time to decide whether to advance to university or return to his homeland, he decided, with little deliberation, upon the latter course.

His reputation as a sports prodigy had preceded him in his repatriation. After a lengthy dinner at one of Mexico City's finest restaurants and a nightcap at its best brothel, he was persuaded, to his parents' unspoken dismay, to join the nation's World Cup team. After only half a season, he was also made captain. By then he was being written about daily in the sports section of Mexico's main newspaper, but his international renown did not really begin until five months later. That year, when the World Cup was held in Italy, the entire United States team was kidnapped and held hostage by a confederation of disenfranchised political groups whose methods were as deplorable as their cause was just.

What had made Santiago Díaz famous was this: When the first demands by the so-called terrorists were delivered by videotape to the news media of Italy and, shortly after, to the world, the leader of the hostage takers, an Algerian who spoke immaculate French, was photographed wearing a tee shirt with a photo-dye-transfer image of Santiago Díaz on it. The shirt showed the Mexican soccer hero leaping into the air, a shower of sweat bursting almost cartoonishly from his forehead. He had just scored the decisive goal in a match against Argentina that Mexico had been given no chance whatsoever of winning.

Once the videotaped demands had been reviewed, antiterrorist analysts from several countries, including the United States, suggested that Díaz be put forward as intermediary between the hostages and their captors. Díaz was approached, he accepted, and when the hostage takers also agreed to the arrangement, stipulating only that they be given a live TV camera to document the proceedings, negotiations began. Satellite TV broadcast every shaky moment between captors and hostages at an undisclosed location fastidiously equipped with soccer posters and automatic weapons. After three days, the hostages were freed, their aggrieved kidnappers were spirited off to a neutral country, and Santiago Díaz was shown by newspaper polls to be better known to the American public than their own Vice President, himself a former astronaut.

Once during these three days of clumsy torment, while Santiago Díaz sat napping in a chair, one of the terrorists had with a single shot blown to pieces a soccer ball lying near the athlete's feet. Waking, Díaz had done nothing more than open his eyes and look at the gunman. This sequence was famous everywhere there were televisions.

"IT IS TIME," Santiago Díaz now concluded, scanning the banquet crowd still gathered before him, "for the two hands of the Americas to grasp one another in mutual respect.

"We have complained too long," he added, "that our borders are porous when it is the skin of our hands that breathes."

Díaz looked up long enough to note that Arévalo had once again left the podium and was gathered with several of his men by the hall's grand piano. The instrument had been pushed up against the wall, and they were peering into its opened top as if viewing a corpse to which they were distastefully related.

When Arévalo met Díaz's gaze and drew his finger across his throat in the gesture of "cut everything short," Díaz felt his heart leap. He had always admired the American football term "sudden death" and relished the redoubled vigor such immediacy—the next point scored meaning victory—gave a match's final minutes. Besides, nothing in his experience, either as a soccer player or as a man, had led him to believe that matters ever ended in a draw.

He shuffled his papers and skipped to the last page of his speech. Whatever was written there, he was quite certain that he could make it say what he meant.

"I detest nationalism," he said, "but I detest also poverty, colonialism, and the lack of mutuality among nations."

He hesitated, touching his ear.

"It is not always true that nations can choose to be prosperous."

There was applause. Díaz was astonished. He understood that he was becoming, like most men, a benign impostor of something he had once intended to be. Perhaps he had been an impostor for some time. Perhaps he had always been a politician.

"I detest political violence," he said, flinging his head upward suddenly as if to free it from the sweat depicted on the famous tee shirt, "but I detest also the suffering of those given no alternatives."

Díaz saw that a *gringo* policeman with a dog had discreetly joined his men at the piano.

"I can find no respect," he said, "for the hand that lacks the courage to seize love, self-interest, and perdition so that others need not fear being strangled by careless fingers."

Arévalo, still standing by the piano, stared at him.

Díaz said: "There are no careless fingers in this room."

After the slightest of pauses, the crowd, clearly relieved, rose to their feet and erupted in applause. Díaz spent some time nodding appreciatively to them before a female aide came to his side and whispered Arévalo's message into his ear. Díaz grimaced, then turned back to the microphone.

"Thank you. Thank you for your support this evening. I am told this auditorium has been scheduled for another event in a few minutes, and we must now retire to the building next door for an informal reception. It is my privilege to have been allowed to speak to you here."

Released at last from their charge of civic duty and transnational self-interest, the members of the audience redoubled their applause. Díaz smiled but said no more.

Within fifteen minutes the hall was empty.

———

IT HAD long been Arévalo's practice to secure two venues for any public event that had been put under his authority. Safety, he believed, begot decorum, and in most cases vice versa. Accordingly, when he had discovered, two days ago, that the banquet hall abutted a prestigious uptown art gallery, he had contacted the director, arranged for a security guard to remain on the premises, and, with the help of the U.S. State Department, acquainted himself with the space's surveillance system. Consequently, the guests who had moments ago been sitting comfortably at their tables next door now wandered about these elegant white rooms with plastic champagne cups in their hands. On the walls: black-and-white photographs of eerily beautiful children wandering naked among dogs and cars in the rural United States.

After receiving the congratulations and enthusiastically uninformed advice of his well-wishers, Santiago Díaz discovered Arévalo by his side. He hesitated, surveying the gallery as he took a sip from his glass, then spoke into his aide's ear. "What was the problem next door really?"

"We thought we had found a bomb."

"But it was not a bomb."

"It turned out to be only a woman's purse." Arévalo permitted himself a chuckle. "A very full woman's purse."

"Strange," answered Díaz. And although he understood that Arévalo meant, by his choice of words, to suggest that the woman in question might be pregnant, his own response had nothing to do with such a possibility.

He cupped one elbow in the palm of his hand and with two fingers covered the tuck of his upper lip. It came to him that he had by chance seen this woman put her evening bag rather carelessly into the piano before dinner.

"Luis," Díaz then said, dropping his arms to his sides in dignified submission, "forgive the inconvenience, but I would like to see this woman's purse."

"¿Cómo no?" Arévalo gave a nod to the operative hovering just behind him, and the man set out for the door.

Waiting, the two friends lingered beside a photograph of a naked blond girl child from Louisiana. As depicted, she stood before an American car (it was hand-colored blue) that had been manufactured before her own mother had been born. Part of the genius of the photograph was that the girl appeared to be aware of the car's antiquity but not of her own youth. Also she had a smudge of coal dust on her cheek.

"My friend," said Arévalo, drawing nearer to Díaz, "I am certain there are no explosives in the purse, but I am concerned to know why you wish to see it. This is a woman with whom you are acquainted?"

"No."

"Her name is Edith Emerson. Circumstantial evidence suggests she is pregnant. You understand my worries."

"Yes. But rest assured: they may be set aside."

"I am glad." Arévalo exercised his eyebrows in an impression of introspection, which he habitually confused with socially expressed sadness and regret. "As you know, I myself have not always been so careful."

"You are a man of the world, Luis. I would have no one else as my campaign manager."

"We make each other laugh," said Arévalo, hoping this was true.

"Yes." Díaz drank from his own glass for the first time. He was beginning to relax truly. "It has always been my feeling that if you cannot say 'fuck the world' once in a while, you are certain to be fucked by it."

Arévalo bowed in grave agreement. "I am glad," he said, "that we have both kept our senses of humor. Because now I am certain that you will not be alarmed to hear that Edith Emerson was the woman sitting directly before you in the banquet hall. The man with whom she came to dinner owns this gallery, but the man with whom she was sitting, if I may put it that way, is unknown to us."

"By 'us' you mean security."

"Of course."

"But if by 'us' you meant two old friends from home?"

Arévalo smoothed his mustache in affected consideration. "Then I would say this man is a prick of no importance."

Díaz looked at his watch, an admittedly effete gift from his wife. It had a silver face, needle-slim silver hands, and a numberless dial so flawless that in certain lights it was unreadable—rather like his wife, Díaz sometimes told himself.

"It is time for me to make my farewells, Luis. When the purse surfaces I would be grateful if you would indulge this impulse of mine to understand our *yanqui* friends."

"There is a small office at the back of this room."

"As always with such rooms."

They laughed together. In the past two years they had spent an absurd amount of time in back offices, windowless rooms, safe houses, and pointless speculation.

"I will wait for you there, in the office," said Santiago Díaz, who had not the least idea why he wished to see the contents of this woman Edith's evening bag. But now he found himself saying: "Is a quarter of an hour too soon?"

Arévalo shrugged. He wanted a cigarette. "This purse you will have in ten minutes."

"Thank you," said Santiago Díaz in English.

And as Arévalo, whose ungainliness was frequently misleading, set out to supervise the recovery of Edith's purse, Díaz lent himself to the company. He kissed the cheeks of the taut-faced women who had doubtless impressed their husbands into attendance tonight. He shook the hands of the husbands, who would be writing checks to his campaign for their own reasons.

It came to him that he missed his wife, who was in Paris. Apropos of nothing, Díaz was reminded that she smoked two brands of cigarettes, one much milder than the other, so that she could more concretely savor her mood. This duality had had an important role in his deciding to marry her.

Of course, he had always loved the name Mercedes.

When Díaz entered the gallery office, ten minutes later, Edith

Emerson's beaded evening purse lay empty on the director's desk, its contents fanned out decorously beside it. A lipstick, a mirror, a jury summons, a comb—the things evoked the woman. Díaz had once sought out the owner of a purse he had found in a taxi, and the experience had taught him that a woman's purse carried more psychic weight than was wise to tamper with. Condoms, throat lozenges, a half-consumed wheel of birth-control pills. Díaz ran his eyes over these things without touching them. A learner's permit to operate a motor vehicle, a pen and notebook, forty-eight dollars U.S., three hair elastics, the torn packaging of a home pregnancy test.

Clearing his throat self-consciously, Díaz picked up Edith's driver's license. He gave it a cursory examination, recited her address sotto voce, and asked Arévalo, who had retired discreetly to one corner, whether she had been contacted.

"*Claro*. Her telephone answering machine is on, but she does not seem to have reached home yet, if that is her destination. We left no message."

Arévalo had had to scrape tomato pulp off the *yanqui* woman's purse after retrieving it from the Dumpster.

Then, because he knew it was fruitless to resist his own intuitive impulses and at the same time unconscionable to send his closest aide from the room while he indulged them, Díaz picked up the tiny notebook.

The first page was blank. He flipped quickly through the rest and was about to set the slim volume down in disappointment when a folded leaf of onionskin fluttered out to land primly upright on the desk.

Near the top of the paper, the date, time, and location of the banquet were written in a hand that struck Díaz as exotic—at once angular and elegant. Farther down the page he discovered his own name, twice underlined and seemingly transformed by the penmanship into astronomical notation.

Díaz swallowed. He felt it incumbent upon him to betray no emotion before Arévalo, since Arévalo had certainly already examined this note in detail. In any case, Díaz did not know what it was he himself was experiencing beyond simple physical agitation.

"You have no doubt done a background check on this woman. Anything to worry about?"

"As far as we can tell, certainly not."

Continuing his perusal of the note, Díaz quickly discovered that the focus of this woman's private attentions was elsewhere than on himself. At seven places on the paper, in varying formulations, the name of Andrew Caldwell appeared—"Andrew C.," "A.C.," "Andrew" (this one circled with a looped garland that suggested either a daydream or a phone conversation), "Call A.," and so on. To the first of these notations a local phone number was appended.

Díaz removed from his pocket a pen and his own leatherbound notebook, in which he wrote Andrew's full name and number. When he was finished, he asked Arévalo to restore Edith Emerson's possessions to her purse.

There was a faint odor of violets in the room.

"Luis," said Santiago Díaz, staring soberly down at the desk before them when it was clear. "I am beginning to think we may win this election."

"The chickens are hatching."

"Are you frightened?"

Arévalo laughed. "No, but my wife is, and I am frightened of her." It was well known that the latter confession was untrue.

"We will have to work harder than I imagined."

" 'Overtime,' yes. But a *gringo* concept. A luxury."

"About that there can be no doubt."

Arévalo allowed a small pause, then placed his hands delicately in the pockets of his jacket. "We are more than halfway there," he said.

Díaz nodded.

"Now if you will excuse me, I must take one last look around the gallery. Then we can all go to bed."

When Arévalo was gone, Díaz quietly closed the door. He looked at the telephone that lay on the desk as if it were a bird announcing a continent to a long-delayed mariner. Not that he had ever actually believed in the details of the Columbus story.

He dialed Andrew's number without having to refer to his notebook.

A woman answered.

"I am trying to reach Edith Emerson," said Díaz.

"This is she." Wearing nothing but her grandmother's necklace, Edith propped herself up on one elbow and considered Andrew. It disturbed her to be getting phone calls here and at such an hour, but on the whole she found that sort of disturbance engaging.

"How did you get my number, and who are you, please?"

"Forgive me for intruding. It is Santiago Díaz. You were at the dinner tonight?"

"Yes." She ran her hand across Andrew's night table for a package of cigarettes. There were none.

"You left your purse at the hall."

She laughed. "Yes. I'm amazed you found it." She drew Andrew's nearer hand to her breast. "I'm told I leave things in eccentric places."

"I could not honestly disagree. And I'm sorry, but my security people felt they had to go through your purse, and that is why I have your telephone number."

"It's not my number."

"I understand."

Kevin was asleep in the far room. Andrew made a move to leave the bed, but his cock was still hard, and Edith took hold of it in a way that he understood at once to mean that she was afraid and in love with him. He had a history of exotic women, and he realized that she would be the cap to it, one way or another. Everything was difficult without being impossible.

"I guess, you know, I'll need my purse back," Edith said.

"Of course," Díaz replied, looking at his watch, noticing it had stopped. "Will you and your friend Señor Caldwell do me the honor of having breakfast with me tomorrow morning so that I may return it? I am staying on East Seventy-second Street, at the residence of Mexico's ambassador to the UN."

Díaz had not known he was going to make this invitation, but having done so he realized that from the beginning he had intended nothing else. Suddenly he was reminded, without knowing why, of the terrorist who in Italy had shot the soccer ball to pieces on the floor before him. Perhaps the same impulsiveness had obtained. Perhaps it was not really impulsiveness.

"Is eight o'clock all right?"

"Yes. I mean, I'll have to ask Andrew, but I think so." Andrew was nuzzling the armpit that in order to hold the phone she had left open to him. He could hear everything on both ends of the conversation.

"Eight o'clock is fine," he said.

"Eight o'clock is fine."

Díaz gave her the address and added, "Such serendipitous pleasures are rarer as one gets older. Or one's eye for them grows more discriminating." He left a little pause which Edith did not fill. "Good night, Miss Emerson. My regards to your friend."

She hung up the phone slowly and turned to Andrew. He looked to her like a man she wished to spend her life with. Was this because he didn't blink before her gaze? Had she already said something like that? "Santiago Díaz sends you his regards," she said for want of anything better.

"Thanks. I'll return them at breakfast." He smiled to himself. For the first time in a long while events seemed to have a logic of their own.

"Kevin's out like a light," Edie said.

"Too much excitement," he replied.

Some seconds passed. Then she said, "Fuck me, Andrew."

But he already was.

THE FOLLOWING morning Santiago Díaz rose at six, as was his custom, took a very cold shower, shaved, brushed his teeth, and dressed.

In North America and Europe he favored a blue suit and red jacquard tie, though he was aware that this had recently been the uniform of the West's business and communications elite. The look was flattering to him in a way he knew to be odd. Because he was an unexpectedly retired soccer player, his muscles were in different places than those of his suit's exemplars.

In all countries, Díaz was amused by the way Arévalo unfailingly slept till at least nine and emerged from his bedroom wearing only pants and an empty shoulder holster. Often this entrance was preceded by the sound of a woman leaving the premises by another exit.

Also, Arévalo snored.

For much of the time that they had known each other Arévalo had been Díaz's closest, if sometimes improbable, friend.

"We'll be having two guests at breakfast," Díaz told the steward. "Acquaintances of mine."

Three newspapers in as many languages had been laid out for him on the mahogany coffee table that occupied one end of the brownstone's rather narrow briefing room. There had been an earthquake in Chile. In his notebook Díaz reminded himself to send a message of regret—aid, if it could be afforded. If it was his to give.

The notion of possession disturbed him briefly. Of course, all sense and exercise of possession was arbitrary.

He was embarrassingly in love with his wife.

"My friends will eat whatever you're preparing for the rest of us," Díaz told the steward in passing. "But I must speak to them in private."

"*No problema.* I'll set up three tables."

"Is Luis awake?"

The man's snores were audible; after a moment the other two men gave in to soundless laughter.

"I'll wake him," said the steward.

"No." Díaz put a finger over his upper lip to suppress a smile. "But maybe it should be four tables."

When Edith and Andrew arrived at the brownstone on East Seventy-second Street, shortly after this exchange, a sidewalk surveillance camera swung leisurely around to examine them with the exactitude and perfect lack of discernment for which it had been invented. After a short interval the house security guard threw open the door to admit the couple, and Santiago Díaz stepped forward to greet them.

"I am so glad you could join me on such short notice," he said.

In fact Andrew had had some difficulty in arranging for the Mexican nanny to come to work earlier than usual that morning, and Edith had adopted an unnecessary (and thus to Andrew definitely suspect) forgetfulness regarding her behavior the night before. By now, however, they had both settled down.

The Mexican ambassador's residence was a narrow building of five stories and half a city block's depth. As Santiago Díaz conducted his guests up a carpeted staircase to the dining room on the second floor, Andrew's hand fell lightly upon the small of Edith's back—as if, it occurred to him, to protect her. Not from the perils of a social breakfast, of course, but from the consequences of other people's claims on them. The grace with which she had resisted James's campaign of seduction now seemed both resourceful and dangerous. Andrew's own clumsiness in marrying and so soon divorcing Susannah, Kevin's mother, presented more obvious difficulties.

The dining room was fitted with a pair of floor-to-ceiling mahogany doors, which Díaz opened for his visitors without flourish. Although he was in some respects a vain man, he had in recent years shed most gestures of physical embellishment except those addressed to his wife.

"Please," he said.

Andrew and Edith entered ahead of him.

Four tables had been set for breakfast—three in one corner of the room, the fourth, somewhat larger, in the corner diagonally opposite. On the farthest chair, the one set to survey the room, hung Edith's purse.

"I'm afraid my speech last night was not my best," said Díaz, shrugging. "It really is like sports; some nights you can do no wrong; others . . ."

"The speech was wonderful," said Edith quietly. "People were actually listening. I'm serious."

She had not decided whether she was serious or not.

Andrew knew this. It was one of the things to understand and cherish about Edith that she hedged her bets in a very professional manner.

As they walked toward the table obviously meant for them, Andrew said, "When I was in high school, I played a little soccer myself. I wasn't really any good, but I remember liking how, when you had the ball, you could control the pace of the game for a short while. Nothing that counted too much, but you could slow things down or speed them up."

Looking down, Andrew saw his shoes needed shining. "Listening to you last night, I thought professional politics must be like that."

Díaz beamed. "Yes, very much like that." He could see they were going to have an interesting breakfast. "And what do you do now?"

"I'm a lawyer with a specialty in probate," said Andrew. "Someone who speeds up the exit from the stadium after the game is over. Really over."

Estate attorneys were the object of some condescension from their colleagues-at-law, and Andrew, routinely watchful for it, now met Díaz's gaze. He was surprised by the gentleness he saw there.

"It is hard to be witty in the face of death and money," said Díaz, seating himself more abruptly than his natural sense of propriety might have dictated. "I feel privileged to make your acquaintance." Distractedly, he made a gesture of abundance toward Edith and Andrew. "Please join me. Life here is often boring, and when it is not, let's not waste time."

Andrew and Edith, momentarily silenced by the passion of these words, took their seats. As she removed her purse from her chair back, it occurred to Edith—who, as a woman with unusually permeable boundaries, was aware of this trait's possible existence in others—that Díaz might have taken something from her. She gave him a speculative glance whose import, she saw, was understood at once by the two men flanking her.

A silverish dust fell through the air.

"You are a gentleman," she said to Díaz.

"Thank you. And I assure you my wife would disagree."

"More's the pity." Edith had never used the phrase before, but it caused all three of them to laugh with surprising force.

Breakfast—sliced fruits and two rough-grained breads—was served.

For some time, no one spoke. Then Díaz, after drawing his napkin across his lips with something of a flourish after all, addressed himself to Andrew.

"Señor Caldwell," he said, putting down his cutlery. "From what you said—and needless to say, from what I saw last night—it strikes me that you are a very brave man."

"Oh no." Andrew laughed. "Bravery I don't claim."

Andrew put down his cutlery. "Here's something, though. I had dinner the other night with a friend, someone I don't know very well. We were talking about this and that, nothing serious—music, I think. Out of the blue she decided I was a hedonist—a 'complete' hedonist, to use her term. She told me that there are far fewer of us out there than people think." He swallowed a slice of papaya. "She scared me. I'd never thought of myself that way."

"So my case is proven," said Díaz. "All hedonists are brave, though, alas, the reverse is not true. Brave men have usually known fear but generally forbid themselves to admit it. They are less acquainted with pleasure."

Lifting her knife as if to admire its silver pattern, Edith ran a quick lipstick check. "Andrew will go as far as any situation de-mands," she said. "Then he'll go a little further, to make sure that what he does is his."

She speared a crescent of mango with her fork. "That's why I love him."

A second silence fell across the table.

"That's why I'm going to marry him."

The windows of the dining room had been thrown open to the day's warm air, and almost as soon as Edith had finished speak-ing a sparrow came fluttering into the branches of the ficus tree that occupied that corner of the room. Then, after a moment of bewilderment, it departed through the same window by which it had entered.

Until that instant Andrew had not really been sure that Edie remembered accepting his marriage proposal of the previous night. Again he was stunned with happiness. Díaz noticed his pleasure with approval.

Tearing off a piece of bread, he said, "My own marriage has brought me far more happiness than I ever enjoyed as a young stud—please forgive the term. The joys of marriage are not something people are eager to tell you about." He looked from Andrew to Edith and back again. "My congratulations."

"Thank you," said Edith and Andrew simultaneously.

The dining room door opened, and Arévalo, dressed in his customary pants and empty shoulder holster, ambled toward their table, yawning. When he saw that his friend and employer had company, he retreated quickly. *"Perdón, perdón,"* he whispered. "I had no idea."

Díaz laughed. "That is Luis Arévalo, one of my oldest friends, and perhaps, should I be elected, Mexico's next Minister of the Interior. Please forgive him. He is something of an exhibitionist."

"Really."

"You sound unconvinced, Señor Caldwell."

"It's a funny term," Andrew replied, addressing himself to the sliced fruit on his plate. "I mean, it's so elastic."

"Oh, stop it, Andrew. This is only *breakfast!*" Edith seemed on the verge of some obscure irritation. "No irony before noon. Tell us more, Santiago."

"Many politicians are exhibitionists," said Díaz, regarding his table companions with an interest he didn't bother to conceal. "So are most actors, most sports stars. I'm sure we can all agree on that."

"Well, they all exhibit *tendencies* toward exhibitionism anyway," said Andrew, who received from Edith an immediate kick to the shin.

Díaz laughed. He saw that he liked Andrew and was liked in return.

Turning to Edith, he said, "Please excuse my asking, but do you work? You seem to me like a woman who works among men."

"I'm a translator at the United Nations," she said. This was true.

"What a coincidence! I'm due there today to make a small speech. What languages do you work with?"

"French," she said.

This was not true.

Andrew, who had quickly become used to her ways, paid no mind to this lie. Edith was employed at the UN to translate from English to Spanish and vice versa, although she could indeed speak French fluently.

"*Tant pis,*" said Díaz, frowning in mock disappointment. "Perhaps Señor Caldwell and the not so United Nations would have allowed me to borrow you this afternoon."

"But you speak perfect English."

"I will be addressing this group, unlike the one last night, in Spanish. It is a more formal occasion, even if it's also a pro forma one. Spanish is required, I think."

"What *I* think is that you preferred being a soccer star to being a presidential candidate," Edith answered, a little coldly.

Díaz winked at Andrew. "Again," he said, "allow me to offer my congratulations. She is a wildcat."

"That's her," answered Andrew without missing a beat.

And perhaps because what Edith had said was true, Díaz was reminded of a time, shortly after he had married Mercedes, when her cousin, a beautiful girl, had lived with them in Mexico City. The cousin slept on the living-room sofa, and Santiago had taken it upon himself to wake her each morning by standing naked over her and dangling his cock in her face. Understandably less amused than he by this routine, the girl had lain in wait for him one morning, feigning sleep, then leapt up as if to bite off the offending member. Santiago had howled in surprise and run back to his marriage bed in such a state of prudish outrage that Mercedes had tormented him for weeks. It was a family story that even now brought a blush to his face.

"You know," said Andrew, putting down the glass of pineapple juice he had just drained, "probably the three of us—you, me, and Edie, I mean—are really kind of alike. Don't you think?"

"You have my fullest attention," Díaz answered.

"Well, when you said that about bravery, I thought, of course, about that TV clip of you and the kidnappers. The guy shooting the soccer ball right in front of you? It's an iconic moment, right? And then Edie saying what she did about how you probably preferred being a soccer star to being a presidential candidate. Maybe true, maybe not. But this I'm sure about: None of the three of us really believes in bravery. What we believe is that certain circumstances produce the *look* of something we call by that name: 'bravery.' "

Edie blushed and put her foot gently atop his. One of her favorite emotional conditions—she was in it now—was startled but receptive conversational abeyance. It invariably had consequences.

Díaz considered what Andrew had said. The steward delivered coffee and, to Díaz, a note written on cream stationery. Díaz apologized to his guests, read the note, then sipped his coffee thoughtfully. His eyes came to rest again on Andrew.

"I would be a ridiculous man, Señor Caldwell, if I did not agree with you about the similarities among the three of us. I would be a cowardly one if I did not agree at least in principle with your definition of bravery."

Arévalo, returning to his solitary table, was this time attired in a blue suit with a fashionably askew pinstripe check. He half-bowed in acknowledgment of Díaz and his guests, who returned the greeting. Arévalo sat down in apparent relief.

"However," said Díaz. "I've just been informed that my wife, Mercedes, will be arriving late this afternoon from Paris. I would like you both to meet her before we pass final judgment on the notion of bravery. Are the two of you free for dinner tomorrow night?"

Startled, Edith and Andrew looked at each other.

"Of course," said Andrew.

"My wife," said Santiago Díaz humbly, "is bravery itself."

WHILE Andrew had chosen the intricacies of inheritance code from among all the law's riches specifically to annoy himself, he found instead that it—like most things constructed by men to bring order to the business of dying—illuminated everything it touched. He had not resisted this discovery. It had confirmed a feeling innate in him that instruction in life's impertinence lay everywhere, indeed could hardly be avoided, so that certain decisions were best made arbitrarily. By the very nature of probate law, for example, dealing as it did with the last wishes of the recently deceased, he had gazed, over the course of his nine-year career, into the eyes of children and adults—whole families—crazed variously by grief, greed, love, expectation, denial, bewilderment, and forbearance. By the age of thirty-eight he had seen as much, in his way, as a street cop in the crime-torn city that had become his home. He had made a considerable amount of money. He had grown from a boy into a man.

"Andrew," said Edith as he opened yet another taxi door for her, outside the ambassador's residence, "maybe now's a good time for you to come get those books you wanted."

He looked at his watch. Her office at the UN was at the opposite side of town from his own, but his schedule today was sparse. "Okay," he answered. "Perfect." He slid into the seat next to her, and the driver swung fearlessly back into traffic.

Andrew was currently working on a troublesome case involving an elderly widow, very wealthy, who had changed her will just before her death so as to settle nearly everything on her sole grandson, a primatologist. This man had for the past seven years been a citizen of Brazil, and Andrew had asked Edith to provide him with certain legal volumes regarding inheritance law in that nation. She had obtained them.

As the taxi began to slip from lane to lane like a fish in feeding frenzy, Edie put one hand palm down on the seat to steady herself. Andrew immediately put his own hand over hers. A further jolt sent her in an involuntary bounce hip to hip with him, atop their clasped fingers. Immediately their lips met in a series of kisses that grew sustained, then passionate.

When Andrew reached around to embrace her fully, he became aware of the driver's darting glances in the rearview mirror.

"I can't keep my hands off you," Edith whispered into Andrew's ear.

There were potholes in the street. The driver began to curse in Arabic.

A couple of blocks later, retrieving an earring from the seat beside them, Edith said, "One of us should tell James."

"Both of us, probably," said Andrew. "Separately, don't you think?"

Edith nodded and rummaged through her purse.

The UN was a place of precautions. Even though Edith knew the guard at her entrance, she would have trouble getting in without her clip-on ID, which she now remembered lay in her bathroom amid the detritus of last night's makeup decisions. "Honestly," she said. She looked at Andrew. "We're trouble, aren't we?"

"Of course." He had closed his eyes and laid his head against the back of the seat. "Whole point, some people would say."

She was struck. After a moment she said, "But not you?"

"No." His eyes, when he opened them, were very blue, but he made no consciously dramatic use of them. "Not me. I wouldn't say it."

Edith's office was on the thirty-second floor of the Secretariat building, a glass-and-steel monolith conceived and built in the last days of imperial optimism. It now looked sadly dated; in a few years it would be quaint enough to be declared an architectural landmark.

Standing before the metal detector at the ground-floor entrance, Edith and Andrew removed the keys and coins from their persons. Edith averted her eyes, faintly ashamed by the obviously morning-after nature of her dress and her failure to bring her photo ID. But the guard greeted her by name, winked at her, and, after allowing Andrew to sign in, passed them politely through the gate.

In the elevator, Edith said, "We're on international soil now."

Her office lay at the end of a long corridor carpeted in a sweetly old-fashioned protozoal pattern. Although the room was small, one wall was almost entirely glass. There was sunlight, air-conditioning.

When they were seated and the door firmly closed, Edith shook out her hair and said, "Lordy. I mean that was one strange breakfast."

Andrew shrugged. "He likes us."

"But he doesn't know us. And dinner with his wife? You don't think—"

"No," said Andrew, choosing the legal definition of his thought processes at the moment. Certainly he was not thinking.

Edith stood, walked around her desk, and sat on Andrew's lap. "Well, everything I said last night I meant."

"Me too."

"So we really do have to speak to James."

"You first."

She laughed and kissed him. "No. You. He didn't really love me anyway; he just thought he did."

"Okay. But still."

"Maybe you're right." She sighed. "And I guess I'll have to go to the gallery, won't I? Shoot the man on his own turf."

"It won't be as bad as that."

She laid her head on his shoulder, unbuttoned his shirt, and placed the flat of her hand against his bare chest. For some minutes they remained like that; he gently stroked her back as if to coax from it whatever wings might be necessary. Her tears were soundless, but copious enough to wet his jacket. She had never even pretended to love James, but she had—it was undeniable—found his attention and persistence deeply flattering, and she knew there was selfishness in the way she had drunk them down.

"Your books," she said, buttoning Andrew's shirt back up. "Sorry, I left them in the delegates' lounge by the General Assembly. We'll have to go back downstairs."

"I love you," Andrew heard himself say, as she pressed herself hard against him.

"I adore you," whispered Edith. She kissed his neck at the collar, leaving half a lipstick mark on his shirt. "Even before I met you I did."

The delegates' lounge was a medium-sized, windowless room at the bottom and to the side of the General Assembly's main chamber. Its ostensible purpose—filled as it was with sofas and chairs upholstered in tones of ocher, sienna, red, and orange—was to provide an informal resting place for jet-lagged delegates, but, just as often, informal negotiations were begun or ended there. All the lighting was indirect and Scandinavian in aspect. Sometimes delegates slept there for hours at a time. Sometimes they argued through interpreters. This morning, the room's tweedy curtain was still flung back, and there was no one inside.

Edith pulled the curtains shut behind them. She walked decisively toward a long sofa facing the far wall. Beside it lay three large legal volumes bound in green. She bent over, picked them up, and presented them to Andrew.

When her shoes and stockings were off, she said, "This is risky, you know."

She pulled a blanket off the sofa's back and covered him as he lay atop her.

"Yes, but we probably meant to do it anyway."

She laughed as she drew his cock into her. "Who taught you this?" she asked.

He shook his head.

"Cover my mouth," she said.

He did.

Sometime later, when they were both once more at interim peace, she asked again, "Who taught you this?"

He drew himself awkwardly up on one elbow and gazed down at her. She was thrillingly alive to his eye. A little scary. "You did," he said, after he had thought the whole thing through.

———

ANDREW had known James since high school, though it could not be said that they had been close friends then. On the day of their graduation, however, talking together through the haze of their first cigars, they had discovered that they were planning to attend the same university in the fall—a sprawling institution at the uptown end of the city where they both now lived. Immediately, they had agreed to rent an apartment together when the semester began. This arrangement, while it did cement their friendship, had not proven immediately comfortable. Though they shared a sense of humor that was dry to the point of evaporation, they were then so different in sensibility that it now seemed remarkable that they had not driven each other mad.

Or perhaps they had. James during that period had devoted himself to drugs, women, contemporary art, rock music played full blast on Andrew's stereo, and whatever pleasures he could extract from the nightlife of the great city. Andrew, for his part, had purchased a secondhand upright piano, a refrigerator, a library of cookbooks, an unusually placid sheltie, and, by Christmas break, a ticket to Paris, where, after requesting an indefinite leave from the university, he lived for nearly two years. James, meanwhile, transferred to a small arts college to the north, from which he graduated with a degree in the visual arts. When he returned to the city, Andrew was already living there, and to their mutual surprise, they found themselves fast friends.

James had been the best man at Andrew's wedding.

Probably by the end of the day they would no longer be speaking.

The breakfast with Santiago Díaz had disturbed and aroused Andrew's instincts nearly as much as it had Edith's, though to her he had downplayed its effect on him. He understood that she was exactly the woman for him. More perilously, he knew that he was perhaps the only other thing she needed besides herself.

"I'm out of my depth," said Andrew to himself as he opened the door to Caldwell, Robinson & Reineger.

"I've thought that too," said his receptionist, as she looked up from the volume of Proust that had lately been keeping her company. "Then I thought, 'Nah, he's really just kind of sweet and naive.' "

He smiled, and she gave him a sheaf of dead-rose-colored phone messages.

"I'm not paying you enough," said Andrew.

"Yes," she said, "actually you are. But this is spring. Can we discuss it again at budget time?"

"You got it. Is Leticia in?"

His receptionist rolled her eyes. Leticia was Andrew's not entirely predictable assistant.

"Okay," said Andrew. "I'll handle it."

" 'It' or 'her'?"

"Luanne, a little *caritas*, please."

"*Longtemps*," recited Luanne, "*je me suis couché de bonne heure.*" The phone rang. "She should give it a try," Luanne added before picking up the call. "Worked for him."

When Andrew reached Leticia's office he discovered his assistant passed out across her desk, her long black hair eerily aglisten with gold and silver bits of nightclub glitter, tiny metallic squares of the sort once used by aircraft to confuse enemy radar.

"Leticia! It's me, Andrew."

"Never again."

"You always say that." Not without sympathy, Andrew placed the three legal books on her desk. "Do you want the day off? It'd be okay."

"I want last night off," she answered, raising her head. She looked at the legal volumes Andrew had placed beside her phone. "What are those? They have UN labels on them."

"Brazilian inheritance law. The Revo case." That was what they had come to call it, from a witticism of Leticia's regarding reverse evolution. "My friend had someone flag the passages that seemed relevant."

"Your friend?" Despite her hangover, Leticia tossed out her

hair, and sparkles flew across her desk, a few settling upon the
back of Andrew's hand. He looked down at it as if Martians had
landed there.

"Don't forget that even utterly filled with regret and self-
loathing as I am at the moment," Leticia said, "I know several languages, and when you say 'friend,' I understand." She opened her
desk drawer and took out a comb. "Probably you want to read
those telephone messages you're slowly crumpling in your hand.
I'll see what's in these books." She was smiling fuzzily at him
through whatever pain she had visited upon herself. "Do you have
a cigarette?"

Although Andrew did not smoke, he usually carried a pack for
Leticia and other people who did. He gave her a cigarette, lit it,
then headed toward his own office.

He seemed to know a lot of smokers.

"Andy, my man!" called his partner Douglas from the water
cooler. "Can we talk about the Gardiner case, maybe this afternoon? I've thrown a few things up on the computer, and I'd like
to run them by you."

"Sure, Doug. But I'll have to get back to you, okay?"

"That's cool. Court date's the seventh."

"We'll talk."

Andrew entered his office and sank into the overwrought
leather chair that his ex-wife had chosen for him. He let the chair
swivel slowly around until his eyes were able to feast unimpeded
upon the city's eclectic, always soothing skyline.

For the first time since the night before he allowed himself to
wonder how Susannah and their son might respond to his sudden
alliance with Edith. And, for that matter, why should he suppose
that Edith knew anything at all about children? It had never occurred to him to ask. He believed, however, as the single son of a
happy marriage, that children absorbed the romantic and sexual
happiness of their parents as sponges, living at sea's bottom,
breathe water.

His intercom phone rang.

"Edith Emerson on line two," said Luanne as neutrally as possible, although neutrality was not her strongest trait.

"Thanks," said Andrew. "Put her through."

"Sorry, Andrew." Edith began. "You must think I'm insane."

"Don't be silly. Anyway, we're beyond that, you and I. What's up?"

She sighed. "I'm going to the gallery now. To tell James."

"He'll handle it. He won't like it much, but what are his options?" Andrew leafed through his messages. They seemed like playing cards from a very poor country, and he had to wonder what stakes were being played for. "He's my best friend and fellow traveler. You want me to call him first?"

"No, that's okay," she said quickly. "I'm just prepping."

"Tell him I want to see him, if he can stand the sight of me."

"I will." A pause. "Andrew, is everything all right? You sound sort of constricted, like."

"There's a message here from Santiago Díaz," Andrew answered, tossing the other slips aside. "Just his name and number. Time he called."

Another pause, briefer than the last. "So give him a ring. After all, he seems to have become our patron saint or something. There *is* a patron saint for people like us?"

"Believe it. We're why there *are* saints."

The line hummed between them.

"Okay, I'm off then. You won't forget about me, will you?"

Andrew, whose profession was in some ways meant to promote forgetfulness, saw that he had a different life now. "Impossible," he said.

When they had hung up, he stared at the screen of his computer as it ran through its boot sequence.

He had surprised himself.

THE FLOORS of James's gallery seemed designed to bring out, if not in some quiet way to challenge, the beauty of the photography shows he monthly mounted on its walls. Planks of perfect grain had been bleached pale, daubed with great swirls of diluted white paint, then covered over with layer after layer of transparent polyurethane—a pickle finish, Edith remembered it was called, because of the vinegar required by the process. She clicked now across the vast and empty space in her last-night heels, hoping that this technical term would have no metaphorical resonance in what was to follow.

"James?" she said as she walked toward his office at the back.

"I thought it might be you," called James, before she had quite reached what she had come to think of as his sanctuary. "Come in."

Instead, for a moment, she stood poised in the impeccably wrought doorway that somehow seemed to frame him, not her. "Hi," she said.

James was wearing a dark suit of Milanese cut, sitting at his desk and drinking the last of the previous night's champagne. He got to his feet to greet her. She kissed him on the lips, and after a piercing look at her he sat back down. "Hi," he answered. "A drink?"

"No, thank you, James." She entered the room and sat in the chair meant for his clients. People who sat in that chair were usually persuaded to buy things from him. He had explained the technique to her. He was very successful at business.

"I know that you've come to tell me something important, but let's let it rest for a moment." James finished his glass of champagne. "Did you have a good time last night? I'm told you did."

"Oh come on, James. That's bordering on the pathetic. Yes, I had a good time."

It was an oddity about her feelings toward James that while he was remarkably handsome and intelligent she had never felt the least sexual attraction toward him. They both understood that this anomaly was why she had just now accepted the champagne after all—not out of guilt, but out of self-amused sympathy. It was a mutually acceptable sentiment, a kind of toast to their futures, and it softened their encounter.

"You've come to tell me that you really are in love with Andrew."

"I've come to tell you that I'm going to marry him."

"Ah." He poured them both another glass of champagne and downed his own immediately. She no longer felt obliged to touch hers. "Till death do you part." He put his hands behind his head and stared contemplatively at the ceiling. "I gotta say, Edie. I gotta say."

"Strange match, huh?"

"Yeah. But I'm thinking about it."

"He asked me to tell you that he'd like to talk to you separately. If you can stand the sight of him, he said."

"Sight! After last night I'd say the two of you are the experts in that department."

"Okay. Enough. We seem to bring it out in each other, him and me."

"I won't ask how literally you mean that."

There was a photograph on the wall behind James's desk, and Edith found herself staring at it, as she always did when she was in this room. The photographer was American, recently dead, and the image, taken in the 1960s, was of a young woman laughing with an excited abandon that had caused her to lift her face partway toward the sky. In her right hand she held a melting ice-cream cone. In the shop window behind her the ghostly image of the photographer, dressed in black, could be seen in reflection.

Edith had always known that there was a sense in which she was that girl, although she was certain the notion had never occurred to James.

"But congratulations, Edie. I'm really happy for you and Andrew. Probably I should have seen it coming; it does make some strange kind of sense." He poured himself another glass of champagne. "Yeah, I'll talk to Andrew. All my life, I hope."

"Thanks, James."

The telephone warbled once, but James made no move to pick up; there was an invisible secretary.

"All those social invitations we used to get, Edie?"

"Business invitations. Art business invitations, really. You got them, I came with you."

"Two years, almost."

"We had fun."

"That we did. We had fun. And everyone thought we were a couple. But then I guess they were supposed to, wouldn't you say?"

"I wasn't trying to fool anyone," she said quietly.

James pushed the champagne bottle slowly away from him. "Did you see the last show here? You didn't sign the book."

"I was out of town."

"It was the real thing—great work. You've met the artist: Marisa de Borba. Anyway, she was going through my files, and she found a picture of you. Then she found some pictures of me and Andrew in Mexico. We looked really tatty—*gringo* guys on the road. But she liked it. And then when she heard about Santiago running for president she got fixated on the idea of photographing him and Mercedes—that's his wife—along with you, me, and Andrew at the U.S.-Mexican border. She wants to fly us down to do it. I think it's hot."

"Am I wrong, or do I remember her as Brazilian?"

"You're not wrong."

"What's the point? What makes you think Santiago would agree?"

"He has."

"Oh James, I don't know; this seems a little bizarre." She began to fiddle with her purse—opening it, rummaging through it, trying to close it again. "I mean is there some polemical point I'm missing? Why doesn't she just take a portrait of Santiago?"

"I believe in my artists. She must have her reasons. Besides which, it seems like an unforgettable image. Maybe we could fit a stop sign in."

Edith froze. "That's beneath you, James."

He shrugged. "What do you know about what's beneath me?"

She forced her purse shut, swiveled in her chair, and left his office at a brisk walk. Against the gallery floor her heels were startlingly loud and final.

"Well, at least consider it," James called after her when he calculated she had almost reached the front door.

BECAUSE of the lunchtime address he was to give at the United Nations, Santiago Díaz was unable to meet his wife that day at the airport—one named, she had pointed out to him, for an assassinated *gringo* president. It was not a secret that Mercedes had initially opposed Santiago's political ambitions. Nor were the press and people unaware that, once he had decided to pursue the presidency anyway, she had embraced his hopes for their country as she had always embraced him and all that he believed himself capable of.

He had sent the delegation's limousine to pick her up.

She had nine pieces of luggage, but even without this excess her driver would have had little trouble picking her out from the teeming, irritable crowd that thronged the taxi depot. She was a striking woman. Six feet tall in her new purple pumps, she had a full yet finely toned figure, a head of hair whose tangled masses were so thickly black that they seemed to extinguish the light for some distance beyond her, and the talent, common to many tall women, of standing with an expectant stillness that enlivened everything else.

"*Hola, Pedro,*" she said to the driver, as he hefted the first pair of her bags. "I've missed you. It's been too long."

"Three months, Señora. And so much has happened! You had a good time in Paris?"

"I didn't really want to go, but it was nice to see my friends." She picked up another pair of bags and followed him to the limousine.

Her air of regal patience was, in general, deceptive.

On the drive back to the ambassador's residence, Mercedes

chatted animatedly with Pedro—first about Europe, which he had never visited, then about Mexico City, where he had not been in over six months, although his wife and children lived there. When Mercedes asked him how the benefit dinner had gone, Pedro said he understood that there had been some difficulty with the lights, but that all had turned out well in the end.

Mercedes caught her breath. Ever since her husband had announced his candidacy there had been a steady stream of threats and violence directed toward his campaign by opposing factions. Indeed she herself had been struck in the head with an egg during a rally in the Zócalo several weeks previously. "But Señor Díaz is well?" she asked with the genial firmness that always defined her moments of anxiety.

"Oh, sí, Señora," replied Pedro. "This morning he enjoyed himself *enormemente* at breakfast with two guests from last night. He is a man who is tireless."

"Yes," said Mercedes, leaning back again in her seat. "My Santiago is tireless." And although her fears were allayed—she had a preternatural ability to distinguish danger from chance—she said little more until she and her bags had been delivered into Santiago's bedroom at the ambassador's residence.

Mercedes had met her husband at Mexico City's National University, at a party held to celebrate his team's triumph that afternoon at the Estadio Azteca. She had for some time been in the habit, evenings, of visiting the so-called *armoría*, a cavernous hall at the edge of campus where commencement speeches and political rallies deemed worthy of surveillance usually took place. At other times, the place was deserted, and Mercedes sought refuge there from the boys and bad air of the locale.

On the night she met Santiago, she had stepped through the building's door to find the room unexpectedly ablaze with light and bright, brassy, self-congratulatory music. A crowd of half-intoxicated men were passing an obviously ecstatic young athlete from shoulder to shoulder. Taking in the scene, Mercedes had gradually realized she was in some kind of pleasant danger. Minutes later, the crowd had dropped the young man at her feet, and, after a moment of shy hesitation, he had kissed her on the lips.

The schoolbooks she had been holding against her chest slid in a stream to the floor.

When he had picked them up and returned them to her, so much already seemed decided that she felt her natural boldness restored to her in a way that throughout her life had caused her to believe in God.

"I am Mercedes Estrada," she had said.

"I am Santiago Díaz," he had answered.

Three months later, in a large ceremony that brought pleasure to everyone in attendance as well as to countless others who saw it on TV news, they had married.

Mercedes now walked about the ambassador's rooms, which she had always disliked for their heavy curtains and overpolished furniture; these were the preenings of self-infatuated men. When the phone rang, and the voice of Luis Arévalo informed her that her husband would be there within the hour, she replied that she would wait. She did not much like Arévalo. However, she did not feel confident that such men were unnecessary to her husband's welfare.

She decided on a bath.

"Señora would like something to eat?" asked the steward over the bathroom telephone.

"No, Tranquilino. I will wait for my husband, I think. *Gracias.*"

Mercedes undressed. Everything she had been wearing but her shoes was black. Draping the bath mat over the front edge of the tub, she sat down upon it, and for a couple of minutes ran hot water over her insteps. When the pain subsided, she slipped into the tub.

She missed her husband.

Often, before the terrorist incident, she had wondered what Santiago would do upon retiring from soccer. Contrary to tabloid rumor, the two of them had made no final decision regarding children. Now, as she neared thirty-three and Santiago drew them into the rigors of political life, she found herself turning inward toward a possible family. He would not resist.

And yet she had lately been troubled by doubts. Although the polls had her husband leading the race by a considerable margin, she did not herself believe he would win. Nor did she feel he would be entirely disappointed to lose. It was this halfheartedness, unexpected and alien, that had begun to disturb her. She knew she would have to speak about children to Santiago before the election.

From the street came the repeated call of a car alarm, and at its sound Mercedes rose dutifully from the bath as if it were she who was being addressed. Drying herself, Mercedes reflected that hers was a life dominated by decisions she made in private and then waited for others to discover. This way of being was innate to her, and it had brought her much happiness.

After she had powdered herself and applied a modicum of makeup in anticipation of Santiago's arrival, she returned to the bedroom, drew her silk wrapper from one of her suitcases, and put it on.

Santiago Díaz entered the room a half hour later. Mercedes did not wake. A towel lay beneath her head, and her hair, which Santiago had always regarded as a splendor somehow connected with her willful nature, had worked its way halfway across the bed's second pillow.

Santiago sat gently down on the side of the bed. It would not help his campaign if it were known that he was a man who took pleasure, especially after lovemaking, in watching his woman sleep in peace. He had seen many paintings, mainly Italian, in which the gender roles were reversed—the man reduced to somnolence—but this had never been his experience with Mercedes.

He touched her thigh with his open hand. She stirred without waking.

Santiago did not judge his speech at the United Nations to have gone well. The delegates he had addressed, the representatives of all South American nations including his own, had asked him questions he considered it premature to answer. He was still only a candidate for Mexico's presidency, not an elected official, and so, with Arévalo's concurrence, he had planned on today's address being no more than a courtesy call. As it had turned out, he had had to skirt certain questions. Worse, he had discovered that his patience for the company of career politicians, with their tedious sense of protocol, had already worn a little thin.

"Mercedes," he whispered, gently massaging his wife's thigh through her dressing gown.

Of course, he was both a player and an optimist—someone whose energies were quickly restored. He understood without sentimentality the enduring challenges and beauty of devotion. He was, he believed, a lucky man.

"Mercedes, it's me. Wake up, my love."

She did, and he watched with deep pleasure as the haze of sleep cleared from her eyes, freeing them to widen to their fullest intelligence. For two full breaths she gazed at him without moving. He felt himself sharply but unconditionally seen, and his own vision quickened in response.

She seemed to him at once huge and tiny.

"I hate Paris," she said quietly.

Santiago smiled, loosened his tie and shirt collar. "How is Coco? You stayed with Coco the whole time?"

"Coco hates Paris." Mercedes slipped the robe off her shoulders in irritation. "She's moving back home to Mexico City next month."

"We will be home soon, too."

"In Los Pinos? In our own house? In prison?"

Santiago removed his jacket and tossed it onto a nearby chair. "In the grip of my advisers: 'Definition and repetition.'" He lay down upon the bed. "That, Arévalo tells me, is politics. '*Definición y repetición.*'"

"Well, at least you have mastered the second part." Free now of her robe, Mercedes pulled his shoes from his feet without un-lacing them, then hurled them one by one over her shoulder into the room's far corners.

Santiago gazed at her breasts with the freshened pleasure of a man looking upon delights that he had as a boy insufficiently imagined. "Two of everything," he murmured.

" 'Two of everything,' " she repeated. "See, I should be presi-dent. *Definición y . . .*" She undid his belt buckle and with a single gesture drew his pants and underwear to his knees. "*Repetición, repetición, repetición.*" She bounced upon his shins in purposely childish time to the syllables she spoke, then fell still. "*Señor Presidente?*"

A pause. He smiled at her.

"We are together?" she said in a more serious tone.

"Yes, my havoc. We are together. Always."

After a moment's mock consideration, she set about removing his socks, pants, and underwear while he laughed softly. He saw the bedroom's pathetic chandelier and was reminded briefly of the previous night, when he had looked up to find a hardly less pathetic chandelier in the room where he was speaking.

Mercedes unbuttoned his shirt and began slowly to cover his chest with kisses. As he ran his thumbs up and under her arms, Santiago thought: *I want to tell her what I saw last night.*

She thought: *I want to tell him that he does not really want to be president.*

From the street below came an incoherent drunken shout. Mercedes put her lips to his ear and exhaled gently into it.

"Speech," he seemed to say. "My . . ." Then, despite the ab-surdity of the shirt and tie which he still wore, he turned her over on her back in bed and, his eyes very wide to hers, allowed her to draw him into her.

"We will have children," she said after a time.

During the pause that ensued she reached up, unknotted his tie, and dropped it off the side of the bed.

"You mean you are . . . ?"

"No," she answered, "not yet." It was then she saw in his eyes that they had, in her absence, been witness to something that had changed him permanently.

Wrapping her arms around his neck, she drew him down close to her. "But we will have children."

They resumed fucking.

"Yes," he said into her ear. "We will."

The decision was made.

Later that night, Mercedes and Santiago dined by long-standing invitation with their hosts, the Mexican ambassador to the UN and his wife, both of whom quietly supported Santiago's campaign against their nation's ruling party. The ambassador was fond of remarking that since the ruling party's candidate was chosen personally by the outgoing president and never lost the election, Mexico was not the oligarchy people complained of but a monarchy gotten up to look like one. Simply by entertaining Santiago and Mercedes, he was putting his career at risk, but he found it impossible to resist the glow exuded by the couple as they sat across from him and his wife at the dinner table, bathed in candlelight. He leaned back, sniffed his brandy appreciatively, then downed it. "The two of you, you could be a photograph."

The ambassador's wife crossed her arms and looked away.

"Mercedes hates to be photographed," said Santiago. He looked at her. "But she sometimes will make an exception."

"You sound as if you have something in mind," Mercedes responded with a laugh.

"Only because this *gringo* art dealer made a suggestion to me last night, and I thought, Why not? None of us is given eternal life."

Mercedes, who disliked liquors of all kinds, peered into her brandy and drank it down in two gulps.

Still later that night, Santiago discovered a Mexican audio-cassette on his nightstand.

" '*Zavalito y Su Banda de Pianos*,' " he read. "What is this?"

"A present. I found it in the flea market in Paris. Aren't you ever going to use that story about his grandmother in your speeches? You told it to me so well." She was already in bed and made a small commotion of rearranging the pillows.

He smiled but did not answer her. He undressed.

"Santiago. What did you mean at dinner about making an exception?"

"Oh, it is nothing. We can talk about it tomorrow. I met a very charming *norteamericano* couple who . . ." He slipped into bed.

The travel clock that Mercedes took with her everywhere ticked audibly.

"Truly, it is nothing. I am very glad to see you."

"I am glad to see you." *What else*, she wondered, *has he seen?*

He drew her toward him.

Edith's encounter with James at his gallery had disturbed her more than she had anticipated. That evening, her second at Andrew's apartment, she mentioned over dinner James's proposal that she, Andrew, and the Díazes allow themselves to be photographed together at the Mexican border.

"I know about it," said Andrew, dressing the salad. "That's what Santiago wanted when he called me at work: the breakdown on James."

"Did you give it to him?"

"Sure." On the phone to Santiago, Andrew had emphasized the professional side of James—his discerning eye, his gift for public relations, his loyalty to his artists. He hadn't had the stomach for a more personal approach. "Look. The border photographs aren't real. They're just James doing damage control after last night. He wants to be seen as still in the game, and I say let it be. By next week he will have forgotten all about Mexico. That's the way he is."

"You just don't understand," Edith said, picking at the label on the wine bottle until it came away in strips. "I don't care if he is your best friend, you don't know the first thing about him." And though she recognized that it was herself she was feeling sorry for—herself suddenly outmaneuvered by everyone around her— she began desolately to weep. She was used to being the focus of events, and intimations of this flaw in her character invariably made her miserable.

"Why don't you go back to your place and pick up some clothes and stuff while I clean up?" said Andrew, smoothing the hair away from her eyes with a patience that shamed her.

She nodded sadly in assent. "I avoid things. I really do."

By the time she returned to Andrew's two hours later, however, a few essential items in her bag, the notion of "home" had already become agreeably fuzzy. She smiled shyly and undressed without comment, wondering if that lost sense of boundaries might not be a sign that she was remaking herself to suit Andrew. They kissed; she decided it was not. He by nature pretended a kind of congenial vagueness which she recognized immediately as a cover. Her own social behavior was reversely composed—it was the vagueness she dissembled—so perhaps she was the one natively fuzzy at heart.

The connoisseur of the hasty impulse.

In the morning, Andrew woke before Edith and left the bed without disturbing her.

He had dreamed at night's darkest, placeless fold of a riotously happy street carnival in a tropical country. The celebrants seemed to be speaking every known language as well as several patois formulated on the spot, and there were fatigue-clad soldiers everywhere among them, firing their weapons joyously in the air. He carried a well-worn soccer ball in his hands and leaned close to Edith to hear what she was saying. As she spoke, the soccer ball addressed them loudly in Kevin's voice. Andrew found himself worrying about where the soldiers' randomly discharged bullets were landing. Still, the dream had been suffused with promise. It was a victory for the forces of liberation.

Draping the dish towel over one shoulder, Andrew set about feeding oranges to the matte black German juicer, relic of his marriage to Susannah.

"I'm wondering what I should do about my apartment," said Edith, walking sleepily into the room.

"Keep it, sublet it, sell it," he answered, tossing another orange half into the garbage. "There's plenty of space here for your personal effects. Or any suitable fraction thereof, pursuant to whatever."

"You love me," she observed.

"Criminals in Love: The Motion Picture." He stepped back to gauge the juice yield.

"I think I want to get rid of the place," Edith said. "The main reason I moved there anyway was because it was near work. How could a neighborhood right in the lap of the UN be so completely lacking in charm?"

"It's the microwaves," said Andrew. "Surveillance frequencies of many lands fouling the atmosphere. You wonder why the pigeons don't get cooked out of the air every time there's a diplomatic crisis."

She moved past him, loosening the belt of her blue silk dressing gown so that it fell partly open as she leaned against the window sash. "Okay, I'll sell."

Her smile folded inward into a look of quiet determination, and after a moment she came forward to press herself against him.

It was only then that Andrew realized how oddly ignorant he was of the intuitions that ruled her life, though she had told him much. Ignorance, for him, was the promise of discovery. The same was true for her. It was ludicrous and cheering to be caught up in such a contradiction.

"Daddy," said Kevin, running naked into the kitchen. "How come she's still here? Is she my new mother?"

Edith drew her gown close about her and waved demurely at her lover's son. She had come, then, to a new life. Very little but work would remain the same, and she saw that she had been preparing for something like this. Kevin, with his tousled red hair and clear blue eyes, seemed to challenge her decision, inquire into her reasons, ask if she was up to it. And though she did not yet know how she would answer him, Edith felt a strange relief pass through her. She had landed safely.

"No, Kevin," said Andrew. "Susannah is your mother. But Edith is a very nice lady who I hope will be around here a lot now. Why don't you say good morning?" He carried Kevin over to her. "You can shake her hand. She'd like that."

"Edith?"

"Hi, Kevin."

They shook hands, or, more properly, he took one of her fingers in his hand and stared at her contemplatively.

"Was she ever little?" Kevin asked his father, who was wearing nothing but black cotton boxer shorts.

"Everyone is little at first," Andrew answered.

Upon receiving this news, Kevin, after the briefest of considerations, burst into violent and bitter tears.

EDITH had been born in rural Virginia to a family of considerable but dwindling means, and though she loved her three younger brothers and had, after her mother's early death by cervical cancer, done much to raise them, she had never really desired children of her own. This disinclination, when she thought about it at all, she attributed to her father.

After her mother's death, he had solaced himself first with bourbon, then with the wives of the clients that his thoroughbred farm continued to attract. More than a few times, Edith had returned from school to find an intermingled trail of men's and women's clothing leading to one of the house's several bedrooms. As she approached college age, these trails ended with increasing frequency at her own room. On the afternoon her father had left the door ajar while taking grim enjoyment in his latest conquest, a blond coloratura whom Edith was able to identify by the scarf flung over the downstairs newel, she resolved to apply only to universities on the continent's farther coast. Choosing a large private institution in California, she graduated in due course, then moved successively, even systematically, to Toronto, Majorca, Paris, and finally New York, which she embraced at once as her home.

She pressed the stop button on the bus that had carried her crosstown and south from Andrew's apartment to the United Nations. Although she had been relieved that the home pregnancy test she had taken a week ago had come out negative, her excitement at becoming a mother anyway now seemed preordained. Excitement, no doubt, was the reason she still had not had her period.

It began gently to rain.

"I guess I should know you by now," said the guard in the Secretariat building when Edith made a show of displaying her ID badge.

"You're way ahead of me, then." She passed through the metal detector's archway and scooped her keys and change from the bin on the other side. "Next time you'll have to tell me all my secrets."

The guard wished her a good day.

Edith stepped into an empty elevator and, when the doors closed, bent over before the thermo-sensitive floor selector. With one warm breath she illumined the button marked "32." *Alive*, she thought. Then she began a mental review of the projects that awaited her on her desk: human rights in Guatemala, starvation in Peru, earthquake in Chile. And next week there was a conference on geosynchronous satellites.

She liked her job, though she aspired to the more interactive position of interpreter. She wanted to be in on the making of events; transcribing them after the fact had, at some point she could no longer identify, ceased to be quite enough. A part of her wanted to know what it felt like to be physically present yet invisible, the indispensable intermediary between whole populations whose grievance was with history but whose redress was each other. Fueled by lives and flesh, history was an unfeeling force that she might nonetheless flirt with, rub herself gingerly against, while remaining as invisible, even nonexistent, as she felt when she was alone. It was a scary thought. Sexy.

Perhaps too much.

The elevator opened, and Edith turned left down the hall, putting the concept of interpreter out of her head as she went. By the time she reached her office, her mind was completely blank.

She opened the office door and froze. A tall Hispanic woman sat elegantly in the chair beside Edith's desk, a rolled-up magazine tucked beneath her arm, her hands folded calmly over the gold latch of the purse that rested on her lap.

"Edith Emerson?"

"Yes."

The woman rose to her feet. "I am Mercedes Díaz. I believe you know my husband, Santiago?"

Edith remained motionless in the doorway. "Yes, I do. I met him yesterday." She was instantly alert. In the space of a heartbeat she had delivered herself to a part of her soul, patient but remorseless, whose dormancy she ordinarily guarded with vigilance. "My friend Andrew and I had breakfast with him."

"Please forgive the intrusion, Miss Emerson, but I wanted to speak with you in private. If you could spare the time I would be most grateful."

Edith made her way past Mercedes to her desk, drawing out her arrival. Try as she might, she was unable to imagine a scenario in which this visit could prove purely social.

Turning to face Mercedes, she felt the force of the woman's gaze as something neutral but unquenchable. No one shared Edith's office, and she had no assistant of her own to interrupt her. Calling security did not even occur to her. All this, Edith saw at once, was as she wanted it.

"I'm thrilled to meet you, Señora Díaz. Andrew and I have really been looking forward to our dinner with you and your husband tonight. Please, sit down."

Huge brown eyes. A long tendril of black hair grazing a cheek. The chair drawn back and occupied in a single fluid movement.

"Thank you," said Mercedes.

Abruptly aware of her own not-quite-over-the-top workplace outfit (black lace brassiere, sheer white blouse, skirted suit of nimbus gray and silver fibers), Edith also sat, groping through her memory of normative conversation for some way into this one.

"Señor Díaz said that you're coming from Paris."

"Santiago worries about my safety now that he is running for office. We have friends in Paris, so he suggested a visit. But after ten days it was too much. *Il me manquait.*"

"Well of course you missed him. He seems like a wonderful man." Edith had made the translation and replied before she realized the linguistic anomaly.

"You were a little difficult to find," Mercedes continued in English. "Santiago said you were a translator of French."

"Yes, I said that at our breakfast. I don't know why. Probably to tease Andrew."

Mercedes considered this a moment, then asked, "Do you mind if I smoke?"

"Certainly not. It's getting harder and harder to enjoy one's tawdry little vices in this country. I'll join you."

For the first time, Mercedes let her gaze stray from Edith. The office had been designed during the era of exigent modernist simplicity, but Edith had nonetheless made it her own. The row of shoes for weathers of varying clemency; the tiny black shopping bag pinned to the wall and filled to floral effect with plastic spoons and forks; the brass hat stand festooned with a transparent raincoat, scarves, and a brilliant blue umbrella—everything spoke of the habits of small transience, rushed decisions. And running along the top of one wall, so that it abutted the ceiling like a frieze, was a series of black oil-stick drawings of a galloping horse, individually framed in pine.

"Those are by my youngest brother," said Edith when she saw

her visitor's eye linger on the strangely glowering panels over-head. "He's still in art school, but he swears he's going into civil engineering when he gets out. Not that we believe him."

Edith pushed the ashtray across her desk so Mercedes could reach it. Mercedes produced a green plastic lighter. Smoke curled into the air between the two women.

"Please, Edith Emerson, this conversation is hard for me. I've never done anything like this before."

"I don't think I have either." Edith swallowed. "What is it we're doing exactly?"

The magazine, still pressed securely under one arm, gave Mercedes an air of inner certainty that, despite her disclaimer, suggested profound self-confidence. She did not fidget.

"I have come to ask if you are having an affair with my husband."

"An affair?" Flattered despite herself, Edith flicked her ciga-rette pointlessly against the ashtray. "What an incredible idea! No. I'm not. The only times I've seen him were at the banquet the other night and at breakfast the next morning. Andrew is my fi-ancé. He was with me both times. You can't possibly be serious."

"Are you in love with Santiago?"

"Me? Why do you ask? Who told you that?"

"Please. If you would . . . I must hear your answer."

"No. I'm not in love with him. Absolutely am not."

"Is he in love with you?"

"How could he be? He's talked mostly about you, about how brave you are. Which now that I've met you seems a bit of an understatement. Your husband is not in love with me."

Without blinking, Mercedes placed her cigarette on the ash-tray's rim and handed the rolled-up magazine to Edith. "I found this in the ambassador's quarters."

The glossy four-colored magazine had been opened to the middle before being rolled up, and even as she took it from Mer-cedes, Edith knew what it was. She unrolled the magazine and spread it flat on her desk. If she was going to be accused of shame-lessness, then there was nothing to do but rise to the occasion and revel in it.

Edith's first thought when she looked down at the double-page photo of herself was that she looked younger now than she had when it was taken, several years previously. She was shown naked except for her grandmother's necklace, reclining on her side across a brown velvet settee. From brow to ankle she glis-tened with what appeared to be lustful perspiration but was in fact the combined effect of massage oil and a thorough once-over with a mineral-water aerosol. Her knees were drawn halfway to her chin and her legs crossed diagonally at the calves, so that her but-tocks and crotch were fully bared to the camera. A pink towel hung over the back of the settee, artfully twisted so that its lower part echoed the curve of her rear end, while beneath her knees a pink pillow drew the viewer's eye to her breasts. Her nipples were erect, her eyes closed, her mouth open. A white pillow printed with violets was convulsively clutched in one well-manicured hand; the other lingered at her clitoris.

The photo session had been grueling. Before it started, there had been a brief debate between the photographer and the art di-rector about whether Edith should shave her pubic hair, but she had refused outright, and nothing more was said about it. They had simply given her a silver goblet two-thirds full of wine, turned up all the lights, and begun. Two hours later, the goblet lay spilled at the foot of the settee, Edith was wondering if she had been drugged, and when the photographer asked her to lower her chin, look into the camera, and for fuck's sake start using her fingers, she had readily obliged. Her own orgasm, sweeping over her a minute later, had astonished her, but not the photographer. That was the shot they had used: double-page spread, full-color bleed, one-time use.

She had been very well paid.

"Well, Señora Díaz, this is all kind of engaging from some

point of view, but do you really think I roam the city's banquet halls handing this thing out like a business card?" Edith tossed the charged relic into an open filing cabinet beside her desk. "I don't."

"So you did not give it to Santiago?"

"Of course not. I posed for this years ago, when I first came to the city. I was working as an artist's model and I needed the money. Besides, these people don't exactly give you complimentary copies of your work on publication." She stubbed out her cigarette. "Where'd you get it anyway?"

"My husband's campaign manager gave it to me. He was the one who found your purse."

"So why don't you ask me if Señor Díaz's campaign manager is in love with me?"

"Security is among this man's duties. And I don't care who he is in love with."

"I see." Edith smiled. "Your husband's handlers think I'm some kind of risky business, I guess. Does that mean I'm being watched?"

Tossing her hair impatiently back, Mercedes answered her quietly. "You are not under surveillance. And nothing you say will ever go beyond this room."

She leaned forward and put her hand over Edith's. "Please, I know you understand men."

There was for the first time a note of urgency in her voice, and Edith was moved to recall, of all things, her encounter with James in the gallery the previous day. She had known without thinking about it that until he had actually heard from her own lips that she planned to marry Andrew—until he had actually seen her speaking the words—the hurt that had accrued from her first refusal of him could not be contained. People were always confessing to her. When she confessed back, it never failed to shock them.

"Understand men?" said Edith softly. "Not me. I just pretend I do. It's reassuring to everyone."

"When I arrived here from Paris, I went directly to the ambassador's residence and waited for my Santiago. I do not need to tell you again that he is the center of my life. I bathed, I waited for him, he returned. As always.

"When we make love—in this we are like any other couple—it is always different. Familiar, but after a certain point different. It was after that point yesterday, when things became different, that I saw something new had happened. Santiago wasn't withholding anything, I don't mean that. But he had changed in a way that was very strange to me. Someone else was with us. In his heart of hearts, where only I have been, there was now someone else too: someone had interfered. I was as certain of it as if he had come to me with her perfume still clinging to him."

Edith eased her hand out from under her visitor's importunate palm. "Do I want to hear this? This intuition of yours? You have no reason to be jealous."

"The next morning Santiago told me about meeting you and Andrew Caldwell. He spoke of you with great . . . appreciation is the word I want. When he left, I went to Luis Arévalo, the man I mentioned to you earlier."

"The one who found my purse."

"They thought it was a bomb. Not impossible under the circumstances. But when they saw it was only your purse Luis pursued the matter on his own. That is how he discovered the magazine." Mercedes was still inclined expectantly toward Edith. "Our sources extend quite far."

"And so you asked Señor Arévalo about me."

"No, it was he who brought your name up. I simply asked how everything had gone at the banquet, and he mentioned that you and Mr. Caldwell had drawn attention to yourselves. He was not specific, but he did let me know in his way where I could find you."

Outside the rain blew in a sudden gust against the window, then settled back to the gentle rhythm of an all-day circumstance. In her mind's eye she saw it all: Japanese and German tourists scampering for shelter, camera lenses lovingly swabbed with chamois, well-behaved children. She saw herself.

"Señora Díaz, to be wretchedly truthful, Andrew and I were a little demonstrative with each other that evening. We are lovers. We were sitting up front. I suppose your husband saw us; in fact, it would be surprising if he didn't. I think he might have identified with us. Would that be like him?"

Mercedes leaned back in her chair like someone who has been engaged in an absorbing dinner conversation and is now making room for the waiter to remove her barely touched plate. "Yes," she answered after a moment. "That would be like him."

"I'm sure that's all it was, then," said Edith gently.

Rummaging through her purse, Mercedes produced two tortoiseshell combs and set about pinning back her hair. She felt as if she had just learned that someone dear to her had died—not Santiago exactly, but a younger version of herself that had been less complicatedly fused with him. It grieved her to let that person go, but retrospection was the enemy of marriage, and there would now be much to do. She let her gaze fall once more upon Edith. "Do you think my husband will win the election?"

The solemnity with which she spoke startled Edith. "The polls say so," she answered.

"But you—what do you think?"

Edith felt a stab of regret. The whole conversation, rife with the calculus of self-esteem, was going to end, after all, in approximation. She laid her hands out before her on the desk, ringless fingers spread. "I think he wants to lose."

Mercedes nodded absently to herself. "Yes," she whispered sadly. "Yes."

Then her dark brown eyes seemed to take Edith in anew. Everywhere there were borders, and all of them were provisional—those between countries, those between lovers and rivals, those between crowds and the men and women they spewed forth onto rostrums to tell them who they were. Mercedes remembered that when she had been struck by the egg that night Santiago had given his famous speech in the Zócalo her first thought had been neither for herself nor for what the insulting act might portend.

It had not even been for her husband. Instead she had imagined with pointless clarity the hen that had laid the egg, already asleep in its rough-slatted coop somewhere in the unzoned depths of Mexico City. Purpose shifted with sudden sentiment, sentiment with aimless striving. But the eggshell always broke.

"Edith?" Mercedes smiled wanly. "If I may call you that?" The force of her feeling grew, enveloping her. "Edith, everything that Santiago said about you is true. You are a remarkable woman. I think you are dangerous, but I am very glad to meet you."

Edith had been called dangerous before, though she had never understood that point of view.

"I would like us to be friends," Mercedes said.

ON THE OTHER SIDE of town, Andrew shut his living-room windows against the rain. Kevin's tears, though, were less easily stanched. The morning's reminder that his world was contingent, and might at any time expand to include Edith or her like—people with their own great glowing befores—had offended the boy's sense of justice and self. When Kevin finally allowed himself to be coaxed from behind the sofa, Andrew decided to dismiss the nanny for the day and stay home to comfort him.

Unearthing a lavish set of building blocks that Susannah's parents had given Kevin, Andrew helped him construct a marble chute. The dominant stylistic influence on their efforts appeared for some reason to be Piranesi's *Carceri*.

"See, Kev?" Andrew said when the edifice was complete. "You put the marble in here and it comes out all the way over there. Here, give it a shot."

Kevin took the apricot-sized marble—he was still prone to testing the capacity of his gorge with any object ready to hand—and stared fiercely at it. Andrew guided the boy's fist over the wedge-shaped starting gate. "You have to let it go now," he instructed the boy gently. Kevin brought the marble to his cheek, savoring its cool surface.

"Does my marble have a name, Daddy?"

"Of course it does. But you have to introduce us, we haven't met."

Kevin rolled the glass orb broadly over his face, squashing it against his nose before smiling wickedly. Then, with that sense of agency whose loss is what adults mourn when they say they were young once, Kevin stood squarely over the chute and dropped it in. "Bye-bye, Susannah," he said.

The marble rolled down the first steep ramp through a series of arches, collecting force as it swept over the drawbridge and the crocodile-infested moat it spanned. Ramps, jumps, and speed curves propelled it into a colonnaded gallery, through an inner bailey, past the court, over the dungeon, and down a long spiral courseway. After passing through rooms both open and roofed, it reached the floor with enough momentum to carry it up the ramp of the pergola in back. There the marble came to rest in the circular bower that Andrew had prepared for it.

Susannah was an interior decorator, with her own firm and showroom twenty blocks south of midtown. She was well-known for her trompe-l'oeil murals.

"Daddy, it worked, it worked! Let's try it again!"

"Okay. But you have to bring the marble back here first."

Kevin ran to the end of the courseway, singing a nonsense song that involved repeating the syllables of Susannah's name over and over in various combinations. "The Name Game." Andrew had taught it to him.

He did not seem an unhappy child.

"When I make it go," Kevin told his father, "it has to pull its legs up so the crocodiles won't *bite* them. And it holds its legs with its arms to keep them there and it puts its head down to look out for trouble below and then it's all in a ball and it goes *fast*."

"Only way to do it. And at the end it comes out safe in that little garden we made, see? That way birds can come and sing to it."

"What kind of birds?"

"Orioles."

"Oreos," repeated Kevin, dropping the glass ball once again into the chute.

Some time later, when the phone rang, its triple-toned warble reminded Andrew of the birdsong he had already forgotten he invented.

"Caldwell and Caldwell," he said when he flipped open the folding cordless phone.

"Hello, boss. How are things in your part of the jungle?"

"Hi, Leticia. Things are okay. We're playing the seven ages of man." He began walking around the room with the phone pressed to his ear. "Right now I'm waiting for reincarnation."

"Daddy!" called Kevin, running after him. "Can I have an Indian tickle?"

"Later, big guy. I'm on the phone."

Propelled by his own momentum, Kevin went hurtling past him into the kitchen.

"You know how I hate to disturb scenes of domestic tranquillity," began Leticia, whose own superheated life in fact involved little else, "but it looks like we've got a serious challenge to the will in the Revo case."

"Shit, I knew it. Who's the aggrieved party? Not that I can't guess."

"Well, it's not the mother, whom I personally was worried about. It's one of her sisters, a Mrs. Beizer."

"The aunt of what's-his-name. The primatologist."

"Right. She's Monkey Man's older aunt, and it is my duty as a student of passionate natures to inform you that she is a charcoal-braised jaguar from hell. Unexampled in my experience. *Oiça.* She's retained Bill Ratner—not, as we know, your favorite person—and he called this morning right after you did."

"If she can afford Ratner what does she need Monkey Man's poor little windfall for?"

"You can ask her. She's been calling."

"She has?"

"Seven times. Then she showed up in the flesh—one of those crepey-necked ladies streamlined for combat. I think you'd better get down here. She's coming back with Ratner himself and they want to see you."

"Oh for Christ's sake. Tell them to make an appointment."

"They already have, my friend. They're coming in at three. There's something they want to show you."

"Okay, put me out of my misery. What is it they want to show me?"

"*Não sei.* But whatever it is, they think they have you all wrapped up. You'd better deal with it now and get it over with." Andrew could hear her lighting a cigarette. "Hey, do you and your new friend want to go dancing with me and Zazie tonight? Or maybe that's too much estrogen for you at one time, cha-cha-cha?"

But Andrew had already decided that Leticia was right—he would have to get down to the office in time to meet this unexpected challenge to what was good and proper and already in motion. He told her that her estrogen bloom was to the legal profession what a field of new meadow saffron was to winter, but that he and Edith had a dinner date that evening; he'd be at work by three. She laughed a loamy laugh; he thanked her and hung up.

Kevin had not been to Andrew's office since the earliest days, when he was still comfortably cradled in Susannah's arms. The firm owned a video camera, which Andrew sometimes used to inventory estates, and Susannah had been pleased when Leticia had offered to record the three of them together. Andrew and Susannah had spent many hours with the VCR during those early homebound days; even the most familiar of movie classics had regained their savor before this tiny third party who had sprung like an automotive air bag from the accident their marriage had already begun to be. Andrew was hardly surprised when Kevin's first word—after the essential "Mommy" and "Dah"—had proven to be "rewind."

"Kevin?" called Andrew, starting for the kitchen. "C'mon, friend, we're going on a little replay expedition."

The kitchen was deserted, the apartment still.

"Kevin, what are you up to?" But the rooms that chambered vastly out around him offered nothing beyond the tick of his grandmother's clock, resonating against the overheated walls.

Andrew began walking systematically through the apartment, his left forefinger against the wall as if he were tracing the architectural plan. The windows were all shut and gated with childproof fronds of wrought iron. In Kevin's room, the brightly colored ceiling mobile of smiling dolphins hung undisturbed by recent passage.

Andrew returned to the kitchen and opened the refrigerator, an appliance that his own parents had warned him against to lasting effect. It held nothing more alarming than a few containers of leftover take-out food.

What a comedy it all was, he thought, what an insidious inheritance. Parents infusing their children with their own preemptive fears, never realizing in time that nothing worth fearing could be prepared for. Probably it was just nature's way of making itself interesting.

Shaking off the thought, Andrew found himself staring at the kitchen's gaping back door. He had failed to close it after taking out the morning trash.

"Kevin!"

He sprinted out past the freight elevator to the floor's open corridor.

"Damn it, Kevin! Where are you?"

After pounding on his nearest neighbor's door to no avail, he hurried down the hall, pushing each buzzer without waiting for a response. Just past the main elevator, as peepholes and latches began to open in his wake, Andrew caught sight of one door that was ajar. He entered without knocking.

Kevin was seated on a sofa next to a lively-looking old lady who was just then handing him a glass of orange juice. She was wrapped in a red silk dressing gown and wore her surprisingly abundant white hair pulled back in a snood.

"Sorry, Mrs. Donoghue. He took off on me."

"Not to worry, not to worry. I'm always happy to have visitors. Ever since my husband died I cultivate the society of others. Of course, I have my standards: your little Kevin is a perfect gentleman."

When the neighbors had been reassured and Kevin was safely ensconced in his own room, Andrew spoke a few words on the subject of unannounced departures. Then he began dressing Kevin in his rain gear, which was neon green and devilishly intricate. A crescent of orange juice topped the boy's upper lip.

"Daddy," he asked, "when Mrs. Donoghue goes out, who does she ask?"

"Mrs. Donoghue is a grown-up. She doesn't have to ask anyone."

"But she told me she never goes out anymore. Is that because she lives by herself and there's no one to ask?"

"No. She's a grown-up. She doesn't have to ask anyone."

"But why does she live by herself? Did she always?"

"Not always. She was married for a long time to a very nice man."

"Where is the man?"

"He's dead now, Kevin."

"Is Mommy dead?"

"Of course not. You'll see her Sunday, just like always."

Kevin kicked the little blue footstool he had been sitting on, then gazed down at his foot in surprise. He enjoyed the springy sensation of his plastic rain boots against his toes. "Daddy, what does it feel like to be dead?"

"What a question!"

"What's it like? What?" He kicked the stool again, and it clattered a short distance across the floor.

Andrew's love for his son was consuming. Neither he nor Susannah had ever really doubted that Kevin would live with him after the divorce, the custody trial notwithstanding. Andrew vividly saw how Kevin's life would pass beyond his, progressively freeing itself from filial custom until he would be only a set of memories for the boy, the memories a set of words.

Andrew squatted down in front of Kevin and put his hand on his shoulder, covering it completely.

"Tell me what it's like to be dead, Daddy."

The boy's eyes were bluer than his own. Andrew willed himself not to blink.

"It's just like how it was before you were born," he said quietly. "Don't you remember?"

THE DECEDENT in the Revo case, a Mrs. Lowell, had lived in one of the city's most exclusive precincts, a stately stretch of middle-sized buildings burnished by time's passage to the aloof inward glow of a sepia-toned photograph. When Andrew arrived at his office, pushing Kevin before him in a stroller, Bill Ratner and the crepey-necked Mrs. Beizer were waiting for him. They had come to take him to the late Mrs. Lowell's apartment.

"Bill, I love it when you get that priestly look," he told his longtime professional rival as the four of them rode uptown. "It does my heart good."

Ratner turned a twinkly-eyed glance upon Andrew. He was having trouble controlling some private hilarity. "My client is a very determined woman."

"Good. I always like it when the people I work with know where they stand."

Mrs. Beizer was not speaking, presumably on the advice of counsel.

"Daddy, I have to go to the bathroom."

"Just hang in there, Kevin. Mr. Ratner is about to show us wondrous things. You'll see."

At that, Ratner laughed outright, and the Beizer woman shot him a vicious look.

"Don't tell me you've already made the kid a partner, Caldwell."

"It's his patrimony," Andrew answered. "Of course I have."

When the car reached its destination, a Deco building with a view of the park, Andrew got out on the traffic side, pushing the folded-up stroller ahead of him like a blind man's cane. He tucked his briefcase under one arm and scooped Kevin up with the other, while Ratner and Mrs. Beizer awaited the chauffeur's ministrations.

"Daddy, who lives here?"

"Just people," answered Andrew, anxious to avoid a reprise of their earlier musings on mortality. "Isn't it a great-looking building?"

"George," said Mrs. Beizer to the doorman, who was actually wearing white gloves and an approximation of livery. "We're going up to my mother's apartment."

The man betrayed considerable relief. "Yes, of course, Mrs. Beizer. I was awfully sorry to hear the news. A spirit like that, she reminded me of my own mother."

"She was something all right," said Mrs. Beizer grimly.

The elevator was of rain-forest mahogany, and Andrew found himself musing over a world in which five-hundred-year-old trees were felled to decorate the appliances of the overprivileged. That was the millennium for you—from the age of discovery to twelve-step programs for mother-dumpers.

"We'll be contesting the apartment, too, of course," Ratner took the opportunity to inform him. "Have you filed for an ancillary proceeding?"

"I'd ask you what your grounds for challenge are, Bill, but I sense a drama unfolding."

Ratner allowed himself a smile. "Like you told young Kevin here—wondrous things."

The elevator door opened upon an intimate hallway decorated with a four-foot bronze Pan on a marble dressing table. There were double doors of the same mahogany as the elevator on either side of the sinuous godling, and the twin pipes into which he solemnly blew seemed to announce the party's arrival.

"I know you haven't been here yet," said Ratner, "which is why I wanted to share the experience with you. Mrs. Lowell owned this whole floor along with the one above." He stood back deferentially while Mrs. Beizer produced a set of keys and addressed herself to the right-hand set of doors. "Why don't we consider ourselves off the record for the time being, Caldwell?"

"Why don't we?" responded Andrew happily. Ratner's unsavory enthusiasms never failed to amuse Andrew on a level that his rival could neither engage nor confidently ignore. This made things interesting if not exactly lofty in their eventual outcome.

The apartment's foyer was fitted out with gray, pink, and black marble floor tiling in a tastefully trompe-l'oeil basket pattern. A massive wooden staircase wound grandly to the upper floor, an incongruous metal bulk attached to the banister. When Mrs. Beizer turned on the lights, the device proved to be an elevator for invalids. Andrew was conscious of Ratner's eyes upon him as he sniffed the sharply fetid air.

"Mrs. Beizer, my son would like to use the facilities, if that's okay."

Now that they were actually in her late mother's home, Mrs. Beizer's anger seemed to trail off into resigned disgust. She appeared disinclined to touch anything, even her own person, and Andrew was able for the first time to see that she was not unattractive. "Sure," she said to him with distaste. "Down the hall on the right." As he walked Kevin to the bathroom he could hear the woman conversing in hushed tones with Ratner, who sounded as if he were trying to reassure her.

An inauspicious locale. Death was palpable.

Andrew switched on the bathroom lights and asked Kevin if he needed assistance, which the boy shyly declined. "I'll be outside, then, bucko," Andrew told him. "Don't fall in."

The apartment, what he could see of it, appeared to have been vandalized, though Mrs. Lowell had died less than three weeks ago and building security seemed perfectly sound. Finger-shaped ammoniac stains ran up and down the rose-colored carpet; several paintings and a set of framed prints had been thrown from the wall, scattering broken glass underfoot, and, in places, what appeared to be shit was smeared across the flocked wallpaper. Andrew could see more of it on the floor, along with festive bits of fruit peel—bananas and oranges, mostly.

As he continued down the hall, past where the light reached, Andrew recalled that Mrs. Lowell had kept a live-in cook and a butler of sorts. They would have had keys.

The stench grew stronger as the light receded. In the dim, heavily curtained library, torn newspaper was gathered together in nestlike heaps. From elsewhere in the apartment, perhaps upstairs, came a high keening voice whose cadence suggested monologue rather than conversation. He wondered why the television would have been turned on; at the same moment he realized the four of them must not be alone.

Starting back the way he had come, Andrew bumped up against a small gateleg table that held a telephone. He stared at it, trying to recall when he had last seen a dial-design phone, let alone a black one that must have weighed five pounds. Still, it was a line to the outside, and he was startled then by a wild desire to call Edith.

Andrew had always taken his responsibilities seriously, and he knew he was perceived as a deliberate, even cautious man. People seemed to need to think of him that way; for the most part he was willing to oblige. He did not take it lightly, however, when someone troubled to look beyond what he routinely put out to the world and engage him on less certain ground. Edith had not even had to try.

Picking up the phone, he realized that talking to her would not be enough. What he wanted was for her to drop everything and rush here in a taxi. He could introduce her as a colleague who would be coming in on the case with him. Then they could continue the tour of this death-drenched place, excuse themselves, and, retiring to the foulest, most completely undone room in the apartment, fuck each other unconscious.

When the dial tone gave way to a recorded message, Andrew hung up. *Second adolescence*, he thought, bemusedly adjusting his erection.

He hurried back down the hall just as Kevin was emerging from the bathroom. Quart beer bottles lay strewn across the floor, and in his haste Andrew nearly tripped over one.

"It's stinky in here," said Kevin, wrinkling his nose.

"We'll open up a window in a minute. Now stick close to me while I see what those two have on their minds. I don't want any more disappearing acts today."

Mrs. Beizer and her attorney were waiting for them at the foot of the staircase, refining their attitude of stoic distemper. The voice Andrew had heard earlier issued intermittently from the upper floor without being intelligible. It sounded like someone's drunken babble.

"Getting the picture, Mr. Caldwell?" said the Beizer woman, holding a handkerchief to her nose.

"No, I can't honestly say I am. But I'm sure you'll help me out."

"We'll have to go upstairs now," Mrs. Beizer answered.

Ratner had withdrawn a bit while he decided how best to deploy the present cast of characters. It was his job to compose the picture Andrew was supposed to get. "You remember Mrs. Lowell died of brain cancer," he said reverently as they ascended the soiled staircase. "She was not in possession of all her faculties."

"Brain cancer, yes," said Andrew, casting a nervous look at his son beside him. "And of course even off the record I can't say anything about her faculties."

The second floor smelled worse than the one below, and was similarly trashed: a large cache of fruit, peels scattered over floor and furniture, more empty beer bottles, damp yellow stains, mounds of shit, torn newspapers. Against the opulent decor—much of it Art Deco, but with older furniture expertly mixed in—this refuse of ordinary life seemed to Andrew inexplicably touching. Objects, by contrast, endured annoyingly long, he thought; they outlasted both owner and heir, persisting into sentimental irrelevance.

As if sensing his father's thoughts, Kevin spoke. "I'm scared, Daddy."

"There's nothing to be afraid of, Kevin. Just hold my hand." Andrew noticed that the drunken gibbering had stopped. Maybe he had imagined it.

"This is as far as I go." Mrs. Beizer stopped several feet from the threshold of the master bedroom, one hand pressed closely to her nose and mouth. "It's in there, I think." She took Ratner's arm and made no move to continue the tour.

"Wait here with Mrs. Beizer, Kevin," said Andrew after a moment. He thought he could discern an instant of silent triumph on the woman's part as Kevin ran over to her and took her hand. Then he walked nonchalantly past them into the darkened room.

Unable to find the light switch on the wall, Andrew stopped at what he judged to be the center of the large space. Here the smell was overpowering, but it was also mingled with a suffocatingly floral perfume, an old-fashioned scent he associated with cluttered drawing rooms and stale petit fours. As his eyes adjusted to the dark, he began to make sense of the large shrouded forms around him: a tall Victorian armoire, a lady's desk or dressing table, three heavy wooden side chairs with upholstered seats arranged around what could only be a bed. The mattress of the huge four-poster, covered with a quilt, tangled sheets, and an excess of pillows, reached to the height of his upper thighs. From the bedding came the snore of someone deeply asleep.

After several seconds of groping blindly about a bedside table, he discovered an electrical cord draped over the near bedpost. He ran his fingers along it until they encountered a line switch. When he pressed it, both bedside lamps and an outsized chandelier overhead blazed on.

The muscular, dwarfish figure in the bed, dark and misshapen, awoke with a hoot, scrambled to the foot of the mattress, and without pause leapt into the upper reaches of the chandelier, where it commenced an ear-piercing shriek.

"God!" cried Mrs. Beizer from the doorway. "Don't let it down! It'll jump! Do something! My hair!"

The creature was a chimpanzee, male. Nearly seventy-five pounds, Andrew judged.

"How could she have lived with that disgusting thing? Don't let it down!"

"Everybody stay calm," said Andrew in a low voice. "Don't move." He tiptoed back to where he had first stood and reached gently upward. "Don't be scared, Kevin," he said over his shoulder. "It's just a chimp."

Screeching in panic, the animal swung easily off the chandelier to the top of the armoire at the other side of the room.

"How long has he been here?" Andrew asked Mrs. Beizer, as he watched the frightened animal.

"Forever! I don't know and I don't care."

"You never visited your mother, then."

"She was crazy, can't you see? Oh God."

"Off the record, Caldwell," Ratner warned him. "We agreed."

"Just don't move. Let him calm down."

The chimpanzee's shrieks were subsiding into a kind of fast-forward singsong of hoots and pants. He looked warily at Andrew, then at the faces clustered in the doorway, then back at Andrew. After a time, he fell silent. Catching sight of a half-full beer bottle on the armoire's opposite edge, he reached one immensely long arm out and retrieved it. Everyone watched raptly as the chimp brought the mouth of the bottle to his eye and peered into it as if it were a telescope. Satisfied, he put the bottle to his lips and drained it thoughtfully. Then, after shaking it a little to be sure it was empty, he threw it to the floor.

"Daddy, give him a banana! I want to see!" Kevin had squeezed around in front of Mrs. Beizer's primly tailored skirt.

"A banana. Just the thing." Andrew found one on the near

bedside table, peeled it, and held it enticingly up to the chimp, who had set the chandelier swinging so that its crystal droplets clashed against one another in distress.

"Anybody know his name?"

But just then, sailing toward Andrew like the bob on a pendulum, the chimp urinated copiously down on him, on the carpet, and on everything within the chandelier's path, marking the terrain with gaudy yellow figure eights of piss.

"Jesus," said Andrew, withdrawing to the doorway. "I think we need a Higher Power here." He herded the others back out into the hallway and shut the door behind them.

"You see the problem, Caldwell," said Ratner, as Andrew tried to pat himself dry with a handkerchief.

"Problem? Unless that's her grandson in there I don't see any problem at all."

"Oh come on, Counselor. Her grandson's a primatologist, he changed his last name to match hers. The guy diddled with her mind."

"From what I can see she had her priorities dead straight. Who says she was mentally incapacitated? She knew who loved her." He started down the hall. "Mind if I use the telephone?"

Without waiting for an answer, he began dialing. The call had already been put through when Andrew noticed Kevin standing by his side.

"What are you doing, Daddy?"

What indeed? Andrew wondered, thinking of his peculiar moment in the library downstairs.

He put a hand over the mouthpiece and said in a voice loud enough for the others to hear, "I'm calling the zoo to see if they make house calls."

LETTING herself into her apartment, Edith already felt somewhat the stranger. The two years she had lived there had been productive and largely peaceful; by any standard it had been more of a home to her than all her previous addresses. Abstractedly, she walked across the living room and back again. *But done is done*, she told herself. Then, her mind made up, she went into the bedroom and changed the message on her answering machine, referring callers to Andrew's place.

After a quick shower, she dressed again, deciding on a black cocktail dress with a bodice of black Venetian lace, and then from her closet chose a second outfit, a possible alternate, for dinner with the Díazes that evening. As she looked at herself in the full-length bedroom mirror, smoothing the dress down over her abdomen and thighs, she wondered if she oughtn't to reassume some at least pro forma relationship to underwear, maybe for the boy's sake. But whatever had led her and Andrew to their present state did not invite half-measures, and they had quite some distance ahead of them yet. She suspected that their shared exhibitionism, if that was the word for it, attached to something far more revealing than one might think.

Anyway, she told herself as she got into the elevator, the real decision had already been made.

When she arrived at Andrew's apartment, it was deserted. There was a note on the mail table:

> *Kevin and I have gone on a short field trip.*
> *Boring, back soon.*
> > *Kisses.*

After a moment, Edith brought the note to her lips and kissed it herself, leaving a lipstick imprint. *We can do this*, she thought, as she put the slip of paper back where she had found it.

On her way through the living room she saw the building-block castle Andrew had constructed for Kevin, and she smiled again at the notion of herself as mother. She should have guessed, by her very failure to include children in her imagined future, that she in fact longed for them. The forces into whose grip she delivered herself kept getting larger all the time, as, she was coming to see, they did for everyone. And who had ever really had time to explain *that* to her?

She laid her fallback dinner dress out on the bed and turned on the television, hoping to catch the world news. When she saw that the network programming had already subsided into lifestyle segments—if one could really use such a term to describe an account of swimming chipmunks—she held down the channel button of the remote control and watched without interest as image after image filed past.

Now might be a good time to call her father, she thought. He would have had his cocktail hour but would still be many glasses from completely sodden.

"Hi, Dad. It's me." She kicked off her shoes.

"Edie. What a pleasure to hear your voice. I was just thinking about you, young lady."

"You must have picked up the vibrations. I have news."

"Lord, Edie. I wish you'd vibrate less and communicate more befittingly. Write us a letter once in a while." His use of the first-person plural was purely rhetorical now that her brothers had grown up, though Edith had lately noticed that he was sometimes given to personalizing the bottle or bimbo nearest to hand.

"I do write, Dad. This is different. I called to tell you I'm getting married."

There was a lengthy silence. "Married? Well that's . . . I'm very . . . Don't you think your young man might have come down here to Vauxhall and spoken to me himself?"

"What, so you could take him into your study and give him a brandy and cigar while he stated his intentions? He probably would have done it, too. He's a good man, an attorney here in town. Andrew Caldwell."

"Caldwell. Have you met his family?"

"Well, not exactly. His parents are dead. But I have met his sister and his three-year-old son, Kevin."

"Edith, for God's sake. A divorced lawyer with a child? What would your mother have said?"

"She would have asked me if I love him, does he make me happy, am I sure."

He sighed. "Yes, I suppose she would have."

"She would have asked me if he was a gentleman," Edith added in a reflexive attempt to stir the coals of her father's own courtliness, a dimmed but unextinguished thing.

"You know, Edie, I'd resigned myself to your flightiness; my daughter is a creature of the sky, I told myself."

She could hear him pouring another drink. "You didn't resign yourself, you prayed I'd never settle down. You used to call me your meadowlark, remember? You never said it but you always thought of yourself as the meadow, me as the lark. But I'm grown now, Daddy. You should be happy. I want you to be as happy as I am."

Just then Andrew arrived in the doorway with Kevin asleep in his arms. Edith waved happily, and when she blew him a kiss Andrew smiled and signaled that he was going off to put Kevin to bed.

"Daddy. I'm getting married."

"Yes, lark, you told me." She heard the bottle clink again against his glass on the other end of the line. "What I'm trying to determine is whether I am to be presented with grandchildren by you and your young man. Eventually, though not soon, I will be old. There's the family to consider, the distribution of genetic felicities, et cetera, et cetera. Not something you think about when you're in love, of course, but it's there nonetheless. Any chance of the two of you moving back down South?"

"Come off it, Dad. Do you think I'm one of your fillies? A promising breeder?" She felt herself blush with resentment. "And please give up this officious old-fart routine long enough to be happy for me! I love Andrew and we know what we're doing."

When her father failed to respond, she added, "I want you to meet him."

"I'd like that, Edith, I really would. When is the blessed event to take place?"

"Soon. We don't have a date yet."

"Well, bring Andrew down to Vauxhall. I'm really very pleased, Edie. I'm certain you know what you're doing. It's just that you're so strong-minded I never thought I'd see the day. Your Andrew must be a very brave man."

"People keep saying that. He is. I love you, Daddy."

"Yes," said her father vaguely. "You must both come down soon. Maybe you'd like to be married here? But do what you think best."

"I will. And Daddy, please don't drink so much; it's not worth it."

"I'll leave it to you to tell your brothers, Edie; it'll be better that way. I suppose I ought to go see about dinner now."

As soon as she had replaced the phone in its cradle, Edith got up from the bed, walked over to the bedroom windows, and threw them open. Elsewhere in the apartment she could hear the shower running.

Once, when she was thirteen, one of her father's lovers had walked in on her accidentally while she was soaking in the bath. The woman had sat down fully dressed on the closed toilet seat and proceeded to ask Edith's opinion of a pair of crotchless black panties she had just received from a mail-order house. "I *think* he'll like them," the woman had said, turning the unnaturally silky garment over in her hands, "but you know his taste better than just about anyone, honey. You're so grown up! Tell me honestly what you think."

Edith took her cigarette pack from her purse and hurried down the hall.

"Andrew," she said, knocking lightly on the shut bathroom door. "Is everything okay?"

His laughter reverberated against the tile walls inside. "Everything's fine. I had quite a day."

"Me too."

"I'll be out in a minute. Trust me, this is a compulsory shower."

"Are you glad I'm here?"

"Glad doesn't describe it."

"Good. Hurry up then."

She continued down the hall to Kevin's room and stopped beside his bed. He was sleeping on his stomach, one small fist half-clenched on the sheet by his nose, his rain gear discarded on the floor. After a while, she found herself trying to imagine Susannah's face by subtracting from Kevin's countenance the features she fancied he had inherited from Andrew. It was an impossible and stupid task. To break her trancelike imaginings, she reached for the baby blanket at the foot of the bed and put it partway over the boy. *Will Daddy come up and tuck me in?* she remembered her own tiny voice asking. Then the memory shifted ground, and she had to catch her breath: it shocked her to find that she could so easily envision her father as a child, even though there had been no photographs of him to speak of. She left the room.

When she heard the shower still running, she took her cigarette outside, into the building's softly lit, branching corridor. The door shut behind her without engaging the lock.

She leaned against the wall midway between two frosted-glass sconces, and in the parabola of shadow there she smoked. After a short time, she became pleasantly aware of the lives humming along behind the corridor's closed doors—a soothing sotto voce cacophony of thoughts, desires, words rushing on, each inner aria intertwining with the others.

As she watched the elevator door quiver with the slipstream trapped behind it, her thought announced itself like a theme reassembled: *I am waiting here.* At the same moment, she heard the door to Andrew's apartment open and gently fall shut again against the chain of its safety lock.

Andrew wore a bathrobe of white cotton woven into a pattern of small squares like windowpanes. His hair was combed but still wet, and the scent of peppermint soap preceded him in a cloud. Edith dropped her cigarettes to the floor as he came to her, then, her back still pressed against the wall, she took him into her arms.

"I have to have you," he whispered.

"Yes," she said. "Yes, I've been waiting here." She worked the hem of her dress up with one hand and reached into his robe.

"You'll never believe what happened to me today," he said.

"I'm ahead of you there," she answered. "I don't believe what's happening to you now."

He kissed her roughly on the mouth, then his lips and tongue made their way across her face to her throat. Over his shoulder, thirty feet away, she saw a man in a lime green sweatsuit come out of his apartment. There was an exercise bicycle beside his door, and he got on it without seeing them. He had his back to them, and he was wearing stereo headphones.

"Give me a ride," she said.

Andrew didn't hear.

"Give me a ride on your handlebars."

Cupping her buttocks in his hands, he lifted her away from the wall and laid her down upon the corridor's beige carpet. Across the hall, just past the elevator, the man in the sweatsuit began to pedal.

"Hurry, Andrew. I can't wait longer." She drew her knees up to her breasts and, as his cock slid into her, straightened out her legs so that they were pinned beneath his shoulders.

"Strange stuff," he said, staring down at her. Then he looked up, and she saw his eyes take in his aerobic neighbor, pedaling away. When Andrew's gaze returned to her, his pupils were dilated.

"Yes," she agreed. "Strange stuff."

As they fucked, the soft whir of the bicycle's flywheel seemed to confirm something they had first glimpsed two nights ago in the banquet hall, though neither of them could have said what it was. Flirtation with shame played its part, but there was something else going on. They had suspended disbelief.

A low breeze passed over the two of them, then became a

steady draft. Andrew's robe had formed a white tent that partly concealed their lovemaking and kept him from noticing the draft, but Edith, feeling it against the side of her face, turned to look. It was coming from beneath the elevator door, pressed out of the shaft by the rising cab.

Edith's lips trembled, parted, and as the elevator rushed past she bit into her hand to stifle her cry. When she opened her eyes again, she stared up at Andrew. "More," she said. "Again."

He sat back to catch his breath, and Edith pressed the soles of her feet to his chest for purchase. For a moment, Andrew was absorbed in the tensile truth of this posture, its exact equilibrium between tenderness and resistance. There was enough moral excitement here for anyone but a simpleton, he thought, when they resumed.

The sound of the bicyclist's cassette player snapping off went through them both like a pistol shot.

"Quick," said Edith, sitting up.

In an instant they were on their feet. Edith smoothed her rumpled dress back down over her thighs. Andrew wrapped his robe around him and, turning just as his neighbor dismounted his bicycle to choose another tape, gave the man a noncommittal wave and stole after Edith back into the apartment.

Some time later, in the bedroom, when they were still again, Edith laughed quietly. "I told James we bring it out in each other," she said. "You and I."

"He didn't like that."

"No, he didn't. He knew it was a placatory thing to say. A lie, really."

"A lie?" They were huddled together on their sides, their faces inches apart.

"It makes it sound as if we both have some sort of recessive trait that burst to life when we came together. I realized how untrue that was as soon as I said it. Nothing about us is recessive. What we are together, we've both been all our lives. Separately." She drew her fingers slowly across his mouth, then got out of bed and began sorting through the jewelry she'd left on the dresser. "I was being childish with James, trying to protect all three of us by appealing to fate or something."

"None of us believes in fate anymore," said Andrew.

"No," answered Edith. "We don't." She sighed. "What should I wear to dinner, this dress or the one there on the bed? I wasn't sure."

"That one. What you had on."

She smiled and began brushing her hair. It was a full minute before Andrew was able to look away and choose a fresh suit for their evening with the Díazes.

"And what lesson should we draw, Miss Emerson, from the demise of fate?"

She didn't even turn around. "Accidents will happen."

"s o w h a t about the poor chimp? It sounds like he's the one who needs a lawyer." Judy, Andrew's sister's lover, had come to baby-sit Kevin while Andrew and Edith went out to dinner with the Díazes, and the three of them were sitting around the living room with a bottle of Meursault. They were waiting for Santiago to call.

"The chimp, as we speak, is receiving the expert attentions of the zoo's detox team. They've got terrific people there, if the woman who came to pick him up is any gauge. Meeting her made me think I've missed my true calling."

"You already work at the zoo," Judy pointed out.

"We both do," Edith added, glancing up from her watch. "I'm in the international wing."

"What a story, Andy. Moral situations kind of seek you out, don't they?"

"They wait for me in doors and alleyways," said Andrew. "How's Sarah?" He had grown close to his sister after his divorce, and despite her obvious strong-mindedness he was protective of her. "She seemed kind of soul-stressed the other night."

"Oh, Sarah's fine," said Judy, draining her glass and putting it carefully on the coffee table. She inspected Edith and Andrew not unsympathetically. "She thinks you and Edie have a hidden agenda is all."

"She said that? Sarah and Edie just met that once. What hidden agenda?"

"Who knows?" Judy shrugged. "Probably whatever it means to you."

Flustered, Andrew looked to Edith, who was now toying with her watch. "I was talking to my father when you came home," she said carefully. "I told him."

"Aha." He poured himself some more wine and sat back in his chair. "Look, Judy. I haven't had a chance to talk to Sarah about this, but Edie and I have decided to get married. I can't imagine how Sarah saw it coming, since we barely did ourselves, but there it is."

"Wow. You two are quick on the draw. Does Kevin know?"

"Not exactly. We're letting him get used to things."

"Susannah's gonna bug. What if she wants him back?"

"We'll deal with that if it comes up, but I don't think it will. You know as well as I do that the maternal impulse is not exactly rampant in Susannah."

"I've got to hand it to both of you: you've got guts." She raised her empty glass to guts and moral situations. "Yay, team!"

The conversation shifted then to other topics, but as the minutes ticked away Andrew thought he saw something furtive and agitated in Edith's face. He was trying to think of a way to ask her what was going on when the phone rang.

"Good evening, Señor Caldwell. It is Díaz."

"Hello. Edie and I have been looking forward all day to dinner with you and Mrs. Díaz. I hope we're still on."

"Mercedes and I have just left the ambassador's quarters. Why don't I tell my driver to stop at your apartment so we can pick you up?"

Brushing past him with the three empty wineglasses in her hand, Edith smiled but avoided Andrew's eyes. He decided that her unease was nothing more than a passing embarrassment at not having mentioned earlier that she had spoken with her father. "Yes, thank you so much. That would be perfect. Do you have the address?"

"*Claro.* We'll be there in fifteen minutes. Mercedes is eager to meet you."

"Same here."

"And my regards to your remarkable *prometida.*" The call cut out with the aeronautic abruptness peculiar to cellular phones.

"You've made a conquest," Andrew told Edith as they waited for the elevator. "He praises you with adjectives."

"Does he?"

"I wonder what his wife is like. Santiago seems determined to—what?—unveil her to us or something."

"I think the unveiling trick is ours, Andrew. But I'm sure she's quite spectacular. Bravery itself, he said. We'll see."

Andrew inspected her more closely. "Edie, is everything okay?"

She hesitated. Then, recovering immediately, she took his hand and pressed it to her breast. "It's nothing. We just haven't had much time to talk is all."

"If it's about your father, please tell me."

"No, really. Everything's fine. We'll have plenty of time later. Let's just enjoy our evening."

They kissed, and like a cat scratch on pale skin, their ardor of an hour ago flared at the touch. When the elevator arrived they were both flushed.

"Andrew!" exclaimed the elevator man archly. "My, my. A night on the town?"

Edith smiled and put a finger to her lips.

"Not a word," Andrew told him.

THE LIMOUSINE was double-parked outside the canvas canopy of Andrew's building.

"Señor Caldwell?" the driver asked when Andrew and Edith approached.

"Yes. And Miss Emerson." Andrew wondered why he was feeling suddenly defensive for her.

"Thank you," said Edith, as the driver opened the door for them.

Santiago, seated comfortably next to his wife in back, leaned forward in greeting. "My friends. Please forgive this idiotic excess, but my security people require it."

"Don't worry," said Edith, stepping into the car. "You can't spoil us. We're just happy *funcionarios.*"

"It's good to see you again," Andrew added when he was seated facing Santiago. He noticed that both Santiago and his wife were inspecting Edith thoughtfully. "I know you must be very busy."

Mercedes, somewhat overdressed in an embroidered purple dress and black rabbit-skin stole, smiled at Andrew as if he had just said something unexpectedly charming.

"Andrew Caldwell, Edith Emerson, this is Mercedes Estrada Díaz. I am no doubt shamefully uxorious, but it is rare for a man to be known so well by a woman. Often we are not worth it."

"As you can see," said Mercedes, giving her hand first to Andrew, then to Edith, "Santiago is a lady's man. I am very pleased to meet you both."

Edith smiled at her, grateful to Mercedes for so quickly divining that she had neglected to inform Andrew of their earlier meeting. It was as they had agreed: nothing of that encounter had passed beyond the walls of Edith's office. She began to relax.

Santiago leaned forward to give his driver the necessary directions.

"Are either of you infected with the political virus?" Mercedes looked brightly from Andrew to Edith. "Tell me everything. I've been vaccinated, so it's okay."

"Me, I'm just an interested spectator." Andrew glanced

quizzically at Edith as he spoke, hoping to coax her out of her silence. "I like to stay informed, but I'm an estate lawyer, which means I spend most of my time sorting out other people's private dramas. The real reason I came to the dinner for Santiago is that a friend of mine bought some extra seats. Edie, on the other hand, works at the United Nations."

"Yes, one can see at a glance that you have the soul of an activist, Edith. How did you persuade Andrew to take an interest in your neighbors south of the border?"

"I didn't. I came with the friend."

The conversation faltered, but Andrew hastened to the rescue. "James Walsh we're talking about. He's the one who called you yesterday about us all having our photograph taken together, Santiago."

"Of course. The gallery owner."

"He's sort of an impresario," Edith offered, struggling to patch over the awkwardness she'd caused. "Andrew's known him since high school."

"Well, I really didn't get to know him till a little later, but he's a phenomenon, that guy. He's got a sort of sixth sense for giving people what they didn't even know they wanted."

"That may be so," said Santiago, looking at Edith, "but clearly he's not as lucky in getting what he wants for himself."

Edith averted her eyes.

"Obviously not," said Mercedes, mistress of the deliberate misunderstanding. "What I can't see is why you're even entertaining the idea of letting him unleash some mad Brazilian photographer on us. Of course, I know you don't really mean to go through with it, but you'll put Andrew in a very uncomfortable position with his friend."

"It *is* a silly idea," Edith added, taking the opening offered her. "Why, Mercedes, are we women always having to save our men from their own vanity?"

"We do it, and then they laugh at our overdeveloped sensitivities." Mercedes gave her husband a smart punch on the biceps.

Santiago smiled, but he directed his words quietly at Andrew, "So it was a *coup de foudre*, you and Edith? No warning?"

"You could say that. We were an accident that didn't wait to happen."

"I thought so. It was the same for us."

The limousine had begun to encounter midtown theater traffic, and Pedro swore softly as he negotiated it. Andrew put his arm around Edith. "Mercedes, I take your point about male vanity. But at the risk of compromising the male mysteries, which Santiago and I, like all men, have sworn a mighty oath to protect, let me say that every day we suffer horrible humiliations of which we never speak. Today I took my little boy to work with me, hoping to instill in him a little respect for the legal profession, which is everywhere reviled. Instead, he now has an indelible memory of his old man being urinated on by a chimpanzee."

Santiago watched his wife as she arched her eyebrows interrogatively at Edith.

"It's true," said Edith, giving in to her amusement. "I think it was some kind of male-bonding ritual."

Santiago was amused. "I would ask you how a lawyer finds himself in such gregarious company, but if politics has taught me anything, it's that questions like that answer themselves."

"Pay no attention to the grand man," Mercedes said, shedding her pose as national headmistress-in-waiting. "Tell us about the chimpanzee."

The restaurant Santiago had booked for them was far downtown, and Andrew drew the story out to suit the trip. He sensed that in taking on the responsibility of social leavener he was performing the function ordinarily accorded Santiago, but the situation seemed to invite, even require, his initiative. As he watched Mercedes wipe tears of laughter from her eyes, he felt grateful that she had not been at the banquet, however much Santiago might have told her about what had happened there.

"Maybe we should get out at the corner," said Edith as they

neared the restaurant. "There's some kind of demonstration down the street."

Santiago spoke to Pedro in Spanish, asking him to pick them up in three hours unless he heard otherwise, and a moment later the two couples were standing together on the wide, pockmarked sidewalk.

For a second, Edith was the only one who saw the young man running toward them in a worn army jacket and sneakers. She touched Santiago's shoulder. "Look out!" she cried. "He's got something in his hand!"

Mercedes had just stepped off the low sidewalk onto the street, and though Santiago made a lunge for her she was out of reach.

"Get down!" Andrew told Edith, shoving her behind a car. He made a move toward Santiago, thinking to protect him, but at the same moment all four of them realized that it was Mercedes who was the target of the young man's charge.

"Killer!" the man shouted at her. He was very pale, with fine ash-colored hair that lifted in the draft of his attack. With one forefinger he pushed his wire-rimmed glasses back up the bridge of his nose as he ran. "Murderer!"

Mercedes sidestepped Santiago's outstretched hand and began walking purposefully toward the man. In three strides she was face to face with him. Shouting incoherently, he pointed at her the object he had been carrying, but she easily knocked it out of his grasp. It fell to the pavement with the unmistakable clatter of a spray-paint can, and for a short time no one moved. Mercedes was more than a head taller than he.

"You are a very rude young man," she said. "What is it you want?"

Across the street, three men sitting on folded-out cardboard boxes were laughing uproariously, pointing to the demonstrators down the block. The men passed a pint bottle among themselves.

"Fur flies, creatures die! Go naked, no fur!"

For a moment Santiago, who had been walking evenly after his wife, thought the overexcited little man was referring to himself.

"You are talking about this?" asked Mercedes, removing the rabbit-skin stole from her shoulders.

"Baby animals slaughtered for your vanity!"

"I agree. It is stupid. Here." She handed the stole to the man and left him there. He was visibly torn between retrieving his spray can and disposing of the offending garment before he was tainted by it.

"It is nothing," Mercedes told Santiago as they walked arm in arm back to Edith and Andrew. "It was not even like the egg in the Zócalo."

THE MAÎTRE D' had recognized Santiago's name among the reservations, and he led them to the table he had set aside for them—private enough for conversation but visible to all patrons. It was the kind of situation Santiago had grown used to. He ordered a bottle of California wine and one of mineral water for Mercedes. They studied their menus in silence for a couple of minutes, then Edith asked Santiago how long they planned to be in town.

"Two more days. After that, we will go home by way of Texas. The border question is always with us in Mexico."

Mercedes looked at Edith and saw her eyes widen. "You mentioned having a son, Andrew."

"Yes. Kevin. He's three. His mother and I were divorced almost two years ago, and the word 'amicable' did not figure much in the process. Still, things seem to be working out, and Kevin will go on living with us."

"Mercedes and I have no children yet, but when things settle down . . ." Santiago made a gesture of unplumbed possibility which now, after his wife's words the previous night, seemed stupid and superfluous to him. In their private life, his wife's desires were decisions that, in discovering them, he ratified.

"I never knew I wanted children until I met Andrew," Edith volunteered as the waiter set a plate of carpaccio before her, "but watching him and Kevin together has opened things up for me. In a lot of ways, really."

During his adolescence, Andrew's mother had often lamented her son's tendency to reveal his secrets only in the presence of family friends. As a result, Andrew's appreciation of those who understood the value of indirection had grown exponentially. His mother had died badly, in a rage of incomprehension that made Andrew's grief an enduring, obdurate thing. He engaged Santiago in a fleeting glance of complicity. "Edith has three younger brothers," he explained.

"I have three sisters," Santiago replied. "All older. As a child, of course, I suffered many indignities at their hands. Really you would have to say that I was experimented upon."

"Don't let him mislead you," said Mercedes over her celery rémoulade. "He had an idyllic childhood."

"And you?"

"I was happy, yes. More solitary."

Edith finished her wine and thanked Santiago as he refilled her glass. "It was impressive, the way you handled that guy out there. How did you know that wasn't a gun he was carrying?"

"I didn't really think about it. At first I assumed he was going for Santiago, but then I saw he was headed for me. It seemed best to find out what he wanted." Mercedes shrugged. "That's just my nature, I guess."

"But don't people often misunderstand? A lot of times I find that straightforwardness gets confused with aggression or boldness."

"Men frequently say that I am a mystery to them, which is fine with me because Santiago knows me very well. With women it's not usually a problem."

Santiago shook his shirt cuff back down over his watch. "Mercedes says that I am sentimental."

"Most men are," Edith surprised herself by saying. "It's how they direct it that counts."

"And you, Andrew? What do you think of all this?" Mercedes smiled at him.

"Maybe it's the effect of sharing a table with Santiago, but I can't help thinking about the role of sports here. You weren't with us at breakfast yesterday, Mercedes. I hope Edie won't be upset with me for repeating her remark that she thought Santiago preferred being a soccer star to running for office. Whether she was right or not, I don't know; it doesn't matter. What struck me at the time, though, was that men do like to set up rules and then measure themselves by how well they do within them, as if we haven't set up the rules in the first place. Women are understandably less likely to believe in regulations they didn't invent. From the outside, our arbitrary devotion has to look sentimental."

For a moment, no one seemed willing to let it go at that.

"Bottom line, though," said Andrew, draining his glass, "nobody thinks it was a woman who said, Winning isn't everything." Edith put her hand on his thigh beneath the table.

The main course arrived, and the conversation meandered amiably. Without thinking about it, the four of them began to speak in a more familiar register, hearing one another out, but knowing when to interrupt. It was an auspicious mix.

The sommelier appeared with a bottle of champagne that Santiago had not ordered. "From the party up front, sir," the waiter explained.

Santiago nodded in the direction of a web of waving hands. Well-wishers. "Please thank them."

As the busboy removed the plates, Edith let out a sigh of annoyance and took off the silver and topaz necklace she had been wearing.

"It's a lovely piece of jewelry," said Mercedes, watching as Edith put it in the spotless ashtray at the center of the table.

"Thank you. Yes, I love it; it was my grandmother's idea of

conspicuous consumption, and she had very good ideas. But my hair gets caught in it."

"Conspicuous consumption," said Santiago musingly. "It's a phrase I haven't heard in a long time, since the fifties maybe. But there's a resonance to it all the same."

"Somewhere between 'Noblesse oblige' and 'If you've got it flaunt it.' " Andrew knew there was no such thing as an evening without politics. "If you take the three expressions together you've got a sound-bite history of the monied classes in this country."

Mercedes appraised Andrew thoughtfully. "You and your friend James Walsh have spent some time in Mexico, I gather."

"Yes, but we were tourists; students just out of college. It was a hegemonic romance. Mexico—land of tequila, Zapata, and chile-tempered women. We weren't disappointed, but if you want an apolitical evening just ask me to tell you about it."

"That is also Mexico," Mercedes allowed.

"Hey, I've got an idea." Edith set her espresso aside untasted. "What if you went on a TV talk show, Santiago? While you're here in town I mean? You could speak to the issues without having to tiptoe around the ruling party types. It would make great footage back in Mexico—just do the show and let the press take care of the rest."

"A talk show, Edie," said Andrew carefully. "I don't know if that's such a great idea."

"Well, isn't our number-one network trying to build an audience for this summer's World Cup? It's a perfect lead-in—sports and politics, as we were saying. I've seen you on TV before, Santiago, and you're a natural. Anyway, I don't mean one of those daytime free-for-alls, I was thinking about *The Oliver Barnes Show*. He's intelligent, and he'd let you call the shots." She took the lemon twist from the saucer of her coffee cup and dropped it in her champagne. "Granted that's not much of an accomplishment except on television, but he'd give you something you could take home."

Santiago appeared intrigued. "Oliver Barnes. I was asked to be on his show once before, after the hostages. Remember, Mercedes?"

"Yes," she said, making no effort to disguise her distaste. "You felt it was a bad idea."

Andrew, who knew quite well the details of Edith's affair with Barnes, cleared his throat and downed his coffee.

"Is he a friend of yours?" Santiago asked Edith.

"Certainly," she said. "I don't see him so much lately, but I believe I still enjoy his fond regard." Glancing uneasily at Andrew, she remembered that her impulse to bring everyone in her life peaceably together had not, by and large, proven helpful. And three glasses of champagne was really quite enough.

"Oh, I don't know. It was just an idea." Leaning back in her chair, she laughed dismissively at her own suggestion. "Anyway I'm sure your campaign manager has already thought of it."

"Luis is concerned that we bring all our efforts to bear on Mexico's local leaders, the *caciques* who have kept our country in solitude for generations. Practically speaking, he is right. But that is not why I am running for office."

Everyone but Santiago was immediately sorry he had offered this confidence. Mercedes helped herself to the other half of his dessert without comment.

"How soon could it be arranged?" asked Santiago.

To Andrew's consternation, an image of Edith came back to him with the force of a holiday memory. She had been peering into a stewpot in James's kitchen, a gauzy blue scarf wrapped around her neck. *This is the girl I've been telling you about,* James had whispered. When he said hello, Edith had put the top back over the pot with a furtive gesture, smiling as if she had expected everything to be just as it was but had prepared herself to pretend pleasantly otherwise.

"Neither of us knows as much as we should about Mexican politics," Andrew told Santiago, "but that's life among the conspicuously consuming."

"I could call him tonight if you like," said Edith, unflustered by what she had set in motion. "Oliver likes last-minute arrangements." She hesitated. "But maybe Andrew's right. I didn't mean to interfere."

Mercedes took a sip of mineral water. She had been upset to be reminded that Edith had so quickly recognized her husband as someone who preferred playing fields to political rostrums, but jealousy was no longer part of what she felt. The terrain of victory lay outside discussion.

"It's not interference," Santiago protested. "Please call Mr. Barnes. Mercedes and I will talk it over with Luis, but my instincts are to do it."

"You're sure?" Andrew realized he was addressing himself to Edith. She avoided his eye.

"Why not?" she said to Santiago. "You can always say no."

"Santiago doesn't like to say no," Mercedes observed quietly, but she pinched her husband's cheek to show she was entering into the spirit of the thing. "He's always wanted to be in forty million American bedrooms all at the same time."

"Gently, Mercedes. I've never said forty million." He turned to Edith and shrugged. "My wife believes I am priapic."

Edith touched her napkin to her lips and set it before her on the table, where it unfolded like a starchy narcissus blossom. "I'll call Oliver when we get home."

"Thank you. And I am most grateful for your suggestion."

Santiago settled the bill, then he and his guests made their way to the coat-check room up front. There the maître d' waylaid them, performing with Santiago the restaurateur's rituals of ingratiation. Andrew was helping Edith on with her coat when she realized she'd forgotten her necklace.

"I'll get it," Andrew said.

When he reached the table, there were three waiters standing around the leavings of the meal in languid discussion. "I mean it's kind of *disappointing*," one of them was saying. "I thought linen was like superflammable. What was that movie where the crazy son torches the whole restaurant?" As he edged closer, Andrew saw the problem: Edith had left her napkin negligently near one of the table's votive candles, and a corner of it had caught fire. Reaching between two of the waiters, he picked up the smoking square of double damask and plunged the tip of it into Santiago's half-empty champagne glass.

"Sorry, guys. Sometimes she gets carried away." He scooped Edith's necklace from the ashtray and, smiling apologetically, returned to the front of the restaurant.

The meal James had been preparing the night he had introduced Andrew to Edith had also ended up in smoke. The company had been too caught up in conversation to notice, and the smoke alarm had gone off.

Of course, none of them believed in fate anymore.

AT THE ambassador's residence, Luis Arévalo paced about the small study he had commandeered as an ad hoc campaign headquarters. The technical staff had set up the laptop system that traveled with Santiago everywhere now, and cables ran in disorderly fashion from the wall outlets to the telephones, computers, and printers perched haphazardly on the furniture. Arévalo was alone except for Abundio Sedano, his chief lieutenant. To everyone but Santiago, Sedano was known as Vendajes because of the arm bandages that concealed the gun he was obliged to carry on security-sensitive occasions. The truth, though, was that he was a young genius. The only reason Arévalo had assigned him hard-security duties as well was to keep him in line.

"Luis, I will have to format another dozen diskettes to back up the last of those databases," Vendajes said, lifting his fingers theatrically from the keyboard to indicate his exhaustion.

"How long?" Arévalo picked up his jacket from the sofa, checked to see that the breast pocket was still buttoned, then slung the coat over one shoulder.

"Ten minutes to format, another fifteen to copy."

"*Bueno*. Do it. Monday is the filing deadline for new candidates, and there are always a few unexpected sons of bitches. We need another copy of everything."

As Arévalo left the room, Vendajes resumed his work, speaking sweet confidences to the computer.

Luis and Santiago had met in a corner of Chapultepec Park during their fifteenth and twelfth years respectively. A sparsely appointed soccer field had been staked out near the few remaining cedars and swamp cypresses. On Saturdays fathers brought their sons there for a pickup game which they watched with relish, drinking beer and shouting good-natured insults among themselves. Luis, heavier in build, invariably played goalie, while Santiago quickly became known as a star forward. They had not played many weekends before Santiago's father, a finely featured, temperate man, had summoned the two boys to the sideline and suggested with an authority that invited no challenge that they see to it they were always on the same team in the future. Realizing that their late-second-half confrontations had become occasion for excessive excitement among the fathers, Luis and Santiago readily complied. Within a month, they were inseparable.

In the summer of his seventeenth year, Luis's cousin had offered to sell him a fighting cock of prodigious reputation, and to purchase it Santiago had stolen the money from his parents. Luis's father, awakened the next morning by the bird's triumphant crows, had shot it dead in its cage. Santiago had been put to work in the local *farmacia* to pay back the money he had taken, while Luis had been subjected to a multiple-installment lecture on the decadence of the rich.

The following spring, Luis had fallen in love with Santiago's youngest sister and had enlisted his aid in gaining her affections. Santiago had persuaded her to leave her bedroom window open, but it was not until late summer that the girl had submitted to his friend's caresses. By fall, when Santiago was sent abroad to school, his sister was no longer on speaking terms with Luis.

Separated by geography, Luis and Santiago pursued increasingly different adventures, but though Luis could never bring himself to answer his friend's letters, the two were as close as ever when Santiago returned for holidays.

That was how it had always been.

At the fourth-floor landing of the ambassador's residence, Arévalo paused to check his watch. A discreet call to his contact at the UN had confirmed that Mercedes had paid Edith Emerson a visit, but since Santiago and Mercedes were at this very moment dining with her, it seemed fair to infer that the women had struck a separate peace. As for Santiago, nothing seemed to intrude upon his happiness. For half an hour before dinner, Arévalo had heard the Díazes' bed thump with incontestable eloquence against the wall.

In a way, thought Arévalo, his father had been right about the decadence of the rich.

It was Arévalo's habit to carry with him everywhere a supplementary door lock so that he would not have to worry about the security of his quarters. In the corridor's dim light he disengaged it and looked about the room for a clean shirt, which he then buttoned up before the closet mirror. From his bedside table he removed a pair of commercial airline tickets and, examining them, sat down upon the edge of the bed. There he brooded over the peculiarities of history, which cared nothing for personal loyalties or the admonitions of one's father. These communions shortly became unsatisfactory, and, tossing the tickets aside, he left the room and walked back down the hall to Santiago's suite.

Santiago's bed remained unmade, and Arévalo sat down upon it in the spirit of agitated inquiry that at times like this governed his thoughts and actions. The sheets bore the chalky stains of lovemaking, but Arévalo was moved to neither envy nor mirth by this testament of intimacy.

Arévalo had always admired the purposefulness Mercedes brought to her day-to-day life in the realm, unreasonably public, she had chosen to inhabit. He was not bothered by her barely concealed distaste for him. His own wife was less assertive, though nearer to the earth.

After a moment he opened the drawer in the nightstand. He had been rebuked by what he perceived as history's coldness, and was reminded that to the discerning man politics resembled a bedsheet more than it did the page of a book. Nevertheless, there was a book in the drawer of the nightstand.

Arévalo recognized the volume by the baroque design of its cover—a purple filigree of decorative flourishes that nearly obscured the title: *Las Obras Completas de Góngora*. Although Arévalo did not care one way or another about poetry, he had become impatient with Santiago for dragging this book with him everywhere. It suited neither the candidate nor his country, and Arévalo personally doubted whether Santiago had read more than a dozen sonnets by this dead European *maracón*. Thumbing through the book with a sigh, Arévalo was about to replace it in the bedside drawer when he saw that Santiago had written in ballpoint pen on the inside of the back cover.

Private property, as guaranteed by a true market economy, is the only invention of mankind that realistically serves the cause of his earthly freedom.

The words, though written in English, bore neither quotation marks nor any sign of attribution. Arévalo concluded they must be Santiago's own. He put the book carefully back where he had found it and commenced pacing unhappily about the room.

Over the course of the forty-eight hours since Arévalo had booked himself and Vendajes on the flight back to Mexico City he had many times rehearsed the conversation he would have with Santiago before leaving. In some versions he had envisioned himself apprising Santiago of the full extent of his plans; he had even indulged himself in the fantasy that Santiago might have understood and wished him good luck. But he saw now that it was too late for expressions of goodwill, even though personal goodwill was part of what he felt. Now, he could not even leave a note.

In his own room, he finished packing. The gun, the diskettes, the portable lock would all come along, improbably enough, under the seal of the Mexican diplomatic pouch. It pained Arévalo to consider that the fictions of state secrecy were so little different from the invention his friend apparently believed to be the genius of man's earthly life. It was not better than Catholicism.

Downstairs, Vendajes had logged out of the computer system.

"I will understand if you have changed your mind," Arévalo said, as Vendajes handed him the backup disks.

"What time is the flight?"

"We must leave now."

"You have not spoken to Santiago."

"No."

"I will get my bag."

N OT MANY hours later, Edith awoke to a dawn refracted prettily by the soot on Andrew's bedroom window, and silently she cursed the invention of champagne. Then she tiptoed to the bathroom and threw up several times. She considered rousing Andrew, but seeing that Kevin too was still asleep and the nanny off for the weekend, she found herself suddenly grateful for the abeyance.

Wrapped in her robe, a glass of water in her hand, she took a slow turn around the living room. Two adjacent walls were lined from floor to ceiling with books—novels and political history—but the rest of the room was so sparsely and strategically furnished that the bookshelves read more as design element than as library. Susannah's touch, Edith wanted to think.

A few framed prints and drawings were hung in out-of-the-way spots that encouraged intimate inspection, and near the end of one long wall, otherwise blank, an Italian angel of leather and wood appeared to be flying through the void. The figure held gilded cymbals in her hand, but Edith felt disinclined to guess at what was being heralded—something beatific and painful, probably.

Again and again in the twenty-four hours since Mercedes had appeared at the office, Edith had felt a cool shadow pass over her thoughts. She had the sense, heady and and cautious, that this shadow was history—history not as tragedy or farce but as the disorderly field of givens from which lives are improvised. Feeling the shadow made her want to see the thing that cast it. It was an immodest thought, but she couldn't quite relinquish it.

"Is my daddy still asleep?"

Startled, Edith spun around to look at the boy. He seemed to expect things from her, and she experienced a moment of panic: Whatever had made her imagine she could be a mother to him? But her disquiet passed.

"Grown-ups like to rest up a little on weekends, Kevin. What's the matter, are you hungry?"

"Yes." He gazed long-sufferingly at his feet, then looked up at her with an earnestness that she recognized as his genetic inheritance. "On weekends, Daddy makes me chocolate *pie* for breakfast."

She laughed. "Not bloody likely." It was something her father used to say to her when she was a child. As she stood, she secured her robe with an extra tuck of the sash. "But come on, maybe we can make some pancakes instead."

"Not bloody likely," repeated Kevin, following her into the kitchen.

As Edith mixed the batter, she and Kevin talked about why chimpanzees didn't really like living alone, even though it sometimes worked out that they had to be by themselves for a while. When the kitchen phone rang, Edith, after small reflection, answered it.

"Edith Emerson?"

"Yes, this is she."

"Oh, I'm sorry to disturb you, I was told I could just leave a message on your machine. This is Oliver Barnes's office, at Fifty-ninth Street? And Oliver wanted me to thank you for calling last night about Santiago Díaz."

"You've talked to Santiago, then?"

"Yes, he's got tonight's hot slot, and Oliver sends you his warmest thanks. We've also set aside some studio passes, if you and your friend would like to join us."

Me and my friend? thought Edith, as Kevin dipped his fist in the bowl of pancake batter. "Thank you, that's very kind of Oliver, but we have other plans tonight, I think."

"That's what he said you'd say. But if you change your minds, my name is Caitlin, and I'll be here all day. At the same number you called last night."

"Okay, Caitlin. Tell Oliver that Santiago is a special friend."

"I think he already knows that, but I'll remind him. Have a nice day, now."

Edith grimaced as she hung up. She had forgotten the oddly adrenal blend of innuendo and naïveté that animated the world of broadcast television. That, in the end, was what had undone her and Oliver, as a romantic slot.

When Andrew appeared a few minutes later, dressed in jeans and a misbuttoned cotton shirt, he was no more than half awake. "Who called?" he asked Edith, while Kevin inwardly rebuked him for not having made the chocolate pie that was pure invention in the first place.

THE MORNING, with its foretaste of summer, had by ten o'clock become something to notice. The three of them packed a picnic lunch and headed to the park.

Just inside the gate was a small, progressively conceived playground constructed of wooden beams, ropes, and rubber tile.

"Help me climb," Kevin demanded, stopping before a pyramidal jungle gym built of cedar timbers. Edith passed the picnic basket to Andrew and hoisted the boy onto the first step of the low-lying structure.

"Hold on to the ropes!" said Andrew. It annoyed him that he heard his own father's voice as he spoke, but he knew the advice was most useful when it was still literal in application. Of course, one's sense of the literal kept revising itself. Edith pressed against Andrew from behind.

"Maybe we should go see Santiago tonight after all," he said to her, though they had agreed to tape the show instead. "Mr. Barnes and I have never been introduced."

"Oliver and I are finished. I told you that."

"But did you tell him?"

"Yes. I mean I didn't need to."

"A good-bye fuck?"

"Now that you mention it."

Although Andrew had known jealousy as frequently as most people, the uncommonly inventive suspicions with which Susannah had showered him had taught him that the truth was a fragile thing, its usefulness easily shattered by those who thought themselves most concerned.

"Look how high I am, Edie!" Fear and defiance grappled in Kevin's face as he peered over his shoulder.

"That's very good. Now why don't you come down, Kevin? All mountain climbers know that the way back down is hardest."

Kevin threw her an irritated look and crawled one step higher.

"That's a record!" said Andrew. "You're taller than me now."

Standing upright, Kevin surveyed his realm. "I want to go to the top, but I'm scared, Daddy."

"Jump and I'll catch you. We can come back later."

Grimly ignoring his father, Kevin hauled himself up one more level, then stood warily, as if he might bump his head on his own aspirations. From this vantage, he could see Edith whole. He turned uncertainly on his perch.

"Daddy, I want to play in the sandbox," he said.

"Okay. Jump."

He did, Andrew caught him, and with a deranged-sounding cry Kevin ran off toward the playground's farther corner.

"Andrew, I think your son likes the ladies," Edith murmured, adjusting the waistband of her skirt.

"Why do you say that?"

She blushed. "We ladies who like the gentlemen always notice things like that," she answered.

By the time they reached the sandbox, Kevin had been discovered by his occasional playmate Lucy, a lithe, honey-haired girl of four. The two of them crouched over a sand battlement, conferring earnestly.

"Beautiful day. Even the lawyers are out." Lucy's father, Paul, whom Andrew had failed to notice on a nearby park bench, waved him and Edith over. Beside him sat Dinah, his wife, looking pleased with herself. They were both psychiatrists.

When Andrew had made the introductions, Paul asked Edith a few questions about the UN. Dinah stared openly at her, eyes aglint with surmise.

"What we really need, though," Edith finished, "is a charisma transplant."

As the adults watched, the two children stood, and Kevin pointed to the parental bench with a stick.

"Uh-oh," said Dinah. "Rebellion in the colonies."

After studying their parents a few moments longer, Lucy, followed by Kevin, walked solemnly over to present their case.

"Mommy, can Kevin come with us to the merry-go-round? He wants to."

"And, she's going to have *ice* cream too." Kevin elaborated. "We never have ice cream in the *day*."

Paul shrugged. "You make the call, Andrew. But if you and Edith want an afternoon to yourselves . . ."

"That's a very nice invitation, Kevin. Can you and Lucy play nicely together?"

The boy looked embarrassed. "Yes."

"Okay," said Andrew, after a systems check with Edith, who smiled abstractedly past her knees. "Promise you'll be a good boy."

They made arrangements for Kevin to be picked up later, and, as good-byes were exchanged, Dinah whispered into Andrew's ear. "Is it possible for a now happily married woman to be jealous?"

"I wouldn't think so."

"She's right for you, I see it. Take care of yourself."

"I will, Dinah. Thanks."

Edith hugged Kevin lightly. "See you later, alligator."

"I'm not an alligator," the boy answered. "I'm an Indian." He smiled delightedly as Lucy dragged him off by one hand.

The picnic basket was an elaborate affair, equipped with tuck-away utensils and wineglasses. A friend of Susannah's had given it to Andrew as a birthday present, and he now wondered, as he and Edith strolled on, whether he could ditch it discreetly on a park bench.

"How long were you with Dinah?" Edith asked.

Andrew was impressed. "Not long. She was having trouble with Paul. Actually we had two separate shots at it—one for her, one for me. Paul doesn't know."

Edith laughed. "I think you're a good guy or something. Does that bother you?"

"No, but you'll find some difference of opinion on the subject."

They waited at the crosswalk for a pack of Rollerbladers to pass, then Andrew led the way around a scattering of crack vials onto an asphalt path.

"What about Mercedes?" Edith asked.

"What about her?"

"I mean are you attracted? She seems like someone you might take an interest in."

"Hey. I just met her, you just met her. She seems like an interesting woman, as far as candidates' wives go. What do I know?"

"Well, I didn't get a chance to tell you, but I met her before you did. She came by the office yesterday morning to ask if I was having an affair with Santiago."

Andrew shifted the picnic basket to his other hand. "We can't get off the subject today. These gorgeous spring Saturdays are a can of worms."

"Oh, Andrew. Don't be absurd."

"Okay, okay. So she heard about our performance at the banquet and took it the wrong way." He was irritated with himself and looked around in earnest for a place to lose the picnic basket. "How did it go? At your office I mean."

"No time wasted, that's for sure. She was there when I got in, and she came right out with it. I said no I wasn't interfering with her husband; she took a few readings and decided to believe me. A little chitchat, densely packed with female signifiers. She left. We communicated."

"So Santiago must have told her."

"No, it was that Arévalo guy. I don't think Santiago knows she dropped in on me at all." Edith tried to experience the park as a good setting in which to tell Andrew about the photograph Mercedes had brought with her, but the mechanics of the thing eluded her. "How about over there, under the tree?"

The spot she had pointed out was at the crest of a grassy hillock that overlooked the intersection of two asphalt paths. Park benches lined the paths below, and a beaten-dirt trail ran by at a tangent. After policing the sunlit area in front of the tree, Andrew produced a rose-colored ground cloth from the basket, and they laid it out.

"What I'm wondering," said Andrew, when they were stretched out side by side in the sun, "is why you made such a project of getting Santiago on the Barnes show."

Edith emptied a take-out container of stuffed grape leaves into a bowl and set it down between them.

"I don't know, it was an impulse. A gesture of goodwill."

"Toward Santiago?"

"Toward Mercedes. Out of deference to their marriage or something. Why, do you really think it was a dumb idea?"

"I was surprised is all."

Edith sighed. By turns she lifted her outstretched legs a few inches off the ground cloth and relaxed them again. "It'll be okay. Probably the champagne had a hand in it."

"I heard you being sick this morning. Are you feeling any better?"

"I'm fine." This was true; in fact the clarity of her mind and nerves made her wonder if she had really had a hangover in the first place. She arranged her skirt high on her thighs for the sun, slipped the straps of her jersey top demurely off her shoulders, and lay back down. "My father was his usual charming self when I called yesterday. The bare ruined choir at full throat."

"So he didn't take it well about us?"

"I wouldn't say that. He took it like a horse breeder. You'll have to meet him."

Andrew helped himself to a grape leaf. "He's probably scared of you," he said.

"He ought to be. Anyway, he wants us to have the wedding down there at Vauxhall, under the swamp magnolias and such. How does that strike you?"

"We could do that. Whatever you want."

She shaded her eyes and gazed up at him. "My father's perceptually arrested, you know. Among other things he thinks I'm my mother."

"I can see how that might be awkward."

"It's not worth talking about."

Andrew leaned forward to kiss her, and she arched her back a little as their lips met. Since Susannah, Andrew had come to believe that if God was in the details, then love was in the context, but by the time he had placed a hand on Edith's rib cage he had forgotten about context.

As if reading his thoughts, Edith laughed a little, tucking in her chin to break the kiss. "Am I doing okay with Kevin?" she asked.

"He's crazy about you."

"I guess since your divorce there's been a lot of basis for comparison."

"No, I've tried to keep surprises to a minimum. As far as his sentimental education."

She smiled and drew her knees up. "What about yours?"

"Oh, mine." The breeze brought the scent of freshly turned earth, salted faintly with diesel and dog urine. Andrew thought it a cheerful smell. "Fall's a good time to get married in New York," he pointed out.

"Couldn't we do it sooner?" said Edith. "Just a few friends; I don't care about coming down the aisle."

Twenty yards away a passerby dropped a gum wrapper, and the sun struck flash from the foil. "That's fine," he said. " 'As soon as possible.' We agreed."

"How strange," Edith answered after a moment. "You remember everything."

He shook his head as if denying it and said, "Yes. I do."

Andrew lay his forearm across her breasts, tucked his hand beneath her shoulder blade, and kissed her. Perhaps because they had been speaking about marriage, or because the ground they were stretched out upon was publicly owned, there was a civic element to their exchange—as if this most ordinary act of human intimacy carried with it the power to elect a more enlightened school board or build libraries.

When Edith closed the kiss, though, they might have been anywhere. "What goes around comes around," she murmured, and her words drifted away like cigarette smoke in still air. Against the inside of Andrew's forearm, her nipples grew taut. His hand set out from beneath her shoulder to her waist, where it encountered a bewilderingly large amount of fabric for a skirt so small. Ignoring this impediment, Andrew slowly stroked the insides of her thighs until Edith drew his hand higher with her own. He kissed her neck, and she tucked her chin against her opposite shoulder in response.

From a few feet away came a firecracker scatter of radio static, followed by silence, followed by a voice.

"Hey, Rizzi. You believe in free love?"

Andrew's neck stiffened, and he twisted to see the two policemen standing before him and Edith. They looked at him as if they were thoroughly familiar with whatever he was about to say or do.

"Chill, Tucker. We got a flag of surrender here," said the other policeman.

It was true. Edith, who had till now ignored her lack of underwear, had jammed a fist over her skirt, pinning it to the ground between her legs. Andrew looked stupidly at her hand, then back up at the police. He sat upright, the blood rushing to his cheeks.

"Look, Officer," he began.

"Looking is why we're having this little conversation," said the one called Tucker. With a sweep of his arm he invited them to consider the park benches below, crowded with accidental spectators. "What is it with you two? The housing crunch so bad you've never heard of bedrooms?"

"It's my fault, Officer," said Edith. "I forgot myself."

Andrew threw her an outraged look, and though he was immediately ashamed of himself, she saw the glint in his eye and fell silent.

"Stand up, please," said Tucker. "I'm going to have to see some ID."

"Listen," said Andrew, handing him his driver's license and business card, "I know we got a little carried away, but it's spring, we're getting married, what can I tell you?" He glanced past Tucker's shoulder at the other officer, who was going grimly through the picnic basket. "I'd appreciate it a lot if you could be easy about this."

"I didn't hear that, Mr. Caldwell," said Tucker, returning the documents to him. "Since you're an attorney, I'm sure you understand why not." He looked Edith sourly up and down. "Your lady friend a client? Working girl, maybe?"

Andrew felt his temper slipping away, but Edith intervened. "I'm a translator at the UN," she said quietly.

"Any ID?"

"In the basket."

As she spoke, Rizzi tossed her purse to Tucker, who caught

it backhanded as if he'd been expecting it all morning. In open violation of search-and-seizure law, he poked through the contents of the small leather bag. Edith and Andrew glanced at each other furtively, both thinking of Santiago performing the same inspection.

"Thank you, Miss Emerson," said Tucker when he was done. Then he called over his shoulder to his partner. "They got a nice lunch packed, Rizzi?"

"Clean."

"Okay." He handed the purse back to Edith and drew a deep breath.

"What's the charge?" asked Andrew.

Tucker gave him a patient look.

"Put your hands together in front of you, Mr. Caldwell," said the other cop. "I've got to cuff you."

"Public lewdness," Tucker informed Andrew.

Edith smirked, put her wrists together, and thrust them out to Tucker. Visibly unhappy at this turn of duty, he handcuffed her. "You people kill me," he said.

The precinct house lay beyond the softball fields, to the north, and the police took care to keep some distance between their prisoners as they walked them over. Not till they reached the long set of steps that descended to the precinct parking lot were Andrew and Edith thrown within conversational distance.

"I have to ask," Andrew said so Edith could hear. "How come you guys didn't arrest the photographer too? He's the one with the explanations."

Edith realized she was being cued, but the gender of the pronoun Andrew had offered threw her. "The guy James hired?" she said over her shoulder. "What's he got to do with it?" She chafed her wrists against her handcuffs, thinking she could have come up with something more useful on the theme of Marisa de Borba.

"Come on," said Tucker, who already wanted to put this arrest behind him. "You two are just a bad hit on my horoscope."

———

THE PRECINCT house was small, even intimate, and despite the weather and day of the week, it was obvious to Edith and Andrew that for the time being they were the only item on the agenda.

Tucker greeted the desk sergeant, a sleepy-eyed young man with a facial tic, then waited for Rizzi and Andrew to join them. "These two were practicing for their honeymoon in front of, you know, everybody." He stifled a yawn as Rizzi put the picnic basket down on a worn wooden settee opposite the desk. "Guy's a lawyer."

The officers released Andrew and Edith from their handcuffs. Rizzi brought Andrew forward and, with a courtly sweep of his arm, indicated that Edith was to join him on the settee while Andrew was booked. She inspected the fatigued piece of furniture, polished smooth by other people's bad days, and sat down.

"Last name, middle name, first name," said the desk sergeant.

Andrew answered and gave his address without being prompted, but when asked for some names of friends or associates he fell silent. He could feel Edith looking at him from behind. "Sergeant, if I was out of line, okay, I'd like to set it right. But I don't want to alarm anyone unnecessarily. I've got a son to pick up later, you know?"

"Don't think too much about it," the desk sergeant answered quietly. "What we've got to do is establish your roots in the community. People we could call."

"Right." But for a moment the only phone number that came to mind was Susannah's; tomorrow was Kevin's custody visit.

"You live with your lady friend?"

"She's my fiancée. You could call my business partner, Douglas Reineger, but he's probably not there right now."

Holding his pen suspended over the arrest ledger, the desk sergeant regarded Andrew with heavy patience.

"Or you could call my friend James Walsh. I've known him since high school, and he should be easy to reach. He runs a photography gallery on the East Side."

"Let's go with Walsh."

In an effort to shake off his misgivings, Andrew rattled off both of James's addresses and phone numbers in a businesslike fashion whose irony he hoped would carry over his shoulder to Edith. Immediately, though, he realized he'd made a further mistake: irony was not the order of the day.

When he had recorded the particulars, the desk sergeant stood up and stretched. "Tucker," he said, "could you see Mr. Caldwell to his accommodations while I process the lady?"

It occurred to Andrew only then, as the officer guided him toward the leatherette-padded door leading to the cells, that he had already had his last private conversation with Edith until they were released.

Edith was deliberately solicitous in spelling out her name, giving her address, producing her ID. Rizzi ambled over to a TV bolted to the ceiling, then, when the desk sergeant asked Edith for phone references, turned around to watch.

She named a friend who worked down the hall from her at the UN and was a part-time professor at a downtown university. Then, mindful of Andrew's comment on the steps and hoping she wouldn't regret it, she said, "And James Walsh."

From across the room Rizzi wrinkled his brow in an impression of deep thought. "Would that be James Walsh the photographer, Miss Emerson?"

"No, as my friend just said a minute ago, James runs a photography *gallery*. He introduced Andrew and me."

"But when my partner and I were bringing you two in, your friend Caldwell said something about a photographer, right?"

Edith sighed. "How big a deal is this? I don't remember what he said. And weren't you supposed to say something just now about my right to a lawyer?"

"Your lawyer," said Rizzi, "is in the lockup just now." He looked at her, and she stared back. "Ah, forget it. It's been a slow morning." Strolling over to the clock, he checked his watch against it.

"So can I be taken to my cell now?"

The desk sergeant struggled with a smile. "Miss Emerson, we don't put males and females in the same cell, besides which your arresting officers have already alleged that you and Mr. Caldwell are intimate. So I'll have to ask you to wait outside on the bench." He called to Rizzi. "Could you do the honors, Batman?"

Rizzi escorted her back to the bench and handcuffed her to the armrest.

"What *is* this?" said Edith, more interested than outraged.

"This," said Rizzi, heading for the coffee machine, "is what we call close observation."

Edith sat very still on the bench. The desk sergeant passed his clipboard to a second officer, who made a few calls, took a few notes, and wheeled himself over to a desk nearer the window. The wheelchair came as something of a shock to her, though she could not have said why.

When the guard brought Andrew out to make his state-ment, Edith tried to catch his eye, but she realized immediately that the room had been designed to make this impossible. She watched Rizzi saunter over to join Andrew and the wheel-chair sergeant, stabbing a plastic stirrer into his coffee without interest.

It maddened Edith that she could not parse the exchange on the precinct steps—whether it was Andrew or herself who had drawn James's name into their immediate predicament—but she knew as well that James would have insisted upon it, in some version.

When Andrew was done, Tucker unlocked Edith's handcuffs. It was her turn.

"But this James Walsh," the wheelchair officer asked. "He's someone special?"

"He introduced me to Andrew."

"Know anything about a photograph? Your boyfriend said something about a picture."

Edith started to shake her head, then willed herself still. Just because she hadn't told Andrew about her excursion into exotic modeling didn't mean he was unaware of it, she suddenly realized. And if Arévalo had done enough research on her to turn it up in the first place, a computer check was probably not desirable.

"A picture?" she repeated.

"What was it, Rizzi?" said the questioning officer. "A photo, a photographer, a major motion picture?"

Before anyone could answer, the precinct's scarred plastic-and-metal doors flew open with a tremendous clatter, and four large white men in their twenties, handcuffed but only partly subdued, hurtled screaming into the room with their arresting officers behind them. Their insults, all but unintelligible, seemed to be directed at one another, and the largest of the four was bleeding profusely from the nose.

"Jesus, Hernandez," shouted the desk sergeant over the din. "What'd you two do, bust a whole rugby team?"

"Me and O'Brien found these tweety-birds piping up over by the softball field," said the first cop, lurching after one of his charges and catching him by the seat of the pants just as he tried to run back out the door. "But I think they're just naturally this way."

As Hernandez spoke, the man with the bloody nose lowered his head, grunted, and charged the officer, delivering a running butt to his stomach. O'Brien's nightstick came down several times on the shoulders of the bleeding man. "Goddamnit, Tucker! Give us a little backup, will you?" he shouted.

Behind the precinct desk, Edith had risen to her feet at the sight of James walking in on the heels of this fracas. He was wearing a beige linen suit and sunglasses. She thought he must be somehow connected to the scene unfolding before her.

"Down on the floor, dickheads!" said Hernandez, trying to catch his breath. "The *floor.*"

"Who the fuck are you?" the desk sergeant asked James. "Their press agent?"

"We got anybody in holding?" shouted O'Brien.

"I'm James Walsh. I received a call about a Mr. Caldwell and a Miss Emerson."

Edith sank back into her chair.

"Yeah, we got this lawyer type stashed in there," the desk sergeant called to O'Brien. "But even he doesn't deserve these scumbags. Let him out, Rizzi." The desk sergeant smiled at James. "You the photographer?" he asked.

NONE OF the three of them wanted to stay in the park after Edith and Andrew's release so they walked without consultation to its eastern edge, then a dozen blocks south to James's apartment. He lived opposite a famous hotel in a small but sunny duplex; it was lightly furnished, suitable for entertaining or seduction, a single man's halfway house.

Edith, feeling defeated, set the picnic basket on the kitchen counter and passed without pause to the living-room sofa, where she lay down at full length and closed her eyes. "Sorry, guys," she said.

James arched his eyebrows and placed his folded sunglasses carefully beside the picnic basket. "Iced tea?" he asked Andrew.

"Why not."

James filled three frosted glasses from a pitcher in the fridge. Carrying two of them over to the sofa, Andrew discovered Edith had fallen asleep. When he touched the glass to her temple she woke and asked him if she could go upstairs and take a nap.

"Make yourself at home," said James before Andrew could answer.

"Just fifteen minutes," said Edith, heading for the stairs. "I know you have to get back to the gallery." She wiggled the fingers of one hand in an abbreviated wave, and as she vanished around the corner, Andrew felt a stab of loneliness.

There were four curly-maple chairs arranged around the dining table, restored inheritances that lent the place an authority it might otherwise have lacked. When Andrew was seated, James said quietly, "My friend, you have a problem."

Andrew sighed. "How do you mean?"

"Well, I don't mean in the eyes of the law."

"I didn't think that," said Andrew, tossing his and Edith's court-date citations onto the table. "A little music?"

James went over to the window end of his apartment and put on a Miles Davis track that opened eerily with a B-minor passage headed for C7—four out, four back. He worked the volume until the music was just loud enough to make their conversation un- intelligible to anyone but themselves.

"Edie already told me the two of you are getting married," James began, when he was seated beside his friend. "I thought I might have heard from you before now."

"I wanted to talk to you in person," Andrew answered. "I'm sorry I waited."

James smiled as if in sympathetic communion with an amus- ing third party. "What the hell, we all had a busy week. But shit, Andrew, the police and everything. It's not as if I didn't know that Edie likes an audience. But you—well, I'm surprised."

"I think today was an accident," Andrew answered.

"How come you guys both gave the cops my phone number?"

"How come I keep hearing about some photo opportunity you're setting up? Marisa de Borba or whatever her name is?"

"We can talk about that," said James.

"How come I'm hearing about problems?"

"I didn't mean Edie exactly." James shook his glass slowly so the ice drew the drink's dextrose strands out like ribbons. "And what happened to simple outrage? Or self-control? Aren't I enti- tled to some grain of social respect in the presence of a business contact like, say, Santiago Díaz?"

"Business?"

"Do you think of me as a connoisseur of politics?"

"I think of you as a connoisseur."

"Fuck you."

Andrew took a long swallow of tea. "I'm sorry, James," he said, putting his glass on the table and pushing it forward like a carefully considered poker stake. "I didn't really know any of this was going to happen."

They looked at each other for several seconds. Then James lay a finger alongside his pursed lips as if thinking about another, more pressing matter. Andrew took the offering and laughed.

"Fuck you," said James quietly.

"James, I've known her for a decent interval. You introduced me to her, I assumed the two of you had worked it out whichever way, and—" Andrew didn't really believe Edith was asleep upstairs, but insofar as he no doubt did have a problem, there was little point in speculating. "You're telling me you always knew this would happen."

"No. As I said to Edie in the gallery, I should have seen it coming. But I didn't." James stood up to take off his suit jacket, folding it carefully inside out as if packing for travel. "Was it her idea to have me bail you out?"

"Actually, I was the one who gave them your number. She took her cue from me."

For a time they sat side by side, looking at nothing, thinking it through. The music brought Andrew back to the early days of their friendship, when they had frequented a jazz club with the evocative name of Slug's. One night, near the end of an after-hours set, a woman had risen from the audience and shot the tenor sax in the thigh. The law was not welcome at Slug's, so James had called a doctor friend who lived a few blocks away. In a tiny room upstairs, with James and Andrew assisting, the friend had operated on the downed musician—successfully, as it turned out—while the rest of the band played an appropriately out version of "My Funny Valentine." Andrew had always loved James for the way he had handled himself that night.

"Edith's way," James began now, "her exhibitionism, to use that idiotic term, it's not meant as a provocation." He spoke musingly, and nothing about his words suggested rebuke or conde-scension. "It's not an exercise of power at all, is it?"

"No," answered Andrew. "It isn't."

"Or narcissism either." James's tone of voice seemed in part a call to reason. He wanted Andrew to be up to this discussion.

"I never really thought I could have her," James continued. "Power, narcissism—these are breakfast and lunch to me. No big deal. But dinner was what I saw in her."

Andrew made a fist of one hand and wrapped the fingers of the other around it. "She said you were never really in love with her."

James stood, walked over to a nearby cabinet, and took a bottle of scotch from it. He poured a small amount into a brandy snifter and downed the liquor without offering Andrew any. "She said that?"

"Yes."

There was a pause, neither awkward nor calculated. An acqui-escence.

"I lied about not seeing it coming," said James. "I knew almost from the start it'd be you."

Sighing, Andrew released himself from the charge of explana-tion. The conversation was exhausted, the subject infinite. After a time he said, "So what did you mean when you said that Santiago was a business connection?"

"I meant," said James, "that maybe for the time being you could take me seriously about the Marisa de Borba photographs."

Andrew stood and went over to turn off the music. "Okay," he said from across the room.

The ensuing silence was a noise that enveloped the apartment as the music had not. Something like a moment of peace settled over Andrew and James. Then the kitchen phone rang—three clipped warbles indicating it was being used as an intercom. An-drew walked back through the room and picked up the receiver without looking at James.

"I can't sleep here," said Edith. Andrew could hear her natural voice and the one in the phone simultaneously. "I want to go home. Pick up Kevin and just go home."

James was staring into space.

"Okay?" said Edith.

THE NIGHT before, the Díazes had returned to the ambassador's residence from their dinner with Edith and Andrew to find everyone but the downstairs guard already asleep. They had passed quickly upstairs, and while Santiago undressed, the day's newspaper clippings laid out before him on the bureau, Mercedes had gone off down the hall in search of toothpaste. Passing Arévalo's door, she had noticed it was unsecured. It did not take her long to decide to let herself into his room; it took her somewhat longer to decide to inform her husband that Arévalo was gone. Together, they discovered Abundio Sedano's departure shortly after.

In bed Mercedes whispered to her husband her misgivings about Arévalo while avoiding any mention of her own conversation with him, the one that had driven her to seek Edith out at the UN. Friendships had a life span, she told Santiago as she curled close to him amid the humid sheets; reason rarely played a part in their demise. When Santiago failed to respond, Mercedes allowed herself to seem partly appeased so that he could come around to her point of view without interference. They made love and fell asleep in each other's arms.

When Oliver Barnes's studio phoned the ambassador's residence in the morning, Santiago took the call in the briefing room to avoid disturbing Mercedes, although he knew she was not really asleep.

No doubt it was their decision to have a child that had made them so newly solicitous of each other's feelings.

Some hours later Santiago and Mercedes proceeded to a purely social brunch at the home of the UN's Under-secretary General for Peacekeeping. Afterwards, Santiago dismissed his car and driver, hailed a taxi, and took his wife to the city's largest museum, where the eccentric paintings of a well-known Mexican artist, at once exuberant and morbid in her tastes, were on view.

The artist in question was widely celebrated for the account her paintings gave of her body, which had suffered both the random injuries of Mexico City traffic and the hardly less chancy torments of her own romantic temperament. Santiago had been to many museums with Mercedes, and it was she who had taught him to love what was to be seen in them.

"So God is revealed in a woman's body," he said to her in Spanish as they descended the museum's steps, their backs to the afternoon sun.

"Revealed?" Mercedes repeated in English. They had discussed their evening with Edith and Andrew in only perfunctory terms; Arévalo's disappearance had intervened. "I didn't know weekend Catholics were susceptible to mystical heresies."

Santiago put on his dark glasses and smiled. "You know I have always felt that the game is won or lost on the field, but that to have saints is a good idea. This is not heresy."

Mercedes looked quickly at him. "You never really told me what you think about Edith Emerson. Did she reveal herself to you?"

"Edith Emerson?" Santiago was genuinely confused. There was a catechism of fidelity that he was sometimes required to perform, but nothing had prepared him to do so now. "She is what you saw. I am your husband."

"You think I am not aware that Arévalo gets your castoffs?"

"My castoffs? But you know I have always been faithful to you."

"I don't mean that exactly."

"And what does this have to do with Edith Emerson?"

Mercedes shook her head impatiently.

"Luis is his own man," said Santiago.

"Truer, it seems, than you imagined." Mercedes regretted her words immediately, and she took her husband's arm. "I'm sorry.

You know my feelings about Luis, and since last night you know also that I am not so stupid as to speak about them again."

A middle-aged white man, conspicuously overweight, cruised across one long granite step of the museum's approach on a gasoline-powered scooter. Several little boys and a small dog ran after him.

"Mexican gasoline," said Santiago unconvincingly.

"Texas refineries," answered Mercedes. They had reached the sidewalk.

"I'm supposed to dislike transnational metaphors."

"But you are a very unlikely candidate." She laughed sadly and put her hand in his pants pocket. "It serves you well."

"No," said Santiago, "the reverse: the man serves the role." He kissed her throat. "There's a café across the street. Let's sit outside."

When their espressos had been delivered Santiago gazed for a moment at his wife, who was making an effective show of observing the sidewalk passersby, smiling patiently to herself. He sighed. "My opinion of Edith Emerson is that she is *una chiflada*. A cockteaser, but an admirable one."

"Luis had her investigated," Mercedes said.

"I asked him to."

"More than you asked."

"That's Luis."

Mercedes took off her own dark glasses and put them on the table between them. "In that case you must have seen the picture."

"Picture? What are you talking about?"

Mercedes held her breath as Santiago twisted a shred of lemon peel into his coffee and downed it in a single swallow.

"Don't tell me the son of a bitch put her under surveillance." Santiago laughed. "What is he doing, playing secret agent?"

As far as Mercedes was aware, Santiago had never lied to her during the course of their marriage, but she had seen him lie to others, his features taking on a mournful gravity as if to compensate for the weightlessness of his words. There was nothing of that now.

"Oh, what does it matter?" said Mercedes, exhaling slowly. "I don't know what I'm talking about." She took a cigarette from her purse and lit it. "But it's strange. She and Andrew Caldwell do remind me a little of you and me. Why did they come separately to your banquet, I wonder?"

"Who can say?" Santiago answered. "Didn't she tell us it had something to do with this James Walsh person? Anyway, surely you remember all the ridiculous ploys you and I came up with to be together before our own wedding. What about the time I had to hide in your closet while your mother delivered every last detail of her marital wisdom to you?"

Mercedes concealed a laugh with her forefinger. "That was at least partly your fault; you're the one who brought her the bottle of cognac back from France."

"Hours of confidences. I had to piss in my own boot. My favorite pair of boots." The memory amused him but also carried with it a hint of regret: he was no longer so young. Catching the waiter's eye, he ordered them both another coffee. "Perhaps it is the kind of story that would go well on *The Oliver Barnes Show.*"

Mercedes looked down at the metal tabletop. When Santiago had first entered her life, it had not occurred to her to resist loving him; loving him, she had married him without debate. In this way she had preserved both her love and her independence. She was a fortunate woman.

"*Querido,*" she said. "I am uneasy about this show. American TV: what good can come of it?"

She had barely gotten the words out when something made of metal and plastic—a piece of costume jewelry, she first thought— fell onto their table from a considerable height, upsetting their coffee cups. Santiago picked the object from the shattered sugar caddy and showed it to Mercedes in bewilderment. It was a key to the hotel of which the café was a part.

"I'm so sorry," said the man at the next table, closing his newspaper and getting to his feet. "I believe she meant that for me."

Following the man's gaze, Mercedes and Santiago saw a young woman leaning out the window some dozen stories up. She was wrapped in a towel, and she waved at them. They waved back.

"Dumb idea," said the man to Santiago. "My apologies."

"No apologies necessary," he replied, handing him the key. "In fact it was quite enlivening."

Watching the man disappear into the hotel lobby, Santiago said, "And people complain that this city is no longer romantic."

Mercedes picked up the tabloid the man had left behind. She studied it, started to refold it, then handed it to her husband without looking at him.

"MEXICAN STANDOFF," said the headline. Beneath it were two photographs, one of Arévalo, the other of Santiago, placed nose to nose so that they looked like boxers in a promotional flyer. The caption read: "Bowing to 'patriotic duty and popular pressure,' Luis Arévalo, till yesterday campaign manager for ex–soccer star Santiago Díaz, vows he'll oppose childhood pal in upcoming Mexican ballot." Beneath these words was a mention of Santiago's scheduled appearance on *The Oliver Barnes Show* that evening.

Santiago folded the newspaper across its middle and handed it back to Mercedes. It was part of the astonishment of loving her that even in his love he sometimes underestimated her subtlety.

"I am beginning to think it is you who should be running for president," said Santiago, taking her arm. "I am sorry. We must return to the ambassador's residence."

OF SANTIAGO'S staff, both those traveling with him and those he was able to reach by phone in Mexico City, all had heard the news, but none admitted to having anticipated it. Nor did any among them seem inclined to speculate on Arévalo's motivations; six-year jobs were at stake, whoever won. Unsurprisingly, there was a general agreement about the moral worthlessness of Vendajes.

Closeting himself in the briefing room with Mercedes, Santiago lingered before the window, tugging at the drapery.

"I cannot call Arévalo without knowing his program."

Mercedes stood with her back to him. She fingered the overwrought gilt frame of a mirror that took in herself, the room, her husband in the room.

Near the center of the space was a double-sided partner desk, a desk with two behinds. Many jokes about Mexican-American relations had been occasioned by this piece of furniture. After a moment's deliberation, Santiago walked to the desk and plucked the handset from one of the three phones strewn across it.

"So you are calling Freddy González?" asked Mercedes, addressing the image of her husband in the mirror.

"I don't have a better idea," said Santiago.

Freddy González was a petroleum engineer and entrepreneur who had been instrumental in persuading Santiago to run for office. He maintained residences in both Houston and Mexico City, and as a man without a family, a man whose only encumbrances were business-related, he could always be relied upon to speak out of self-interest.

"You said yourself that Freddy can't be trusted," observed Mercedes.

"Not past a certain point," answered Santiago as the phone in Mexico City rang. "But he will know about Luis."

Mercedes hesitated before the mirror, surveying herself and the effect her presence exerted upon her surroundings. The green silk blouse she wore had been given to her by Santiago during the stormy period that had preceded his decision to run for office. She unbuttoned it and regarded her bra, a butterfly filigree of black lace she had bought in France.

"Freddy, it is me. Yes." Santiago walked the phone to the end of its tether. "No, Luis said nothing to me before he left."

Mercedes walked slowly over to the cowhide sofa and stretched out upon it, listening.

"I must have grown stupid overnight, Freddy. How does he plan to nationalize an economy that is already nationalized?"

With part of her mind Mercedes was thinking about her breasts. To be pregnant, her mother had told her, was to assume a degree of femaleness that for a time made men irrelevant. Their abashed discovery of the nipple's true function, for example. And yet even thinking about having a child only increased her desire for her husband's embraces.

There was an Italian fashion magazine on the rug beside the sofa, and Mercedes picked it up without enthusiasm.

"Okay, my friend, okay," said Santiago into the phone. "But now is the time for you to pull your cock out of the oil fields long enough to think about our country. Where can I reach Luis?"

Mercedes tossed the magazine aside and, rebuttoning her blouse, left the room.

IT TOOK Santiago three calls after speaking with Freddy González to locate Arévalo's temporary campaign headquarters in Mexico City. Then he had to wait, repeating his name to volunteers who deferred to other volunteers. By the time the voice on the other end of the phone was Arévalo's, Santiago had finished mourning his friend's defection, though he knew he had not yet tended to the friendship itself. Neglect had its own consequences.

"Luis. I feel we should wish each other luck." Santiago sat in one of the partner desk's two ascetic chairs, straight-backed wooden things from New England. "Tell me what is the situation down there—tires burning in the street, ad hoc committees, position papers being written by *pepenadores*?"

There was static from the line. From Arévalo, a melancholy silence mixed with embarrassment.

"Okay," said Santiago. "I know there are no burning tires. And needless to say, my present advisers would have counseled me not to make this call."

Arévalo, who had been shaving in preparation for his imminent appearance on Mexican TV, wiped the soap from his jaw. "I did not split with you out of malice, old friend. And fuck our advisers. I will beat your ass on personal principles alone: all goalies ought to have their own penalty kick."

This was a sentiment that Santiago, under the circumstances, could appreciate. "So it is our ideological differences?"

"If I am wrong in my ideas, Mexico will reconcile us."

Santiago considered the history of personal reconciliation in Mexican politics and grew morose. Perhaps he should not have said that about position papers written by garbage pickers.

"Do you remember the time your father shot the rooster your cousin sold us?" he asked.

"*Hombre*, how could I forget?" Arévalo's voice tightened. "We suffered like donkeys the death of this bird. His blood was everywhere. My mother tried to make me change shirts before going to school, but I would not. And you, afterwards, working at the *farmacia*. A stupid business."

"Yes. That is how we felt at the time."

A silence.

"But it is not how our fathers felt," prompted Santiago.

"Not so much has changed for Mexico since our fathers were young," said Arévalo.

"Still less for roosters."

The comment did not invite reply.

"I have yet to issue a statement," said Santiago after what he judged to be a sufficient interval. "But I am told you will be addressing the nation shortly."

"What I have to say may surprise you."

"Surprise has its value. In the eyes of the world."

" 'It has always been my feeling,' " recited Arévalo, " 'that if you cannot say fuck the world once in a while, you are certain to be fucked by it.' "

Santiago did not laugh. The image of Edith Emerson, who a few days earlier had indirectly caused Santiago to voice this sentiment, passed through both men's minds.

"I will miss you, *compañero*," said Santiago. *"Buena suerte."*

Santiago had once been told by Mercedes, regarding his presidential candidacy, that he was a rooster discovering the dawn.

"Suerte," responded Arévalo, as he wiped the sweat irritably from his newly shaven jaw.

SANTIAGO then summoned to the briefing room those he still numbered among his traveling campaign staff. He said that he and Arévalo had spoken, but in a largely personal vein, and that he, Santiago, continued to believe that victory was the only goal worthy of his attention. Otherwise, he added, he would be endorsing athletic shoes and growing rich, as was expected of him.

His staff laughed, and Santiago was marginally relieved. Morale was almost always salvageable, he had learned, but one had to be careful not to misplace one's sense of reality in the process.

Mercedes entered the room again, wrapped unseasonably in a shawl of azure wool, and began pacing distractedly back and forth. Observing her movements, one of the staff, a university student named Carlos, discreetly turned off the air-conditioning. Santiago and Mercedes had many weeks ago picked out Carlos as a possible campaign manager should Arévalo's talents be required elsewhere.

Clearing her throat, a sensibly dressed young woman, whom Santiago had his eye on for finance minister, wondered aloud how they ought to handle *The Oliver Barnes Show* that evening, given the circumstances. A brief silence ensued.

"We must remember that the broadcast is live," said Carlos in a soft voice. "People watch it with the hope of seeing something unplanned, a gaffe of some sort. It goes without saying, then, that Santiago will be questioned about Luis." He seemed to be speaking, however indirectly, for the approval of Mercedes.

She stopped pacing and drew her shawl suddenly close in a gesture of self-shelter. Nakedness, she had come to see since meeting Edith, was something that could be so variously offered as to contradict the frankness it implied. One could be publicly naked like a statue—Paris was a city where this was well understood—or one could be nakedly public. Arévalo, for example. But modesty, which was recognized by everyone, conferred a kind of power that was at once more reliable and less negotiable than nakedness. Perhaps love was less than modesty. Certainly politics was only a public facsimile of love.

She bit her lip, looking around the room at the people she and Santiago had pressed into the service of a Mexico not yet fully imagined. For the first time since her husband had announced his candidacy Mercedes found she was absolutely set upon his victory.

"This television show tonight," said Santiago, resuming his walk. "*Gracias*, Magda, Carlos, for reminding us. My own sense is that the timing could not be better. While Luis conducts politics as usual, as the *yanquis* say, we have a casual forum from which we can address the issues however we see fit. Mexico is ready for a leader who welcomes international exposure."

"I think we must make a statement," Mercedes suggested quietly. "We do not want to look oblivious."

"Agreed," said Santiago. "But let's wait for Luis to fire the first shot. He's scheduled to make his own press statement within the hour. We'll see what he has to say." Kicking balls filled with air had been Santiago's most successful profession. It was a peculiar thing to have done.

He realized he was angry.

"What about that paleolithic television over there?" he asked suddenly of the room's corner. "Is there a satellite feed?"

Carlos lifted one leg in a martial manner and gently kicked the TV's housing to indicate that such electronic arrangements indeed existed. The gesture was perfectly calibrated. Afterwards, no one present doubted that Carlos would be taking over Arévalo's duties.

"*Entrámoslo,*" said Santiago, turning away. Let's get down.

A lunch was brought up—*chilaquiles* and beer—and an atmosphere of mild abandon was encouraged by Mercedes and those she could press to the cause of cheerfulness.

Luis announced his candidacy alone at a rostrum in a studio. Behind him was a convincing if sentimental image of El Monumento a la Independencia—*El Ángel*, as it was known to all—on the Paseo de la Reforma in Mexico City. Santiago's crew joked about the well-known fact that while the city itself was sinking into the ground at a rate of twenty centimeters a year, the monument rested on a base so thick that it remained fixed, regularly seeming to climb above its surroundings. Another step had to be added every twelve months to keep the monument accessible. Arévalo presumably had not had this in mind when he decided to name his program "The New Step."

As Freddy González had intimated, this step involved the nationalization of certain enterprises that had till now been privately owned. Arévalo also vowed to stop the sale of the *ejidos*, or communal farmlands, to corporate agribusiness—a promise that implicitly allied him with the campesino rebels to the south. The rebels exerted a certain romantic appeal in the capital, but while their cause was just, Santiago believed it was also antihistorical. The hope of Mexico lay in looking forward, not back.

Love of one's country was a peculiarly disturbing passion, thought Santiago as he watched Arévalo. So seldom did it come to a good end.

After Arévalo's broadcast, Santiago and Mercedes spoke at length with their campaign staff. Whatever surprise Luis had hinted at to Santiago on the phone, he had either decided at the last moment to withhold or, more likely, only imagined in the first place. The speech itself, apart from the fact that Luis was giving it, had fallen conspicuously short of the sensational. He seemed to have packaged himself as a man of the left, proposing variants of the standard opposition programs—incontestable at heart but tactically dubious. However, the threat he now posed to Santiago's candidacy was undeniable, and, inevitably, there would be further unpleasantness. When Santiago had heard his staff out on the subject, he and Mercedes excused themselves and returned to their bedroom for a nap, though neither was sleepy.

They removed their clothes and lay upon the bed in each other's arms. It had been a grueling business.

"Perhaps I should withdraw my candidacy," said Santiago. "Out of personal considerations."

"Don't be idiotic. It is out of personal considerations that you are running." She took his balls gently in the palm of one hand. "Consideration number one, consideration number two."

"I was under the illusion that there was a moral element at work as well."

"You are charmingly romantic."

"Another reason for quitting."

"No," she said. "Now I require you to win."

SANTIAGO'S colleagues on *The Oliver Barnes Show* that night were to be a natural blond American actress of still-emerging comedic talent and, in a triumph of legal maneuvering, a serial killer recently released on bail from a Texas prison. When told of this arrangement, Santiago had to laugh. He imagined himself trying to persuade Arévalo of the moral vitality of a country that entertained itself in such a manner.

The show was broadcast not from the network studios but from a refurbished theater in midtown. The Díazes were admitted through a back entrance, where they were greeted by a young woman in harlequin-frame glasses and asked to sign in.

A few minutes later, a production assistant asked Santiago and Mercedes to join the other guests for sushi in the green room. "It's just better if you eat before we do makeup," she explained, leading them briskly down the hall.

The scene in the green room suggested to Santiago a seventeenth-century Dutch painting of doubtful provenance. The actress was sprawled forward from her chair, facedown across a teak conference table, her famous hair flipped over her head to spill before her like new coins. Across the room, the alleged killer sat stiffly upright in a wooden armchair, his own forearms resting formally on the chair's. His posture and unfocused stare gave him the presence of a minor dictator or, Santiago could not help noticing, a man about to be electrocuted.

"Oh, and if you could all sign these releases?" said the girl, loudly enough to rouse the two from their reveries. She passed out three single-spaced, machine-stapled documents and a set of black roller-ball pens. "I'm sure your press people have already taken care of this, but, you know, just in case?" She touched her hair in an insecure but hopeful way and appeared satisfied by the experience.

When she had everyone's signature, she realized she had forgotten the introductions. "Miss Holmes, the actress. Mr. Deitcher, whom I'm sure you've all been reading about. And Mr. and Mrs. Díaz, of Mexico." She smiled with nearly aerobic satisfaction. "Please give a shout if you need anything. Oliver will be in before you go to makeup. Just, you know, to say hi."

When the production assistant shut the door, it became evident to Santiago and Mercedes that the room was soundproofed.

After a while, gazing down at the black-and-pink platter that had been laid before him, Mr. Deitcher asked, "What's sushi?"

CERTAINLY the last emotion Mercedes had expected Oliver Barnes's handshake to inspire in her was sympathy, and she allowed him to draw out the greeting so that she might consider him more closely. He was not an especially handsome man—slight, ash blond, gray eyed—however, Mercedes saw immediately why Edith had cared for him. It was rare to meet a man more interested in the woman he was looking at than at the effect his interest might have upon her. Mercedes allowed her smile to grow purely social.

Barnes next directed his attention to Santiago. By now it was unclear to everyone in what order Barnes was made uncomfortable by Mr. Deitcher, Miss Holmes, and his own on-screen personality, which seemed to follow unacknowledged at his heels. "Again I have to thank you, Señor Díaz, for agreeing to be on the show with so little advance notice. I guess I owe that one to Edie Emerson."

"Certainly. I've just met her, as I told you on the phone this morning. But she is a persuasive woman."

"I knew it was something like that. Okay, good." Barnes turned to the alleged serial killer, who was smiling shyly in a medicated fashion. "We're all very grateful to you and your lawyers for giving us the go-ahead tonight, even though your trial is still pending and all that. Any objections if we put you on first?"

"None by me," said the man.

"But, Ollie, I thought I was your first," whined the actress winsomely. "That's what you told me. Your very first on your very new desk."

Oliver Barnes regarded her with a life-may-be-longer-than-you-think look. "Julie, I would encourage you not to pursue that train of thought right now. And you did bring a clip from your new movie, I hope? The one with the poodles and black-leather cadettes?"

Miss Holmes giggled. "I'm sorry. The studio wants to open it exclusively in Singapore. The whip thing is very big over there, as you probably know." Biting her lip in an impression of modesty, she added, "So. First me, then Mr. Deitcher? If he doesn't mind?"

"No problem," said Deitcher. "I'm just so flattered to be on the show, Mr. Barnes."

Arching his eyebrows telegenically, Barnes agreed to let the actress go first. "And we'll end with Santiago Díaz," he said. "Next President of Mexico." He looked at Mercedes and Santiago. "You do take opinion polls as seriously as we do up here, don't you?" he added, curious to see what effect these words might have on his guest of honor.

Mercedes intervened. "We are less certain of our destinies

than are your countrymen, and so we are much more . . ." She gig-gled at the pretentiousness of her delivery. "Sexy," she finished after a moment's thought.

"Okay. Perfect." Oliver Barnes smiled his real smile then. "Señor Díaz, I've always wanted to meet you, and now I'll have to fire my assistant for not booking your wife, too." His assistant, Billy, threw him a self-consciously arcane look, and Oliver said, "Good-bye, Billy."

Billy smiled and withdrew.

"But is that something you could say on the air?" Barnes then asked Santiago. "I mean, about 'more sexy.' Just generally speak-ing, it's funny and true."

"I could say it," Santiago answered. "But I don't think many of your viewers would know what I meant."

Oliver Barnes nodded thoughtfully. On his way out he clapped Deitcher lightly on the shoulder. "Luck," he said.

Deitcher looked back at him as if about to cry. Instead, he ex-plained to the other guests, "Good, bad: luck is just luck to me."

Santiago, Deitcher, and the actress were seated behind a cur-tain stage right, where they were able to watch the run-through by video monitor. The show's rock band, a little heavier on the metal than was usual for late-night TV, was set up opposite them, fussing over the sound check.

When Oliver Barnes made his entrance, everything around him subtly realigned itself. His opening monologue, over the course of the show's success, had developed into a national insti-tution of sorts, with its mixture of topical jokes, ritualized per-sonal meditations, and social commentary that, while funny enough, carried with it something of the moral authority of a statesman's critique. Watching him, Santiago had the sudden in-tuition that Oliver Barnes and Edith Emerson had had some sort of romantic interlude. No doubt Mercedes had already consid-ered this possibility, but he was glad nonetheless that she was not there to see him smile.

When Barnes's monologue was finished, three men in white

short-sleeved shirts came out to confer with him. Despite the audience's dutiful applause, it was decided to drop the first two
jokes about the U.S. Congress, as well as the one about abusive
baby-sitters.

Barnes walked back to his stage desk and announced each of
his guests in turn so that they could get the hang of stage entry and
of moving down one seat at the proper time for the next guest.

Microphone booms and cameras on cranes moved through
the air like starved prehistoric creatures.

When it was Santiago's turn to appear, he walked out onto the
stage and, as the crowd, cued by the applause sign, welcomed him,
he experienced an insight. The insight embarrassed him, and he
was obliged to steady his voice as he discussed technical protocol
with Oliver Barnes.

People lived out a subtle dignity in conferring their attention
on the displays, both personal and public, of others. To admire
was to give measure to one's own strength and so to make it actual. These were the needs of an audience and, to some extent, of
an electorate. Santiago had disappointed Arévalo in this regard,
both as a friend and as a candidate. Without question it was why
Arévalo had left to start his own campaign. Also without question,
it was why Edith Emerson had made such an impression on Santiago: she had forced him into the position of audience.

"And I think we could finish up," said Barnes, "with something about cultural difference. The 'sexier' thing, if you can work
it in. But I'll just leave it to you."

"*Gracias.* Yes. I think that will be fine."

Santiago suddenly desired above all things the sight of his
wife's face. When he looked for her, he saw her making her way
politely but rapidly out of the third row toward an exit.

"EXCUSE ME," Mercedes asked a guard standing outside
the studio, "but I would like a cigarette before the show starts up.
Is there a place?"

He directed her to a small room down the hall, where, cautiously pushing open the door, she discovered Mr. Deitcher's mother, already ensconced on one of two beige sofas. She was halfway through a pack of menthols.

"It's just hard to sit there in the audience and watch," offered Mrs. Deitcher, a fleshy, dough-colored woman in a batik housedress. "You keep wanting to jump in and say, 'But Oliver, I've made *breakfast* for that boy.' " She flicked an ash into a paper coffee cup and seemed to retreat into her own reflections. "Well, I'm sure you know what I mean."

If Mercedes was now somehow newly invested in her husband's winning the election, then this was cause for one or two thoughtfully smoked cigarettes in the cartoon privacy of a TV studio's smoking room. Of that she had no doubt.

"I guess that's a Mexican cigarette," Mrs. Deitcher said without shifting her gaze.

"French," said Mercedes.

What Mercedes had seen in her husband's eyes while making love to him two nights ago had not exactly been, she now realized, an infatuation with Edith Emerson or someone she might represent. It had been a rough awakening within him to the disparities between his own public and private selves, disparities of which he had become, without realizing it, increasingly fond. Mercedes had for some years desperately wanted this sign of self-awareness from him; she required it absolutely in the father of her child. So if she had herself become a supporter of his vision—she could think of no other word for it—and if his vision at this moment involved coming here, to an American TV talk show, okay.

Hearing music start up onstage, she stubbed out her cigarette and, silently wishing Mrs. Deitcher well, left the room.

Immediately there were difficulties of a surpassingly stupid nature. Because Mercedes had removed herself from the audience after the run-through, she could not now, for security reasons, be allowed to return to her seat. Instead she was redirected to a VIP screening room, a place equipped with theater seats, a video projector, and an indistinct sound relay.

Mercedes argued her case to the guard who presided over this otherwise empty room, but he explained that bodily harm had sometimes come to those who had tried to return to the broadcast studio at the last minute. He was sorry, but there was nothing he could do to reinstate her.

When Miss Holmes appeared onstage for her interview, Mercedes realized that she had seen several of her films, which were quite popular in Mexico. Now, during a short improvised sketch in which the actress pretended to be a schoolchild napping at her desk, the band's saxophonist interjected a repeated two-note figure that suggested klaxons. Startled, Holmes ducked under the desk, where she turned the sketch into a reminiscence of the air-raid drills of her childhood.

The Deitcher segment was predictably more harrowing, and Mercedes was forced to light another cigarette in order to sit through it. No one on the show except Deitcher seemed comfortable with his presence there; innocent or guilty, he was certainly not bedtime entertainment, although he seemed, in his way, neighborly.

"Well, no, Oliver. I never wanted to be famous," said Deitcher with the guilelessness of a spelling-bee contestant. "My purest desire was always to inherit Daddy's farm. I didn't think life would turn out like this."

For a moment, Mercedes thought she glimpsed a more interesting Oliver Barnes, a genuinely curious man who wanted to believe that all stories had at least a kernel of enduring moral worth. She looked closely at Barnes on the screen. He appeared young for his age.

"Well, it hasn't turned out yet, has it?" said Barnes to Deitcher, who seemed, by the squint in his eye, to be aware for an instant that he presented some sort of difficulty for Barnes.

"No, sir, I don't suppose that it has."

"Ladies and gentlemen, please join me in thanking Mr. Deitcher for sharing his views and personal trials with us tonight." Barnes nodded balefully, Mercedes noted, in the manner of a U.S. presidential candidate. "Mr. Charles Deitcher."

There was a storm of appreciative hand clapping. No doubt, thought Mercedes, the applause sign was flashing helpfully, though she could not see it.

"And now, a man known to all of us for his prodigious accomplishments in sports and his personal bravery in helping free the American hostages at the Olympics only a few short years back. He is currently running for the presidency of Mexico, a country that has never before elected an opposition candidate. Please welcome Santiago Díaz."

Mercedes was pleased that her husband, though running for office, strode to his on-set seat with the cocky pace of a former soccer player. The applause that greeted him seemed to her independent of any electronic prompting.

After an exchange of pleasantries, Oliver Barnes asked Santiago if he minded looking at a film clip from his time with the terrorists. Santiago said he did not. The clip, predictably, was the one of the soccer ball being shot to pieces at Santiago's feet, and the sequence was frozen at its most famous moment, when the whites of Santiago's eyes seemed to outshine the light that fell on every other object and person on the screen.

The audience exploded in spontaneous applause. It was a celebrated event that they recognized and admired.

"Does it make you uncomfortable to recall those days?" asked Barnes. "It must have been a frightening time."

In fact, Santiago appeared briefly nervous, but what he said was: "Actually I am quite stupid about fear."

"You saved many lives."

"No. I diverted attention long enough for them to be saved by others." Santiago smiled modestly. "I was a soccer player."

"But now you are running for the highest office in your nation," said Barnes gently. "Have you always been ambitious?"

"No. I am not ambitious in the way you mean."

Mercedes, alone in the screening room, stood and, despite the hold exerted on her by what she was seeing, started to pace. She lit another cigarette.

"Okay, I'll buy that," said Barnes, "but you're not exactly opening a restaurant in Vegas either."

The actress, now seated to Santiago's far right, gave a hiccupping whoop, which she immediately pretended to stifle.

Barnes looked at her quizzically. "Julie, I think I know the restaurant you mean, and if you'd called ahead I'd have advised you to stay away from the steak Diane."

The audience found this uproarious.

"Well," said Barnes, when they had quieted down, "I guess everybody here who follows politics knows you were in the news today, Señor Díaz. Your closest adviser, Luis Arévalo, reportedly—and I'm just going by what the papers say here—*reportedly* has left your campaign to run against you for the presidency of Mexico." Barnes touched two fingers to his temple in a thoughtful and fastidious way. "Did this come as a surprise to you?"

"As a personal matter, yes, Oliver, it did." Santiago realized he was abandoning vigilance in some temporary way, but he felt the necessity of that freedom as keenly as he had moments ago yearned for the sight of his wife's face. "Luis and I have known each other since we were boys, and of course like all friendships ours has had its difficult moments. But we did not discuss his leaving my campaign."

"*Mierda,*" said Mercedes to herself.

"So you read about it in the papers, too."

"So I read about it in the papers, too," agreed Santiago.

Barnes gave him another thoughtful look, somewhat less convincing than the earlier one. "Difficult stuff, difficult stuff." He paused. "And would you agree with the papers that the differences between you and Señor Arévalo are basically economic ones? He's quoted as saying that your free-market policies are too extreme for Mexico, that extensive governmental controls are still needed in a country that, let's face it, has been dominated by the U.S. for a long time. What do you think about that?"

Santiago smiled, then relaxed. His intuitions about himself, about the world as it had presented itself to him today, had been correct: as one got older, the responsibilities one had accumulated through the joys of youth were to be savored in a different, weightier way. One had been observed; one was fated to be an observer. The important thing was to understand the value of the latter role as much as one had luxuriated in the former one. This, he felt, he could do.

He said: "Last night, my wife, Mercedes, and I had dinner with a young *yanqui* couple—you will forgive me the term—and the woman used the expression 'conspicuous consumption.' It had been a long time since I had heard those words put together in that way, but they had a strong effect on me. We in Mexico have long been a captive audience to the conspicuous consumption in your country. This has not been good for us. But I would like to bring this same conspicuous consumption to Mexico."

Mercedes, in her media cell, stood perfectly still.

"I believe we Mexicans are lovers of the conspicuous," Santiago continued. "To bring such examples more readily to our own rich country is my desire."

Barnes appeared briefly at a loss. Then he said, "Well, if you open a restaurant in Acapulco I'll lay you ten to one that Miss Holmes would be happy to consume conspicuously."

Again the audience erupted in hilarity. But Mercedes could bear no more. Throwing her unfinished cigarette to the ground, she fled the room.

When she reached the end of the hall, Mercedes, with as much aplomb as she could summon, asked the guard for the ladies' room. It was kept locked, he told her, and he would have to let her in with his key.

Mercedes and the guard made an unlikely couple, she in her black dress and spike heels, he in his olive-colored uniform, as they walked together to the ladies' room.

Inside, Mercedes placed her purse on the glass shelf above one of the sinks and looked at herself in the mirror for a long time.

Living with your own distorted self-image was bad enough, and everybody had to do it, but to have to watch your husband passionately declare his own misreading of himself before an audience of tens of millions was absurdly painful, more than could be borne.

After a while Mercedes washed her face. She opened her purse and carefully reapplied her makeup. It was in her to deal with all of this, if only she could know with certainty what occasion she was being asked to rise to. She had done more difficult things.

James and Marisa de Borba walked up the avenue together, their shoulders touching haphazardly in a way that suggested that nothing of value happened only once.

It was Sunday morning.

"You should have told me I'd be too hot," said Marisa. She stopped to adjust the knee-length leggings she wore beneath her much shorter skirt. The leggings were printed with a fantasy jungle pattern; the skirt was black. "Why do you torture me?"

This was something she said often, though comfort was her natural state.

"Probably I like the challenge," James answered. He put his arm around her, and she pressed his hand to her breast.

At twenty-eight Marisa was ten years younger than James, but also more keenly possessed of a sense of purpose. "You have a very dirty mind," she added by way of afterthought.

James had been Marisa's North American dealer for almost two years, and though they never made any special effort to see each other they had been lovers for much of that time. What they had most in common was an appreciation for the kind of physical

passion that ensues when a man and a woman connected by circumstance and temperament are left alone at the end of an overly
eventful day. Because they laid no claims on each other, however,
they never spoke about their liaison; friends who inquired about
it were answered with irritation or sudden hilarity, both genuine.

James let Marisa into the gallery. While he deactivated the
burglar alarm, she glided toward the back of the space, turning on
the lights as she went.

"When are you going to get a new assistant? That guy is never
here on time."

"It's his day off. Besides, people like him."

"Not me. First he dyes his hair silver, now he wants me to
photograph him."

"Maybe it's a decisive moment. Exercise your artistic instincts." He followed Marisa into his office, where he found her
sitting in the chair Edith had occupied three days earlier while
telling him she intended to marry Andrew. Marisa's natural sense
of sexual entitlement, rare enough, was made startling by her perfect awareness of it.

James unlocked his desk drawer and wrote her a check for
thirty thousand dollars. "I'm thinking maybe we should suspend
operations for a while," he said, handing it to her.

"Why? Are you feeling criminal?"

"Certainly not. Is your father feeling criminal?" Marisa's father owned a company that was logging and burning the Brazilian rain forest on a semiexclusive basis.

"Of course he is. But he likes the feeling."

Part of the profits from her father's enterprise was being sent
to Marisa's brother, who was a highly placed trade representative
in Mexico City. Then various things would happen, and another
part of the money would show up in U.S. dollars at James's
gallery. James's cut was thirty percent. The checks he wrote
Marisa were drawn on the gallery's account.

"I'm trying to remember why it was a good idea to buy a table at Santiago Díaz's banquet the other night. In retrospect, things turned out funny."

Marisa laughed and cocked her head, waving the check dry in a gesture she had learned from her father, the only person she knew who used a fountain pen. "Oh come on, they were already funny. You promised I could have my border photographs, right?"

"I'll promise you anything. Then occasionally I'll ask myself why."

"Spoken like an art dealer."

"But you know I'm bad about politics." James had no interest in parsing his connection to Marisa; what he liked was to let himself be a bit ignorant without abandoning his wits. Love had lain that way for him before. Imagination, as he understood it, always did. That was why one asked the little questions.

"What did you really think about Santiago's performance last night?" he inquired of Marisa.

She sighed. "I told you already, okay? I didn't know Arévalo was going to break with Díaz. Anyway, it doesn't affect us."

When Marisa used the first-person plural with James it was to remind him that the life allotted them lay in never being quite sure what they were doing with each other, apart from bed and business.

"But what if Arévalo wins? Let alone Santiago. Your brother will feed us to the press." James made the gesture of ruefully repudiating his own shirt cuffs, though in fact they were pristine. He was a fastidious man.

Marisa laughed and came over to sit on his lap. "The opposition does not yet win in Mexico."

"Yes, it does."

"But it never takes office."

James pressed his thumbs gently to her armpits, through her blouse, turning her toward him. "These border photographs. Even for you it's a strange setup. All of us down there at some no-place Mexican town. Am I missing something?"

She laughed softly and brought her mouth down upon his.

There are kisses that subtend the whole grammar of convenient misunderstanding. Afterwards, for a time, neither party is deceived by anything worth speaking about.

"You have lipstick," she said, touching her fingers to his mouth a bit later.

James withdrew one arm from their embrace and wiped his lips on his shirt cuff.

Marisa laughed. "You still don't love me, do you?"

"No."

"Good." She kissed him again and removed herself from his lap with the tiny flourishes of someone who feels thoroughly understood. "Now. What about those photographs you were going to show me?"

"Oh, I forgot. Your dramatis personae." He walked over to a bin full of black print portfolios, each of them about half the size of a folded-out exercise mat. "Him. Him and me. Her. Me. Her and me. Mexico."

James placed the portfolios he had selected on the desk before Marisa. "Archival only, okay?"

She smiled the smile of lean greed at him.

"Don't forget I know you well, Marisa."

"I'd rather be known than loved."

James left the office, then walked across the street to buy a couple of take-out cappuccinos. When he returned, Marisa was sitting cross-legged on the floor, surrounded by the portfolios she'd asked to examine. All but two of them were open, and she leaned so closely over the one in front of her that James wondered if she didn't need an ophthalmologist.

"I like this one," she said without otherwise acknowledging him.

He put the coffees down on his desk. "Maybe you'd like a loupe? If you really need to look at it that closely?"

She glanced up at him and smiled. "This one," she said,

putting her forefinger down on the plastic-jacketed photograph she'd been inspecting. "Why haven't I seen it before?"

Crouching beside her, James surrendered to her appreciation. "Yeah. I like that one, too."

It was a photograph of him and Andrew in a bar in Mexico City. They were about to be in trouble, but they had asked for it and then had survived it. Andrew was playing an upright piano, and James, a shot of tequila in one hand and the customary complement of spiced tomato juice in the other, was singing with his eyes closed. Actually he had only blinked. Andrew was playing from sheet music that had been given him, and James was improvising the words in Spanish. The faces of their nearest listeners conveyed their assessment of the situation.

"You were two bad guys, huh?" said Marisa.

"We were younger than you are now."

She narrowed her eyes at him melodramatically, then smiled. "Also, I like this one," she said, throwing open one of the two portfolios she'd left unfastened beside her on the floor. "It goes with my interest in—what did you call it?—'vernacular photography.'"

Looking down at the picture of Edith, not an original print but a carefully spliced-together tear sheet from the magazine for which she'd posed, James had the sensation that he'd never known her at all. Of course this was opposite to the intention of the magazine's publishers, but Marisa de Borba was adept at giving things an unexpected spin.

"She's pretty, isn't she?" said James.

"Certainly yes. But maybe this was a while ago, right? Do you think she'd mind undressing for the camera again?"

"In a border town in Mexico?"

Marisa gave him a look that involved an ironic pursing of her lips, which she knew to be beautiful enough to improvise with.

"Yes, I think she would mind," said James, smiling into the middle distance. "But what do I know?"

"So maybe I can ask?"

"Your call."

"*Obrigado.*"

He stood, and at the same moment she seized his trouser cuff, fixing him to the spot and claiming his attention. When she felt him settle she kissed the inside of his thigh through the fabric.

"I won't say we deserve each other," James offered, "but we are a kind of match."

"Us?" She laughed and bit his leg.

From the front of the gallery a voice called out for James.

"Well, don't think about it too much," James told Marisa, drawing a hand roughly through her hair. "It was just an observation."

"Hello? Come out with your hands up! This is a raid."

Although he recognized Andrew's voice, James waited until the video camera in front had swung around to focus on the gallery's entrance before he responded.

"Let the boy go," called James, when he saw that Andrew had brought Kevin with him, "and I'll surrender peacefully."

Marisa smirked unhappily, rose to her feet, and, taking a hairbrush from the bag she had left on James's desk, vigorously addressed her own self-image.

"Hello, Mr. Kevin," said James, sweeping Andrew's son up in his arms. "What's happening?"

"Daddy's taking me to see my mommy." Kevin looked with curiosity at Marisa, who had bent over to finish brushing out her hair. "Who's she?"

"Hi, James," said Andrew.

Advancing upon the situation, Marisa used her foot to flip shut the portfolio containing the picture of Edith. "Hi, Andrew Caldwell," she said. "Remember me?"

"Of course I do. You're the one who wants to ship us all off to Mexico so you can photograph us, right?"

"That's right." She was delighted. "I didn't know James had spoken to you."

"Maybe it was Santiago Díaz? I can't remember. Anyway it's nice to see you again, Marisa."

While Andrew did not recall being told that Marisa was sleeping with James, it seemed a natural turn of events and, since no one was making much of the matter, it also seemed something to be quietly encouraged, like dandelions growing on a highway median strip. Andrew smiled at her.

"James was just talking about how you saved his life in Mexico when some guy in a cantina wanted to cut him up because he had said something terrible. You sat down at the piano and made him sing his way out of the whole mess in Spanish." Marisa put her hairbrush away and shrugged. "I think."

"Yeah, that's always advisable with James." Andrew winked at her.

"How come you're in such a good mood?" said James irritably.

"Because my good friend came to my rescue yesterday when I was being accused of various indecencies."

Marisa was staring at Andrew with long-exposure eyes. "My mother tried to find a piano teacher for me, but it didn't really work. I played the finger exercises backwards for fun."

"Daddy, I want to play the piano backward!" said Kevin, propelling himself out of James's embrace into what had become a neutral space among the adults. "Can I?"

"Sure. But maybe you'd like to try forward first."

"Mommy has a piano."

"Yes, she does."

The adults looked at one another.

Kevin began to stroll around the space he had created. "Can she play it backward?"

It was the kind of conversation that responsible parents hasten to redirect, but Andrew was distracted by the sense that he'd made an insufficient impression upon the present company, who'd clearly been talking about him. "James remembers that piano. It was the one I bought when we were in college."

"The one you'd play till two in the morning and leave beer bottles on."

"Yeah. Susannah got it in the divorce."

Kevin made a break for the main gallery, and no one stopped him.

"Well, fuck, man. How come? She can't play."

"She likes props."

Marisa began to feel comfortable. "Who took the picture of you and James in the cantina?"

"Oh that's a story."

"Daddy, if I take my shoes off I can skate!"

"Then don't," called Andrew.

"Marisa likes stories," James offered.

"I can tell. I hope we get to do another version of the cantina photograph sometime."

Marisa blushed charmingly. She had a full and sulky figure that responded well to attention of most kinds. "I just follow my impulses."

"Daddy! Everyone in these pictures is *naked*!"

"Kevin, please don't shout at us from another room."

"Naked!"

"Well," said Andrew, recrossing his legs. "It's a piss. Being a father and so on."

"Bravery is always honored."

Andrew looked closely at James. It occurred to him that maybe James was actually more involved with Marisa than the casual observer might think.

"Anyway," said Marisa, who hated to lose even an imaginary advantage, "James and I are hoping you'll let me photograph you in Mexico. You and your friend Edith and, um—"

"Kevin," said James.

"Yes," said Marisa. "Your son would be a wonderful addition."

"Santiago and Mercedes—are they still part of the arithmetic?"

"I hope so. Of course, after yesterday, with Arévalo leaving like that . . ."

"Yeah, hard to say, I guess." Andrew rubbed his scalp in good-natured bemusement. "You know, I don't see as much art as I should, but the concept here eludes me. What would we all be doing together, and how come down there?"

James and Marisa exchanged another look, but it was obviously her cue, and Andrew was surprised to note that James looked relieved.

"I like to photograph people who belong together without knowing why. It's . . . what, James?"

"Eloquent, probably."

"Don't be sarcastic." She tilted her head so that her hair fell over one eye, and then she couldn't help but laugh. "I'm sorry. James is funny, don't you think?"

"He's got a rare sense of humor, definitely."

"Anyway, I hope you'll think about it."

"We will. All of us, I mean." Andrew turned to James. "I just wanted to thank you for yesterday, at the police station and all."

"Hey, no problem. A friend in need."

"I appreciate it."

"Daddy, what's this?" said Kevin, returning to the arena of attention with a black leather ankle weight of average size.

"Oh. That's a beanbag. You know, like at your birthday party? You can throw it around if you're careful not to hit the pictures. Okay?"

"Yeah!" He returned to the other room.

"Is there a story that goes with these photographs we're talking about taking?" asked Andrew after a suitable interval. "Lawyers—you know how we are—we love stories."

Marisa looked scared and said nothing.

"Well, there's always Edie's Texas stop sign story," responded James. "That might be apropos."

Andrew was acquainted well enough with the stop sign story. "Maybe," he said. "But Edie might wonder in what way, though."

There seemed to be an arrangement about who could look scared at a given moment because now it was James who did, and Marisa who swept up.

"I don't know anything about this—what did you call it?—stop sign story, but I thought the thing to do would be to get everyone together and just feel it out. Sometimes the setting is everything. Right now, I'm interested in borders."

"That's because you think we're all borderline cases," James said cheerfully.

"Just you, my friend."

Andrew relaxed. He again felt certain that this project of Marisa de Borba's had never really been meant to be taken seriously. "Let's see how things go. Anyway I've got scheduling conflicts. Edith and I have to be in court later this month, and we'll need James as a character witness."

This appeared to be the right thing to say, since both Marisa and James laughed without the customary exchange of cryptic glances.

"Of course, 'witness' is probably not the word I want," Andrew couldn't help but add.

Kevin came rushing into the room. Mercifully, he had lost the ankle weight. "Daddy," he announced, "I want to laugh and talk, too."

"C'mon, bucko. Put your shoes back on. It's time to go see your mother."

While Andrew tied his son's shoelaces, James and Marisa stood formally by, adopting the respectful attitude of those who have no children and don't intend to.

"Everything okay?" Andrew asked when things at ground level had been squared away.

"*De positivo,*" said James, stepping forward to embrace his friend.

For a moment this gesture surprised everyone.

Then Marisa said, "It was very nice to see you again." She gave Andrew her hand. "We'll talk soon about the photographs, okay?"

He looked for a long moment at Marisa. She was young

enough for the features of her ambition not yet to have seized hold of her face. "Yeah, okay. I'll think about it."

James gave Andrew the nod of someone acknowledging a debt partly repaid.

"I don't make deals," called Andrew over his shoulder as he and Kevin headed out of the gallery. "I just enjoy the thrill of the chase."

"He's stealing my lines," whispered James, kissing Marisa on the throat. "But I guess you've already figured that out."

She unbuckled his pants. "Fuck you," she said.

ANDREW hated the ritual of the custody visit as it had been legislated by his and Susannah's conflicting temperaments. She lived in a building with an overly appointed lobby and poor services, and the deal was that Andrew was to deliver Kevin to the guy at the desk downstairs, who would then send him up to Susannah when Andrew was gone. The whole thing smacked of something read in a paperback self-help book, but Andrew tried to make allowances for the ways of mutual heartbreak.

"Daddy, am I going to spend the night here?"

"Sure. Why not? Don't you want to see your mommy?"

"Yes."

"Well, okay then. Are you my boy?"

"No! I'm a dinosaur!"

"What kind? A brontosaurus?"

"Yes. I eat *vegetables.*"

This last was patently untrue—Kevin hated vegetables—but Andrew saw the seeds of dignity here, and he hugged his son good-bye.

"Call me if you want to," Andrew said. "I'll be at home."

It was an impossibly stupid arrangement.

Walking uptown from Susannah's neighborhood Andrew encountered a homeless woman with whom he had become passingly familiar. She asked him to buy her a chocolate milk, and when he did she thanked him politely. Her requests were always modest and specific, which set her apart from many of the people in his life.

Hailing a taxi, Andrew gave the driver his home address. Then he thought better of it and asked to be taken to his midtown office instead.

"In my country," said the cabdriver, whose country no longer existed, "today is the anniversary of our betrayal by the West."

Andrew couldn't remember when he'd lost his mood.

After he'd signed into the building and negotiated the lock on his firm's office door, Andrew walked down the hallway turning on the lights. He was alone there. That suddenly seemed to be the point.

Why should he have expected everything he was doing to fit together like an air-traffic controller's perfect day?

"Hello?" he called out, just to be sure.

Then he stopped by the fax machine, which was delivering itself of an information hair ball.

"Pointless piece of shit," he told it absently.

It answered immediately in kind: page two of a tedious memo from the firm's accountant, who lived upstate and dreamed in numbers. Andrew set this communication aside in annoyance, realizing he probably deserved it for coming in on Sunday, although he had hoped for better. This low-grade optimism was an aspect of Andrew that amused most people.

"Don't even think about it," he said to the voice-verification phone that had at that instant begun to ring. It stopped.

He found two other faxes of interest in the delivery tray. Both were from Brazil, both dated earlier that morning. This was the kind of thing Andrew felt he could have predicted, but useless foresight was his métier, in a sense.

In the first instance, Brad Lowell, problematic heir to his grandmother's estate, had notified Andrew that he wanted the money bequeathed him to be set up as a foundation for the protection of the golden monkey, current object of his research. The species was imperiled by the destruction of the Brazilian rain forest.

The second fax suggested that Brad Lowell felt himself similarly imperiled. There were overtones of a loneliness that might elsewhere be thought paranoid or ridiculous, but for some reason this was the syntax of Andrew's office. It inspired a kind of bad-attitude bonhomie, and Andrew encouraged it.

Death-related litigation was like that.

"I'M *NOT* on the other line," said Edith into the first line. She wasn't talking to anyone she knew.

"I'm not on *this* line," said the other voice. And almost immediately it was true.

"Get well, girl," Edith told the ensuing dial tone.

She rang the switchboard downstairs and asked for a caller ID, but it was Sunday at the UN. No one had been keeping track of the incoming.

Edith had come into the office this morning, nearly noon now, to give herself some breathing room, though there was basically the same amount of oxygen all over town.

She lit a cigarette.

That morning, while she and Andrew were watching the videotape the VCR had made of Santiago's appearance on *The Oliver Barnes Show*, Edith had drunk a liter bottle of Italian mineral water. The show, because neither of them had till then heard of Arévalo's defection, had startled them into a number of competing witticisms. After Santiago's comments about conspicuous consumption, Edith had excused herself and been quietly sick in the bathroom.

She and Andrew had intended to watch the program live, since that was its point. But at show time they'd been busy planning their future together. Late-night television existed for people who didn't have such options.

Edith leaned forward precipitously and seized a computer diskette from her ASAP file: a report on the northward tide of illegal aliens in the Americas. She translated a couple of paragraphs without interest. Some things were obvious in any language.

The word "subsistence." The word *esperanza*.

Edith cleared her computer's screen temporarily and sat back in her chair.

Her and Andrew's arrest the day before had not been as much of a surprise to her as it no doubt ought to have been. Exposure was her avocation. On the other hand, law was Andrew's profession, so without thinking much about it she had left him in charge of that part of their picnic. A natural division of labor.

Edith's phone began to ring again, and after trying to stare it down she snatched the handset from its cradle. "Hello?" she said.

The caller sighed heavily and hung up.

Maybe Sunday really was the Lord's day because Edith rarely had a good time then. She looked at her fingernails, which her manicurist had lacquered that morning with an iridescent glaze, then she drank deeply from a glass of water she'd set by her desk, grabbed her purse, and left her office for the ladies' room.

It was hard to know what might be a good time in the Lord's eyes.

In the bathroom stall Edith put her hands underneath her blouse and touched her breasts as if they were presents from someone she loved. The presents hurt.

She raised her skirt, lowered her underwear, and sat.

The way the pregnancy test worked was you had to urinate on the absorbent tip of something that looked as if it had been a cigarette filter until the day before yesterday. You had to do it for at least five seconds. Then you were informed of your fate by the appearance or not of a thin blue line in what the instructions gravely referred to as "the large window."

Edith let the opening bars of *Also sprach Zarathustra* run through her mind while she peed, but irony was not really helpful under the circumstances. She knew she was pregnant even before the thin blue line appeared.

Afterwards she threw the little plastic test away and wept. She'd never really envisioned having a child of her own, and now to have conceived under circumstances so compromised by accident made her feel undermined, supplanted by a self for which she had not prepared. She had no idea what she would tell Andrew, or when, but accepting matters was a way of hoping for the best. And the best was a fugitive item. In her opinion anyway.

SANTIAGO and Mercedes were putting on their underwear in a combative manner.

"You know I hate those—what are they, underwires?"

She threw the brassiere he had thus condemned out the window of their room at the ambassador's residence. "I hate you and those ridiculous underpants," she responded.

He took them off. He knew they were ridiculous.

"I didn't buy them myself."

"Oh, your lover bought them!"

"No, my lover was in Paris."

She threw the underpants out the window, too.

"I hate you!" she said.

This was the kind of interchange they tended to have when Santiago's plans shifted suddenly.

"Listen," he said, trying for the conjugal tone he'd mastered often in his daydreams and a few times in actual practice. "You know I must go back to Mexico City and see what it is with Arévalo. Okay? I can make no important decisions without you, but I ask you to stay here in New York for the time being. I do not want to worry that you are in danger."

"Danger!"

"Please trust my judgment on this," he said, walking to the window, though admittedly his nakedness did not help his case. "Things have changed too quickly in the last twenty-four hours.

From here, in this city, who can know? I would be grateful if you could indulge my worries for a day or two. I will call you."

"Don't be moronic. If I were afraid of the kind of danger you mean, do you think I would have married you at all, Señor Co-jones?" She began to put on a new pair of panty hose. Because she was a long-waisted woman this was always an arresting occurrence.

Santiago tried to remember if he had any clean underwear left. "I promised your mother that I would never involve you in—what did she call it?—my 'hostage politics.' "

"Too late, *querido.*"

Santiago decided that dressing without underwear was the best option available to him. He started with his suit pants. "I think it would be better if we didn't rush back to the capital together in a panic. What I am asking is that you help us achieve our aims."

Mercedes stood stunningly still, naked but for her panty hose. "Our aims? Please, after last night, tell me what they are. I will not leak them to the press."

She and Santiago had discussed many aspects of his performance on *The Oliver Barnes Show.* They had argued without communicating, embraced without restraint, wept, made love again, laughed at the life they had blundered into together, and proposed several names for the child they had yet to conceive. But nothing between them was settled in a way that could be given a name of its own.

"Okay. I should not have said what I did about 'conspicuous consumption.' It will be misunderstood." Santiago shook out a newly pressed shirt. There was the usual problem with over-starched buttonholes, and under the circumstances he made the most of it.

"Misunderstood is not the word I would have chosen." Mercedes selected a brown silk blouse from her suitcase and put it on.

"You are not yet my speechwriter," Santiago reminded her.

"More's the pity."

"What an expression!"

"You've never heard it before?"

"It is a fucked Euro-television way to speak."

Mercedes smiled faintly. "Can you help me with my necklace? The clasp too is fucked."

She handed him the necklace, he approached her from behind, she held her hair up from her neck while he fastened the golden garland. They had reconciled in this way countless times.

"I can't stay here at the ambassador's," she said after they had kissed.

"No. I would not allow it."

"With or without Arévalo we are still the opposition as far as our government is concerned." They both knew the state party had been using the ambassador's staff to keep an eye on them.

"Of course," Santiago replied, trailing a hand across her torso as he turned away.

"Still, I don't think I want to go to a hotel."

"Why would you have to? We have many friends here."

"Yes." She stepped into a tiny skirt of black suede. "The zipper sticks," she said. "Could you help?"

Santiago understood he was about to be asked for something else. A fond warmth flared through him. Because he had given her this skirt and had with reverence removed it from her hips many times, he knew that the zipper was sound.

"I'm fat," said Mercedes as he closed the skirt around her.

"Yes, very fat."

"*Cochino!*"

"What is it you want to tell me?"

"Until I join you in Mexico, I will stay with our new friends, Andrew and Edith."

"They have invited you?"

"Not yet." She took the phone from its cradle and punched in a number.

Mercedes, reflected Santiago, was a warrior.

"Hello," she said into the phone, "it is Mercedes Díaz."

But Santiago could hear the recorded message on the other end of the line. It was Andrew Caldwell's voice, introducing his home in a neutral-sounding way. Santiago shook his head sympathetically and, reaching out a finger to the phone's plunger, terminated the connection.

"*Gracias, mi corazón.*" Mercedes turned her back on him with the full force of her alarming beauty.

"It is not good to be so dramatic."

"No doubt."

"Let's try him at his office."

"Let's try her at her office."

"*¿Cómo no?*" He offered her the phone, which in her pique she had thrown down on the bed.

It would have been impossible for either of them to say when they had begun fighting over Edith Emerson as if some part of their lives depended on it.

"BUENAS TARDES," Edith told the phone, hoping to throw off anyone who might still be calling her anonymously.

"*Buenas tardes, Señorita Emerson.* It's me, Mercedes."

Edith stood, laughed, remembered she was pregnant. It was like hiccupping and sneezing at the same time. "Hi," she said. "*¿Qué tal?*"

"We're okay. You saw the TV show last night?"

"We taped it and watched it this morning. I'm really sorry about Arévalo."

"Yes. Thank you. We all are." Mercedes paused long enough to remind Edith of Arévalo's unpleasant resourcefulness in regard to lost purses and forgotten photographs. "Anyway, as you can imagine, we've had to change our plans."

"You're going home early," said Edith, shamed even as she spoke by the note of accusation in her voice.

"Santiago has a flight out in two hours, but I'm going to stay a few days."

"Is there anything we can do to help?"

"Well, Santiago feels I should not remain here at the ambassador's without him. And it's true: our government has almost certainly been using the ambassador's staff to spy on us."

"Yes, I'd wondered about that." But actually Edith was thinking about other things.

"So perhaps you could suggest a hotel," Mercedes continued. "I'd like to be away from the press."

Edith reached for her cigarettes before she remembered she'd thrown them away. Breathing for two was the excuse she'd given herself, but she knew it was more complicated than that. "You can't stay in a hotel," she said peevishly.

"Of course I can," Mercedes reminded her.

"But stay with us instead."

Mercedes glanced at Santiago, who was gazing unconvincingly at a nest of neckties he'd left in the top drawer of the dresser. "It is very generous of you," she told Edith. "But as I'm sure my husband would tell you, I'm more trouble than I am worth."

Santiago received his wife's blown kiss. "She never sleeps," he announced loudly. "And she calls her manicurist in at midnight."

"What was that he said?"

"Nothing. He feels guilty about going home without me."

"So tell him you'll be in good hands. When should we expect you?"

"Really? Are you sure it's all right?"

"Absolutely. Andrew loves impromptu house parties." She didn't actually know if this was true, and she wondered why she'd said it. "I should be here another hour or so," she added, "why don't you call us at home a little later?"

After a triumphant silence Mercedes accepted, thanking Edith profusely. Before she was done Santiago wrested the phone from her to express his own gratitude and high regard. It was all interestingly overdrawn. They hung up.

Not for the first time Edith reflected that what she most liked about being a translator was that the task was technically impossible, an exercise in approximation. Increasingly, the only completely literal utterances she knew came from her own body. For example, since her menstrual cycle was short and unusually regular, she could be as much as six weeks pregnant. Of course, the first test had come out negative.

A wedge of brilliant sunlight made its way across her office floor.

Edith again scrolled rapidly through her computer agenda, trying to pin down the date of her farewell encounter with Oliver Barnes.

OUTSIDE the ambassador's residence someone had made a sidewalk fresco in colored chalks. It was an interpretation of *Mona Lisa*, with particular attention to the smile. Mercedes stood in one of the implausibly green regions of the composition, her luggage beside her, and Santiago stood upon an eye.

"We'll tell Pedro that you're going with me," he said as the limousine pulled up to the curb. "After he's dropped us off, I'll get you a cab."

Mercedes nodded once in brisk assent. Santiago could see, though, that she was reviewing her options: whether to insist that he take her with him right then to Mexico or to linger a while longer in what he was coming to see as a kind of reverie they had created involving Edith, Andrew, and whomever else.

Pedro stowed their luggage in the trunk of the car, then, when Santiago and Mercedes were settled beside each other in back, maneuvered the absurdly large vehicle into traffic.

Santiago had decided to take the helicopter shuttle from the city's eastward river to the airport. His aides would catch the next day's flight.

"How far do you think Luis would go?" asked Mercedes suddenly.

"Go?" repeated Santiago.

"To win, I mean. For example, would he blackmail you?"

Santiago laughed, but a wakefulness ran through him. He knew he loved the unexpected as few men did and that in a sense this enthusiasm made him vulnerable. Not to blackmailers, whatever Mercedes was referring to, but to the moment when the ball, patched together from black- and white-dyed leather, spun suspended above the players and the field, a nearly perfect object of anticipation.

"Luis has no reason to blackmail me," said Santiago. "And what would he blackmail me with?"

She leaned her head on his shoulder.

When they arrived at the heliport, a featureless place flanked by haircutting salons and hamburger bars, Santiago had Pedro unload the luggage. There were whitecaps on the river. Mercedes put on her sunglasses.

"*Buena suerte, Señor Díaz,*" said Pedro.

"*Gracias.*" Santiago shook the young man's hand. "I will see that you come home soon."

Mercedes smiled. "*Hasta luego, Pedro.*" Pedro returned to the limousine and left the asphalt lot.

"Maybe I should go with you after all," said Mercedes, approaching her husband in the wind.

"No, *alma mía.* I can't allow it. Not yet." He gestured to one of the cabs idling nearby.

"But you don't mind my staying with Edith and Andrew."

"Why would I mind?"

She moved forward into his arms. The cabdriver began loading her luggage into his trunk. Santiago's bags were already onboard the helicopter.

"I'll call you every day."

"Twice a day," she corrected him.

They kissed, the helicopter's engine started up, and in the sudden downwash the black-and-white chiffon scarf Mercedes was wearing lifted from around her neck and wrapped itself across the upper part of Santiago's face like a blindfold.

For a moment neither of them made any attempt to correct this awkwardness.

"Are you scared?" asked Mercedes, pressing the scarf closer to his face.

"No. Are you?"

She kissed him hard. He couldn't see. The scarf flew away.

"Yes," she said.

It wasn't until he was halfway to the airport that Santiago noticed the length of black-and-white chiffon caught on one of the helicopter's skids.

SOME hours later, Edith, Andrew, and Mercedes sat in the cocktail lounge of a much-esteemed hotel listening to an even better known pianist interpret Cole Porter. Sometimes the man sang, but a lot of what he did seemed to be about leaving things out.

Mercedes was staring at one part of the room's mural, where it appeared that two of the bunnies that formed the narrative motif of the room's decor were mating.

"You're sure you won't mind being plunked down in the middle of domestic life?" Edith asked her. "Because there's always my old apartment. It's not much more than a studio, but no one would bother you."

"I live very badly when I am not bothered," answered Mercedes.

"Good. It's settled then." Andrew handed her a set of keys. "There's a fold-out bed in the study and a separate phone line. We'll show you."

The piano player began a version of "Night and Day" that seemed to be mostly night. There were not that many other patrons present, and Andrew got the feeling that they were being treated to an autobiographical statement.

"I used to play piano," Andrew announced then. "But it's such a complex proposition, trying to figure out how hard to hit the keys and whatnot."

Edith, who was drinking soda water to Mercedes's kir royale

and Andrew's scotch, affected puzzlement. "Well, the guitar is the international instrument of choice now. You pluck it."

Mercedes lit a cigarette. "When I was growing up in Mexico City, my uncle used to take me some nights to see the *mariachis* in Plaza Garibaldi. Lots of guitars, more strumming than plucking. People think the *mariachis* are a creation for *yanqui* tourists, but it is not so. The real customers, even now, are Mexican."

"You liked the music, though," said Edith.

"Oh, no!" She allowed herself to complete the laugh she'd almost stifled. "What we liked was the companionship."

The waiter arrived with another round. "On the house," he said.

Mercedes saw the piano player smile at her, and she smiled back. A stripped-down version of "Begin the Beguine" immediately ensued.

Swaying a little to the music, Edith found herself wondering what, exactly, had caused her to insist so adamantly upon Mercedes staying with them at Andrew's apartment. Maybe what she wanted was the companionship.

"I got a couple of funny hang-up calls at the office today," she said then. "Before Mercedes called."

"Man or woman?"

"Woman. Portuguese accent, I think." Edith swiveled in her seat so that she was half facing the piano.

"Anyone we know?" asked Andrew, suddenly alert.

"Not me."

Andrew downed his drink in a couple of swallows. "That reminds me. I ran into Marisa de Borba today at James's gallery. She's really set on this idea of photographing all of us together in Mexico. I forget whether you know about this, Mercedes."

"Don't you remember? We discussed it on the way to dinner the other night."

"Right. Of course. So what do you think?"

"I believe in art. Artists sometimes are a different matter."

"That's the creative impulse for you," said Edith.

There was a party of what appeared to be prep school students at a nearby table. They were well dressed, genetically mannered, and quite drunk. One of the boys was staring openly at Edith.

"Anyway," Andrew continued, "are you and Santiago really going to accommodate our Miss de Borba?"

"I don't think it's the first thing on anyone's list."

Andrew and Mercedes exchanged a bright, infected look and laughed.

It was only then that Edith realized that being sober and pregnant gave her a leg up on the situation, whatever it was.

"I've begun to think we should do it," she said. "Just for the record."

"Really?" said Andrew with fond unfocus. "How come?"

"Because it's senseless. It doesn't translate." She made an exculpatory spiral gesture with one hand. "Because everyone needs to do something like that once in a while."

"A lot of people would probably tell you that's why Santiago is running for president," said Mercedes.

Edith found herself suddenly caught up in a memory of the banquet at which she had first laid eyes upon Santiago Díaz. As she recalled it, he had explained his political ambitions in terms that involved the words "plain view."

"People get to say anything when you put your personal fate in their hands," she pointed out. "It's the arrangement."

Andrew was delighted. "It is?"

"Of course it is," said Mercedes.

Across the room from them, one of the prep school students—two were girls, the other four boys—was trying to knot the stem of a maraschino cherry in her mouth. This drama was being watched with rapt attention by everyone at her table but the boy who was still fixated on Edith.

The pianist abandoned Cole Porter for a medley of Thelonious Monk.

Andrew looked at his watch and said something to Mercedes.

What Edith felt next was so ordinary it was like reading the weather report in a morning newspaper while having lunch outdoors. And in fact weather was not far from her mind as the pianist glided from one song to the next. Certain rains stirred her; usually they were island rains; they dampened the insides of her thighs and made her breasts ache.

She was aware of her heartbeat.

The prep school boy who had been watching her stood suddenly, martini glass in hand, and lurched forward in a direction that might have been calculated to bring him to their table. Instead, he stumbled against the piano and dropped his drink into the instrument's open case.

For a moment the musician kept playing. The sound was like something that might be produced by an ingeniously broken dishwashing machine. Then the celebrated man gave up in disgust and walked over to the bar, where a brandy had already been poured for him. "That's why I don't take requests," he told the bartender. "People just don't know what they want."

Because of the way Edith was seated, neither Andrew nor Mercedes could see her face, but they had the sense that she might be laughing. Her shoulders quivered. Also, everyone facing her was looking at her.

But when she turned around everything became obvious. Her blouse was unbuttoned, her breasts were bare and beautiful, her lips had composed themselves into a smile of angelic absence.

"Edie! What the hell are you doing?" But Andrew's question was immediately transformed as the words of it climbed into the air and hung there like votive candles. He felt his cock stir and stiffen. The emotions he felt—anger, embarrassment, excitement—swallowed one another successively like the ever-larger fishes in the food-chain cartoon.

"Gosh, I—" Edith buttoned her blouse back up with the natural speed of a seamstress or a teenage girl. "I'm so sorry." She felt frightened and beautiful. "I didn't know I was going to do it until it happened."

Mercedes put one finger over her mouth as she laughed. "I think we're going to have an interesting time together."

"Really I'm a serious person," Edith explained.

For some reason it was Andrew who blushed.

LATER, at home, in bed, with Mercedes safely asleep in the study and Kevin at his mother's, Andrew tried to think of a way to express what was in his tangled heart. "I guess I thought you only did that for me," he said.

" 'That?' What do you mean?"

She spoke gently, but Andrew understood that he was being asked to let it alone. He sighed and kissed her temple. Not that he'd ever imagined things with Edie were going to be simple.

There was a silence then. When it had run its course, Edith, as if belatedly offering an explanation for her behavior, told him she'd been beside herself all day. Saying so made her realize it was true, and she moved closer to him.

"I had the idea you might want to ask me about Texas," she said.

"Texas? You mean Oliver Barnes?"

"Right."

"Why would I want to do that?"

She bunched the pillows together and tucked them underneath her chin. "You said you talked with James and Marisa de Borba about those photographs she wants to do of us in Mexico. At the Texas border."

"I did. So what's the problem?"

Closing her eyes, she shook her head slowly. "Nothing, I guess. It's just me. Sometimes I remember unkindly."

The period she had spent with Oliver Barnes had brought with it a strange mix of unfamiliar pleasures and constraints. His celebrity had constituted a nagging third party to their affair, and they had determined from the outset to keep their liaison secret. Privacy had been their aphrodisiac.

They had been seeing each other about a year when his producers conceived the idea of sending him out to do the show from a number of other cities across the country—an essay in regionalism and boosted ratings. For reasons she could no longer remember, she had decided to join Oliver in El Paso the week they had sent him there.

The show went well, but afterwards, while driving along the chain-link fence separating Texas from Mexico, they'd been stopped by the Border Patrol. The patrolman had accused them of running a stop sign a couple of miles back, and the standard harassment had ensued: Oliver was intoxicated, Edith was underage, a drug shipment meant for them had been intercepted just across the border. Things had been running their course when the policeman suddenly shone his flashlight on the fence behind them, picking out a young Mexican boy poised atop it, ready to jump down into a new life. The officer had shouted for him to stop. Then, after seeming to think about it, he had shot him in the chest.

The boy had fallen off into darkness with a moan of such sadness and disappointed hope that Edith would never forget it.

Afterwards, when the patrolman had ordered them on their way, Edith had wanted to circle back and look for the boy, but Barnes had been fearful of the possible publicity. So although there had been no stop sign, not even the flimsiest of pretexts for their being drawn into the whole terrible incident, Edith thought of that night as one long admonition to halt. It had marked the beginning of the end of their affair.

Andrew did not know that Edith was crying until the first tears trickled onto his shoulder.

"Edie, what is it?"

"This last week. Everything."

He stroked the back of her head. "It'll slow down soon."

"I don't think so."

When she fell asleep, he gently disengaged himself, put on his bathrobe, and walked into the living room. Behind the study door he could hear Mercedes snoring faintly. It occurred to him that he should have called Kevin at Susannah's, but just as quickly it occurred to him that probably that was a bad idea.

He took Volume One of his *Complete World Atlas* down from the bookshelf, opened it to the page marked by the bound-in ribbons, and looked at the colors for a long time.

As it turned out, Andrew had been mistaken in not calling Kevin the night before, or at least in not ringing up Susannah while Kevin was in her charge, because Monday morning, despite their usual arrangement, Susannah delivered their son to Andrew's apartment door personally.

Mercedes was still asleep, Edith already off to work. She had a midday appointment with her gynecologist.

"Hello, bat of my belfry," said Andrew, kissing Susannah on both cheeks, as was his custom when he perceived her to be in a rage. Sometimes old endearments really did express whatever was left of them.

"Daddy, can we play with my blocks again?" Kevin ran to his father and wrapped his arms around one of Andrew's legs.

"Not right now, bucko. Maybe later."

"I want to speak with you," Susannah informed Andrew. She had a way of cutting her eyes from side to side when she was angry; the effect was a little comical, but no one had ever had the heart to tell her so.

"Sure." He looked at his watch. "Okay."

At that moment, Dorotea, the Mexican nanny Andrew had

hired after the divorce, let herself into the apartment, singing under her breath to the empty orchestra that scrolled through her stereo headphones. Weekend nights she liked to go to the karaoke rock clubs—they were as fashionable here as in Mexico City—and sometimes she practiced her sing-along routines for Kevin, to make the day go.

Kevin ran to her now.

"This won't take long," Susannah told Andrew in a way he knew she meant to be alarming.

They walked the length of the apartment and sat at the kitchen table, the second best place either of them knew of for having alarming conversations.

"Kevin talked a lot about his new mother," Susannah said. "Is she here now?"

Andrew sighed and tried to remember the mistaken, lovely things that had caused him to marry this woman and, out of what had seemed the sheerest harmony, father a child by her. "Does that sound like something I'd say? 'New mother?' "

"Am I a social worker? Can I read your mind? Is this a daytime TV show?" She was wearing her hair in a French braid that reached partway down her back and seemed dense with rebuke that her last shampoo had only burnished.

"I live here with Edith now. She's already left for work. The three of us have spent some time together, but no one's confused about who Kevin's mother is."

A flitter of interest passed through Susannah. "Why do I know you're going to marry this Edith woman, Andrew?"

"Because you're you," he answered.

"Lawyers," she said. But it was not clear to either of them whether she was describing him unflatteringly or summoning reinforcements.

"I'd like Kevin to go on living with Edith and me," said Andrew. "I think our arrangement has really been working out well for him. Nothing need change that wouldn't have anyway."

"Great. Glad you let me know." She drew herself up in her

chair with an exaggerated rectitude that raised even her eyebrows. Her hands contracted into fists, and she rested them before her on the table as if challenging him to a guessing game. In Andrew's long experience of her, this posture usually portended a blinding bout of tears and accusation.

"Stop, Susannah." He enfolded one of her fists in his own hand. "Let's not do this."

"I hate you."

Andrew shook his head sadly. "No, you don't."

"Yes, I do. It's not subtle, but I'd forgotten. You use our son as point man. Why don't you fight your own battles?" She jerked her hand away from his.

"Gently. He'll hear us."

"Always lawyering your way through life. Don't you get tired of it?"

"This argument is what I'm tired of."

"Good. Good. How long have you been fucking her?"

Andrew sighed in the face of his ex-wife's recklessness. She was profligate with her energies, and she failed to pace herself. It was a trait that had thrilled him at first, but in the end it had cost them both dearly. "Does how long make any difference, Susannah?"

Just then Mercedes emerged from the study in a red bathrobe and, waving sleepily at them, slipped into the bathroom.

"She's discreet, your Edith. Leaving us alone together like this."

"That's not Edith," Andrew answered.

From the other end of the apartment came the sound of Dorotea and Kevin counting in Spanish. A propitious sound, promising in cadence.

"So," said Susannah, forcing herself to look Andrew in the eye, "what if I want Kevin to come live with me now? What with you getting married and everything."

"That might be difficult."

"Difficult? Why is that?" She tilted her head and frowned in mock puzzlement.

"Are we speaking hypothetically?"

"I don't know yet."

"Then let's stop here before we ruin each other's day."

She lunged at him, but he was able to catch her by the wrist before she slapped him. A silver and turquoise bracelet he had given her one long-ago birthday fell to the floor; he had not noticed she was wearing it.

"Bastard," she said when he released her. She turned on her heel and hurtled down the hall, almost colliding with Mercedes on the way.

As he listened to his ex-wife say good-bye to their son in strained tones, Andrew felt his mood shade toward the philosophical. Presently, he reflected, it would be time for all concerned to take their fears in their arms and jump for the white water.

AT THE OFFICE Andrew made a private show of throwing himself into his work. After the morning partners' meeting he sent a lengthy fax to Brad Lowell in Brazil, updating the primatologist on the state of his inheritance. Then he sketched out a preliminary defense of the late Mrs. Lowell's will.

At lunchtime, he called Edith. Not until her voice-mail service began telling him which buttons to press did he remember her saying she had a doctor's appointment. He hung up without leaving a message.

Edith's performance in the piano bar the night before continued, in the light of day, to trouble Andrew slightly. Not the act of display itself, which, after all, was part of what he sought in her, but something else. She had thrown herself with apparent fearlessness into a life with him; she had accommodated the incidental wreckage such a life entailed, and she had not complained. Yet what he now sensed in her ran deeper than either self-control or its feckless breach. He had come to imagine her naked body as a voice. This voice was asking a question, addressing him in the most straightforward way, and he was expected to make sense of it. Under the circumstances, he was moved to wonder if Mercedes had not been called in as interpreter. An attorney might say so.

An attorney, he thought, might say it had something to do with the prospect of matrimony.

"Boss, your devoted staff is ordering out for lunch," Leticia told him over the intercom. "They're worried about you. 'Doesn't he eat anymore?' they ask themselves."

"Tell them he has a lunch across town."

"You really should have come dancing with me and Zazie the other night," she pointed out before hanging up.

Andrew did not in fact have lunch plans, but now on impulse he decided to take a cab over to James's gallery. Not until he got there did he remember it was Monday, the art world's day off, but he pounded on the gallery's plate-glass window until he attracted the attention of Rickie the Assistant, who seemed to be hanging the forthcoming show all by himself.

"Look what the cat dragged in," said Rickie by way of greeting. He favored Japanese couture, rings, and artfully arranged dramas of self-regard. "Would it like to make itself useful?"

"I'd only spoil things for you, Rickie. Any idea where your master is?"

The youth rolled his eyes and redirected Andrew around the corner to the racquet club where James was regularly to be found cultivating clients and the aerobic arts. Andrew was also a member, and though he disliked the air of privilege that attached to the place, he wouldn't resign. It was James who had put him up.

"Greetings, Counselor," said James when Andrew had located him coming off the squash court. "If you'd phoned ahead, I would have reserved our favorite table."

"Sorry. I'm still on primary process."

"Hey, no problem. Just let me get changed, and I'll meet you in the dining room."

The lunch went well. In simpler days, the two had made a point of taking lunch together once a week at the club as a way of shedding the pressures of work and ordinary disgruntlement. Lately they had let the ritual lapse.

"You should have been here last Monday," James told his friend. "Two whole tables in violation of the briefcase rule. One guy had to be thrown out bodily."

The club's bylaws strictly prohibited its members from conducting business in the dining room. Briefcases, legal documents, and personal digital assistants were banned.

"Must be the economy," Andrew suggested.

"Nah. People are just getting greedier."

Andrew ordered a bottle of wine. The casual drift of the conversation encouraged him to hope that his friendship with James remained intact. Susannah's visit was sitting badly with him, but when he found he could put it aside for now, he did. Andrew's native optimism began to flow.

"Hey, Walsh. How come you've been keeping Marisa de Borba under wraps like that? You never mention her."

"Never mention her? Who's staking his reputation on her artistic whims?"

Andrew had to smile. "I meant something else. Am I wrong, or are you two an item?"

"Oh, yeah. Well, it's just a sex-type thing."

They laughed together.

"She's Brazilian," James explained.

Over dessert, Andrew told his friend about Brad Lowell. The story of being taken to meet the grandmother's grief-maddened chimpanzee had by now acquired the luster of a traveler's tale, and James was suitably entertained. But what really seemed to engage his interest was the thought of Lowell alone in the rain forest, hunkered down on the battle line between nature and civilization.

"So this guy's sending you daily dispatches from the front. What's he got to say?"

"About what you'd expect: corruption, waste, indiscriminate logging, festive burning. He's studying this certain species of monkey. Its habitat is in the line of fire, and he wants me to use his grandmother's money to set up a conservation fund."

"You going to do it?"

"That's the plan. He says his life is being threatened."

"Who'd want to do that? The government?"

" 'Certain foreign interests,' I think he said."

James laughed outright. "Guy's been in the jungle too long. He's a bug."

"Maybe." Watching James pour himself a last glass of wine, Andrew thought he detected a tremor there. "I didn't know you knew so much about it."

"I don't. Just what I read in the paper. Speaking of which, what's the word on our friends from Mexico? I'm told they decamped."

"Just him. She's still here."

To Andrew's relief, James did not pursue the topic. "Hey, you and Edie coming to the opening tomorrow night? Strictly A-list. You'd like it."

"Your parties are always A-list, Jimbo."

James's eye settled on his friend with something like amusement. "That's okay, I know you're usually tied up on Tuesdays." He reached for the check before Andrew could claim it. "But, hey. I've got to give you and Edie your engagement present. How about I drop by your place after dinner tonight?"

It occurred to Andrew that maybe he and Edith would end up going to Mexico after all.

"*Mi casa su casa,*" he said.

EDITH'S VISIT to the gynecologist had left her obscurely dissatisfied and on edge. He had drawn blood samples and asked her all the routine questions, but she couldn't shake the feeling that she'd been condescended to. Doctors didn't ordinarily have that effect on her.

Still, she was wearing red fuck-me pumps, and they gave her a boost as she passed again through UN security. No one could say she didn't appreciate the theater of redundancy. She was a lover and an incipient mother and she knew her rights.

"Edith!" said a woman she had just passed on her way to the elevator. "I thought you'd be over at the General Assembly."

Turning, Edith recognized Billie Chang, an acquaintance from late nights around the coffee machine. Billie experimented with vitamin regimens in a way Edith associated with recovering addicts. Also, Billie collected everybody else's hot-shit information.

"I guess I've been out of circulation," said Edith. "How come the General Assembly?"

"I don't know. People are saying." She smiled brightly. "Anyway, see you at Enrico's tomorrow night, okay?" Billie Chang's new haircut made her look like the star of a Hong Kong cult film.

"Sure," said Edith. "Usual time." She had no idea whether Enrico was a person or a place, but she liked to help Billie out with her routines.

Back at her desk Edith addressed herself to the migrant populations report. The work went easily, and when she finished, an hour or so later, she logged off the computer. The resentment that had come over her at the doctor's office had not left her. It felt primordial in nature, not to be argued with. On an impulse, Edith grabbed her purse and headed for the General Assembly.

The session had been called to discuss bringing the administration of geosynchronous satellites under direct UN control. As Edith understood it, there were only a limited number of spots in space where you could park a telecommunications satellite on a more or less permanent basis. Naturally the richer nations had already snapped up most of them, and the developing nations were demanding their share of the swag. It was an issue whose time had come.

Seating herself in the visitors' section at the back of the vast chamber, Edith fixed her attention on the speaker, whom she recognized as the ambassador from Belarus. The man was turning red in the face from the force of his own oratory.

Although Edith knew some Russian, she shortly lost the rhetorical thread and was forced to take up the earphone plugged into the jack at her elbow. The interpreter's voice was female, incongruously sibilant and measured. Edith at once identified it as belonging to her friend Hannah.

I've been out of circulation, Edith reminded herself.

After fidgeting her way through the last of the speaker's allotted time, she took herself quickly upstairs to the interpreters' booths.

She didn't have to wait long.

"Ah, Edith, it's you. I was beginning to count you among the missing." Hannah smiled and closed the door of the booth behind her.

"Have a minute?" asked Edith.

Hannah took Edith's arm in hers and guided them into a stroll down the nowhere corridor. "It's been quite a day. Were you here for the morning session? An actual altercation on the Assembly floor. Fisticuffs and whatnot. I think that's a first."

Hannah was a good ten years older than Edith and had seen the sights.

"Really? A fistfight?"

"Well, something physical, anyway. Mexico and Brazil. As far as I could figure out, it had to do with Mexican pollution and the Brazilian rain forest."

Edith was startled to realize she'd lately come to think of Mexican matters as her own special province. She hoped it didn't show. "I don't get it," she said.

Hannah gave her friend a wise little look. "So where've you been?"

Edith felt for Hannah a respect that was only deepened by the older woman's refusal to let it define their friendship. In her twenties she had been married to a well-known sculptor, a German, who, two months after the wedding, had been crushed to death beneath a one-ton steel plate he'd been positioning outside a museum. Although Edith had not known Hannah then, she did not need to be told that the loss had been complete. A lesser woman than Hannah might have made a career out of tending the dead man's considerable reputation. Instead, she had turned his estate over to her in-laws, diversified her passions, and cultivated what Edith thought of as an attitude of receptive willfulness.

"I'm afraid to speak," said Edith. "What about the good opinion of my friends?"

"What about it? I think you're covered."

"No. I've become a gusher. I'm an inward gusher about to gush publicly. Does that word summon up anything for you—'gusher'?"

"Well, maybe. Certain pictures come to mind."

"Hannah, I'm getting married. And I'm pregnant. But the guy I'm marrying isn't the father." It was the first time she'd said it aloud. "Also, I think I hate men."

"Goodness."

"Goodness the fuck is right."

They sat on a backless bench upholstered in turquoise plastic and talked for almost half an hour. As she explained what had brought her to her present pass, Edith found she was handling it well enough. During the night she'd had flashes of blind panic. People would be wanting things from her and she didn't know what they were. Now, in a concession to clarity, she was trying to meet those expectations head-on. Maybe they applied.

Hannah asked if Edith planned to see Oliver Barnes again. She absolutely did not. "That last time was just a fluke," she explained. "A fuck for auld lang syne. And anyway I've already told Andrew about it."

Hannah, who had also been Edith's confidant during the Oliver Barnes period, grimaced. "But you haven't told him anything about being pregnant."

"I was hoping you might have a few thoughts on that."

"Well, I'm supposed to say something here about honesty. If you're going to marry this guy, you're going to have to tell him sooner or later."

Edith shrugged, a slow underwater kind of movement. "I guess so. But don't you find that men are kind of dumb about counting?"

"About counting," repeated Hannah blankly.

"Counting back, I mean. They think the menstrual cycle is an offense against reason. You and I know that Oliver Barnes is the father because I haven't been with Andrew long enough for the tests to show positive on his account. Even though theoretically Andrew is at least as likely a candidate."

Hannah shook her head vexedly, refusing the notion. "I don't know, Edie."

"So if in a couple of weeks I gave Andrew the good news, Oliver's name wouldn't even have to come up. Ever." Seeing Hannah's finely cut features cloud with skepticism, she felt a surge of impatience. "I know that Andrew wants to have another child. He's told me. So what I'm thinking is, Why not this one?"

"And you could live with that."

"I'd have to."

Hannah was shaking her head again. "It's such an indelible lie, Edie. The kid would be living his whole life under false pretenses, not to mention you and Andrew. You'd suffocate."

Edith said nothing.

"How much does this have to do with you not spoiling the picture you've imagined? Are you afraid that if you tell Andrew the truth he won't love you the same way?"

"That's part of it."

"And I'm assuming from the way you're talking that abortion is not one of the things on your mind."

"Maybe not. I don't know yet."

A brace of media people passed by, tightly knotted around

three men walking side by side down the corridor. The reporters were asking questions, half-falling over one another in their bid for attention, while the man they were addressing informed them repeatedly that he would have no comment. Sometimes he said it in English, other times in Spanish.

Edith looked down to see that Hannah had taken her hand. "What are you so angry about?"

"Am I angry?" asked Edith.

"Maybe you feel you've rushed into this thing with Andrew."

Edith said nothing. For a moment she was tempted to ask Hannah if she'd ever been to Mexico, but she quickly thought better of it.

"If the baby's what's tying you into this maybe you should reconsider."

"No, it's not the baby. And anyway I do want to be tied in." She realized she wasn't ready to pursue this conversation further. "Probably I'm just mad that I won't get to show my tits in public anymore."

Hannah was amused. "There's always breast feeding," she said.

ANDREW and Edith arrived home late but within minutes of each other. Andrew had phoned Dorotea, asking her to make dinner for Kevin and herself. Now Mercedes and Dorotea were deep in conversation at the kitchen table, Kevin was riding his hobbyhorse up and down the hallway, and Zavalito was directing his band of pianos over Andrew's not exactly state-of-the-art stereo system.

"Holy hell," said Andrew appreciatively. "It's domestic life."

While Edith took a shower, he cooked a quick meal of stir-fry shrimp for whomever might still be hungry. No day was predictable, and satisfaction lurked in the strangest corners. It could not be managed. The more you tried to direct the course of things, the more likely you were to fall victim to your own insufficient imaginings. That was the problem with last wills and testaments, but for the living there were compensations.

Dorotea was expressing enraptured disbelief that Mercedes was acquainted with the music of Zavalito. To lend weight to her opinions she delivered them in English.

"But no joking," she said. "He is the only guy from home I can listen to. Everybody here thinks Mexican music is maximum *mariachi*."

When he was done cooking, Andrew put enough plates around the kitchen table to accommodate present company, relieved Kevin of his broomstick mount, and delivered him under only minimal protest to bed. Knocking on the bathroom door, though, he had a moment of unease. The water had stopped running some time ago.

"Edie? You going to eat with us?"

He could hear the medicine cabinet close. Then she said, "Sure. I'll be out in a sec."

For a moment he hesitated. He wanted to tell her she was needed, but he realized how such words might sound through a closed door. "Okay," he said. "We long for your presence."

In the kitchen Andrew addressed himself to Dorotea. "*Señorita bonita*, please dine again with us."

"*¿Cómo no? Gracias*," she said, entering into the spirit of things.

Mercedes was staring at him with amused speculation. "You are a man with a kitchen table full of women."

"Bitter with the sweet," he said. He was putting a bed of arugula on each plate so that there might be something underneath the shrimp. "How was your day, Mercedes?"

"I saw some of my friends. But mostly I just walked around. Also, of course, I called Santiago."

"Yeah? How are things?"

"I guess Santiago is your husband," said Dorotea, who was beginning to enjoy feeling free with her opinions.

The Zavalito tape clicked loudly off.

"Hi, everybody," Edith offered, taking her place at the table. She was wearing a blue silk wrapper with a paisley figure, and no one but Dorotea thought this a good sign.

Andrew hastened to put down wineglasses. He understood Edith was presenting herself in the aspect of anger, but he didn't have time to consider why because he himself was growing irritated in a low-key kind of way.

"You missed meeting Susannah today," he told her. "She came by when she dropped off Kevin."

"Is that good?"

Placing the bowl of shrimp at the center of the table, Andrew sat down opposite her, next to Mercedes. "Usually she sends him up by himself. This time she wanted to talk to me about redoing the custody agreement."

"Because of me."

Andrew saw he was leaning too hard on her. "Nah. It's just the way she is sometimes." He laughed. "Anyway, I think she's under the impression Mercedes is you."

"She is?" Mercedes was delighted.

"She ran into Mercedes in the hallway. I tried to explain, but Susannah listens kind of selectively."

Edith was amused despite herself. There was something here for everyone tonight, she reflected. *"Los camorones son muy rico, querido."*

"Thanks."

Dorotea snuck a look at her watch. She was having a good time, and Edith, noticing, decided to make it a little better.

"You're really talented with kids," she told the young woman. "You must have grown up in a big family."

Blushing, Dorotea nodded. "I am the oldest."

Mercedes was still sorting through the ironies available to her in being taken for Edith, and her smile had grown pleasantly speculative. "How many are you?" she asked Dorotea.

"My five brothers and me."

The telephone intercom rang with a three-burst downstairs *buenas noches.*

"Are we expecting anyone?" asked Edith. Among the more defined of her present grievances was Andrew's failure to ask about her visit to the doctor, even though she had told him it was just a routine checkup.

"Shit. I forgot. James said he'd be coming by with an engagement present." Andrew picked up the phone and without consultation buzzed the party in.

"You two are engaged to be married?" Dorotea inquired after downing her glass of wine. *"Fantastico!"*

"Everything just kind of fell into place," Edith explained.

"I've been wanting to offer my congratulations." Mercedes raised her glass. "I've always believed that the best marriages announce themselves immediately. It's a great gift."

It was a sentiment no one wished to quarrel with. They drank the toast.

James and Marisa arrived immediately after, looking flushed and a little predatory. While James at first appeared not to recognize Mercedes, Marisa fixed her at once with a smile so nakedly expectant that it cast light.

"I tried to lose her on the way," James explained to Andrew and Edie, "but when it comes to parties Marisa will not be denied."

"Glad to have you, Marisa," said Andrew. "Glad to have you both." He performed the introductions.

"My husband has spoken to me of you," Mercedes told James and Marisa. "You are photographers, no?"

"Not me," said James. "I stay away from the creative end of the business."

Marisa stepped over to shake her hand. "I have wanted to meet you for a long time. What an unexpected pleasure." She was wearing one of her especially burnt-down-looking outfits. It brought out her figure.

"I'll get a couple more chairs," said Dorotea.

The engagement present James had brought was a thing of

truly weird beauty, and unwrapping it Edith was unable to stifle a cry. It was an antique Indian mask from southern Mexico, hand-carved from balsa and lavishly decorated with polychrome paint, leaf both gold and silver, and bits of semiprecious stone. From the forehead to the nostrils it was a single face, with a startling pair of blue crystal eyes and slits in the forehead for the wearer to see through. But below the nose, the face bifurcated, Cubist-style, so that there were two jaws and mouths. One mouth, rendered in excruciating detail, completed a face of blissful tranquillity and beauty, while the other, no less evocative, showed the same face in a snarling rage. It was uncanny and more than a little scary.

Andrew had seen it before. James had bought the piece during their youthful journey to Mexico, and Andrew knew how highly he prized it. The mask, as he recalled, had a name.

"God, James," Edith said, staring at it. "You've outdone yourself."

"May I see?" asked Mercedes.

Everyone fell silent while she examined the object, holding it before her as if it were someone she had just been conversing with unsatisfactorily. Then she flipped it around and held it before her own face. When she put it down she was smiling.

"La Máscara de la Danza de la Dualidad," she said. "It represents the interior and exterior of the personality. Very beautiful. Very Mexican."

The calm with which she spoke rattled Edith. She realized she had no definite idea what Mercedes was capable of when fully engaged. "I guess it's not worth asking which side is which," she said.

As the evening progressed, Andrew's mood darkened. James was making free with the wine, but he had always been something of a drinker, and it only sharpened his performance. The effect was bracing. Andrew noted that he directed his charm at everyone except Marisa, who apparently preferred it that way.

It had long been James's pleasure to lace his badinage with enough darts and probes to keep things interestingly off balance. He was attentive to the unspoken thought, and in his presence,

Andrew had observed, people often felt themselves possessed of a subtlety that otherwise eluded them. Sometimes, when they got to know him better, they felt violated.

"Actually," Mercedes was saying, "it was Edith who arranged for Santiago to be on the show."

"No kidding. I didn't know Mr. Barnes was still worthy of your attention, Edie."

Glancing at Andrew, she roused herself to reply. "We'd all like it a lot," she told James, "if you kept your filthy thoughts to yourself."

After Dorotea excused herself and went home, Edith relaxed noticeably, yielding bit by bit to James's pleasantries while continuing to withhold herself from Andrew. At one point, she loosened her bathrobe, crossed her legs, and hiked the hem up well past her knees. It had probably been inevitable that Andrew's impatience take on a sexual dimension.

He glanced at Mercedes, and her eyes widened in unspoken comment. She seemed to understand his position thoroughly.

"Marisa," he said, "what do you know about the rain-forest situation down there in Brazil?"

James, who had been relating a lengthy art-world anecdote, fell abruptly silent. After a moment Andrew continued.

"The heir in a case I'm handling works as a primatologist way back in the jungle, and he thinks somebody's put a price on his head. He's an obstruction to progress or something. Does that kind of thing go on?"

The temperature of Marisa's calm surveillance rose a couple of clicks—just enough to ripple the air. "Brazil is an unreal place, sick with beauty. We have Stone Age cultures living in the middle of a computer society. Not everyone behaves well, but our problems are sometimes exaggerated by outsiders. I doubt your primatologist is in any serious danger."

"That's good to know." Andrew found himelf disinclined, for now, to pursue the matter. "I'll tell him."

The evening ended, as Andrew had known it would, with

James's pitch. He wanted them all to spend a day or two together in a Mexican border town so Marisa could photograph them. It could be coordinated with Santiago's schedule, and there were ways it could be put to the advantage of his campaign. He emphasized the need for a record, not just of the personalities involved but of the forces that had brought them together.

"Sooner or later," he concluded, "I'm going to persuade you. So why not just say yes and let me and Marisa worry about the meaning of it all?"

Aware that she was being deferred to, Mercedes laughed softly and shook out her hair. "Why don't you just settle for no one saying no, Mr. Walsh?"

Later, in bed, Andrew and Edith found themselves still at odds but too tired to talk about it. They lay side by side in the darkness, unable to sleep. After a while, she spoke.

"You remember I told you I got a couple of hang-up calls at work yesterday? It was Marisa. I didn't recognize her voice at first."

"You must be mistaken."

"No. I don't think so."

For some time Andrew tried to think what Edith's words might portend. He was still turning it over in his mind when she sighed and moved into his arms. "Anyway, it doesn't matter now, does it? They're all going to be part of our lives whether we like it or not."

"Why?" it occurred to him to ask.

"Because we invited them."

OVER the course of the week that followed, the household they had created and the rules that governed it evolved according to the prevailing mood of expectancy. Everyone had a separate agenda, but like skaters on a rink they had to accommodate one another's momentum. It was a surprisingly intimate situation.

The opening at James's gallery had received a good deal of advance publicity, and, in the end, when Mercedes expressed a desire to attend, Edith and Andrew decided to come along. The photographers were a pair of pastiche dandies straight out of art school. They affected bowler hats and oversized black tee shirts; their taste in subject matter ran to eviscerated forest animals, over which they superimposed uplifting slogans in gothic type. At the dinner afterwards, Mercedes and Marisa amused themselves by reciting these apothegms at the least lull in the conversation.

They can kill you, but they can't eat you. Today is the first day of the rest of your life.

The next day Marisa called Andrew at the office and asked if she could drop by. He was on the point of declining when it struck him that twenty minutes alone with her might afford him a better sense of what she and James had in mind.

She arrived half an hour later with a camera, tripod, and quartz light.

"You're impossible," he told her. "Aren't you ever off duty?"

"Just one roll. Ten minutes. You can think of it as a warm-up routine."

He arranged himself against the window casement for her, gazing out over the litigious city while she snapped away. "The other day, when Edie and I were at James's, he referred to Santiago as a business contact."

"Did he? Tilt your head toward me. Good. Don't move."

"But seriously. What do you think he meant?"

"He knows how much I want to photograph Santiago. And despite what you may think, I too am a business contact in James's eyes."

Andrew sensed at once that she was telling the truth, and he couldn't help but wonder what he had to offer in exchange. "That's not the James I know," he said.

"Come to dinner at my place tonight. James will be there."

"I don't know. Edith wonders what your interest is."

"She's already said yes. Bring Mercedes and Kevin."

Marisa had him sit at his desk for the last few shots. It was a place where he was comfortably double-hearted, tolerant of ambiguities. He was a man who understood productive disruption, and it seemed to him, as Marisa held the light meter to his face, that she was aware of his watchfulness.

THE DINNER at Marisa's was a success. Her and James's campaign to insinuate themselves into the lives of Edith, Andrew, and Mercedes took on a momentum of its own, partly comic. The protocols were those of irony and sport, which made it unseemly and finally irrelevant to delve too deeply into purpose. Kevin began asking when James and Marisa could spend the night.

Mercedes talked daily with Santiago. As anticipated, Mexico's ruling party had been quick to take advantage of the split in the opposition, and while so far the polls did not show them picking up support, there was a growing stream of defections from Santiago's camp to Arévalo's. One evening, Mercedes let slip the fact that state television was running clips of Santiago's interview on *The Oliver Barnes Show*, believing it would help Arévalo's cause. The "conspicuous consumption" segment had become the inspiration for jokes, editorials, and even an ad campaign for a bridal accessories outlet. Shamed, Edith hastened to apologize: she had been wrong in suggesting Santiago appear on the show, it was an act of self-fascinated ignorance.

Mercedes reached out and placed a finger across Edith's lips. "No," she said. "We can't help each other if you think like that."

On Thursday, Andrew heard from Susannah's lawyer. Disinterested inquiry had brought to the attorney's attention Andrew and Edith's indiscretion in the park the previous weekend. While Susannah wished Andrew to know that she believed new custody arrangements could be amicably reached, it was the attorney's duty to inform her ex-husband that she would be petitioning the court to reopen the case. Andrew, who was not exactly surprised, decided to wait for Susannah to call him before he made his next move.

"What makes you think she *will* call?" Edith asked him the next morning. He was shaving and she was leaning against the bathroom doorjamb.

"Susannah's the creature of her anger. She expends. What she is wouldn't work if she didn't always upstage herself."

They'd all been up late the night before viewing a film Marisa had made a couple of years previously. "I'm like that too, aren't I?" said Edith. "Maybe you're repeating."

The film had concerned the special dissonances occasioned by Brazil's recent census. Some of the rain-forest tribes counted their dead as mouths that still needed feeding; conversely, some of the city census takers had viewed their task as an opportunity to settle personal enmities on a house-by-house basis. Marisa's camera had adopted the aesthetic approach to these events.

"You couldn't be more different from Susannah," Andrew answered. "You'll see when you meet her."

"No, I can do a really first-rate irritable bitch if I put my mind to it. I know you've noticed."

"I've noticed you trying; that's true enough." Turning to her, he wiped the shaving cream from his face with a hand towel. "How come? What're you so pissed off about?"

She took the nail scissors from the shelf over the sink. "Hold still. Your eyebrows need trimming." Her brow furrowed in concentration as she snipped. "God, they're like wire."

Andrew laughed quietly to himself.

"What's funny?"

"Nothing." Then he said, "You were talking in your sleep last night."

"No kidding. Was I interesting?"

"You sighed a lot. I didn't know it was possible to sigh while sleeping."

She smirked. "Stress, I guess. What else?"

"I think what you said was, 'Fuck the music, just keep playing.' Also, 'The show must go on.'"

This time they both laughed.

"Didn't Susannah ever talk in her sleep?" Edith wanted to know.

"When she was pregnant she used to recite A. A. Milne into the pillows. It was a preemptive strike."

Edith stole a glance at his sky blue eyes. What she saw there was her own intransigence reflected back at her. She was a woman who had never yet been naked enough, and here was someone who seemed willing to watch her turn inside out.

"I bet Susannah never trimmed your eyebrows, though," she said. All at once she was dizzyingly calm. "Stop squirming. I'm nearly done."

THAT afternoon, after lunching on carpaccio and asparagus with the wife of a former tennis star with whom Santiago had become friendly, Mercedes took a taxi downtown to Marisa de Borba's studio.

When Mercedes was a little girl she had imagined for herself a life in which men would die for her in extravagant ways. She would beseech them to abandon duty and rest with her, let her care for them. Their gallantry tended to fall into certain occupational categories. Soldiery was one. Socially enlightened drug smuggling was another. But none of these imagined men had ever heeded her pleas. Glory was their lot, and grief was hers. She had been a romantic child.

Marisa came down to let her in. "I'm so happy you've come," she said.

"I was interested to see your new work. The other night at dinner you promised to show it to us, but I think James got too drunk."

The elevator was an old one, dating back to when Marisa's loft had been a fish-packing concern. To engage the mechanism, a rope was yanked, and to keep other tenants from leaning into the shaft, a shout was obligatory. "James is such a sweet man," said Marisa. "You mustn't pay any attention to him."

Upstairs, Marisa's studio belied the building's age. It had been renovated during her most recent sojourn in Rio, and its walls presented variations on the theme of white—a purely professional decor that had been lost on Mercedes during her earlier visit.

"Sorry. I'm a chemical hazard," said Marisa, who had been in the darkroom when Mercedes buzzed. "I'll just wash up."

A portion of one wall had been turned into a bulletin board, and pinned to it were the photographs Marisa had taken of Andrew at his office. Inspecting them, Mercedes found herself growing impatient with aesthetic prerogatives. "When did you take these shots of Andrew?" she called out to Marisa, who had vanished behind a Sheetrock partition.

"The other day at his office. Tell me what you think."

"I think you must have scared him."

"Yes. They're terrible, aren't they?"

Mercedes again felt left to her own devices. Waiting to rejoin Santiago was an activity she'd been forced to make interesting, and she walked now through Marisa's loft with an eye toward the entertaining detail.

"There's coffee," Marisa called.

Everything Mercedes had done lately she thought of as practice for something else. "Thanks."

The way Marisa had set up her studio made it seem that her photography was something as closely guarded as the secret of birth. Her living area resembled a waiting room more than a site of social pleasure, although Mercedes herself had recently passed a perfectly agreeable evening there with Andrew, Edith, James, and Marisa.

Spying a photographer's portfolio halfway under the sofa, Mercedes, in the spirit of international exchange, pulled it out and opened it.

The magazine tear sheet of Edith naked was on top of a series of Cibachrome prints that looked as if they had been commissioned by a travel magazine. After inspecting the tear sheet for a photo credit she put it back and slid the portfolio under the sofa again. She had long had an unpleasant gift for prognostication.

Never mind whether Arévalo had a hand in the way Edith's photo moved around like a marked bill, never mind why people's plans collided. Mercedes took a cigarette from her bag and sat down at the kitchen table.

"Now you've got me here you have to come out and make a good time," she called.

Marisa emerged from behind a partition, wiping her hands uncertainly on a dish towel.

"I want to hear about you and James. I must hear private things. Everything you don't want to tell me, you should."

Not used to being outdistanced, Marisa laughed. "Okay," she said, sitting down beside Mercedes as if compliance were a dangerous private joke they could both enjoy.

Which in a sense it was, since Mercedes now distrusted Marisa completely. The things that were political built themselves like crystals in the dark; the things that fed their growth, though, were flesh.

Mercedes sat back in perfect confidence.

Nakedness was the last secret.

"I DON'T CARE what the crew boss wants," Andrew said. "This call was booked days ago."

He and Leticia were on a conference line to a noplace dry goods store in the Brazilian jungle. Leticia repeated Andrew's words into the phone in Portuguese.

"Please, Mr. Caldwell. I have a visitor," said the American ambassador to Brazil, who had been patched into the call from his office in the capital. "I'm sure you will keep me apprised." He hung up.

Leticia rolled her eyes at Andrew.

"Okay, fuck him," Andrew said.

"What?" she said. "Remember I'm a student of the law."

"Figure of speech."

The air in Andrew's office was thick with luminously broken language, as if an important firework had misfired.

"Are we still connected to whatever the fuck it is?"

"The store doesn't have a name, but I'll pass along the suggestion."

"Hello?" said a voice over the speakerphone.

"Yes," said Andrew, picking up the extension.

"Brad Lowell here. Can you hear me?"

"Hi, I got your faxes. You understand your aunt is challenging the will."

"Yeah, that's the kind of thing she does." The phone line swallowed an emotion so adaptive that maybe no one had actually had it. "You have to realize it's a war zone down here," Lowell went on. "One of my research assistants had an accident yesterday involving a poison toad. It wasn't an accident. She wasn't the first."

"Okay, I've been in touch with the American ambassador about getting protection for you."

"Forget government channels. U.S., Brazilian, Mexican; it makes no difference. I need money to hire locals."

"Mexican?" said Andrew. "What do you mean Mexican?"

Leticia walked over to the window and gazed out at a blimp that appeared to be about to drape itself over a midsized office building thirty blocks downtown.

"*Locals*, not Mexicans. I said locals." Over the speakerphone, Lowell's voice took on the overly patient tones of a primatologist obliged to refresh his funding. "These are the last four hundred golden lion tamarins on the face of the earth. Magellan's logs describe them. The reserve here is twelve thousand acres, and the logging interests have bulldozers and chain saws and utility-sized flamethrowers on all sides. What I want to do is hire as many local people as I can so that the microeconomy here gets tied into preserving these monkeys. That way, when something does happen to me, the project goes ahead anyway."

Andrew found himself looking at a mind's-eye image of his son swinging from a crystal chandelier, an expression of grief and rebuke cast across his features like thin snow. Something happened to everyone.

"Mr. Lowell," Andrew said.

Leticia turned her back on the view. The blimp had collapsed without ceremony over the water tower atop the building next to the one it had almost made famous.

"Mr. Lowell. As far as setting up a foundation for the reserve, we've done the paperwork. And I understand your concerns. Now as you know, your aunt contends that your grandmother was not mentally competent when she made out her will. Is there anything you want to tell me about that?"

The phone warbled, and Leticia pounced on the sofa-side extension. Covering the mouthpiece with her hand, she said, "It's your ex on the other line."

"Get a number and I'll call her back."

"My grandmother," said Brad Lowell, "was completely sound. Funny and smart. Iconoclastic, obviously. She never told me about the will."

In the electronic middle distance of their phone call a conversation in Portuguese was taking place. Andrew made out the word *luminoso*. Leticia handed him a square of paper with Susannah's work number on it.

"Is there anyone who might give us a deposition?" he asked.

"Call her first husband. Call her housekeeper."

"Did you give her the chimpanzee?"

"There are no chimps in South America. A colleague of mine arranged for the transfer after his research project was done. Biolinguistics. The papers are totally in order."

On another square of paper Leticia wrote, "If he dies, who kills him?"

Looking at her in surprise, Andrew wondered, not for the first time, what kind of future she was planning for herself. Leticia lit a cigarette in acknowledgment of his appreciation.

"Yes," said Andrew into the phone. "I'm very optimistic that we will get your grandmother's will admitted to probate. But as an attorney I really have to ask you about these threats against your life. How serious are they, and who's making them?"

"I just told you they fed a poison toad to my research assistant. What counts up there for serious these days?"

"Who's they?"

"A few people in this country are making a fortune cutting down the jungle. Government people, logging concerns, highway contractors."

"You said something about Mexico earlier."

"The Mexicans are not the problem. Forget about them. If it weren't the Mexicans making the financial arrangements it would be someone else."

Acquaintances became friends, friends became mysteries, light fell unpredictably upon exposed surfaces, the nighttime was the right time to be with the one you loved.

"Maybe it would be good if we got you some press exposure," said Andrew.

"Counselor, you are out of touch. Exposure is the coin of the realm down here. What we need is hard currency. Will it happen?"

"As I said, I'm optimistic. Can we arrange to speak again next Friday, same time?"

"Better make it Thursday. Friday's payday for loggers, and things can get out of hand."

When Andrew hung up, Leticia put out her cigarette and hugged herself. "This man is scary. He's the kind of person who knows his fate and tells people about it."

"Maybe he's a harmless idealist."

"Same thing."

Andrew loosened his tie. "I keep hearing about Mexico in relation to Brazil. Why would that be?"

"I don't know what he meant," Leticia said, "But, to use his phrase, I'm out of touch."

"Leticia is never out of touch," he said. "She's haptic."

"Please. No English lessons." Leticia regarded her reflection in the glass of a framed photograph Andrew had bought from James. She adjusted her scarf. "You'll like this, though. This year inflation in Brazil is twenty-five hundred percent. And according to an article in *Isto É*, the frequency of sexual relations among Brazilians has dropped from three times a week to one-point-six." She smiled at him as she headed for the door. "It's because of the stress. Just imagine if you were a monkey."

Andrew sat by himself for a while in his office. This was the hour in which sunlight drenched the room and brought a chemically fresh smell out of the carpet.

There was a point in every case that Andrew handled when it was time to settle up. People had their programs, and in the face of inheritances or other prospective windfalls certain yearnings tended to emerge. It had long seemed to Andrew that he would have been a better lawyer had he not been so moved by people's willingness to reveal themselves. Professionally he acquitted himself perfectly well, but he could never quite contain his own curiosity.

He punched James's office number into the phone. "Hi, *compañero*, it's me."

"Andrew, what's happening?"

They talked a bit about someone they both knew, a photographer whose name had been in the papers that morning. He'd been caught smuggling hard currency into an Eastern European nation and had had a hand cut off for his trouble. Neither Andrew nor James could think of much to do for him.

"Listen, James," Andrew went on in a different tone, "Edie and I really appreciate you guys looking after us this last week. And your Marisa's a treat. Sometime soon you're going to have to tell me what she's really up to. But right now we need a few days off, okay?"

James mounted a feeble protest but didn't sound particularly surprised. "Maybe we can come by over the weekend and shoot a little film," he suggested.

"We'll see."

After he had hung up Andrew reflected that if there was a poison toad in your future you really had to watch whom you kissed. He sat there for a moment with his forehead pressed to his palm. Then, because he was settling up, he called Susannah.

"MY DADDY always lets me drink coffee when I take my bath."

"Is that so?" said Edith, giving Kevin a wink. She was leaning up against the sink, sipping a double espresso while he bathed. Neither Andrew nor Mercedes was home yet, and she'd let Dorotea leave early.

"Mommy says that when I'm four I don't have to take a nap. Do you take a nap?"

"Sometimes."

"If I take a nap now I'll drown."

"And you'll go down the drain and end up in the ocean. Then what would happen to you?"

"All the fish would kiss me."

"Kiss you?"

"Yes! On my skin!" He laughed wildly—a brilliant sound in the tiled room.

There was nothing to suggest to Edith that she knew enough to be custodian of this small boy who was holding his erect cock in both hands and sloshing water out of the tub. But she had helped raise her younger brothers, and, while her instincts were agony, she trusted them.

"Okay, Kevin. Out you get or you'll wrinkle up like a prune. Here's a towel."

She showed him how to mop up the sloshed water by skating across the floor on the bath mat.

In Kevin's room she helped him choose clean pajamas. Dorotea had told her he liked best the ones with a blue and red windowpane pattern, because they had a drawstring at the waist. It was true that he did. He showed Edith his monster trap, which was made out of shoe boxes and rubber bands. He still had an erection, but he didn't seem to notice it. He sat in his boy-sized rocking chair. The erection subsided.

"Is your mother dead?" he asked.

"You're not much on small talk, are you, young sir?"

"My mommy's still alive."

"That she is. Mine's dead."

"Did you burn her up when she was dead?"

Edith stared at him. In fact her mother had asked to be cremated, but Edith's father had insisted on burying her on the property, in a bower, near to him yet far. It was hardly the first time he'd disregarded her wishes. "No, Kevin. She has a grave on my father's farm in Virginia."

With this last bulletin, Kevin appeared to tire of the subject. "I'm too hot," he said, standing up and taking off his pajama bottoms. He sat back down again.

"You're your father's son," said Edith.

"I know. If you marry him does that mean you're my mother?"

"No, Susannah's your mother."

"I know." He got up and went into the kitchen. Edith made him a dinner of tortellini and marinara sauce. They talked about the behinds of different animals.

"Say 'so what.' "

"So what."

"So chicken butt."

Mercedes and Andrew arrived home together as Edith was washing the dishes. They'd run into each other downstairs in the lobby, and they carried with them the air of people inventing suitable remarks to avoid talking to each other about their days.

"Aha. I should have known you two were keeping company. There was a sudden pressure drop."

"Yes," said Mercedes, coming forward to kiss Edith once on either cheek. "He's been following me everywhere."

"Never mind. He's backward in these matters."

Andrew had set off with his son in search of pajama bottoms.

The evening was episodic, punctuated by incidents of mutual deference: nods, polite smiles, full attention given to small tasks. There was leftover Indian food, and Mercedes ate it. Andrew made veal scallopini for himself. Edith took a shower.

"I'm too old to go to bed," Kevin suggested as his father tucked him in.

"Let's sleep on that one, bucko. See you in the morning."

The call to Susannah had unsettled Andrew in all the wrong ways. He'd prepared himself for a tight-lipped colloquy whose themes were rage, the best interests of the child, buried grudges that had now unearthed themselves in the form of self-help entitlements. It was not exactly so. Susannah had been summoned by a client to Seattle for the weekend. She would not be able to take Kevin that Sunday, as was the custom, and she wanted to arrange to make up the time the following weekend. Her voice, an anthology of grievance and seduction, had touched him more than any argument she might have mounted.

"Andrew?"

It was Edith calling him now. It was she standing framed in the far doorway of the living room, wrapped in a lilac towel. "Andrew, aren't we expecting Marisa and James at eight?"

"No, I canceled."

She gave him a startled look that an instant later became a lopsided smile of approval. "Well," she said, turning back toward the bathroom to dry her hair, "good for you."

When, over the phone, it had become clear to Andrew that Susannah was not going to mention her bid to reclaim custody of Kevin, he had brought it up himself. The conversation had then deteriorated rapidly, though within the limits of their respective self-interests. Andrew had wanted to know how she had found out about the incident in the park, but he could see no useful way to speak about it. Susannah had wanted her lawyer to be the bad news. In the absence of other options they had split the difference.

Mercedes was sitting in the living room with a Spanish-language newsweekly open in her lap. On the coffee table was a tray that held a pot of tea, a cup and saucer, a jar of honey, a spoon.

"*Digame, estimado Señor Caldwell*," she said, tucking her bare feet beneath herself on the sofa. "It is true you told James and Marisa not to come tonight?"

From the bathroom, the banshee whine of the hair dryer. Andrew sank into the armchair opposite Mercedes.

"We've all got a lot on our minds. It was getting distracting."

"Yes, I agree. Do you know where I spent my afternoon?"

"Hit me."

"At Marisa's studio. I was curious, you know? I was beginning to like her; I do like her. But she moves by her own compass. When I watch her I see her mind working: it is like an ivory globe spinning, spinning, spinning. Very fast, very quiet."

"You have my full attention."

Mercedes looked closely at him, as if checking just how much attention he was capable of. Something fleshly passed between them then, a sudden opening up of their gaze so that it became like a vase that they were filling together, each daring the other to keep pouring, both of them aware that it must not brim over.

She tilted her head a little, and there was a crimp in her mouth, not a smile but nearly so.

Andrew inhaled sharply, a half-spasm. He understood that Mercedes was offering to take him through a place that he'd been wandering toward anyway. And though the nonverbal syntax was that of a come-on, he understood as well that he was expected to extrapolate.

"I think," said Mercedes, "that Marisa is not our friend."

"That's what Edith said the first night, the night they brought over the mask. Or maybe she didn't say it, she implied it."

"You're not telling me everything."

"Because you're not telling me anything."

Mercedes smiled. "I'm sorry. I have to be difficult first."

In the building across the street a woman skipped rope in pro-file before the window, in the street a car alarm spoke to the night.

"When Edith posed nude for that picture . . ."

"Excuse me?"

"The one our friend Arévalo showed to me after you and Edith caught his attention at Santiago's banquet dinner."

"What, he had a tie-clip camera or something? Not that any-one wears tie clips anymore."

"You don't know what I'm talking about, do you?"

"Yes, I do."

They both knew he didn't.

"Anyway, Marisa has a copy of this picture. I found it—accidentally, I think. I didn't let Marisa know. But it's strange to think that someone like her has the patience to do background research."

"Background to what?"

"I don't know."

"Let me get this straight. There's a photograph of Edie naked, and Arévalo showed it to you, and Marisa has a copy of it too."

"It was in a magazine. A few years ago I think."

"What magazine?"

"The magazine doesn't matter."

"Something here does. What is it?"

Mercedes frowned. It was a look more porous than her smile. The things it invited were costly, deep, multiple. "Are you a jeal-ous man, Mr. Caldwell?"

"I thought all us X-Y types were."

"In my experience, yes."

"So go on. What about this picture?"

"A woman takes her clothes off for a camera, or she decides she doesn't see the point of underwear, or she is inventive in pub-lic places with the man she loves. These are things that matter.

They are easy to make fun of. It is always a little comic when the private and the public switch places."

"Are we beginning to talk politics?"

"I'm worried about Oliver Barnes."

"Barnes? Don't tell me he collects dirty pictures too."

She looked at him with what might have been a grain of appreciation, then poured herself another cup of tea. "When I met Edith, she said to me that maybe Santiago identified with you. I think now she was right."

"Thanks. I don't remember her saying that, though."

The hair dryer had stopped, the bathroom door bumped audibly open against the towel rack, Edith's footsteps sounded down the hall to the bedroom.

When the bedroom door slammed shut, Mercedes said, "I think really you are not a jealous man after all."

"Probably I'm just selective."

The phone in the study rang, Andrew went to answer it. It was Santiago, calling for Mercedes. Andrew summoned her and left her alone at his desk.

When he entered the bedroom, Edith did not look up. She was sitting naked atop the thigh-high cherry-wood file cabinets that ran just below the windowsills on the street side of the room. She'd caught a sliver in her heel and was picking at it with a needle in a way that illustrated a whole range of dogged inquiry.

"Now see?" she said. "Here I am all naked and disobliged."

The halogen reading lamp was trained on her foot, and she was using the unshaded window glass as a kind of mirror. For anyone with an across-the-street point of view she was a community event.

"But you have an audience," he said.

"I think I do, yeah. Isn't that something? A girl my age."

"Interesting," he observed to the wall beside him. "Compliments cling to her, clothes don't."

Edith furrowed her brow and addressed herself with renewed

vigor to her tiny wound. She still had not met Andrew's gaze.

"Hey, Mr. Caldwell. Why don't you come here and join me in the late-night wrap-up."

His tie was undone, and he took it off. He removed his shirt and pants, and when she looked up he abandoned his underwear as well.

"You think we're playing tag," he said.

"No, but all the same." Edith had heard from her doctor that afternoon. Her pregnancy was confirmed and conception dated at between five and six weeks previously. She didn't want to speak about it.

Stepping forward, Andrew kissed her on the corners of her mouth, down the side of her throat, across one nipple and then her thighs.

When Edith found herself on her feet, standing atop the file cabinets, fully naked in the window, she thought at first that what she wanted to do was to pace. She wanted to go somewhere, but distance was a hard job. So she stopped and reached a hand down to Andrew.

He joined her in the illuminated space framed by the window.

"Show time," she said shyly.

"Yes," he answered. "It's strange, isn't it?"

Lacing his fingers together, he cupped her buttocks and, still standing upright, lifted her to him.

For a time they fucked like that, slowly, almost without movement, he standing upright, holding her in the basket of his hands, she with her legs up on either side of him, knees nearly to his armpits. The tops of the four file cabinets together formed a narrow walkway before the window. Finding he was able to negotiate this path with Edith still in his arms, Andrew walked the surface, then turned around and walked it back.

She bit hard into his shoulder. When she looked back up at him her gray-blue eyes seemed the size of butter plates.

"Kisses," she whispered. "On your skin."

He lowered her, letting her feet again support her weight. As his cock slipped out of her, she continued her improvisation with gravity until she was kneeling in front of him. She took his cock into her mouth.

The windows in the building across the street were points of light in Andrew's leftward glance, markers multiplying now with the simple avidity of habitual things. His fingers sifted lightly through Edith's hair. *Counting souls*, he thought, though he couldn't think where the thought had come from.

When he stepped back from her, lay down, and drew her on top of him, a transparent thread of first sperm was flung by her head's drowsy toss from her lower lip to the windowpane.

Witnesses weren't hard to come by, it occurred to him, but you had to have enough of them.

Edith said his name and then said something unforgettable to him and then said his name.

It was he who came first and she, the truthful witness, who followed.

Afterwards, when they turned off the lights, they could see their audience milling before the windows across the street: a few lone figures silhouetted here and there, two couples, an apparently disrupted dinner party of people wearing black.

"Scared?" Andrew asked.

"Not yet," she answered.

It was the kind of exchange that exerted its intimacy retrospectively, giving ease to lately unspoken things. Still in the dark and without speaking further, Edith and Andrew dressed. While he was rolling up his shirtsleeves, she kissed the back of his head in passing, and for that moment they might have known and loved each other since they were children.

They wandered into the living room. Indirect lighting made the ceiling radiant, tiger lilies on the mantel advertised a different time frame.

Edith had brought home from work the galley proofs of a translation she'd done for the UN, and, sitting at one end of the sofa, she began to pick at them with a red-leaded pencil. It was like picking out a tune on a piano left out on the sidewalk, if the sidewalk were a place you could designate as a personal zone. At his end of the zone Andrew was clipping newspapers and experiencing difficulty. The thought of the photograph Mercedes had mentioned nagged at him.

"I was thinking we might want to change our phone number. In recognition of we're starting a new life and so on."

"Sure," she said. "I'm for that."

"Our sense of privacy may be a little funny," he went on, "but we've got to have room to maneuver, just like anybody else."

Edith attempted a smile but ended up sneezing instead.

Later it would seem to both of them that somehow they had anticipated what happened next, that they had courted it and arranged the circumstances of their lives to receive it. That it was inevitable.

Mercedes, when she got off the phone at last, came into the living room where they were sitting, hesitated, then took the brandy decanter and three glasses from a side table and joined them on the sofa.

"*Con permiso?* I don't usually, but tonight I think I would like to have a drink." She poured one for each of them.

"How are things with our Santiago?" Andrew asked.

As Mercedes raised her glass, Edith, who had stopped drinking, surprised herself by raising hers too.

"My husband would like you to see for yourselves," said Mercedes. "I am returning to Mexico City Monday night, and it would please us very much if you would accept our invitation to stay a few days in our home."

Andrew and Edith knew right away: they would discuss it through the weekend, tell each other why it was impossible, impose reciprocal conditions—only if we bring Kevin, only if we don't tell Marisa or James. They would make the whole plan into an enemy that finally they could only reconcile with.

Monday morning they got gamma-globulin injections and took Kevin to his pediatrician. Edith had a friend at work who owed her a favor. Leticia, her heart on her sleeve and her sleeve on her smirk, updated the work directories on Andrew's notebook computer.

That afternoon four plane tickets arrived at the apartment by courier. Andrew, Edith, Mercedes, Kevin.

By sunset they were gone.

ON THE WIDE quiet streets of Lomas de Chapultepec, in the westernmost part of Mexico City, the Díazes' house lay like its neighbors discreetly sprawled behind ivy-topped walls the height of two men. Windows faced in toward the central courtyard, a blue-eyed cat patrolled the roof. Wind chimes were silent, hallways were dark, men and women whose names Santiago did not know stared into the screens of laptops and drank coffee from Styrofoam cups.

Since returning to Mexico City, Santiago had given over the north end of the house to his campaign staff. At all hours there were people speaking quietly in caffeinated cadences, holding meetings, arranging demonstrations, canvassing by phone and fax. The wood and bull-hide furniture was given new point by all this activity. The shelves of soccer trophies and the game-action photos that were clustered on the walls recommended perseverance. Everybody smoked.

Santiago was wakened just before dawn by the first of several explosions, a deep thunderous sound from the center of the city, a dozen kilometers to the east. While he shaved and dressed for his morning run he counted seven more blasts, spaced about two minutes apart.

"The minister of methane must have resigned," Santiago said as he tossed his car keys to the slender young man who had been covering the phones. "What's our position on spontaneously detonating sewers?"

Without waiting for a reply, Santiago hurried through the door.

He was able to get halfway through his run before his bodyguard caught up with him, wielding the Volvo sedan as if it were an instrument of medieval battle, prolonged and pastoral. At the intersection that marked the three-kilometer point of his course, a TV crew from an international cable network had set up an ambush interview. Santiago cut to the right. The Volvo went straight for the cameraman. Nobody was hurt.

In the week that he'd been back in the Distrito Federal, Santiago had been obliged to stop answering the phone at home. Inventive threats had become a sport. The voices were always different. Castration for him, rape for Mercedes, shattered kneecaps for his associates and former teammates. He thought it interesting that most of the callers made a point of identifying themselves with Arévalo's campaign. The ruling party's anointed candidate, a genial antique named Gutiérrez, had a clumsy grasp of field tactics.

While Carlos briefed him on the day's schedule, Santiago wrapped an elastic bandage around one knee.

"So lunch will be at Bellas Artes," Carlos was saying. "Televisión Azteca is sponsoring, and we expect a full complement of our free-market friends."

"My wife is flying in today. What time?"

"Yes. We have wanted to talk to you about this."

Santiago assumed a mien more sportive than he felt, strictly speaking. He flexed his bandaged knee. "Where is the difficulty?"

"No difficulty. We are unsure how to arrange for your friends, Señor and Señora Caldwell."

"Edith Emerson, Andrew Caldwell. They are not married."

"Exactly."

Suddenly irritated by his aide's gingerly manner, Santiago walked over to the refrigerator, selected a bottle of vegetable juice, and drank deeply from it. Despite everything, he missed Arévalo.

"These are very good friends of ours, and Mercedes and I would like to return their hospitality. They will stay in the bedroom next to ours. Another bed can be put in for their son."

"*Claro que sí.*" Carlos appeared embarrassed. "It was the security arrangements that I was concerned about."

There were two armed guards in the house at all times and half a dozen more patrolling its peripheries. A private protection agency, owned by Israelis, had been hired to coordinate Santiago's movements and public appearances. Although he conceded the prudence of these measures, Santiago found them increasingly suffocating.

"There is no reason my friends can't come and go as they wish," he said, tossing the empty juice bottle into the garbage as he left the room.

The week had been a difficult one for everybody. While there had been no further defections from his staff, Santiago had not been long in realizing that Vendajes must have provided Arévalo with a duplicate of the campaign's computer database. The engineers, physicians, economists, and entrepreneurs who from the first had been consultants to the Díaz camp were now the subject of daily press releases from Arévalo's headquarters. The word *perfumado* was being used in regard to them, the word *egoísta*.

In the southern states, the campesinos had killed eight of Santiago's local organizers and half again as many Gutiérristas. When the army came in by helicopter to chase down the insurgents they could find no one to arrest but a few teenage boys, barefoot and armed with antiquated carbines. Meanwhile, the leader of the real agrarian uprising appeared on Cable Network News, an orange-and-black bandanna tied below his eyes. He declared his movement's provisional solidarity with Arévalo. Of course, this was both bad and good from Santiago's point of view, not to mention the government's. Short on options, the army had arrested the news team. This was stupid from anyone's point of view.

Strolling to the open door of his bedroom, running a belt through the loops at his trousers' waistband, Santiago stared out into the heart of his home. In places he couldn't see, people were working or napping on his behalf, on Mexico's behalf. It made him feel combative.

"*El candidato* has canceled all his appointments for today," he shouted into the tiled and planted space of his courtyard. "In consideration of his testicles."

After that it was a day in which he was never alone. On the esplanade of the Insurgentes metro stop, he spoke of education to a crowd of morning commuters. At the Mercado de Merced, among bins of chiles, pigweed, onions, *zapotes*, and tiny dried fish, he greeted, singly and in small groups, the women and elderly men who had come to buy their groceries. The small bodily traits of the people he spoke to exhilarated Santiago: a freckled hand, a permanently raised eyebrow. In one of the long, ambiguously outside-inside corridors of the market he watched three plump young women, temporarily freed from minding their vegetable stands, reduce themselves to helpless giggles while chasing after each other and pulling one another's aprons.

His security agents pressed their earphones closer to their tympanums, spoke into their sleeves.

Lunch was at Bellas Artes.

In the afternoon, at the university, Santiago's address on economic development got a mixed reception from the students. A sizable contingent, gathered beneath a banner that juxtaposed Arévalo's likeness with Zapata's, hurled tomatoes and tried to get a bad-blood soccer cheer going. "*Cu-lo, cu-lo,*" went the chant; "*Lo-co, lo-co,*" was the response.

"Señor Díaz," said a man Santiago did not remember hiring. "Please, will you come with us?"

Four men in sunglasses hustled him into a car. Carlos, running close behind, shouted after Santiago, "They are not ours!" But Santiago was already in the car. Carlos dived in after him. The car, a black Chevrolet, left rubber on the cobbles of the street.

"To whom do we owe the pleasure?" asked Santiago after he'd had a look at the state-of-the-art assault pistols strapped handily across the chests of his abductors.

The driver was speaking into a cellular telephone.

Carlos was reviewing emergency procedure.

"The eagle is with us," the driver told the telephone. "We are returning to the nest."

"I am Juan Oiticica," said the man sitting to Santiago's left. He took off his sunglasses and offered his hand. "My partners and I do not feel your security has been adequate, and we respectfully offer you our services."

Carlos heaved a huge sigh and gave Santiago the nod. He had been waiting to hear from this man.

Santiago shook the hand of Juan Oiticica. "Do you know the American football term 'sudden death'?" he asked.

The car raced off toward the Díaz home while the passengers discussed a few famous moments in the history of soccer.

His irritability, his physical restlessness, his newly mordant pleasure in risk and disruption: Santiago knew he was playing too far upfield. Even as a forward on an aggressive team he was. Whatever he meant now by "team."

When Mercedes had suggested that she bring Edith and Andrew down to the capital with her, Santiago had experienced a flash of pride in his wife. She knew better than he how to rush ahead, how to bring distracting business to its ripeness. He understood that this talent of hers was not easily appreciated by, for example, his political advisers, his sisters, or the Spanish-language sports press. But as a public property, which is how he'd lately begun thinking of himself again, he ignored the niceties of individual taste. Running for office was like soccer in that he couldn't exercise his gift if he was obliged to know how he did it.

Mercedes had once told him that nothing was worthier of protection than a gift casually possessed. She'd been explaining her theory of marriage.

AT CUSTOMS travelers were required to press a button on a small stoplight device, which then flashed red or green. Edith got red, and the official, a *medio-moreno* of grim dignity, laid open her suitcase for inspection. When she was slow to hand over her purse, he took it from her patiently and upended it over the counter.

"I could have done that for you," Edith informed him. People were always wanting into her purse.

"*Bienvenidos a México,*" he intoned when he finally waved her through.

Andrew, Kevin, and Mercedes had all drawn the green light.

The arrivals hall was packed with people craning their necks to catch sight of the passengers they had come to meet. Women on the shoulders of their boyfriends held up signs, businessmen loosened their ties and barked into cellular phones. Every fifty meters or so an officer of the *policía* was stationed, his automatic rifle slung across his back.

"Santiago is speaking at a dinner at the Museo de Antropología," Mercedes explained to Edith and Andrew, raising her voice over the din. "The driver will take us home, then if there's still time we can join him."

She was now closely attended by two men in bulky windbreakers. A third was loading their luggage onto a handcart. Andrew gathered Kevin up in his arms.

"How're you holding up, *hombre?*" Edith asked the boy.

He regarded her with an incomprehension verging on outrage. "This is very gigantic," he told her. Minutes later he was asleep.

At the house the guard standing hard by the carport saluted when Mercedes emerged from the limo. "Please don't do that," she asked him in Spanish. From somewhere inside they could hear a radio softly playing music that seemed to have wandered down from across the border thirty years ago and gotten stuck. It urged San Francisco–bound travelers to wear flowers in their hair.

"Are you glad we came?" Edith asked Andrew when they were settled in their room. They had put Kevin under the temporary care of Rosária, the Zapotecan housemaid.

"We did it. Let's make the most of it."

This was the tip of the argument that they had decided not to have. They had talked each other into this trip, they had guided each other through the logistics of departure, smoothing the way as if it were something they had planned from the first, the logical outcome of their affair. But they both knew that the truth was otherwise.

Surveying herself in the mirror, Edith said, "I feel kind of blond."

"I bet you do." He laughed a little. "*La Dorada* Descends into the Covetous City."

The room was done in functionalist pueblo style, with hot pink plaster walls and an unembellished concrete stair that ran to the roof. From one wall a garden faucet protruded.

Edith poured herself a glass of *agua mineral*.

"You know, I wasn't really sure I could handle you when we started this. I'm used to doing things my own way."

"No shit. Scare me to death."

She looked at him as if he presented a problem in translation, an idiom she couldn't render. "What are you used to?"

Andrew had said nothing to her about his conversation with Mercedes regarding photography. "I tend to go on the evidence."

"Well, then we're okay, aren't we? That's the point of me lately. I am evidence." She was wearing a double-skirted slip dress and she held an off-the-shoulder jersey top pressed against her chest. "What do you think? With or without?"

When he didn't answer she came over close to him. "Andrew, we needed this. I needed it and now you do too." She leaned down and kissed him across the mouth, a slow, wet wipe like a brushstroke.

It was dawning on Andrew that while they had a lot to talk about, he and Edith, they were going to have to earn their conversation. Show and tell was what they knew. They had to have both, but that had to be the order.

He put on a fresh shirt.

"You know, you probably could lose the jersey. We've got friends in high places."

"Better not," she said, putting it on and walking to the door.

In the living room, a double-story space of egg-yolk yellow, Mercedes was pacing up and down before a group of young men, staffers, who were settled casually in the cypress-wood chairs and settee. One of them had a computer open on his lap, and he was working the keyboard in a way that suggested some kind of competitive gardening.

"*Buenas tardes,*" offered Andrew companionably.

During the fractional silence that ensued, Edith saw the man with the laptop do a stylized double take and say to his colleagues, in a voice perfectly audible to her, "*Coño. Aquí está la Conspicua.*"

She had no choice but to assume she was the conspicuous one referred to. The guy who'd said it, it seemed to her, had been seated on the stage behind Santiago at his banquet.

"Mr. Caldwell and Miss Emerson are friends of ours," Mercedes was telling them. "Anything you would say in front of me or my husband you can say in front of them."

THE CENTRAL patio at the Museo de Antropología was a dramatic affair, partly sheltered by a huge concrete canopy supported by a single column. From around the top of the column a curtain of water rained down upon the granite flagstones to a concealed drain.

"I don't see him," said Andrew, as the three of them made their way into the gathering.

"But hey, it's all *caballeros* here." Edith scanned the company with a delinquent glance. "What is it, they don't let the women out after dark?"

Tables had been set up and lavishly turned out with linens, china, and silver, but dinner was over, Santiago had already spoken, and the dishes were being cleared. It was true that the guests were mostly men, professionals who had staked their futures on a new Mexico and now wanted to see if there was such a place. They poured one another brandy. They conferred in exploratory tones.

When Mercedes caught up with Santiago, he was standing just inside the entrance to the Aztec galleries. He was locked in close conversation with a man maybe ten years his senior and he was refusing a newspaper that was being offered him by an aide.

Edith thought she saw Mercedes throw a cool little look her way before stepping into Santiago's line of sight.

"Ah, there you are, *vida mía*. Excuse me, Emilio. I believe you know my wife?" Santiago kissed her attentively. "And our friends Edith Emerson and Andrew Caldwell."

"*Encantado.*" In fact the man did not look much enchanted. "Señor Díaz. We will speak about this matter tomorrow?"

"Certainly."

When the man left, Mercedes threw her arms around her husband and put her lips to his ear. A kiss and a whisper.

"Of course," he replied. "Can you doubt it?"

"And you see," said Mercedes, drawing back and inviting him to share her satisfaction. "I told you I'd persuade them."

There were a couple of silent seconds while she and Santiago appraised their guests. "The two of you could be a picture," Santiago said at last. Stepping toward Edith, he bowed, took her hand, and, without quite touching it to his lips, kissed it. She blushed.

"What kind of picture?" Andrew inquired.

"I'm sorry we missed your speech," Edith said, ignoring him.

"But you've heard it before," said Santiago. "Then again, repetition is the soul of politics."

He exchanged a light *abrazo* with Andrew. The greeting held a considerable intimacy, complicity even, and Andrew reflected that when in contact with cultures other than his own he frequently fell back on a more feral self. Out of impatience, he supposed, and because he could. "Santiago, it's a real pleasure."

More of the guests were drifting into the gallery from the patio, continuing their conversations, casting curious glances at Edith and Andrew.

"What was on Emilio's mind?" Mercedes asked casually. But the high, tight smile with which she fended off an approaching supporter was not at all casual.

"He's unhappy that I didn't stop at the border on my way home. You remember, Luis arranged for it. I agree that we've got to make the border issue our own. But it will keep. And, from the present point of view, Luis can go fuck himself."

They walked together, Santiago and Andrew, Edith and Mercedes, skirting the gathering on the central patio. They moved through dimly lit galleries where stone figures, golden insect ornaments, and a massive calendar wheel, centuries old, counseled larger judgments.

"I've been reading about your friend Arévalo."

"Yes, yes. He is Zapata now." Santiago shook his head vexedly. "Who could have predicted?"

"But are your positions so different?"

"We are each other's consciences. He is the goalie, I am the forward. When we were boys, my father instructed us to be always on the same team. It was good advice."

In the illuminated display cases, fist-sized effigies looked on with chthonic pettishness. Jaguars, cicadas, hummingbirds, snakes: the interestingly defective Aztec gods.

"I've been meaning to ask you, Santiago."

"Good, good." He put his arm around Andrew's shoulders and steered him around an exhibit of earthenware shards.

"When Arévalo was working for you he handled security, am I right?"

"Among other things, yes."

"Well, see, this is awkward. What I'm wondering is whether, in the course of things, he might have run a check on me and Edith, maybe put us under surveillance."

Santiago was silent. The last of the dinner guests were filtering into the gallery, waiting for an opportunity to buttonhole him.

"I mean why shouldn't he have taken an interest in us, when you think about it. We invited it. But I'd like to know anyway."

Edith and Mercedes were following several paces behind, the click of their high heels strangely eloquent amid the relics and eager voices.

"He went through her purse in my presence. Afterwards, I am told, he made further inquiries." Santiago loosened his tie and shrugged. "Sometimes I think Luis really is the soul of Mexico. He feels a spiritual obligation to be suspicious."

"Is that good?"

"Maybe so. Why not?"

Up ahead, a woman in a red satin dress was talking very rapidly to a semicircle of politely poised men. Her hands flew about before her in excited semaphore. On the thumb and first two fingers of her left hand she wore several silver rings.

"That's my youngest sister, Felicia. When we were kids I pimped her to Luis." Felicia returned his wave without interrupting her monologue, and Santiago sighed. "Why are you worrying about him?"

"Your wife told me that he's flashing around a rocks-off photo of Edie. From her party days."

"I don't understand."

"She posed for a center shot in a men's magazine."

"This is the first I've heard of it."

"Apparently Oliver Barnes has a copy too."

"What does Edith say?"

"Nothing. She's winging it."

Santiago considered this, and as he did Andrew began to feel he had failed to communicate his current approach to things.

"I'm afraid I must apologize for Luis," Santiago began.

"Hey, no need. Really. I just wanted to let you know."

They had stopped before a pedestal that held an intricately carved figurine in pale blue chalcedony. The creature it represented, its teeth bared in a rictus of permanent appetite, appeared half asleep. Andrew identified with it.

"Edith had a really bad time up by the border once, and Barnes was with her."

"I see. Did it have to do with conspicuous consumption?"

"She saw a kid get shot on the fence. Barnes wouldn't let her help out because he and Edie were having a hot-pants late-night thing at the time and he was afraid of the publicity. It put a lot of mileage on everybody."

Interposing himself between the two men, a tall *blanco* with the brisk and cultivated air of an *internacionalista* inclined his head toward Santiago. "Díaz. A few words."

"Not now. I'll find you later." He grimaced at Andrew in apology. "The only time I'm alone anymore is when I shit."

Mercedes had been intercepted by some friends, and Andrew watched as she introduced Edith around. A sudden vertigo assailed him. Simple fatigue was part of it, and the effort involved in reshaping his life to accommodate Edith. But he felt also the trill of impending calamity. Presently he would be offered the opportunity to set things right for himself.

"Santiago, let me ask you this. If you knew, in your heart of hearts, that you weren't going to be elected, would you run anyway?"

"Say that again?"

"I'm sorry. It was a stupid thought."

"Edith has nothing to worry about from Luis. Please tell her I said so."

Andrew swallowed. He thought he might have difficulty finding his voice.

"You're being set up."

"I am? How do you know?"

"It's just . . . a feeling." The words sounded weak and sickly in his own ears. "I'm probably wrong."

"Maybe not. But the point is, it doesn't matter if I'm being set up or not. We've got an agenda, and we want to pursue it."

Andrew hastened to agree. "Right," he said. "Oh yeah, absolutely."

From across the room Edith's voice came wafting over, her lush Virginia vowels somehow exaggerated by the floors or the context. She seemed to be speculating on the reciprocal pieties of the Aztecs and Spaniards. The one had bet everything on death, she said, the other on destiny.

Santiago smiled darkly at Andrew and excused himself.

LATE the next morning, in the pleasantly upscale neighborhood of Polanco, Marisa and James sat watching Jovãozinha de Borba run an electric razor over his cheeks. He had arrived at his office directly from last night's assignation to find the two of them waiting there beside their luggage, aspiration in their eyes.

"The next time you might give me a little notice."

Ignoring her brother, Marisa opened her cassette player and flipped the tape over. "Jovãozinha is without *question* the most notorious playboy in Mexico City," she told James, punching the play button.

James yawned. "Climb every mountain," he said agreeably.

The night before, curious at Andrew's failure to answer his home phone, James had let himself into his friend's apartment with the key he'd been given for emergencies. There he had startled Dorotea and her boyfriend, who were watching a budget western in the dark. After tears and repeated reassurances she had been quick to inform James of her employer's whereabouts. Marisa had booked tickets for the 7:00 a.m. flight.

"Last night at dinner I met a man who said to me, 'Information wants to be free.' "Jovãozinha shut off the razor and giggled. "This is such a beautiful idea, don't you think?"

Marisa smiled from between the headphones. "I sense a hustle struggling to be born."

"No, no. I am completely sincere. 'Information wants to be free.' It is so true it is almost erotic."

Jovãozinha de Borba was a tall, lithe, tobacco-colored man with a startlingly full mouth. His hairline was receding, and his heightened brow, together with the tinted aviator glasses he wore, gave him the look of a debauched eaglet. In the upper rim of one ear he sported two tiny earrings.

"What do you suppose he meant?" James inquired.

"We were talking about the writings of Thomas Jefferson," replied Jovãozinha, "and honestly I don't know what he meant." He took a bottle of sparkling lemonade from the refrigerator beside his desk and, when he had poured them each a glass, sat down in a leather club chair opposite his guests. "It could have been anything from software to slavery."

"How's our father?" Marisa asked.

"Gilberto is in love. Sending forests to the blade does remarkable things for his libido. A tree goes down, his dick goes up." Jovãozinha winked playfully at James. "Seriously, he's the original fucker."

"I thought you were."

"Do I know the girl?" Marisa wanted to know.

"French. A lapsed anthropologist, I think."

"Eek."

Jovãozinha shrugged. "He's a visionary, and women find that compelling. It doesn't concern us."

The newspapers had said nothing about the squabble between the Mexican and Brazilian delegations at the UN a week ago, but James had not been able to put it out of his mind. His own part in Marisa's father's profit-skimming scheme was negligible, a bookkeeping courtesy to one of his artists, as he saw it. But people were emotional about the rain forest. Andrew and Edith had made no secret of their curiosity the night he had come over with their engagement present.

"You don't think we should chill until after the elections?" James asked.

"Why? The elections are a month away. Anyway, we're minding our own business. The money comes to me by diplomatic pouch, I send it to you, your gallery makes an unexpected sale. Are you telling me somebody cares?"

Marisa poured herself more lemonade. "Poor Jojo. Don't be sad; of course someone cares."

"All right, all right," said James. "Forget I mentioned it."

The treble register of Marisa's tape was nattering out into the room from her headphones. She closed her eyes and began moving in some half-acquainted relation to the music.

"Don't let her fool you," Jovãozinha advised James. "She can't hear a word we're saying."

After dropping their bags off at Jovãozinha's town house, Marisa and James strolled through la Zona Rosa, where the *vanidad*-for-lunch bunch lingered over coffee and every other corner was occupied by a rebozo-wrapped grandmother selling gum.

James tried to imagine what they might be walking into by following Mercedes, Andrew, and Edith down to Mexico, but in the end, he knew, such speculations were irrelevant. The urgency of their pursuit was bogus, but it required believing in.

Sometimes James suspected that the true wonder of the world had moved forever beyond his reach. Others had implied as much. He was, as gallery owner and sometimes seducer, an impresario of longings, the more inchoate the better. This was no doubt as he had invited it, and regret was beside the point. Still he was not immune to sentiment. The very readiness with which he saw through the dumb-fuck errantries of others, people who ought to know better, lent their recklessness a force it might not otherwise have had. Maybe, he thought, they were on to something.

At Reforma they caught a *micro* for the city's central district.

———

"ARE WE really going to see witches?" asked Kevin.

"These aren't witches like at Halloween," Edith explained. "They're more like doctors."

"But no vaccinations," Andrew added quickly. "These are friendlies."

They were headed across the concrete plaza to the Mercado Sonora, where the paraphernalia of ordinary sorcery was for sale in bins and cages.

"Daddy, can I ride on your shoulders?"

Earlier, Kevin had walked in on Edith being sick in the Díazes' bathroom. She had felt sharply guilty, as if it were he whom she'd been deceiving by her secretiveness. The child she was carrying seemed addressed by Kevin's presence, and she was encouraged to think that a whole range of ambient misunderstanding might soon be cleared up.

Passing under a sign that read "*Herbolaria,*" they were at once swept up in a stream of women, the matter-of-fact consumers of remedy. Candles in the shape of faithless loved ones, aerosol sprays promising *paz en el hogar,* amulets, bobbins of colored threads and hair, soaps, powders, dried lizard carcasses, roots: the very banality of these things endowed them with a poignancy that made their magical properties moot.

"I feel suffused with sorority," said Edith. "Sisterhood is powerful."

"You won't get any argument from me."

"Do your sisters live in Mexico?" Kevin wanted to know.

"No, I don't really have any sisters, Kevin. I was just teasing your father. But I do have three brothers."

"That's good. Are they still alive?"

In the course of a slippery second, she was able to see just how carefully he was appraising her. It wasn't suspicion that animated this inventory, but something more nakedly adaptive. He was trying to gauge what kind of loyalties he might be called upon to manufacture.

"Well, sure they're alive," she said. "Why wouldn't they be?"

The path between the stalls was very narrow, its center worn down to a shallow trench. They wound their way through the labyrinth. A little girl sorted through a tray of dried chicken feet, a woman held a goose egg up and pointed to Edith's stomach. Cats lurked, cages held back flourishing weeds, beads were strung, smokes contended, pinches of white powder flung into the air made the way safe.

At a turning in the passway a woman asked Edith in Spanish if she wanted to be told the sex of her child.

"But anyone can see he's a boy," she answered, glancing nervously after Andrew and Kevin as they forged on without her.

The woman shook her head to indicate she didn't mean that, then handed her a packet marked *"Legítimo Polvo de las Dos Marías."*

"Which two Marias?"

"La Virgen y La Magdalena."

Edith pressed ten pesos into the woman's hand.

"I think this is the market with the live animals," Andrew said when Edith caught up with them. "Do you want to see?"

"I insist on it."

She put an arm around Andrew's waist, and simultaneously Kevin reached down and grabbed a handful of her hair.

The animal market looked as if it had been going on forever, like a night thing that couldn't be bothered anymore to explain itself in daylight. Some of the creatures for sale were connected, in Edith's mind, with the blood faiths of witchcraft—chickens, turkeys, lizards, snakes. But as the rows of stalls stretched on, anything resembling purpose fell away.

"Maybe this isn't such a good idea, Andrew."

"It'll be okay. Anyway, the same thing goes on in the States; you just don't see it."

Goats bleated in pens too small for them, badgers slept, rheumy puppies crawled shakily over one another, cats hissed and fought while men in soiled straw cowboy hats watched the passing throng for customers. The smell was very strong, and Edith, though not by nature squeamish, was repelled.

"I guess the animal rights people triaged this place."

"Shit, the *human* rights people triaged it," Andrew said. "But I don't need to tell you that."

Work seemed very far away. She had almost forgotten about it.

"Edie, look! Baby goats! Do they have names?"

"Sure. That one there is Pablito. And the one next to him is Julio. And in the back you've got Paquito, Olga, Ramón, Chalo, Josefina." A broth of feeling swept over Edith as she christened these incidental lives, so little buffered against the world's scatterings. Startled, she found herself in the middle of a childhood memory: she was being led by her father across thin snow to the stables, where a roan foal was halfway born.

"I want to pet them," Kevin announced. "I want to see their *behinds.*"

"They're too little, sweetheart."

"Are you all right, Edie? You look pale."

"I'm fine."

"Daddy! I want to pet the baby goats."

"Hey look, Kev! There's a little lamb over there. See? On the boy's shoulders."

The shock came up through the dirt floor of the market and into their bones. Edith's slo-mo scan intersected Andrew's as they sought the source of the blast, a sharp blurt of sound smeared down to a rumble. When it was over, they were facing in different directions. Andrew had swept Kevin into his arms and pressed him close without realizing it. Dogs were barking.

"Not thunder," said Edith.

Nobody else seemed to have registered anything amiss. Kevin stared in citizenly outrage as an escaped chicken tried to flutter its way past him to freedom.

"Everything's fine, you two," Andrew said. "Stay cool."

Kevin burst into tears.

"*Emanaciones de las cloacas,*" a man told Edith. He was sitting on a wooden packing crate sharing a bottle of mescal with a couple of *compadres.*

"Sewer gas, he says," she informed Andrew. The men had fallen silent, and she was aware of their collective gaze running frankly over her.

"Hush, my little friend. We're on an adventure, okay?" As he comforted his son, Andrew struggled visibly to maintain his composure. "Really. You're safe with us."

"Here, let me take him for a while."

But being in Edith's arms reminded Kevin at once of what he was unhappy about. "Where's Mommy?" he screamed. "I want my mommy!"

Still surging with adrenaline from the explosion, Edie set about calming the boy as she had done each of her brothers years ago, cooing into his ear, cradling his head. Andrew pressed a hand into the small of her back. She felt grateful to him for understanding her need to do this, to calm herself by comforting the boy.

They were standing still in the middle of the aisle, people passing on either side without complaint. "Don't you remember missing your mother when you were his age?" she asked Andrew.

"I'll tell you about it sometime. You'll cry your eyes out."

Kevin's tears were subsiding, but the dark thrill that had entered her, just before the explosion, persisted. At first she had thought the explosion *was* the feeling. Other possibilities—an earthquake, a bomb—had come to her only after.

"My mommy has a baby goat," Kevin said petulantly.

"She certainly does," Edith agreed. "And his name is Kevin."

The boy considered this. He uttered a tentative bleat, and in it she heard something of herself. The trying on of a role offered and accepted only because of the multitude of ways it might be rejected.

"Goats like to be on the ground," Kevin declared. She put him down, and he began running through a repertory of goat sounds.

"Edie knows all about goat talk," said Andrew. "She's a translator."

Kevin bleated. "And when I'm hungry I eat tin cans!"

What stayed with Edith from the night her father had taken her to see the roan being born was summarized in her mind by the steam. It had poured off the mare and the foal struggling out of her like a luminous announcement. Edith had felt it between her own legs, then and for a long time after.

"*Mamacita.*" It was the man who had told her the sewers were exploding.

She walked over to where he and his two friends were sitting. "*Sí. ¿Cómo le va?*"

One of them was selling a couple of chickens to a young boy. As the campesino held the birds out by their heads the boy fit a burlap bag around the fluttering fist of feathers.

"I wonder," said the man who had addressed her, "if I might be of assistance to you on this beautiful day, in our capital city." He said it in Spanish. His words were slurred.

"Oh, I don't think so. We're staying with friends."

"You and your husband and your little boy?" he inquired, peering pointedly at her ringless fingers.

She forced herself not to glance back over her shoulder at Andrew and Kevin. "That's right."

"*Pues . . .*" He looked her slowly over. "*Qué lástima,*" he concluded, his gaze locked with hers.

His friend with the mescal bottle laughed and leaned close to him, knocking both their hats askew as he pronounced his assessment of the situation loudly into his ear. "*¡Pobrecita! Tiene la chocha caliente.*"

Andrew was instantly beside her, tense and volatile. "Did he say what I think he said?"

It took her a moment to tear her eyes away. "No," she said, linking arms with Andrew. "Definitely not. Come on, let's go."

When they were outside again, Andrew bought a mango from a street vendor and cut it into thirds with his pocketknife. "Here, *mi cabrito,*" he said to Kevin, seating him on a crookedly settled wrought-iron bench. "Take five."

Edith watched Andrew consume his portion of the fruit.

"What were you planning to do back there, defend my honor?"

"It was a reflex. I was pumped."

"Well, don't do it. I'm flattered, but don't do it."

They stepped aside to let an Indian woman pass. She was pushing a standard-issue grocery cart jerry-built with a kerosene camp stove and a steaming caldron of neon green liquid. *"Rico Ponche Caliente,"* said a hand-lettered sign taped to the cart. Delicious hot punch.

"They say this is the site of the original Aztec market. Bernal Díaz writes about it in his history of the Conquest. You know it?"

" 'All is overthrown and lost, nothing left standing,' " quoted Andrew.

"The guy goes on for pages, describing what he saw. Silver, gold, slaves, spices, furs, fruit." Edith waved her slice of mango at him meaningfully. "Now *that's* an estate inventory. Montezuma wasn't even dead yet."

"Poor old Montezuma. He sent Bernal Díaz a concubine, as I recall."

"Of great beauty and good family. Bearing a feather mantle, several crickets in a golden cage, and a quantity of freshly made soap."

"Hegemony and sighs. Cocoa in the mornings."

"It makes you wonder, doesn't it? On the one hand, you have a situation. A culture that has calculated the exact year of its erasure collides with one that thinks it's the wrath of God."

"I heard you advance this theory at the museum last night."

"On the other hand, we've got Bernal Díaz in the arms of his cherry-eyed beauty. What does it mean?"

"Blue-eyed babies."

"Exactly. Blue-eyed babies." Edith sighed and pressed herself close to him. "Hey, what time do we meet up with Santiago and Mercedes?"

"We should head over there now."

A man with a battered Polaroid offered to take their picture but Andrew declined. Edith raised her chin to him, inviting the kiss. The man released the shutter anyway and began demanding money. Andrew ignored him.

"*Tienes la chocha caliente?*" Andrew asked Edith, drawing back to look at her.

"No."

He moved his hand slowly over her buttocks and squeezed. She quivered.

"Yes you do."

MERCEDES snipped the red plastic ribbon and declared the new medical clinic open. It wasn't much to look at—a five-by-eight-meter structure of tangerine concrete, nestled among the auto-parts stores and chicken take-out shops of Nezahual-cóyotl—but it had been built without government help, by a church group. Somehow, they had found a doctor as well. He wore an Ohio State tee shirt and carried his instruments in a woman's clutch purse of blue vinyl.

"An ophthalmoscope," said the doctor. "I don't hope for a phone, but we get so many eye infections because of the *contaminación.*"

"Yes," replied Mercedes. "And the forceps. We will get them for you."

Felicia Díaz, accompanied by her bodyguards, led a group of concerned wives across the street to inspect the open ditch that served here as a sewer. The press photographers followed. Except for a handful of teenage boys playing soccer with a plastic jug, the neighborhood regulars kept their distance. They were Zapotec, newly arrived from the countryside, and had little Spanish.

"Señora, I do not think we should linger here," said the bodyguard who had been assigned to Mercedes for the afternoon. "I myself would not have suggested coming."

"Ah. You feel the occasion is too populist?"

"We make very conspicuous targets, Señora. That is all I meant."

Embarrassed, Mercedes hastened to apologize. "Let me tell my sister-in-law."

As she crossed the street one of the soccer players kicked the jug her way. The boys' laughter, as she kicked the jug back to them, flattered her, and she was led to wonder what kind of victory she might in fact settle for.

On the drive back into the city's central district, Mercedes encouraged Felicia, whom she had detached from the rest of the group, to share her opinion of Santiago's emotional state. While she was well aware that Felicia, mother of five, read her own childlessness as a refusal to assume her proper role in the family, and that among the Díazes such obstinacy spoke darkly of sexual appetite, Santiago's obvious devotion was the only rejoinder Mercedes needed.

"Of course he is upset by Luis's betrayal," Felicia told her. "How could he not be? Just yesterday, before you got here, I heard him tell someone on the phone that if he had known that this would be the price of his candidacy, he might never have decided to run. It was beautiful what he said, but very sad."

"Do you think the split was personal, then?"

"Without a doubt it was personal! Luis has always been envious of Santiago. If anyone should know that, it's me, believe it. From day one."

Mercedes understood this to be a reference to Felicia's adolescent affair with Luis, a fling she happened to know Felicia cherished precisely because of its overtone of surrogation. She lit a cigarette.

"But Fifi, don't you think Luis and Santiago have real political differences?"

"Now they do. 'Conspicuous consumption, conspicuous consumption,' it's all anyone talks about now. Is it true that *gringa* you brought with you put that idea in his head?"

"No."

Felicia glanced quickly at her. "She is very pretty. A little forward for my taste, but I like her husband. And their child is perfectly adorable. Kevin. How old is he?"

"Three and a half."

"Ay, she has kept her figure so well. Exercise is what does it. All *gringas* have a mania for exercise." Removing a lipstick from her purse, Felicia freshened her own appearance, which the poisonous air of Neza had noticeably marred. "Of course, their sense of family is not as strong as ours."

"Darling Fifi," said Mercedes, unable to suppress a smile. "It is always refreshing to see the world through your eyes."

"A word to the wise, that's all. There's a first time with every man, even Santiago."

SANTIAGO first learned of Arévalo's plans for the *maquiladoras* at midafternoon following a speech he had given at the Stock Exchange. Word had come in from campaign headquarters that sometime before the end of the week Luis would propose nationalizing the string of foreign-owned factories that stretched along the Mexican side of the U.S. border, 3,326 kilometers of unregulated manufacturing and assembly shops positioned to take advantage of cheap local labor. As Carlos hustled him off to the car, Santiago spoke into a cell phone. "Are you sure of it? Has anyone talked to Freddy González?"

The voice on the line informed him that Freddy was apparently on his way to Washington, but messages had been left.

"Luis is not one to fuck himself up the ass like that. The *gringos* would blowtorch his campaign before he could get his pants back up." Realizing he did not even know the name of the staffer to whom he was talking, Santiago made an effort to control his irritation. "Has the press got hold of this?"

The leak had come through an informant that Carlos had contrived to place in Arévalo's innermost circle. As far as could be determined, no one else knew about it. Of course, Gutiérrez, as the ruling party's candidate, had both Mexican and U.S. intelligence at his disposal.

"Try to find out Luis's schedule for the next couple of days," Santiago said disgustedly. "This can't be what it looks like."

At a parking garage off Reforma he changed cars for his rendezvous with Mercedes, Edith, and Andrew. Oiticica was unhappy with the arrangement.

"At least the Volvo is armored. Why not take that?"

"Because the Volvo is back in Las Lomas," said Santiago as he relieved himself against the concrete wall of the garage.

Another explosion shook the ground.

"Along with the bathrooms," Santiago shouted over his shoulder.

It had been a bad day for the sewers.

"Leave him alone," Carlos told the security chief. "He's got a long week ahead of him, and he needs the distraction."

Even before Mercedes returned from New York, Santiago had chafed under the constant supervision and scheduling now necessitated by his campaign. As a *futbolista* he had been notorious for disregarding curfews. He said they were the enemy of brilliance.

Firing up the Chevy's throaty engine, Santiago rolled down the window and beckoned to his campaign manager.

"Carlos, do you know how to make God laugh?"

The young man looked at him impassively and raised an eyebrow.

"Tell Him your plans."

Santiago edged out into the anarchic, hacking sprawl of Mexico City traffic.

Arévalo's perfidy, which Santiago had tried to reconcile with his love of the man, ate away at him. He sorted through what he remembered of their discussions, worrying out their moments of disagreement, trying in hindsight to construct a pattern that might explain the divergence of their hopes for Mexico, their ambitions for themselves. When he had returned from England, brushing aside his chance at university in favor of the game that had made him famous, Santiago knew that he had done so in part because of Luis.

From the start, their friendship had assumed Santiago's eventual success in the world. It had also assumed that such success would include Luis. And although the life that had been laid out before Santiago at his English boarding school had offered much and promised more, while he never doubted the variety of his abilities or the satisfactions they might afford him abroad, he had balked at abandoning his boyhood theater. So many graces, so much thought, and in the end it had come down to a scratched-out playing field in Chapultepec Park.

The goalie's role, as long as his team had the ball, was like that of the spectators, only more so. He was the embodiment of audience. The forward, dribbling the ball, faking, passing the ball, and charging upfield to receive it again, was always aware of his counterpart, stationed behind him at the other end of the field, intently fixed on his progress. An invisible line connected the two players like an alternating current. Whenever the forward had possession, everyone but him forgot about the goalie, who might as well not have existed. But each moment also held the possibility that the forward might fail to score, and the direction of the current reverse, leading to a series of eventualities that, in the furthest case, would end in a scoring attempt by the other side. Then, from the instant the ball left the shooter's foot until it was caught, blocked, or let by, the goalie became the only man anyone present saw. The only one alive.

Santiago steered the Chevy into the traffic that swarmed around the *glorieta*. Accelerating, he savored the rush, then shot back out the other side onto the avenue.

It was hard not to wonder about what Andrew had told him. So like Luis to have followed up on Edith. If there hadn't been a photo to find, he would have imagined one, but telling Mercedes about it had been a mistake. Luis had always underestimated her.

Poor Luis. Maybe he thought there was some leverage to be had from a dirty picture. The failed self-esteem such a notion implied embarrassed Santiago. This was not *gringo* land, where they could turn you out of office for having a hard-on. Surely Luis knew that.

During the World Cup crisis, when Santiago was holed up with the U.S. hostages and their captors, Luis had been discreetly approached by the *yanquis*. They asked him the usual sordid questions: mistresses, drug use, gambling. Luis had laughed in their faces. Afterwards, he had threatened to go to the press, and it had taken Mercedes the full force of her outraged Latin womanhood to dissuade him.

Santiago shook his head over his friend. An impulsive and extravagant man. At bottom, a romantic. No doubt there was a lesson to be learned here about the kinds of promises a man could keep, but Santiago didn't have the stomach for it.

Bringing Edith and Andrew down had been a good idea. Together they inhabited a space that traveled well, a zone worth admiring. Maybe it was fatuous to admire something so familiar from his own spiritual scavengings; after all, it was just some kind of erotic miscue that he shared with them. An audience, a witness, an aversion to boundaries. As badges of honor went, these were petty enough. Not to mention the misunderstandings they covered over, the fuckups past and present.

But of course there was more to it than that. A man found strength in unlikely places, and lately, for better or worse, Santiago had found it in this pair of *yanqui* rarities. Nothing in particular about them seized his fancy, but somehow, taken altogether, they were hypnotizing. They had a whiff of mortality about them, Santiago considered, and a readiness to improvise that made you wonder if they knew it.

The radio Oiticica had insisted he stow under the seat as a precaution erupted in static, then just as abruptly fell silent. Santiago grimaced. As if he might forget the promises he had made, even if he wanted to.

Border factories worked by indentured labor, air and water tables poisoned, babies born brainless with heads the size of soccer balls. *La frontera.* Nationalizing the *maquiladoras* would just mean that the people who knew how to run them would scurry back to Houston or Detroit or wherever they came from. And that was already supposing the *yanquis* wouldn't march their army in to recapture their goods in time for the evening news.

Arévalo would have heard by now about Andrew and Edith's arrival in the city. Maybe he'd release another fucked-up video to make a point. *Chica de la Frontera,* he could call it. Border Girl.

Turning off Cárdenas onto the worn streets of *el centro,* Santiago had to laugh. The image of Luis gravely presenting a girlie shot of Edith to Mercedes while affecting tones of fraternal concern almost made up for the betrayal. He wished his father were alive to hear about it.

A couple of blocks away from the Plaza de la Concepción, Santiago eased the car up onto the shallow sidewalk and parked.

"I DON'T see any piano," said Marisa. She and James sat at a little table in the Tira el Pianisto with a couple of tequilas. The clientele was various, from businessmen to the odd early-bird *mariachi,* but excepting Marisa, it was all male. A sign over the door declared the place off-limits to men in uniform, children, and women.

"Maybe they put it in the back room," James answered. "Anyway, this is definitely the place. I can't believe it's still here."

"Are you overcome with nostalgia?"

"My youth doesn't affect me that way. Hey, what's the deal with the *botanas* here, I wonder. They used give you these bull's blood tacos from yesterday's *corrida.* Challenging but delicious."

Marisa discreetly slipped a fresh roll of film into her camera. "I want to hear about the good time you and Andrew had here. You provoked an incident, I think."

"We're close enough to provoking one now," said James in a low voice. "Promise me no pictures."

"No pictures. So what did you do anyway?"

James glanced unhappily over the room. "I was pretty loaded at the time, and I don't remember much. First mistake, we let some guy buy us a drink. The way they do it here is first they spend what's left of their money on you, then you both start in on yours. It's very bad form to quit before you're cleaned out."

"*Mi dinero, su dinero.*"

"Right. So a whole lot of little glasses later we're all *compadres*. I'm buying tequila for fifteen, twenty guys. Andrew's at the piano banging out chorus after chorus of 'No Vale Nada la Vida,' which is like the national anthem of Mexican drunkenness. Everybody's singing, or at least sobbing helplessly, and a lucky few have already passed out. Traditional situation, give or take."

A flicker of amusement crossed Marisa's face. "I hope this story doesn't have a moral."

"Suddenly this guy, El Mosco, who started the whole thing, asks me to lend him a hundred dollars U.S. I'm a little surprised, even though by then we're comrades forever and so on, so I ask what he needs it for. Clearly the wrong approach. A friend doesn't question a friend's need for money. Anyway, he tells me that he needs the hundred to buy a gun to shoot my pitiful bean-sized balls off, because any faggot who doesn't trust his own friends in this shitty life is a waste of the whore's milk that his slut of a mother suckled him on. Or words to that effect."

"You boys and your balls. But you kept your composure."

"Actually, I did. I asked him why the gun cost so much."

"And that calmed him down?"

"No, it was the last straw. He grabbed me by the neck and started shouting. Literally frothed at the mouth. What kind of fucked-out dog's son was I that I thought he'd shoot a friend with a cheap, shitty pistol? Did he look like some dirt-eating pubic hair who would settle for less than the best in a matter of honor? *Two* hundred dollars. Extra for bullets.

"That's when Andrew came to my rescue. He told the guy I was a famous singer, and he couldn't let him wreck my throat. Anything else, but not that. So I went back to the piano with

Andrew and improvised about a billion verses of a song about the futility of striving, the heartlessness of women, and the consolations of drink. Even you would have wept. It saved my neck."

"I didn't know you were so gifted."

"I respond well to deadlines," answered James. "Drink your tequila."

The other patrons of the cantina were bad-eyeing them openly by now, but Marisa managed to appear oblivious to their inspection. Running the length of one wall was a lurid mural done in the heroic manner of Siqueiros and Rivera. With its unlikely mingling of motifs from the Spanish Conquest, California surfing culture, and vampire lore, the painting was an authentic treasure. It might be amusing, James thought, to track down the artist. He could not remember if the mural had been there on his first visit, seventeen years ago.

Trouble, such as it was, came eventually from the bartender, a young, fire-hydrant-shaped *machista* with close-set eyes and a cauliflower ear. After watching James and Marisa for a while he called his son over and had a word with him. The boy arrived at their table with another round and named a price four times what they had paid earlier. An unwholesome silence fell over the room.

"*Gracias, amigo,*" said James when he had counted out the bills. Looking up, he blundered into eye contact with a party of domino players at the next table. "*¡Qué trato!*" he observed to them in a hearty voice. "*Gasofia mexicana al precio americano.*" Mexican gasoline at American prices.

The sally was well enough received by their fellow patrons to buy at least a temporary peace. "This will be the last one," James told Marisa, who had assumed the glittery-eyed look of someone anticipating entertainment. But she wasn't looking at him.

"Andrew!" she said with as much aplomb as she could muster. "We were just speaking of you."

With Kevin in his arms, Andrew stopped and stared. "I can't believe it! What are you two doing here?"

"Us?" James struggled visibly to take hold of the situation.

"We're revisiting the fields of my youthful glory. Sit down and let me buy you and your sidekick a *copita.*"

A squeal of dissent issued from Kevin. "Daddy, I gotta go *right now*! I gotta go to the *bath*room!"

Shaking his head, Andrew set out toward the urinal that protruded from the back wall like a dirty vegetable. "Be right back."

Marisa bit her tongue in silent mirth and winked at James.

"Okay, you've got a sixth sense. Just don't look so pleased with yourself," he told her sourly.

As it turned out, Kevin's social instincts set the tone, and shortly he was seated in Marisa's lap discussing the dietary habits of witches. Andrew pulled up a chair beside James.

"So how'd you find us?"

"I had a heart-to-heart with Dorotea. She's got boyfriend problems."

"Please don't tell me about them."

"What happened to Edie?"

Andrew looked him over irritably. "You got reason to be concerned?"

"Hey. Unarmed."

"Yeah? You're probably the only one present who is, then." Chuckling darkly, Andrew scanned the cantina as if he had just noticed it. From one corner came a loud snore. "This fucking place. It looks just the same. Remember that peyote death-wish mural?"

"Hand of a master," James agreed. "But what happened to their music program, I wonder."

"They shot the piano player." Andrew tried to make out what Marisa was saying to Kevin, but their voices were lost in the general din.

"Shot the piano player?"

"Forget it. Edie's over at Concepción, a couple of blocks down. We're meeting our hosts for coffee and whatever. Where you staying?"

"Polanco."

Andrew took a pen from his jacket pocket and wrote down Santiago's number. "Call us after eight. We'll get together, maybe tomorrow."

"Don't be pissed," said James. "It's all in a good cause."

"Art? That's the good cause?"

"Art and, you know, human purpose. Why we do the things we do, what our stories are, and what they look like. We're enthusiasts."

Andrew looked thoughtful for a moment, then broke into laughter. It was an inclusive sound and a relief. "Actually, maybe you two are just what we need." He got to his feet. "Marisa, a pleasure to see you again. C'mon, short stuff. We've got places to go."

As they watched Andrew and Kevin leave the cantina, Marisa said, "Your friend Andrew is sort of a throwback, isn't he?"

A Mixtec woman in a brightly colored but soiled rebozo was making the rounds up front, displaying her baby at each table and collecting coins from the delighted customers before moving on. The child, no more than ten months old, was plump and healthy, with a vigorous patch of coal black pubic hair.

"No," James corrected her. "He's an enthusiast."

WAITING for Andrew to return, Edith walked back and forth in the sleepy little *plazoleta* where he had left her. Planted with trees and fronted at one end by a partly riven eighteenth-century church, the little square spoke to her gentler appetites. Half a dozen high school students had commandeered its far side as a rehearsal space for a play of some sort—Calderón, she thought. She found herself touched.

Since coming to Mexico, Edith had let her thoughts play out without censure, without design. What had seemed in New York a debacle, a misfortune whose consequences would undo her all the more quickly if she considered them, here offered dividends. A truth to live with, if she wanted it.

The last time she had seen Oliver Barnes he had taken her riding in the park. His horsemanship had proved adequate but no better, and she had had some fun at his expense, inciting both their mounts to a gallop that had ended with him ingloriously un-horsed by a forsythia bush. Contrite, she had brought him home. Their lovemaking then had struck a studiously inventive register that somehow turned everything polite and valedictory. The image of the shot Mexican boy falling off the fence into darkness had visited her repeatedly, as if it were he she was taking leave of. Afterwards, alone, she had cried a little.

As last times went, very high concept, ha-ha. Though they'd been careful about birth control. Edie paused to retie the scarf she had wrapped around her hair.

The fact was, she thought, Oliver hadn't any right to know about this child of theirs. He would be gratified and upset in all the wrong ways, and he would offer embarrassing declarations. About what to tell Andrew, though, she was less sure. *Such an indelible lie*, Hannah had said.

The *plazoleta* players were giving Calderón an athletic inter-pretation, forming a human pyramid atop which the female lead, a ponytailed extrovert with an untroubled glance, might more suitably reflect on her passage to heaven. She threw her chest out, back arched like a gymnast's, and recited with relish her sober lines.

When Edith saw Santiago striding unaccompanied toward her, she realized she had been expecting something like this. He carried his suit jacket over one shoulder and walked with a bounce that seemed less jaunty than restless. As fit as he was physically, his face looked gaunt, its planes angled in a hawkish ratio, and a lock of oiled hair had fallen across his forehead. She had never looked at him so frankly before.

"The guys went off to find a bathroom," she told him. "What happened to the shades brigade?"

"My bodyguards. I gave them the afternoon off."

A small silence settled over them. Finding no reason to look away, Edith continued to stare into his eyes. Other, more superficial greetings failed to suggest themselves. After what felt like a long time she said, "How strange."

"Yes. We seem to be the same kind."

They turned toward the young actors, who, having finished their scene, were boisterously elbowing one another into line for a curtain call. Seeing they had attracted Edith's and Santiago's attention, they bowed quite professionally. Edith applauded. When Santiago did not join her, she took a quick step to the side, faced him, and redoubled her applause. The actors, catching on, added their handclaps to hers, and Santiago was forced to take a bow.

"Maybe you handle it better than I do, though," Edith added as the youths began to drift away.

"I've been wanting to tell you," said Santiago. "You mustn't worry about Luis."

"Really? But I do. I got you into Oliver's silliness, which believe me I've had ample experience with myself. I wasn't thinking straight."

"My problem with Luis really has nothing to do with the things I said on the show that night. Besides, I said them."

"So you did." She looked away. She had tied the scarf around her hair after leaving the marketplace, to make herself less conspicuous. "I wonder about you," she said. "Literalists don't normally like—"

"You're mistaken."

"—don't like to be recognized." Again they stared at each other.

"I'm sorry," she continued grimly. "Recognized as opposed to seen, I meant."

"Yes. I understand."

Edith rubbed the back of her hand across her forehead in annoyance. "Where's Mercedes?"

"She should be here any moment. We were coming from different directions."

Again Santiago was aware of his wife's organizing intelligence in the scene now unfolding. She had penetrated swiftly to the core of the woman with whom he had this unlooked-for kinship. By presenting her to him in this way, so clearly at crisis, so passionate in her display, Mercedes had posed the problem in its purest terms, factored out to primes. Solve for x, where x is the sum of self-love divided by trust.

"I hope you will forgive us for being such negligent hosts," Santiago said.

"Please don't apologize. How did your speech go?"

"Political oratory is a highly stylized art in Mexico. People expect to be moved, and they communicate that readiness. It's surprisingly easy to bring them to tears, and a moment later to laughter. Anger is easier still. But ideas—to speak of anything that might require thought or hasn't been said a thousand times before—that is not permitted."

"I thought every place was like that."

"Perhaps. But in Mexico we make it a point of honor."

Edith smiled. "So which did you go for?"

Instead of answering, Santiago took her arm. She inhaled sharply, surprised suddenly by the impulse to hit him, the citric sting of adrenaline high in her throat. But an instant later she mastered the spasm.

A young mother with her several children had staked out a spot under a struggling ash and was carefully washing her feet in a rain puddle. As Santiago and Edith passed, the woman let out a low moan, the same sound the boy on the fence had made, falling away.

"Hey, Señor Díaz. I'm in a state."

"As you said, we are literalists."

"You knew this right away."

"About you, yes. That evening at the banquet, watching the two of you during my speech. It gave me an emotion. The shock of recognition, I think I'll call it. I've never been a man who looks closely at himself."

"You're not going to start now, I hope. Because I don't think it will help."

Santiago considered this. "You're wondering if I know about this photograph of you."

"Oh, no I'm not."

"It couldn't matter less."

"I agree. Let's talk about something else."

"Oliver Barnes?"

"Not much to talk about. We had an affair, it ended, your problems with Arévalo have nothing to do with what you said on his show."

"I liked him. I saw why he might appeal to you."

"Really? Tell me."

"He is a responsive man, one with respect for the unconscious gestures of others. He does not use what he sees. Interpretation and meaning do not interest him because he does not like power completely. This is a man of two minds."

Edith did not reply. They walked the perimeter of the little park arm in arm like old friends who found themselves inexplicably at odds. That this was the first time they had been alone together occurred to neither of them.

"Why does—"

"I already—"

Shaking her head in undisguised irritation, Edith said, "You first."

"Nothing. But I'm coming to think that none of us is given the luxury of choosing our audience. Your friend Oliver Barnes believes otherwise, which makes him a coward. And you don't have much patience for cowards."

"Do you?"

"In a way, yes. I appreciate the problem. But there's nothing to do about it."

Edith laughed sharply, one syllable. "You make me want to slap you."

"Yes, I imagine I do."

They walked a few paces in silence.

"So what about you?" she asked. "Do you like power completely?"

"I'm trying to find out. I used to believe it didn't matter, since power has always liked me so much. But I've had to think again." He shrugged. "It takes a long time for some things to sink in."

Wincing, Edith touched thumb and forefinger to her temples as though suffering from a headache. "Did Mercedes tell you that she came to my office at the UN? Before we all had dinner together I mean. She wanted to know if I was having an affair with you."

"I see. And what did you tell her?"

"Well, I told her no, of course," said Edith matter-of-factly. "What else would I tell her?"

"Nothing else, nothing else."

"She's become a friend."

"I'm glad."

Looking at him, Edith saw that he was. "When James Walsh first invited me to your banquet, you know what I thought about you? With all due respect? A dilettante. Another spoiled celebrity who thinks he's got the answers."

"But that's what I am."

She glared at him.

"I'm an athlete—no, a former athlete. A man who can act without thinking. A literalist with a talent for self-display. A dilettante."

She shook free from his grip. "Deny it, damn you! Defend yourself!"

"My famous intervention on behalf of the hostages, putting my life on the line, living with them while the so-called terrorists strutted up and down for the camera. People always want to know if I was frightened. I will tell you what I felt."

Turning abruptly from him, Edith stalked off several paces, then just as suddenly wheeled back around, shaking her finger at him as if to make a point. "I know what you're doing. I know!"

"I was bored. Nothing to do. Shitty audience. I couldn't wait for it to end. Whichever way it turned out."

His crooked smile infuriated her, drew her. "You can't play coldheart with me," she said. "I have more energy than you."

"Good."

"Don't do this, Santiago, okay?"

"People always ask what I felt."

"Fine, fine."

"*Definición y repetición.*"

"Where's Mercedes? Aren't you worried about her?"

"She is on her way."

"All those explosions."

"Sewer gas. What about Andrew and Kevin?"

"On their way."

"Good, good."

They circled around each other, arguing with themselves. Later Edith would remember this scene mainly for the silence surrounding it, extending from the *plazoleta* in all directions. Only then would it come to her. Mexico City, maximum metropolis, choking on its own car exhaust, was a place where the drivers never used their horns.

CHET BAKER was singing "But Not for Me." Yellow street light fell in raked diagonals across the floor of Jovãozinha de Borba's town house, and the air smelled of fresh sweat and mulberry.

The big question on Jovãozinha's mind as he listened to the frail tenor was how a white Californian of the nineteen fifties, poisoned with heroin and invidious loves, had meant such a voice to be taken. Innocently, as it sounded; ironically, as the life suggested; or some third way that disregarded silly distinctions. Jovãozinha reached out to turn on the bedside lamp.

"Jojo, what time is it?"

"Seven-thirty. A little after."

Marisa raised her head from his chest and sat up, still astride him. She combed her tangled hair out with her fingers. "What's the matter?"

"I can't make up my mind about this fucking music."

Smiling, Marisa slowly lifted her hips until he slipped out of her. "Poor Jojo. You think so much." She bent over and carefully removed the condom before taking his slackening cock into her mouth.

"Ai! You're excruciating." He caressed her neck. "Besides, that defeats the whole point of condoms. Or one of the points anyway."

She let him go and giggled as she bounced out of bed. "I always was a dirty girl," she said, dropping the condom into an ashtray.

Jovãozinha watched his sister, her lips still glistening with his semen, seat herself cross-legged in an armchair by the window. She plucked a pomegranate from the sill and tore it greedily open.

It had been a trying day. He had heard a rumor at his squash club that a major devaluation of the peso was planned for after the election, and no one that he had been able to reach had denied it convincingly. What disturbed him was not the devaluation itself but that he hadn't been the first to know about it. He trafficked in access. Appearing to be uninformed could be quite as bad as the real thing.

Throwing a silk dressing robe over his shoulders, Jovãozinha walked to where his sister sat and began idly rearranging the vase of yellow roses on the table beside her. "Where did you say our James went?"

"He's having a drink with the director of the Centro Cultural."

"Oh, yes. The American."

"You don't like him?"

"I don't think such pretension is becoming in an expatriate."

"I meant James."

"Ah, James. No, I love James." He smiled slyly at her. "Don't you?"

"Sometimes. Not really." She busied herself with the pomegranate.

Whenever Marisa returned to Jovãozinha after a separation she found she had to readjust her thinking. The ease with which she wound her way through other people's daily star wars, touring the spectacle and taking note, could sometimes lull her into complacency. She never explained herself. She avoided judging others, not out of principle but because things were more entertaining that way. And so, in the end, it was Jovãozinha, her witness and confessor, who kept her honest.

"Andrew asked me about the rain forest," she told her brother. "Back in New York. He said he has a client, some sort of save-the-jungle scientist, whose life is being threatened. I got the feeling this man has attracted our father's special attention."

Jovãozinha took a small, thin cigar from the pocket of his robe and lit it. "It's a shame. People go where they don't belong and disgrace themselves. It's embarrassing." He shrugged. "But so what?"

"Mercedes Díaz was there for this conversation. Edith too. Edie saw the fistfight at the UN, or at least she had heard about it. And Andrew all but asked point-blank what Mexico and Brazil could be up to, messing around in each other's domestic affairs." A rivulet of crimson pomegranate juice ran down Marisa's right breast, and she wiped it away. "Really, Jojo, it was tight-squeeze city. We're just lucky the UN thing didn't run in the papers."

Wiggling his eyebrows Groucho-style, Jovãozinha blew a smoke ring and smiled. "Lucky?"

"Aha. Okay, I'm impressed. But even you can't keep the press off this forever."

"That won't be necessary. We'll see to it."

"We will?"

" 'By any means necessary.' That's Malcolm X, the great American *negro.*"

She sighed. "Honestly, Jojo. Don't you think your reading is getting a little eclectic? I can't keep up with you at all anymore."

They took coffee together while Marisa leafed through a portfolio of prints she had brought Jovãozinha as a present. The previous summer she had conceived the idea of a series of formal portraits of fathers with their daughters. For strategic reasons she had chosen fathers who were public figures—sports stars, poets, politicians, artists—men of whom the viewer could be expected to have a strong preconception. She had then made sure that each shoot took place in the father's home, where she encouraged her subjects to arrange themselves as they saw fit. Once she saw what she wanted, she had pared it down, patiently adjusting limbs, fingertips, hair, and clothing until the bewildering bloody bond itself was laid bare. What had come of it was her best work to date. Looking at the prints unsettled her.

"They smolder," agreed Jováozinha. "These pictures make me think of arson. Of Lear on the heath. Have you shown them to James?"

"Not yet. Of course, he helped me with the introductions, so he knows all about it. But I wanted to wait." She flashed a mischievous smile. "In case he needed an incentive."

"And here you are. I wonder if his other artists receive such special attention."

"They'd better not."

Stroking her thigh, Jováozinha let his eye wander across the room to the row of Indian masks he had recently installed on an otherwise bare wall. In principle he was holding them for a Swiss buyer he had met in the Dutch Antilles, a spindly fanatic with long-range plans, but now he wondered if he could bear to part with them. Stoic, casually cruel, their features suggested a familiarity with the forces Jováozinha had come to think of, not without sorrow, as his special domain. Sometimes he thought it was history he glimpsed in their curly faces, but he knew what he hoped for was sympathy.

"You really want your border photographs, don't you, Marisa?"

"I've worked for them," she replied. "It's right."

He thought about that. "What about your personnel? A motley crew, when you get past all that grace and high-minded purpose. Can they really give you what you think they can?"

"I'm certain of it. They can't help it."

"But seriously, Marisa. They bumble. Suppose you get them all up there together and instead of bringing each other out they just present their own failures. You run the risk of silliness."

She stared him down, a tuck of tender amusement at one corner of her mouth. "Failure is not silly, Jojo. Not from where we stand."

Jovãozinha sighed. "Touché."

"Anyway, I don't expect it to come to that," she said. "I told you, I've got a feeling about this one. Synergy. That's the word for this project."

"Well, if anybody can do it, you can."

The phone rang, and Marisa answered. She listened intently, her head cocked, then held the handset out to him.

"Gutiérrez," she said.

IT WAS after nine when they all got back to the Díazes' house. Andrew and Kevin had shown up at the *plazoleta* more or less simultaneously with Mercedes and her bodyguards, and an afternoon of sightseeing had ensued. Santiago had instructed the driver to take them to Teotihuacán, where Andrew, Edith, and he had climbed the ruined Pyramid of the Sun. Afterwards they had dined on eel fry, termite eggs, and *gusanos de maguey* at a restaurant in Tlalpán. The press had been nowhere in evidence.

Andrew worked at his laptop for half an hour after their return, faxing instructions to his office in New York. When he was done he found Edith in the music room. She was reading Santiago's copy of Ortega y Gasset's *La rebelión de las masas*, heavily annotated in hot pink and green ink. On a plate at her feet, the pit and peel of a *zapote*. Andrew took the book from her and sat down.

"I've been trying to catch up with you all day," he told her. "What's going on?"

"Nothing much. I mean I'm absorbing things." She winced at the lameness of her reply.

"You and Santiago seem to be hitting it off. He likes you."

"He likes you, too. Anyway, it's not a question of like. We have the same screw loose is all."

Andrew appeared to think about it. "Could be."

The mood of rebellion had stayed with Edith through the

afternoon and into the evening. She hated Andrew when he was like this, attorney with no meter running. The effort of containing her frustration made her eyes go soft and polite; they would never give her away. The care he took not to claim possession. She would never grant it, but his failure to ask for it was inexcusable. She detested cleverness.

"Kevin and I ran into some friends of ours on our quest for sanitation, back there at Concepción. Want to guess who it was?"

Edith didn't answer.

"Marisa and James."

"You're joking."

"They got it out of Dorotea. I think James has actually lost his mind."

"Wow." Edith stood and walked to the center of the room, her arms folded. "Can this really be about a bunch of photographs? I mean Marisa just doesn't strike me as the art-for-art's-sake type."

"She's hard to read," said Andrew, watching her closely. "Maybe we do her a disservice."

"Where did you find them? Or did they find you?"

"In a cantina. I have the impression it was more or less an accident."

"But there must be half a million cantinas in Mexico City."

"It's a place James and I have patronized before. Remember that picture of him and me, I'm playing the piano and he's singing? Marisa asked me about it once in the gallery. Maybe they were scouting locations."

A baby grand presided over the side of the room that looked out on the landscaped patio. Feeling Edith's eyes on him, Andrew went over and stood before the keyboard. He played a couple of chords.

"Andrew," she said, circling the piano to face him across its bent side. "Have you asked yourself why we've drawn them into this? James and Marisa I mean. They're extraneous."

Andrew's fingers sketched out the chord changes to "Mack the Knife" while he looked equably at Edith. "Don't forget Oliver Barnes. As long as we're doing the books on this."

"Right. And Oliver." She swallowed. "But the point is, we've been running an open house right from the get-go. What's that about?"

"You got me." With his right hand he picked out a few bars of the melody. "Family feeling?"

"Oh, please."

"Hey, Edie." He stopped playing. "You should have told me about that odalisque you did for the nice men at the jack-off magazine."

"What?"

"I said," he repeated slowly, "you should have told me about your nudie shot."

She snorted in exasperation. "What am I, surrounded by children? How big a deal is this?"

He caught her by the arm as she tried to turn away. "I was hoping you would tell me."

His hand on her biceps aroused and angered her. She shook free and, when he tried to speak, put up a hand to block out both him and his words. "Do you really think I'm in need of moral instruction? I'm not."

"You know me better than that," he said.

"What, then?"

He studied her curiously, then crossed the room again and poured himself a glass of water. "Did you know that Marisa has a copy of that picture? Mercedes told me just before we left."

She felt her features thicken, but she was determined he would get nothing this way.

"Not impressed. Okay. But then there's the highly networked Oliver Barnes. According to Mercedes he venerates the same picture. It worries her, and given the way things turned out for Santiago on Barnes's show I can't say I blame her."

"Stop it, Andrew. It was in a fucking magazine, for God's sake!" She hugged herself, begrudging him the sight of her sudden goose bumps. "And, if it makes you feel any better, I'm the one who told Mercedes that Oliver had seen the photo. When it was published he had his assistant track me down to set up lunch. That's how we met."

"I get it," said Andrew. "Field notes."

"Look, you. Mercedes came to my office waving that picture around like a dirty sheet. There was a lot of opportunity for humiliation on both sides, thanks to Arévalo. I did what I could to fix it."

"That's okay, Edie. I know you did." Seeming suddenly to lose interest in the subject, he returned to the piano and seated himself on the bench.

"Are you going to tell me what you talked about with James and Marisa?" she asked.

He rolled up his sleeves. "They said they'd call. Maybe we can all get together tomorrow."

"Really? And what would we do?"

Without answering, he launched back into the song he had begun earlier, feeling it out. Edith leaned against the mahogany case to watch. As his fingers took surer hold of the melody, coaxing home the notes and improvising a little, she felt her mind race to contradict them.

"Do you know the words?" he asked.

"What *words*?" she demanded. "Could we stay on the subject, please?" She wanted to slap him. She realized the impulse was sexual, and the recognition only exacerbated her impatience.

Letting his gaze drift past her and through the floor-to-ceiling window to the illuminated patio beyond, Andrew teased the notes apart as if looking for something. The music spoke of weariness and pleasure, of last things gamely embraced and relinquished. It was a half-sarcastic hymn to knowingness, and playing it you had to be careful not to splash it around. Andrew braided the melody back together and nodded over his efforts.

"I liked the look on your face when you undid your blouse that night," he told her. "In the piano bar."

"I liked the one on your face," she answered.

He laughed a little. "Indulge me."

When he behaved this way, everything she did in response became a comment on his buffoonishness. Smirking, she untied the string fastener at the back of her dress and let the bodice fall down around her hips, where the fabric caught and clung like an apron. She shook her hair back over her shoulder and leaned into the open piano, daring him with her eyes.

"To answer your question," he continued, "I'm inclined to tell our artsy friends that we'll do the border photos."

"Whatever you say, boss."

"Just to clear the air."

"With them or me?"

"Both."

It came to her that she was being offered a range of options and that whatever mixy business had brought James and Marisa to Mexico was beside the point. She had a debt to pay off and an opportunity to do it. Her spirits rose. Sometimes you could only explain yourself after the fact.

She wriggled the rest of the way out of her dress and backhanded it across the room. "Okay, Mr. Caldwell," she said, pressing close to the piano and shaking her tits a little for good measure. "I'm ready for my song now."

He brought the melody back to the top and watched raptly as she fit the words into place. She knew all the verses.

Afterwards she walked to the window while he undressed behind her.

"Not very Mexican, is it?" she said of the song. From the patio a pair of Aztec stone figures stared back at her. In fact, they seemed quite conversant with the sentiments conveyed by the music.

"When we get home," said Andrew, turning her toward him, "I've got to get my piano back from Susannah. You remind me."

On the floor, her legs wrapped tightly around him, Edith flashed on herself as a teenager, picking out radio tunes on the family piano while upstairs her father serviced whichever of his clients' wives had lately made him her project. Edith would try not to hear, but by the time they were done, and she along with them, fresh underwear was usually her most pressing concern.

Andrew tended her closely, intent on her pleasure, anticipating its gait by half a heartbeat. At one point voices drifted in from the patio's far corner, but when Edith turned her face to the window she saw nothing beyond her and Andrew's reflection. Her unexpressed resentment goaded them both on, and she came twice before he spent himself.

As they dressed, she sensed the strength of their bond. It made her feel uncomplicated and younger than her age. The child she carried might, from this slightly less jaundiced point of view, be considered compensation for the Mexican boy she had failed to save from falling off into the night. That Oliver Barnes should be its accidental father might then be tolerable, even just. Andrew would understand as much. She would make him.

"What are you thinking?" he asked her, as if on cue.

She stared at him, wanting to speak.

"Is something the matter?"

"I was thinking about my mother. What it might have been like if she hadn't died so young."

"It must have been hard for you."

"Yes and no. The testosterone got very thick in that household after she was gone, and I could have used a bit of female reinforcement. On the other hand, it wasn't all bad. I learned that you don't reject something just because it comes to you a little tainted." She tried to shrug. "I mean things are sordid sometimes. So what?"

"Amen to that." He drew the cover over the piano's keyboard.

"Andrew," she said. "Andrew, look at me. Do you feel we've been bulldozed into this?"

"By whom? I don't know what you're talking about."

She was an arm's length away from him.

"If you're having second thoughts about us just say so, Edie."

"It's not that."

"Glad to hear it." Stifling a yawn, he bounced up and down on the balls of his feet a couple of times. "As for your mother, you talk as if you betrayed her somehow. Want to tell me about it? I mean I sort of know what you're thinking. You took over her role as mother, and now, with Kevin, you're doing it again."

"Don't be clever."

"Yes, you hate that, I know." He chuckled.

"What do you hate?"

"Sentimentality about the dead. If my professional life has taught me anything it's what a great alibi grief makes."

Her fist flew out and caught him full force just below the left eye. In his surprise he fell back a step, his hands still at his sides. She saw she had hurt him. She supposed she had meant to.

"Sorry," he told her. "I don't know why I said that."

A blaze of red had risen across his cheekbone, with a raw, darker patch running to his eye. Edith, awry and panting, stared at him.

"Maybe I was thinking of my own mother," Andrew added. "When she died I shut down for a long time."

She put a hand up to stop him. "Don't. Just don't." Snatching her shoes from under the piano stool, she started for the door, then thought better of it. "You know, when I was in high school, my father used to fuck his girlfriends in my bed. I'd listen from the living room, playing the piano so he could hear. I mean it was obvious who he was really fucking, right?"

"He saw your mother in you, Edie. He couldn't help it."

"No doubt. But you know what else?" She heard herself laugh. "Neither could I."

WHEN Santiago arrived for his luncheon meeting at the roof garden of the Hotel Majestic, he found his staff peering gloomily over the balcony at the Zócalo below. Arévalo had minutes ago announced his plan to nationalize the *maquiladoras*, and crowds were already pouring into the vast square to show their support. Demonstrations in the Zócalo, once the center of the Aztec capital, were always a stirring sight.

"Our troops are disconsolate," Santiago observed jovially. "Eh, Carlos?"

His campaign manager smiled and shrugged.

"All right," Santiago said when he had everyone's attention. "You've all heard the news. I don't need to tell you that if it's what it seems, our friend Arévalo has just burned his bridges for a few moments of glory. That it's an effective gesture in the short run you can see for yourselves. But nobody likes to remember that the *gringos* have a string around our balls. We're confident that as soon as they jerk it a couple of times Arévalo will be pissing Coca-Cola. Our job is to stay out of the way and see that Gutiérrez takes the blame for whatever pressures the U.S. brings to bear."

There were a few snickers and some rueful head nodding.

"By the time the smoke clears," Santiago continued, "those Jurassics in the Palacio Nacional are going to think Arévalo was working for us all along. It's up to us to stay loose and play as a team. Silence and cunning. We'll leave the exile part to our former colleague. Questions?"

From the square below a chant rose up, faltered, and died away in confusion.

"Should we be contacting Arévalo privately?" someone wanted to know.

"Good question. I'd like to hear your thoughts."

Although thoughts hardly seemed to be in short supply, none were spoken.

"Okay, I understand your reticence. Let me assure you that I'm sensitive to the risks presented by my personal association with Luis. So for now, the answer is no."

Interrupting his boss, Carlos leaned forward and spoke a few words into his ear. Santiago winced but didn't miss a beat.

"Some of you may have heard a rumor about my impetuous sister Felicia. As far as I know there's no truth to it. And if the time does come for us to approach Arévalo in private, she would not be my first choice."

The staff allowed themselves a little nervous laughter followed by light applause. In the Zócalo the crowd had taken up the chant for *tierra y libertad*. Whatever Zapata's old chestnut now lacked in pertinence, Santiago reflected, it more than made up for in heart.

"What's our official position on the *maquilas*?" asked the young woman whom Santiago was grooming for finance minister.

"We support the sentiment but prefer a more complete solution. No need to get specific. By next week the stock market will be in free fall and even the *Maoistas* will want everything back the way it was." He looked thoughtfully at the fresh young faces of these people who believed he should be president. A surge of confidence passed through him, and he found himself thinking of Trotsky, who had lived out his years of exile not five kilometers from this very spot.

"To paraphrase the old man of Coyoacán," Santiago concluded, "everyone has a right to be stupid on occasion, but Comrade Arévalo abuses it."

FROM a corner banquette, Andrew and Edith watched Kevin march the perimeter of the cocktail lounge, pausing every few steps to speak to the neo-Aztec monsters woven into the carpet's figure. It was five o'clock, just past lunch local time, and except for a table of elegantly groomed businessmen, they had the place to themselves.

"What if you just call her and explain?" Edith asked. "Tell her you'll bring him over next weekend instead."

"You don't know Susannah. Lawyers give her delusions of grandeur. Which, I will spare you the trouble of pointing out, is why she married me."

Neither of them had mentioned the events of the night before. A lurid bruise had appeared over his left cheekbone, and, looking at it while shaving that morning, he had been oddly fascinated. It was as if he hadn't seen his own face in years.

Andrew finished his tequila. "All I'm saying is that if I don't have Kevin on her doorstep day after tomorrow, I'd better get my story straight."

He was watching the entrance to the lounge in disgruntlement when the fire door nearby opened and James sat down next to him.

"Sorry we're late," he whispered. "Had to pick up something at Garibaldi."

Marisa, who had slipped in beside Edith, suppressed a giggle. "He's so bad," she told her.

"See that guy talking to the two German dealers?" James asked, pointing to the other occupied table. "That's the director of the Centro Cultural Arte Contemporaneo. I met with him last night to try to put together a show of my artists, and he was, shall we say, underly receptive. That fuck, I knew him when he thought art was somebody's first name. Now he's an *internacionalista.*"

The man was addressing his table companions in an English whose arch inflection did in fact suggest that he held himself in good opinion. Mexico City, he confided to them, had attained a level of sophistication that would soon leave Köln and Berlin blushing. He signaled the waiter for more champagne.

Marisa had trouble containing her mirth. "If only Jojo were here."

"Who's Jojo?" asked Edith, warming to the mood.

"This was sheer inspiration, an idea so fine I'm almost ashamed to claim it as my own." James looked to see if Andrew was suitably respectful. "Hey, what doorjamb did you walk into?"

Before Andrew could answer, the doors to the cocktail lounge swung open, and in walked five *mariachis* in full *charro* regalia: sombreros, mustaches, black suits with silver buttons running up the seams. Carrying their instruments tucked formally under their arms, they seemed to bear the weight of a serious and mildly tragic duty. Without ado they surrounded the table of the museum director and his friends.

"Excuse me? What exactly do you think you're doing? This is a cocktail lounge, not a drunken wedding." The man signaled vainly for the proprietor, who, along with the rest of the staff had discreetly absented himself. "No. Don't play. Please."

Violin and trumpet were raised, guitar, *guitarrón*, and *vihuela*, and at a nod from the trumpeter the band burst into a thunderous chorus of "Cielito Lindo."

"Hell of a job getting them here," James shouted over the din. "Three taxis, one for the hats."

His lip curled in an actual snarl, the unhappy internationalist at last managed to shove past the musicians and lead his bemused guests out of the lounge. The *mariachis*, who had been paid in advance, serenaded the empty table. They felt obliged to complete the song.

"A signature moment," Andrew told his friend. "I'd recognize your work anywhere." Edith and Marisa leaned against each other, weak with laughter.

"Thanks," said James modestly.

"Daddy, can they play at our table too?" Kevin had recently taken to standing with his feet planted firmly apart, hands on his hips like a tiny contestant. He seemed to expect an assault on his balance.

"I think once is enough, Pancho. Come say hello to your uncle James."

When the *mariachis* decamped and the management, who had also received James's consideration, saw fit to return, Andrew ordered drinks. Edith had perked up nicely and, after insisting that chairs be brought over for James and Marisa, she inspected her compatriots with dark glee.

"So. You've run us to earth."

"We thought you might need us," replied James, who was

showing Kevin how to work the balsa-wood jack-in-the-box he had brought him as a gift. It involved a gold-and-turquoise skeleton playing a harp.

"What James means," explained Marisa, "is that you have an opportunity here. As your friends, we can't let you pass it up."

"What opportunity?" said Andrew.

"I think we know what they're talking about," Edith told him. She put a hand over his and, addressing herself to Marisa, said, "What opportunity?"

"You have a chemistry going with the Díazes, some sort of involuntary connection that gives the four of you a, what shall I call it, a grace."

"A grace, definitely," agreed James.

"To talk about this is not so easy. Sometimes people come together accidentally in a way that seems to make a point. Maybe they're partly aware of it. That might even be a requirement, I don't know." Marisa twisted a cocktail napkin in her fingers as she spoke. "Anyway, when this happens, people around them notice. Maybe because they recognize needs of their own that it's usually inconvenient to think about. Or maybe they're just drawn to the spectacle. A kind of momentary transcendence, to put it that way."

"Marisa's a very spiritual person," James explained helpfully.

"I'm embarrassing him," Marisa continued, "but he, more than most, knows what I mean."

"So you want to photograph us and the Díazes in this edifying state." Andrew shrugged as if amiably perplexed. "That's it?"

"That's it," said Marisa.

"Are we still doing it at the border?" Edith wanted to know. "How are you going to work that?"

"Let me worry about the logistics. All I ask is that you put a word in for us with Santiago. The sooner the better."

"I don't know," said Andrew. "We're scheduled to leave tomorrow. Kevin's mother is expecting him, and lately she and I have been having philosophical differences. If you take my meaning."

Putting the folkloric harpist down on the table, Kevin struggled out of James's lap and took a few steps toward his father. "Daddy has a black eye," he told James seriously, pointing at it.

"Yeah, I was going to ask about that."

Marisa and James glanced reflexively at Edith, who had her best wicked-auntie smile waiting for them. "He says he slipped in the shower, but Kevin and I think the housekeeper did it."

Andrew waved for the check.

"So the housekeeper is a cookie, is she?" James said, plainly intrigued. "Do you like her, Kevin?"

The boy looked at Edith. "I don't know."

"Drop it, James," said Marisa. Turning back to Andrew, she assumed the briskly reverential manner of a rogue graduate student. "What can I do to convince you?"

Andrew affected concentration on the bill he had just been handed. "Hey, did you guys hear about Arévalo and the *maquiladoras*?"

"Yeah, very strange. We saw the demonstration at the Zócalo. I didn't peg Arévalo as a forgotten-masses kind of guy."

"I did," said Marisa.

"Quixotic, don't you think?"

"Maybe. We'll see."

Edith nuzzled Kevin, making him laugh. It was a pleasing sight, and, as the table fell silent to take it in, Andrew recalled the casual cruelty of his remarks to her the night before. His own professed indifference to grief had surprised him thoroughly. Still, he thought, that was primary process for you. It cut both ways.

"Okay, we'll hit up Santiago. Because we're sympathetic to the arts and on account of your being such an entertaining guy, James."

"And because you got the girl," James added.

They all looked at Edith, who appeared to think about it. She lifted Kevin into her arms and held him close. "That's right, Andrew," she said. "Because you got the girl."

———

THAT NIGHT the Díazes' house was more than usually animated. Carlos had decided to restructure the staff into individual task forces, and they had spread out everywhere with their cell phones and laptops, working up strategy and lists of talking points. Mercedes, who had abandoned all pretense of trying to maintain a private household, circulated from room to room with a sandwich platter. During Santiago's playing days, she had performed this role countless times, for the team, as the team captain's wife. Together they had been the bride and groom of victory. Winners. It was beginning to feel like that again.

At nine o'clock Santiago shut himself up in his study to tape a TV interview. Deciding that a cigarette smoked in peace might do her good, Mercedes headed for a small alcove off the north staircase. The space included a fountain and shallow turquoise pool above which Mercedes had hung a crucifix, crudely hewn in the *art brut* manner and bound with barbed wire. Because of the frequency with which Santiago's more convivial teammates would be found passed out there after parties, the place had acquired the colorful nickname of La Gruta Sagrada de los Olvidadizos. As it turned out, the grotto already had a supplicant this evening.

"Fifi! When did you get here?"

They embraced.

"I didn't want to be in the way in case the press was around. Is Santiago angry with me?"

"No, no. Don't worry. Everything's fine. Well, not fine exactly, but we think Arévalo has cooked himself."

"Let's talk about that." Felicia shook her hair free of the hooded black cape she favored on occasions of state or family crisis. "*¡Condenado!* This place makes me feel like a nun."

Mercedes lit her cigarette. In their shared love for Santiago, she and Felicia sometimes fell into a collusive irritability that seemed to comment on the grossness of everything else. "Is it true you were alone with Luis last night?" Mercedes asked.

"I arrived, he had to let me in. Luis is a man who cannot be given choices." Felicia looked sharply into her sister-in-law's eyes.

"Of course, he is very full of himself right now. We watched a movie together—¡*The Grapes of Wrath, si puedes creerlo!*—and we talked things over."

"I'm surprised he didn't ask you to vote for him."

Felicia gave a dainty little snort. "That, at least, he did not ask for."

"Fifi! You're joking." Mercedes stared at her, trying to imagine the scene. "Aren't you?"

But Felicia waved the question off. "Luis expects to win, and he wants to do it in the style of *un macho auténtico*. The crowds, the three-hour speeches, the songs of land and blood. And all the time he has Vendajes running the computers. Plus or minus three percentage points, he should do this, he should not do that. *El charro electrónico.*"

"Yes. Having it both ways is a thing Luis likes. What else did the great populist say?"

"He knows you brought the *gringa* and her husband down with you. He wonders what is Santiago's attachment to her."

Mercedes had the clear sense that in this question, at least, Felicia and Arévalo were united. "If it were what you are implying, Fifi, do you think I would have invited Edith and Andrew into our home? After all, it was my idea."

"But you have to admit that she seems to have a strong influence over our Santiago."

Bending down before the fountain, Mercedes scooped up a double handful of water and splashed her face. "I think of it as homeopathy, Fifi. Like cures like. For now it is best that Santiago and I keep Edith and Andrew near to us. We will all benefit."

"So you will be taking them with you to Juárez tonight?"

Mercedes stood, the water running down her face and neck in rivulets. "And why not, since they want to come?"

SANTIAGO'S decision to fly to Ciudad Juárez, where he could attack the border question head-on, had boosted everyone's morale. By upping the ante, Arévalo had handed him the opportunity to reprise his most famous role. When crisis loomed and just minds quailed, it was El Díaz once more into the breach. Never mind, thought Mercedes, that Santiago himself seemed bent lately on shaking off the hostage crisis and the falsifications that had ensued. She did not require him to be a hero, but, if others did, let the solemnities begin.

On her way back through the house to see if Santiago was done yet with his interview, Mercedes caught sight of Marisa de Borba, deep in conversation with the security man Oiticica. Instantly alert, she went over to say hello.

"Congratulations, Marisa. It looks as if you'll be getting your photographs after all."

"Thank you, Señora Díaz. I am honored." The perfume Marisa wore, languid and densely floral, clashed arrestingly with her urchin-model street chic. Oiticica put his arm around her.

"This one, Señora, allow me to tell you. She comes from one of Brazil's finest families. When I was a boy in Rio, before I came here, the de Borbas were like royalty to us."

Mercedes inspected him innocently. "But Juan, I didn't know you were Brazilian."

"And do you know who her father is? Gilberto de Borba, the great visionary. He is building a highway right through the jungle. A modern man, very progressive."

"People make too much of it," said Marisa.

Mercedes, who guessed that people made of it whatever Marisa's father wanted them to, studied her thoughtfully. "It's a pity. Society is very hard on those we suspect of being forward looking. Such people make us feel inadequate, and we question their motives. Do you find that happens to you a lot? As an artist?"

"Not really. Anyway, I don't think of myself as having motives. Ideally, I try to become the instrument of my subjects."

Nodding sympathetically, Mercedes turned to Oiticica. "You're right, Juan. She reminds me of royalty too."

He smiled uncertainly at his employer's wife and, as if recalling pressing business, excused himself.

"You understand, don't you, Marisa? We're on twenty-four-hour call here. Events are moving quickly. We need to anticipate, and we want to avoid distractions."

"Of course. I'll stay out of the way."

"Edith and Andrew are here because they are our friends; you and James, because you are their friends. It would be very troubling to Santiago and myself if, at the border, we had occasion to regret bringing you."

"Don't even think about it," said Marisa quickly. "Believe me, I understand."

Relaxing a little, Mercedes surveyed the room. Three groups of staffers were meeting simultaneously, talking over one another and juggling sheaves of green-and-white computer printout. Two televisions flashed in synchrony; a man shouted into a cell phone.

"Not very restful, is it?" Mercedes observed. "But it's our home."

What she had been longing for from Santiago, it seemed, was that he capture anew for them the animal grace of their marriage's early days. Anew because it couldn't be gone back to, or, if it could, she didn't want it. Successes, like pleasures, rejected mere repetition as inadequate, or at least imaginatively suspect. Santiago's standards for calculating victory were not less exacting than her own.

"Marisa," she said. "Excuse me, but I am curious to hear your dreams for yourself. Ours are so evident, you see."

Though she arched an eyebrow, Marisa didn't seem at all surprised by the question. "You think I don't have any, I bet."

Mercedes tried to protest, but Marisa waved her off. "No offense taken. I know that's the impression I give. Often it's what I think myself."

"It's just that you're still so young," Mercedes continued. "When I try to see all this through your eyes, I realize I have no right to assume you could understand."

In a gesture that startled Mercedes by its simplicity, Marisa took her hand. "People make such a big deal of youth these days. It wrecks the moral climate. Not that I'm one to talk."

Mercedes stared. "Why do you say that?"

"Oh, because I'm weird that way. I've never felt young. And my character's bad." She smiled as if she were repeating someone else's assessment. "But I have a good eye for a certain kind of person. Not so much the forward-looking ones we were talking about before. No, it's the people who put themselves on the line to find out what they want. They fascinate me. I admire them."

Santiago's voice could be heard in the hallway, expansive and jovial. His interview was over, and he was telling a joke that had something to do with rowboats in the desert.

"Perhaps," said Mercedes, "such people photograph well."

As they stood there hand in hand, gazing at each other like imperfectly reconciled schoolgirls, Mercedes had the sudden sense that she was being asked for forgiveness of some kind. She tried to imagine what it could be.

"When I was in France one time, a man told me something I've always remembered. He said that photography is where God went when religion let Him go." Marisa laughed. "Only in France, right?"

Touched, Mercedes squeezed her hand. "So is that your dream? Photography?"

"My alibi," Marisa corrected her. A trace of sadness seemed to pass over her face, but an instant later Mercedes wondered if she had imagined it. "I get the two mixed up."

THE SUN was just up, the desert chill already dissipated, when they pulled up beside the chain-link fencing that surrounded the *maquiladora*. Some distance away, the day-shift workers were arriving by the busload, in silence, pausing at the guard booth to be clocked in before they passed through the gate. Closer to the factory itself, uniformed men with automatic rifles stood about smoking and chatting in the pale, drought-blasted light.

"Can we get out?" asked Edith from the backseat. With the corner of a bandanna she wiped a silver trail of drool from Kevin's chin as he slept. Beside her, Marisa fooled with her light meter.

"Let's ease around back," James suggested.

Andrew let out the clutch, and they edged along the perimeter fence, broken concrete popping and crackling beneath the tires.

Since arriving in Juárez, Edith had found herself prey to a swarm of contradictory notions. She had not been back here since coming down to El Paso with Oliver Barnes, and now, pregnant with his child, she struggled to take efficient hold of her situation. The shooting of the Mexican boy had made her feel angry and stupid. Much of what she had done since, it seemed to her, had been at the service of erasing those feelings. But erasing them was not the way.

"There's our guy," said Andrew. "That must be the boss man he's talking to."

On the other side of the fence, fifty meters away, Santiago and Carlos stood conversing with a jackal-faced fellow in a battered straw cattleman hat. Even at this distance his all-weather grin marked him as a Texan. Oiticica and a half dozen of his men fidgeted beside their cars, looking on.

"Are we going on an airplane again?" asked Kevin. Waking, surveying his terrain, he reminded Edith of a prairie dog.

"Not right now," she answered. "This is a factory where they manufacture cloth. Or clothes maybe, I can't remember."

The factory was emitting a rapacious howl that made any comparison to airplanes seem like wishful thinking.

"I'm just going to take a look around," Marisa informed them. She hopped out of the car and walked away from it without closing the door.

Andrew watched her go until she disappeared around the corner of a concrete blockhouse, windowless and oil stained. "Hey, did you tell her to look out for the scorpions, James? I bet they really like it out here." He smiled affably at his friend in the seat beside him.

"Okay, okay. Don't get pissed, *amigo.*" James opened the door and got out. "All you got to do is ask."

Andrew gave him a cheery little wave, and James trotted off in the direction Marisa had gone.

"What are we doing?" Edith asked him as he backed the car up. "Wait! The door!" Holding Kevin tight with one arm, she lunged to close it.

"We're indulging my protective instincts." He turned the car around and proceeded at a businesslike clip back along the fence to the main gate. "Kevin, once we get inside I want you to stay close to Edith and me. No wandering off. Okay?"

The billowing cloud of dust raised by the car had engaged the attention of the guards, but, just to be sure, Andrew drove through the gate and over the customary speed bump before coming to a halt. When the first of the uniformed men caught up with them, Andrew had their passports at the ready.

"*Buenos días, Capitán,*" he said in a tone suggesting manly zest for the day's prospects. "My family and I are with Señor Díaz. We took a wrong turn back there."

The rest of the guard detail, who appeared to be soldiers of the Mexican army, surrounded the car as if expecting orders to lift it on their shoulders and bear it away.

"You all got a fine-looking operation here. Everything squared up?"

Edith was about to ask what the military was doing guarding a U.S.-owned concern when, in the middle distance, she saw Marisa and James hotfoot it across the pavement, through a loading dock, and into the factory.

"*Está bien,*" said the officer, returning their passports and gesturing briskly toward Santiago's entourage. "*Por allá.*"

"Very impressive," Edith told Andrew as he parked. "Not that I have the least idea why you did it."

He laughed. "Me either. I must be practicing for something."

Whatever negotiations had been taking place between Carlos and the mongrel Texan had reached, if not an actual outcome, some acceptable mix of authority asserted and relinquished. Mercedes, who was speaking rapidly into Santiago's ear, caught sight of Andrew, Edith, and Kevin, and beckoned them forward with a quick double scoop of her hand. Without thinking about it, Edith lifted Kevin into her arms. Andrew was beside her, his cheek, where she had hit him, livid and exposed. Together they were walking into the mouth of noise.

On its two-hectare work floor the factory supported hundreds of machines, attended by a thousand people, brought there for the purpose of cutting, assembling, stitching, riveting, and folding indigo-dyed denim into dungarees. From the open-work second

story, a web of catwalks allowed access to the machinery and observation of the help, all of whom were women. Staring down at
them, Edith was assailed by the unhelpful urge to ask who looked
after their children.

"Do this!" Kevin instructed her amid the terrible din. He
clapped his hands on and off his ears as fast as he could. "Wah-
wah-wah-wahhhh."

Edith did as she was told, playing her head as if it were a trumpet from which issued the immense sound of clothing manufacture. The alliance she and Kevin had entered into, droll and a
little dark, encouraged tampering with the obvious whenever
possible.

"You know who makes that sound, Kevin?"

"Hell!" he shouted gleefully. "Hell does."

"No," she corrected him. "Hell with hiccups."

"Hey, you two. C'mon, shake ass." Andrew shepherded them
down a corrugated-steel walkway to a kind of mezzanine where
the rest of their party waited.

"No, sir," the Texan was saying to Santiago. "No way in fuck
am I gonna shut down for a goddamned speech. We're twenty-
four, seven, three-sixty-five here." He spat tobacco juice. "Shit,
mostly Indian anyway; don't half of them even speak Spanish."

Carlos had a hand on Santiago's shoulder and was talking into
his ear as if reciting some other conversation from some other
place.

"Did Santiago really plan to make a speech here?" Andrew
asked Mercedes. "What for?"

"No speech. We just want the local *caciques*, the ruling-party
functionaries, to get wind of us."

"Then what?"

Mercedes dodged a frantic barn swallow, one of several that
flew pointless loops around the factory. "*Con ayuda de Dios*, we
find out who our friends are."

Andrew was about to press the issue when Santiago, assuming

his most dashing bad-boy athlete manner, walked abruptly away from Carlos and the foreman, took Edith by the elbow, and steered her over. She had Kevin in her arms again.

"*Con permiso,*" Santiago said to Andrew, "I would like to borrow your *prometida* and son for a few minutes. They have graciously volunteered their services."

"Daddy, he's going to show us the machines!"

"Why don't we all go?" Mercedes started to say. But she bit her tongue.

"Are you sure it's safe?" Andrew asked.

"Perfectly," said Santiago. "You have my word."

"Please, Daddy!"

Andrew and Edith exchanged a long look. "Me, too," Edith told him. "I'm practicing for something, too."

Andrew nodded. "Okay. Don't get saddle-stitched."

Watching them set out down one of the catwalks, Andrew bit his thumb pensively. "How about those two? You think they know what they're doing?"

Mercedes turned her startling brown eyes on him. "You mean here, at the *maquila*?"

"No. In the larger sense."

"Of course," she said. "Don't you?"

When he neglected to reply, she looked politely away. "You and I are in the same boat, Andrew. We have to let them be."

TWO OF Oiticica's men, one in front and one behind, created a protective slipstream within which Santiago, Edith, and Kevin walked, oblivious to caution. Whatever resentments or suspicions Edith had entertained toward Santiago now fell away, exposed as senseless vanity, and she was seized at once by the memory of the open piano on whose strings she had laid her purse that first night. The instrument, with its expectant curves, its lid propped open over its taut insides, had been her friend and familiar, an odalisque like herself. She could hardly pretend surprise that her own postures of readiness and display had brought her to so troublesome a pass.

"Edie," said Kevin, indicating the factory workers with a sweep of his tiny arm, "why don't those ladies take a *rest!*"

"This is their job, Kevin. They're making blue jeans."

"But it's too *loud,*" he said. Mock angry, he shook a fist at them. "If you don't stop that!"

On the work floor below them, villagers from Oaxaca, Chiapas, Guerrero, women who had surrendered all citizenship except that conferred on them by the machines, labored without talking, a shadow population. They submitted enormous bolts of denim to the pitiless dentition of mechanisms that scissored out, in countless multiple, the twenty-one pieces of shrink-to-fit blue jeans. Other mechanisms sewed the pieces together beneath the women's darting fingers, and, as the conveyor belts looped endlessly past, thread waste continually threatened to foul the needles. It was impossible work. Watching it, Edith could not imagine how the women escaped injury.

"I'm very glad you came with us," Santiago told her. "After our conversation at Plaza de la Concepción, I was afraid you might not."

"Isn't this what we were headed for, right from the start?"

"It certainly seems so now."

She grimaced, aware suddenly that there was no time to waste. "The point is, we both have the fire in the belly now, as we say in *gringo* land. We both want to win. Let's not go into exactly what, but we know we want it. And we both happen to love people who appreciate our methods."

"God help them."

"Yes, God help them." Edith gave Kevin's hand a reflexive squeeze, but he was absorbed in the spectacle of capitalism. "You remember what we talked about the morning you returned my purse?"

"You told me I preferred being a soccer star to running for office."

"Did I? Well, that was then."

"We talked about bravery," said Santiago.

"Bingo."

They had come to a place where the factory opened out and the catwalk ended in a steel staircase leading to the floor. Seventy meters distant, sliding doors were drawn back on a view of the esplanade outside. A bright red semitrailer with mutant artichokes painted on its sides glided across the framed space. Against the violent white Chihuahua sky it seemed a charmed thing, unreal but outrageously physical. *The frame makes the picture*, Edith reminded herself.

"The gist of our little chat," she continued, "was that bravery lies in the eye of the beholder. It's circumstantial, therefore a shuck. You excepted Mercedes, which I think was very chivalrous of you but also, since she's not like us in this way, maybe a little dishonest?"

"Maybe so," Santiago admitted. "A false comparison."

"The whole thing was false. I mean, where do we get off, speaking philosophically? We're praxis-type people."

"Literalists, yes. As you said." Santiago cleared his throat. "Did Andrew tell me," he asked her, "that you have unhappy memories of the border?"

"I was here once with Oliver. On *el otro lado*. We were stopped by the Border Patrol for running a stop sign that didn't exist." She waved away her own words dismissively. "I don't know why, but I've always been fixated on that moronic pretext. Why a stop sign? Anyway, while this patrolman harassed us, a Mexican kid tried to climb the fence. The patrolman shot him, probably killed him. Afterwards, I wanted to get help, but Oliver wouldn't go for it. He didn't want to get involved."

Santiago sighed. "It's cruel. Some of the things we see never leave us."

"Squalid is what it was. I didn't know how easily a life could be reduced like that and tossed away. Vulgarized."

"Yes, and people aren't in a hurry to tell you about it, either."

A cattle truck carrying soldiers crossed the esplanade outside. Edith glanced nervously over her shoulder, but there was no sign of Andrew and Mercedes. Santiago's attention fell on Kevin.

"So, *compañero*. What do you think of Mexico?"

Shaking himself loose of Edith's grip, Kevin assumed his feet-apart stance and inspected his inquisitor warily. "Are you really going to be the president?"

"Maybe. We'll see."

Kevin received this answer with a dissatisfaction bordering on suspicion. "The president is boss of everything," he pointed out.

"People think that," Santiago agreed. "But it's not strictly true."

"When I am at my house, sometimes my daddy lets me play boss of the *skeletons*, and we fight a giant war. If you get to be president you could come over and be on our side. Then we could fight a lot of battles and rescue people and come back here and *blow this place up!*"

Santiago and Edith exchanged a look.

"Why would we want to do that?" Santiago asked.

"*Because*," said Kevin, pointing to the women at the machines, "then the mommies could be with the daddies again."

"*¡Precisamente!*" Santiago was delighted. "You've put your finger on it, Kevin." When Edith failed to respond, he explained. "The *maquiladoras* prefer to hire women because they are less likely to form unions. So, the men go to hell and the family suffers. We plan to fix that."

"That's probably harder than it sounds," she said soberly. Kevin's vision of returning mothers had sent her thoughts careening off toward Susannah. All at once Edith understood that getting Kevin back to his mother on time had now, without a word from Andrew, become her responsibility, hers and no one else's. How oddly apt it was, Edith reflected, how clearly in the cards.

"People want a better life," Santiago offered as he guided her and Kevin down the steel steps. "You see it at borders everywhere.

As soon as you put up a fence, you'll have people with reasons to climb it."

A commotion had broken out at the number six assembly line, where five women struggled to subdue a machine that, rather than folding the jeans fed to it by conveyor, was flinging them to the floor seriatim like a triumphant child. Right up next to this problem, becoming part of it, was Marisa. She and the section boss were fighting over one of her cameras, which they both had hold of, and Oiticica was trying to intervene on her behalf.

"Our photographer seems to be making quite a vivid impression," said Santiago, as he took Edith's arm. "Is she good at what she does?"

"Marisa? I think she is, yes."

"Good. Let's go help her out."

When they arrived on the scene, though, Oiticica had already prevailed and Marisa had her camera back. The jean-folding machinery continued amok while the workers stood away from it in attitudes of fatalistic disapproval. Edith observed that they were careful to keep their faces averted from Marisa.

"Sorry, Señor Díaz," said Marisa, who in fact looked anything but. "A misunderstanding."

Two meters away, the section boss barked into a telephone while James, the picture of reason in his cream linen suit and brown wing tips, discreetly pressed a folded U.S. bill into the man's palm.

"Don't be sorry," Santiago told Marisa. "We came here to get attention, and now we can be sure we have it."

A horn blasted, and the number six line came to a halt, incrementally diminishing the din that encased the factory. Close by, a song alleging fealty to brown sugar emanated from someone's tortured transistor.

"*¡Cuidado, Señor, cuidado!*" Santiago's bodyguards threw themselves in front of him as a forklift came wheeling down the aisle at full speed. Perched on one blade of the lift like an avenging angel was the Texan.

"Goddamnit to hell," he said, hopping off in front of them. "Are you dirtbags on drugs?"

"Five minutes," said the section boss over his shoulder. While he probed the machinery's rebellious innards with a wrench, Edith edged over to James.

"Are you out of your mind, giving that guy money?"

He shrugged sheepishly. "I just thought a little grease might help the situation."

"Get straight, will you! You were supposed to keep her *out* of trouble, not pick up the tab. Why do you think Andrew sent you after her in the first place?"

At the mention of his father's name, Kevin began to cry. Picking him up, Edith sympathized thoroughly.

"Actually," said James, "I think Santiago kind of digs it. Look at him."

It was true. Leaving Oiticica to handle the Texan, Santiago was chatting up the women on the stalled assembly line. They listened politely, their dark eyes aglitter with highland caution, but when Santiago mimed rocking a baby in his arms, they tittered and pushed one of their number forward for his inspection. She had an infant strapped to her chest, under her work smock, and Santiago admired it. After a few more words with the mother, Santiago beckoned Marisa to come over and take a picture.

"Hey, you can't do that here!" The Texan made a lunge for her, but Oiticica interposed his considerable bulk, throwing him off balance and nearly to the floor.

"Why, you ignorant dog-butt," said the Texan to Oiticica. "Don't you know this whole fandango is U.S. owned and U.S. run, and it's got a U.S. boss, and I'm him?" He turned to Edith in weary frustration. "God*damn* but sometimes I'd swear being Mexican is a social disease."

"Probably you're just assimilating," she told him helpfully. "Why not go with it?"

James leaned close. "Don't look now, *chiquita*, but I think we're about to get our ticket punched."

A barrel-chested Mexican in a guayabera strode jauntily their way, an expression of boundless goodwill illuminating his puggish features. Mercedes, Andrew, and Carlos followed unhappily in his wake, like reluctant conscripts in a show of amateur entertainment.

To her confusion, Edith thought she saw the man exchange a fractional nod with Oiticica, an acknowledgment of some kind, but an instant later she wasn't sure she had seen it at all.

"Señor Díaz. On behalf of the workers of this plant, please allow me to welcome you to Juárez. I am López Hidalgo."

Accepting the hand extended him, Santiago glowed with false cordiality. "*¡Maravilloso!* Who says Gutiérrez has lost his marbles? This, Carlos, is what I call local party structure."

Carlos shrugged. "They've been in power for seventy years. What do you expect?"

"It is a pity, Señor Díaz, because *personalmente* I would like nothing better than to spend time in your company. The final ten minutes of the Mexico-Argentina match . . ." López Hidalgo rolled his eyes heavenward in wordless reverence. "Who can forget your performance? But unfortunately, because of Luis Arévalo, I must ask you and your staff to leave."

"Because of Luis?" repeated Santiago. "What are you talking about?"

"I cannot guarantee your safety here. Even now, outside . . ." Feathering his hands vaguely in the direction of the esplanade, López Hidalgo seemed to suggest matters so inconvenient as to be already passing from his recollection.

About one hundred thirty citizens from the shantytowns of southeast Juárez had gathered just beyond the perimeter fence, where they were hurling abuse and the odd soft-drink bottle at the startled troops standing guard within. Draped over one of the buses that had apparently brought them was a banner impressively emblazoned with the likenesses of Emiliano Zapata and Luis Arévalo, rendered *muralismo* style, and the reflection *"Dejar de Luchar es Dejarse Morir."* To stop struggling is to let oneself die.

The sentiment occasioned in Edith a neck-prickling moment of *solidaridad*. Fatuous though such fellow feeling might be in a *privilegiada* like herself, she was quite unable to let it go. She caught Andrew's eye, and for a moment she could have sworn he knew what she was thinking.

"This is not exactly a media consultant's dream, is it?" said James to no one in particular.

"How's that?" asked Andrew.

Oiticica and his men clearly felt they should be calling the shots now, as they took up a modified nickel defense on the sun-beaten esplanade in front of their charges. Ignoring these deployments, Mercedes and Santiago carried on a hushed conversation that verged on argument.

"Well," James elaborated, "over there you have your basic disenfranchised *paisanos* with God on their side, and here we are with the soldiers and neocolonialist stooges. How good does that look?"

"God, James. You make me so mad." Marisa slipped a fresh plate into her 4-by-5 Deardorff view camera, which she had discreetly retrieved from the trunk of their car. In her other hand she held a tripod. "Come on, guys. I want you over there by the other principals."

Kevin, with a child's eerie sense for the cadences of adult conversation, abruptly ceased whimpering. "Why are those men shouting?" he asked in a bell-clear voice. "Are the soldiers going to shoot them?"

Andrew and Edith stared at him as if they had just been addressed by a sphinx.

"Forget about the camera," Marisa counseled them. "Just get up close to the Díazes and be yourselves. Edie, are you with me?"

"I haven't decided," Edith answered, though at that very instant Santiago looked up from his conversation and caught her eye. He seemed pleased but puzzled to find her there. "Come on," she said to Andrew, taking his hand.

The confrontation between the soldiers and demonstrators was undergoing a subtle change in character as both parties realized that, barring some reckless, self-destructive gesture on the part of the aggrieved, the range of possible outcomes would quickly dwindle to anticlimax. The bottles had been exhausted, and with no other projectiles ready to hand, the crowd seemed momentarily to falter while it reviewed its options. Some of the younger men were tying orange-and-black bandannas across their faces.

"James had a point, didn't he?" Edith said.

"It's a no-winner for Santiago," agreed Andrew, bending down to tie Kevin's shoes. "He can't afford to lose his business support either."

To leave, it would be necessary to pass through the same gate they had used on the way in, a prospect manifestly distasteful to Oiticica, since it put them on a service road that ran right by the demonstrators. Edith had the impression, watching him, that he felt unfairly put upon, as if someone should have told him he was going to have a bad day. Of course, a little countertransference was probably just what you wanted in a security guard.

Her exchange with Santiago concluded, Mercedes turned to Edith, Andrew, and Kevin with a smile whose radiance momentarily confused them. "You see? We often have to improvise in Mexico because events are so . . . fluid."

"Sexier," Santiago corrected her. He appeared to be in the grip of some private amusement that caused his eyebrows to twitch roguishly.

With a flourish, Mercedes scooped Kevin up in her bangled arms. "What about you, darling? Are you having a good time?"

"I think so." He threw Edith a look of shy concern, for which she was at once sharply grateful. "Yeah. It's exciting."

"Excellent," said Santiago, coming around to drape his arms lightly over Edith and Andrew's shoulders from behind, team-captain style. "Because we were thinking we might all go down there to have a word with those *caballeros* at the fence. That is, if your father approves."

Marisa, who had set her camera up right in front of them, was shooting away. With each exposure, she pulled the plate and exchanged it for a fresh one fed to her by James.

"I don't know, Santiago. I—" But with the steady-state sun beating down on them like God, Andrew knew himself to be inextricably part of this accidental coalition: six people stubbornly complicit in their own exposure as soft and unprotected things, having only their wills to work with. It was what he and Edith had come for, in a sense, and he wanted his son to be part of it. The desert light compelled it.

"Kevin, you hang tight with Mercedes," he said. "Edie and I will be right beside you."

Hissing at James to follow her, Marisa snatched up her camera, tripod and all, and hurried ahead to reposition.

"Oh, and let's not bother Oiticica and the gang with this," Mercedes added. "They're awfully busy."

The demonstrators quickly regained their collective voice at the sight of Santiago and his retinue headed their way—something pithy about *el pueblo unido* that a moment later acquired a taunting counterpoint. At the front and center of the crowd, a gangly youth in an AC/DC tee shirt was working away on the fence with an outsized set of wire cutters. Cutting from the ground up, one link at a time, he had opened a diagonal tear to about shoulder height.

"Am I hearing what I think I'm hearing?" Edith asked.

Andrew nodded and held her close. The taunt that the demonstrators had improvised into their cheer gave the words *consumo conspicuo* a particularly unpleasant gloss.

"Don't worry," Mercedes told them. "Santiago knows what he's doing." In her arms, Kevin surveyed the scene with an expression of sublime detachment, as if it confirmed expectations he had harbored for some time.

Two of Oiticica's men came loping alongside Santiago. Without breaking stride, he politely asked them to leave him the fuck alone. Sounds of military confusion, orders voiced and immediately contradicted, could be heard issuing from behind, but the demonstrators, who had succeeded in bending back the flap of fence that they had torn open, fell abruptly silent, startled both by what they had done and by what it might require of them next. A moment later, Santiago stood before them in the breach, Mercedes and Kevin on his right, Andrew and Edith on his left. A shelf of fine dust drifted past at knee level, quickly settling.

"Compatriots, I am Díaz. This is my wife, Mercedes, and three friends of ours from *el otro lado.*" He might have been addressing acquaintances at a christening or some other small community event. "We were inside inspecting the conditions. What can you tell us of this place?"

It was a puzzling situation by any standard, and for the space of two breaths no one spoke. Marisa had set up again. James held a light meter out, and when he whispered the reading to her she released the shutter without acknowledging him.

"Are you with us or not?" a voice called out. Immediately several others repeated the question approvingly.

"Certainly I am with you," replied Santiago. "You who spoke first, do you think if we seized the factories you would be better off?"

The crowd parted to produce a lean, rather mournful-looking young man who had a puckered, oyster-hued scar running from the corner of his mouth to his ear. He was one of those with an orange bandanna, which he wore loosely rolled around his neck. "We want only what is ours," he said. "The right to form a union, the right to protect ourselves and provide for our families. Arévalo has promised us those things."

"No, he has promised to seize the factories. Who will run them then?"

"We will, of course."

Santiago shook his head. "Even if it were possible, who would buy the jeans? You propose to sell to a population that lacks even basic necessities? And what about the cloth to make them with? Where do we get that?"

A murmur had risen among the demonstrators, but with a soft chop of his hand their spokesman silenced them. He let his eyes rest in turn on Mercedes and Kevin, Andrew, and, for a longish moment, on Edith. "There are those of us, Señor Díaz, who are disappointed that you refuse our cause. But it *is* our cause."

Santiago was just opening his mouth to speak when the first of the tear gas canisters clattered to the pavement beside him. That, of course, had been the reason for the bandannas.

Because the seven of them were positioned so close together, and because Oiticica had anticipated the army captain's orders, evacuation was a simple matter. Andrew had a moment of panic when he heard Kevin cry out for him, but Edith took hold of his hand and placed it firmly in Mercedes's free one. Santiago, holding a handkerchief to his face, personally conducted each of them—Edith, Andrew, Mercedes and Kevin, Marisa with her camera, James—to the car Oiticica had brought around, and was about to get in himself when he was stopped by a familiar figure with a bandaged arm.

"Ah, Vendajes. I see Luis has broadened your portfolio."

Vendajes, his eyes streaming, gave a perfunctory bow. "And I see that you've made the *yanqui chiflada* part of your staff."

The two men coughed together a bit. Santiago began to have an inkling of what might soon be required of a praxis-type person like himself. In any case, the circumstances did not encourage witticism.

"Luis is flying into Juárez as we speak. May I tell him you have agreed to meet with him?"

The soldiers had donned gas masks and were now engaged in beating senseless as many of the demonstrators as they could get their hands on. It was not yet ten o'clock.

ARRANGEMENTS had been made for Santiago and his crew to be put up at his campaign's Juárez headquarters, an incompletely restored Porfiriato mansion east of *el centro*. The place belonged to the friend of a friend, an entrepreneur who owned a string of boot-making concerns celebrated for their way with exotic skins.

"The sheriff's nephew just tried to sell me dope," said Andrew, who had been out to buy drinking water.

Edith was washing the chemicals out of Kevin's hair. "Very hospitable," she said over her shoulder. "Did he introduce himself that way or what?"

"No, the sheriff did. He'd been watching us from the corner and wanted me to appreciate his personal commitment to the war on drugs. Even though it is a fact of history that there is no drug problem, only *gringo* decadence."

"I feel safer already. What's going on downstairs?"

"Mercedes is listening to the radio to see if we made the news. Otherwise it's *siesta*." He watched Edith pull Kevin from the tub, an old-fashioned cast-iron affair with griffin feet. "Feel better, Kevin?"

"Sort of. It itches."

The gas had carried some sort of additive that had worked its way into their clothes, fouling them thoroughly. While Edith sponged down her own body, Andrew helped Kevin into a fresh shirt and jeans.

In the course of allowing the Mexican army to tear-gas his son, Andrew had been surprised by a memory of himself at very nearly Kevin's age. His mother had just returned home from giving birth to his sister, Sarah, whom he had been summoned into his parents' bedroom to meet. Maybe he had expressed some misgivings about siblinghood, because his father had then marched him over to the full-length mirror on the closet door and, standing there beside him, explained that, having grown so big, Andrew could now be counted on to help take care of the women.

It was a lesson he had thoroughly absorbed. Never mind that years later, with his father dead and his mother witless with brain cancer, the promise had proven impossible to keep. The look of concern he had seen Kevin direct at Edith outside the *maquila* had made his own childhood suddenly so palpable to him that he felt absurdly large, buffoonish. How delicate, he thought, were the understandings that shaped a life.

Seeing that Kevin was about to fall asleep on his feet, Andrew carried him to the cot pushed up against one wall of the little room.

"Yes, James. I know," said a voice. "All I meant is I didn't appreciate your pointing it out."

Startled, Andrew looked up to find Edith lurking beside the partly open window, a hinged square of cracked stained glass in amber and green. She put a finger over her lips and did a quick eyes-right to indicate the source of the voices.

"I was worried, for Christ's sake. Your brother I can understand being nonchalant about it; he doesn't have his nose stuck up *in* the situation the way we do."

"Leave my brother out of it, please."

Their voices sounded quite close. Andrew pointed at the wall questioningly, but Edith shook her head and mouthed the word "outside."

"Why is it I get the feeling that he'd be a whole lot happier if I came with an expiration date—something clean like cancer or impending bankruptcy?"

"You are such a paranoid. Jojo knows you are my dealer. He loves you."

"Thanks, Marisa. That was very reassuring."

Her laugh had an agreeable splash to it, good to hear. "Could be worse, right, Mr. James?"

They were moving off.

"Sure," said James. "*You* could love me."

Edith waited until their voices could no longer be heard, then closed the window. "I didn't know Marisa had a brother," she said. "Did you?"

"First I've heard of it."

Tossing the sponge aside, Edith took the dress she had laid out for herself, a jade green number cut to midthigh, and threw it on over her bare skin. While Andrew did the buttons, she watched Kevin sleep.

"He's a good boy," she said, running a hand over his curls.

"Damn straight. He keeps his own counsel, and he's concerned about his fellow man. One of these days he'll astonish the world."

Touched, Edith turned to face Andrew. "You're a believer, aren't you? You believe things work out."

"Sometimes they do work out. I try to use my modest influence to nudge them in that direction."

"But what about when they don't?" she asked. "What then? Cut and run, make the best of it, take up tai chi? Tell me."

"Oh, come on, Edie. You know the answer to that one as well as I do."

"No, I don't. Seriously, I need help in this area."

For the space of a heartbeat, she thought he was going to try to laugh it off. She almost hoped he would.

"Well, I guess I think disappointment is as negotiable as anything else. You pay what you think is a fair price for the experience, everything you can afford usually, and then you move on."

"I see. And that's how you think of your marriage to Susannah?"

He eyed her thoughtfully. "Regret isn't an option, if that's what you mean."

"No, I suppose not." The sense she had had at the *maquila* that Andrew was privy to her thoughts returned now with a force that rattled her. "Would it please you, sir, to see a little of Juárez with me? Maybe take a drive?"

"Certainly."

"Just the two of us, if that's all right."

"Well, okay." He checked his watch. "I don't know what's up for this afternoon, but maybe Mercedes could be persuaded to take Kevin for a couple of hours. Now that they've been to war together."

While Andrew saw to the baby-sitting, Edith took herself downstairs, lingering over the incongruous detailing of the entry hall. Dark wood panels, sinuous Art Deco panes of cracked stained glass, an ironwork balustrade broken in several places: the building's aspirations were grossly European. As if to apologize for such folly, both barrels of a shotgun had been discharged against one wall, tearing away much of the imported wood and badly scarring the rest. Mexico was a part of the world, Edith reflected, where the impulsive gesture was well understood.

Outside she found James seated on a tiled bench in the building's shallow shade. His panama hat made him seem to be part of the same misapprehension as the room she had just left.

"Enjoying the excitement?" she asked.

"Not as much as you," he answered sourly.

She shook her head, refusing the bait. "What's the matter? Trouble with your lady friend?"

"Someday I'll tell you all about it. When are you guys thinking of leaving?"

"I don't know. Andrew's supposed to have Kevin back to Susannah sometime tomorrow. What about you?"

"Marisa wants more pictures. We're going out in a little while to scout locations." He gave these last words a sibilant lilt, as if mimicking Marisa's inflections might make the prospect more alluring. "Because we are people who belong together without knowing why," he pronounced, widening his eyes imperiously at Edith. She was amused.

"That girl has you all figured out," she told him, patting his knee. "Whoops. Here's my ride."

She hurried over to the car Andrew had just brought around.

"Hey, where you going?"

She waved without answering and ducked in on the passenger side. Andrew peered at her curiously through his dark glasses.

"Everything *tranquilo*?" she asked him.

"Yeah," he said, easing into gear. "Everything is."

It was just past midday, and the desolating sunlight had driven pedestrians from the narrow sidewalks and robbed the visible world of depth. Andrew took them west on Triunfo de la República, a six-lane *paseo* lined with bridal shops, dental clinics, and haircutting establishments—the three signal industries of Hispanophone impoverishment. As they approached *el centro*, Edith was reminded that in Juárez legal services constituted a special-case fourth, and local attorneys took the refreshingly straightforward approach of billing not by the hour but by the crime.

"How much time have we got?" she asked, inclining her face over the air-conditioning vent. She had found it worked best fully cranked with the windows open, an arrangement that struck her as somehow appropriate.

"A couple of hours. Mercedes gave me the address of a social club or something where they're meeting Arévalo. We'll hook up with them there."

"What do you make of it? I thought Arévalo's campaign was supposed to self-destruct about now."

"Maybe it already has. We're too close to tell and we're not all that well informed."

She bit her thumb. "It looked to me as if Arévalo has done some pretty decent organizing. With the right people, if that makes a difference. Are you going to say Santiago can afford to ignore that?"

"Afford to, yes. But we'll see."

The traffic on the main drags was heavy. Local taste and circumstance favored vintage American sedans, the larger the better, and custom dictated that they be driven bumper to bumper at bracing speeds. With a little concentration, Andrew found he was good at it.

"I was thinking," said Edith, "that we're going to have to get serious soon."

"Hey, I'm for that." He kept his eyes on the road.

"I mean, I have to get back to work. Don't you?"

"You bet. If I don't get state probate law rewritten by sundown, my assistant tells me, I'll have the extinction of the golden monkey and who knows what else on my conscience. Death of the ecosystem and such. Bad stuff."

Edith was taken aback. It was not the sort of reply she had expected. "The guy in Brazil. Yes, I remember."

A bus had stalled in the intersection ahead, and Andrew turned left onto a lesser street, where a row of rickety vegetable stands, attended by old women and boys, marked the outer fringes of the *mercado*.

"He told you his life was in danger," Edith prompted him when Andrew failed to continue. "Did you call him?"

"Not yet. I've got a phone appointment with him later this afternoon." He slowed the car, looking over the bins of chiles, beans, *napoles*. Unshucked corn spilled from a stall onto the sidewalk and street. "How do you mean, serious?"

"Tell me about your mother," she said after a moment. "How'd she die?"

"Brain cancer."

"Was it pretty bad?"

"Yeah, it was." He sighed. "The old man was long gone already, and she was living alone. The doctors misdiagnosed it at first, but it wouldn't have made any difference. The way it was positioned, the shape of the thing."

He made a right.

"It took her forever to die. She had friends, but friends sort out unpredictably around real illness. My sister lived nearby, so she was there a lot, and I went down when I could. But it was excruciating, like watching someone get run over by a steamroller."

Edith looked at him in surprise, wondering if he had spoken more bitterly than he had intended. "Were you there when she died?"

"Not technically. But that kind of death is relative, really. We set her up in a hospital bed in her living room. She was funny about it in a terrible way, but the air was thick with uninvited truths, let me tell you." He laughed. "Want a sample?"

She reached over and ran two fingers over his lips until he kissed them. "Yes."

"Mornings began early, four-thirty or five if I was visiting. She'd press a buzzer and I'd come down to kick things off. Carry her to the toilet, wait till she was done, wipe her, get her washed and dressed. Then I'd put her in a wheelchair and park her in the dining room while I made breakfast. Still half asleep, as you can imagine."

Andrew was driving by reflex now, taking them through streets so belabored by light that they shimmered with imaginary puddles.

"This one time, long before the end, I put her breakfast on the table and—she had dropped her fork so I was squatting in front of her, looking right into her eyes—and she said, 'You know, don't you, Andrew, that I'd much rather this were happening to you than to me.' "

"Good Lord," said Edith.

"Yeah, old Mom had a gift for the fascinatingly extra. And as an attorney who has dealings with the death industry, I've given that one quite a bit of thought."

"She was frightened, Andrew. She didn't know what she was saying."

Andrew nodded. "The fear was impressive, definitely. Over into the area of religion. What I think is she had a moment of clarity there in the dining room, and she wanted to communicate it. She was always very big on communicating. After a while I stopped taking it personally."

Stunned to silence, Edith felt the side of her body closer to him flare up in goose bumps. It was easy enough to picture—the shadowed dining room, the dying mother desperate to lay claim to her firstborn's attention, the son himself desperate to find excuses for her annihilating confidences.

"I'm so sorry, Andrew," she said.

"Thanks." He smiled. "Anyway, I got over it."

They had arrived by default at a shadeless *plazoleta* bordered on three sides by quiet commercial streets with arcaded sidewalks. Loitering in the shelter of these arcades, small groups of men in jeans and sun-beaten straw cowboy hats watched impassively as Andrew drove by.

"Any of this look familiar?" he asked Edith.

"I think that might be the market building." She pointed across the square to a two-story concrete structure, open along its front, where tables had been set up to form a kind of café. A man with a guitar was serenading the only customers, an American couple who sat bickering over a tabletop crowded with empty beer bottles.

"Andrew, stop the car."

He pulled over to the curb. "What is it?"

Turning in her seat to face him, she struggled not to cry. "There is just no other way to do this," she said, reaching out to remove his sunglasses. She folded them carefully and put them with hers in the glove compartment.

"Look at me," she said.

He did.

"I'm pregnant, Andrew. It was an accident. That last time with Oliver, before you and I were lovers, before the banquet. It meant nothing, fucking him then, but I'm pregnant, and he's the father."

Andrew tried to speak; she put two fingers across his lips to hush him. "I've known for certain since Sunday before last. Oliver hasn't a clue. I haven't talked to him at all, and I don't want to. What matters is that you know." She took her hand away. "I've wanted to tell you, but I just didn't know how."

The engine was still running, and when Andrew turned it off the heat, light, and silence seemed to open up for them on all sides.

Her breathing was audible but not labored. He touched her cheek. "Well, you're not conspicuously pregnant yet, are you?"

She smiled and leaned the weight of her head into his palm. "Walk with me," he said.

They left the car in the care of a small boy wearing aviator shades and headed across the square. At the café, the American woman, alone now, tried to engage them in a compatriotic chat, but Edith made the gesture of *no hablo* and they passed around her table into the market.

It was a surprising space, graceful, even airy, with rows of plain concrete pillars running its length and breadth in a grid. Curved staircases on either side of the entry arcade led to a mezzanine overlooking the market stalls, and an unglazed clerestory made the roof, a dozen meters overhead, seem to float.

As they started up the stairs a boy with a shoeshine kit darted after them and pointed at Andrew's black loafers imploringly. When Andrew shook his head, the boy began daubing on polish anyway, catching the left foot every other step until resistance became pointless. They stopped on the landing to let him finish.

"The thing is," said Edith, pressing close to Andrew as people streamed past, "I want to keep the child."

He nodded. "But have you thought this through, Edie?"

"I thought we might do that together."

"Okay. What role do you see for Oliver Barnes?"

"Godfather, maybe? He should be accessible but underinformed. Like a UN press officer."

"You're not going to tell him he's the father."

"No." She put her arms around him. "There's no point."

"What do you tell the kid?"

"Adopted. Which has the advantage of being half-true. Later, when she's reached the age of reason, there'll be time to go into the niceties."

"Age of reason, that's a good one." He had to switch feet for the boy and steadied himself with a hand on Edith's waist. "And what makes you so sure it's a girl?"

"I just think it is, that's all." She released him and walked around the shoeshine boy, arms folded. "This is really bad, Andrew, isn't it?"

"Don't say that."

"Look, I'll understand if you want nothing more to do with me. I don't know what I'd do in your position."

"But you are in my position," he said, realizing it. "I've got Kevin. We're each bringing along someone we can't leave behind."

She stared at him. "You mean you'd do this with me?"

"Only with you. She'll be Kevin's sister. After all, they're not born asking questions, are they? After that, we can play it by ear."

The boy popped his rag one last time over Andrew's shoes and told him *cinco*, which Andrew tried to render in pesos. The coins lay there on the boy's palm like a litter of stillborn mice until Andrew relented and gave him five dollars U.S.

"You understand, don't you?" Edith said as they walked along the mezzanine. "After what happened last time I was here, I just couldn't have an abortion."

"No need," he said. "We can do this."

As the time of *comida* and *siesta* approached, there was a spasm of activity on the market floor below. Women hurried through the aisles with their lurid plaid shopping sacks, children sold tortillas, old men stood up from rickety chairs and yawned.

"You know what I've been thinking, Edie? Ever since we started this road show?"

"Tell me."

"Sometimes more is the only game in town." He looked pensively at her and smiled. "I'm not talking about self-indulgence here, even though we both could do that one in our sleep."

"Not me," she said. "And not you, either."

"All right." He seemed to be amused.

"But I know what you mean, Andrew. Believe me."

"We're reasonable people," he told her. "It's just that in our particular circumstances reason gets us only partway there."

Across the market, descending the stairs, a group of teenage girls sang the chorus to "Hotel California" before dissolving in laughter. One of them waved.

Edith led Andrew to a bench overlooking the activity below, and they both sat down.

"Do you really want to be a father to this child?" she asked him. "All the stepfather's laments—you'd have a right to them."

"No. I'm certain."

A man with a sheaf of pink, purple, and green umbrellas strapped to his back handed one to Edith. *"Para el sol,"* he told them. Andrew gave him three dollars.

"So what do you want to do, Edie?"

She laid the furled umbrella on the floor. "Pick up where we left off?"

Rising from the bench then, Edith walked the few steps to the rail and surveyed the doings on the market floor. She leaned out over the railing, balancing precariously, as though she were looking for someone on the market floor below.

"We're lucky in what we know," she said over her shoulder.

Her posture, bent over at the waist so that her upper body was parallel to the floor, had caused the hem of her dress to ride partway up her naked buttocks—a jade green curtain rising on a beloved drama.

"And also in what we don't, probably," Andrew added.

When she turned around, Edith held a twist of fabric in her fist, pressed to her stomach, and her skirt in front was bunched above her navel. With her free hand, she reached behind to be sure her dress covered her in back. "I've never loved anyone like this. The way I do you, Andrew. It's a shock to the heart."

"The heart has its reasons." He looked quickly to either side and discreetly undid his belt. "Mine, too."

Her eyes fixed on his, Edith drew the first two fingers of her free hand up between her legs, through her cunt, and her gaze grew hazy for the length of a breath. "I think I know now why we like this," she said when her head cleared.

"Really? Don't tell me."

"Why not?"

He had unbuttoned his pants and was lowering the zipper when two women neither he nor Edith had seen approaching passed arm in arm between them, leaving a smear of whispered Spanish and printed-fabric colors in their wake.

"Why not?" repeated Edith, sincerely puzzled. Her fingers, glistening and pale, asked another question.

"Because if we're some kind of aberration, I don't want to know about it," he said.

"But we're not. What everybody else feels, we feel too."

"Then come over here, Edie. Now would be a good time."

"Show me," she said.

Andrew lifted his hips and slid his pants down to the tops of his thighs. His cock sprang free of his underwear, and for a moment, as it thrashed back and forth in the air of the Mercado Juárez, the full comedy and sorrow of love rose up to do their bidding like the genie from the lamp in an animated cartoon.

Edith walked over, put her hands on his shoulders, and lowered herself onto him.

"I really, really open up for you, Andrew," she said.

They fucked slowly, sitting upright on the backless bench. What they by degrees relinquished to each other, with each slight rise of Edith on him, with each descent, they seemed also to be giving up to the ordinary life of the market. Far from growing oblivious to their surroundings, they found themselves increasingly attuned to the building and the lives it momentarily contained.

Voices floated up to them with bewitching clarity: an elderly woman calling for her grandson to help fold up her display table, two men trying to persuade a third to join them at the dog track, one woman remonstrating loudly with another over her refusal to extend credit, someone repeatedly calling out the name Ignacio.

"Edie, look at me."

She paused in her movements and drew back just enough to meet his eyes, her features hazed with sensation.

"Now tell me," Andrew said, trying to catch his breath, "what you were going to tell me. Before."

She slipped one strap of her dress off her shoulder. "I just want you to be complete," she said.

As he kissed her, she lowered her dress's bodice on one side, baring a breast, then drew his hand to it.

"But why we like this," he said at last. "You said you knew."

"Oh, Andrew. Because grief is not an alibi. It's not." She clasped him tightly to her. "Fuck me more."

It was as she had said, the night of Santiago's banquet: they would never be done with each other.

In Andrew's mind, even though his eyes were open, a thin red ribbon began to unspool itself. He followed it mentally as it snaked along the mezzanine's walkway, back the way they had come. Slipping down the staircase, the ribbon wove itself festively through the legs of the shoeshine boy and out onto the floor of the market.

A man with a bullhorn was there, urging the citizens of Juárez to vote for Gutiérrez. The people he was addressing seemed to think this was an idea so obvious it hardly bore mentioning. *"Para seguridad total,"* the man insisted. But that was obvious too.

Edith whispered something in Andrew's ear, and when he whispered back she gave an involuntary lurch that caused him to slip out of her for a moment. Descending, she found him again immediately.

"See?" she said.

Andrew realized the ribbon could be any length he wanted, and he tracked it in his mind as it began to make loops around, and actually decorate, the people he could see below, over Edith's shoulder.

She bit through his shirt into the tendon at the base of his neck and held on.

When the girls who had earlier been singing started up the other staircase together, Andrew was hardly surprised to see the ribbon tie itself around them, a bright red zip that resolved itself into a bow. These girls had exactly the right idea. They walked the length of the mezzanine, egging one another on and dragging the whole ribbon, which had bound everybody present into a raucous, ribald whole, taut behind them.

Edith dug her nails into his back.

As the girls passed them by in single file, giggling and whispering, Andrew caught sight, across the mezzanine, of two men he had not till that moment noticed: one fat, one thin. They watched intently with expressions of sorrowful outrage on their faces.

Andrew was in the middle of realizing that nothing was beyond him in the teeth of love when the last of the girls tapped him on the shoulder and waved. Then she ran off after the others, the ribbon snapped, and he and Edith were lost to anything but each other.

"WHY NOT just two cars?" asked Mercedes.

She stood hand in hand with Kevin beside the gas pump, watching a boy ride off on a bicycle, the crankshaft of the third car lashed to his handlebars.

"Security," said Santiago over his shoulder. "Oiticica. Let it be."

The gas pump was hand-painted green and bore the words "*Magna Sin*" across its face. Super Unleaded.

"That lady over there has orange drinks," Kevin observed with affected indifference.

Since the events at the *maquila*, Mercedes had felt compelled to keep Kevin close beside her, an impulse frequently at odds with her other big concern right now, which was to keep her place in the decisions Santiago and Carlos were trying to make. Theoretically, they were all on their way to meet with Luis Arévalo.

The gas station, itself kind of theoretical, seemed to exist on both sides of, and possibly on, the white dirt road that had brought them here, hardly a kilometer from Texas. Worn-out cars were scattered across the lot, their parts laid out on oily tarps.

Under the only shade tree, a savaged cottonwood hung with broken Christmas ornaments, two boys smoked in silence, washing metal parts in gasoline.

"I wonder if she has grape drink, too," said Kevin of the soft-drink seller.

"Well, I guess we'd better find out, hadn't we?" Mercedes answered. She watched Carlos pace up and down in front of her husband, arms folded across his chest. Santiago appeared to be reciting his version of things, and Carlos was manifestly skeptical.

"When the soldiers fired gas at us," said Kevin, "and made our eyes cry, did they *hate* us?"

"No, they didn't hate us. They had to do what the captain told them to do."

"Did *he* hate us?"

"Everybody was confused, Kevin. Maybe the captain was just scared, like us."

Beneath the straw cowboy hat that someone had produced for him, Kevin's face darkened. "*I* wasn't scared," he reminded her.

The woman with the *refrescos* was set up under a simple *ramada* of saltbush branches and mesquite poles—a sunbreak that raised a prism of dark space from the bleached salt ground.

In the desert, Mercedes reflected, and in places like it, a certain moral authority accrued to those who had staked out a bit of shade. It made them seem smarter than oneself and hardier.

"*Dos Fantas uvas, por favor,*" she said.

They sat with their grisly purple drinks on a plank-and-cinder-block bench at one edge of the *ramada*. Seven meters off, Carlos had stopped pacing.

"How come," Kevin inquired, after a sizable slug from his bottle, "that our eyes can cry without the rest of us?"

"You mean like with the gas? That was just a physical reaction. You didn't feel sad, did you?"

"No."

"So you see. The gas irritated your eyes, and tears came out to soothe them. That's why they call it tear gas."

"Can it happen without gas?"

After a moment's thought, Mercedes gently removed the boy's hat so she could see his face. With his high forehead, full mouth, and prominent but delicately turned nostrils, he bore an almost indecent resemblance to his father. "The eyes are a window on the soul. Didn't anyone ever tell you that?"

"No," he answered solemnly.

"Well, it's true." She smoothed his damp red hair and kissed him lightly on the top of the head. "In Spanish we say *ojos*. Eyes."

"*Ojos*," he repeated.

"*Habes los ojos de tu padre.* That means you have your father's eyes."

A sly smile stole across his face. "No, I don't," he confided to her. "They're mine."

In the twenty-four hours since Luis had announced his promise to nationalize the *maquiladoras*, his candidacy and the persona attached to it had taken on a curiously double life. The media in the Americas, Germany, and Japan had seized at once on the story, making Arévalo's face and this point of his program instantly famous. He was variously portrayed as a populist, a revolutionary, a dangerous marginal, a Quixote, and a Mexican. From the quarters most concerned, however—governmental, financial, and commercial—there issued only a low-grade silence. Even the big guns on the Bolsa had made no move toward a sell-off, hoping, maybe, to stick it out one more day until the market closed for the weekend.

A dilapidated motorcycle carrying three men, a load of firewood, and what looked like a dead raccoon turned into the gas station. Lacking a muffler, the bike made an enormous racket as it headed for the gas pump, overshot it, and, apparently unable to stop, did a wobbly figure eight around the lot before finding its way onto the road again. There it accelerated and, a moment later, was gone.

Not till she saw Oiticica putting away his gun did Mercedes understand what had happened.

"We may not yet be regarded as the people's hope," she said when she stood before him in the shattering sun, "but is it necessary to threaten them with guns?"

She lowered Kevin, whom she had snatched up and carried from the *ramada* like a bedroll, to the ground. Somehow she had spilled grape soda down the side of her mouth and throat.

"*Perdón, Señora Díaz,*" said Oiticica with a slight bow, "but I must do my duty." He excused himself and set off purposefully toward a truck pulling in across the road.

"Ignore him," advised Santiago, arriving at her side. "He's a necessary unpleasantness."

"I can't help it. I dislike him."

Carlos looked pained.

"Our campaign manager shares your sentiments," Santiago replied. "But time is short. We need to sort our cards one last time."

"Allow me to deal them, then," said Carlos, addressing himself to Mercedes. "Face up we have Arévalo, Champion of the People. Perhaps he is a demagogue, perhaps not. Certainly he cuts an appealing figure: rough around the edges, romantic, dedicated to justice. Also, if I may say so, he is ugly, which helps."

Mercedes permitted herself a smile.

"Face up on our side we have Santiago, the Reluctant Crusader, a Cincinnatus. He has solid support and we know that his public votes. When we look at our hole cards, they are just as strong: powerful friends, an economic program, a gift for leadership. We assume his sense of justice, but if necessary we can draw to it."

"Does Gutiérrez have a hand in this game?" asked Mercedes.

"He's the bank," answered Santiago. "With the usual odds."

Kevin, who had finished his soda, held the bottle to his eye telescope-style. "You've got purple-mouth," he told Mercedes.

"So our problem is to guess Luis's hole card," she said to Carlos.

"Exactly. He's standing pat. He's satisfied with his hand."

Mercedes glanced at her husband, who shrugged and nodded slightly. She turned on Carlos.

"You mean Santiago? You think Luis is counting on Santiago to win it for him? How?"

"That's not so clear," Carlos admitted.

"Carlos has had second thoughts about my meeting with Luis. Maybe the practical consequences of saying he would nationalize the *maquilas* have not yet been driven home to him."

"Or maybe," ventured Carlos, "they don't matter."

While she thought about what these two men, one of them her husband, were trying to communicate to her, Mercedes watched Oiticica roust the driver from the truck across the way. At this distance, their mirror-lensed shades made them look like insects with faulty laser weapons for eyes. Painted on the back of the truck, though, in melodramatically inclined script, were the words *"Ave sin Rumbo,"* Bird Without Direction, presumably the driver's professional credo.

"Carlos, if you don't mind, I must speak to my husband alone." When Carlos was out of earshot, she turned to Santiago. "I hate that look on your face, like a guilty teenager. Tell me what's going on."

She saw her husband's eyes fill with her. He was choosing his words. Not a good sign.

"Mercedes, I'm done!" said Kevin, brandishing the soda bottle. "Where do I put this?"

"You can give it back to the lady," she answered quietly, letting him go. "But don't get lost."

"Alma mía," Santiago began. "I haven't forgotten my promises to you."

"I don't want to hear that now. What is going on?"

He grimaced. "Carlos feels it's not wise for me to go. He thinks it's a trap."

"What kind of trap?"

"Who knows? It's an intuition at best. Luis's confidence makes Carlos suspicious."

"Carlos is young," she answered softly. Saying it launched in her the unhelpful thought that she was as much Kevin's mother as Edith was. With a glance she ascertained that the boy was under the *ramada* with the *refrescos* woman, each of them speaking a language unintelligible to the other. "But of course," she added, "Luis's confidence has always been suspect."

Mercedes allowed herself to be drawn by Santiago into an aimless stroll across the white dirt.

"Meeting with Luis face to face," he said, "is the only way I can know for certain what he's got in mind. It's true I thought he'd be out of it by now, but Los Pinos is playing this one well. Gutiérrez has got his ducks, as the *gringos* say, very much in a line."

"Big ducks. The U.S. government, international finance."

"Exactly. The longer the ruling party can keep them from panicking, the more legitimate Luis looks. When our vote is sufficiently split, they crush us. Luis has got to open his eyes to this. I'll force him to."

They parted to avoid a puddle of brake fluid, shimmering with malignant greens and yellows.

"Santiago, are you leaving something out for my benefit?"

"No, of course not."

She looked at him quickly. "I'm afraid someone will try to hurt you."

"Oiticica assures me there is nothing to worry about."

"Oiticica!"

"You may not like him, but in his profession he is a rocket scientist, I promise you. And don't forget who my previous security man was."

They had come to where their crippled car stood, hood open, awaiting the return of the bicyclist. Mercedes leaned over to look at herself in the driver's-side mirror. "So you're going anyway."

"It was meant to be," Santiago answered. "And besides, I owe Luis an apology."

"For what?"

"He had a point about the *maquilas.*"

Straightening up, repositioning the combs in her hair, Mercedes took stock of the situation: herself, a woman with grape-soda stains on her face, standing in a derelict gas station with her husband, a man whose future at the moment depended on a crankshaft and a friendship, equally faulty, while a child belonging to neither of them helped an old woman sort bottles.

Mercedes put her sunglasses back on.

"You're right," she said. "It was meant to be."

THE UMBRELLA Andrew had bought for Edith cast a lilac haze over her as they made their way on foot up Avenida Juárez. The late-afternoon heat had cleared the streets, but wherever there was a bit of shade—in the doorways of the tourist discos, under the awnings of half-imaginary shops—sidewalk hustlers loitered, making snap judgments and offering services to match. Behind Edith and Andrew, very near in most senses, were the Franklin Mountains of Texas.

"I hope you realize what a venerable route we tread," said Andrew. He had bought a white straw Stetson outside the *mercado*, and it was giving Edith the giggles.

"The path of righteousness?" she suggested.

"No, the path of uncontrollable greed and conquest. This was part of the Camino Real, which ran from Chihuahua to Santa Fe. Don Juan de Oñate came through here in 1598, looking for gold. When he decided the natives were holding out on him, he killed them one by one, waiting for someone to give him the good word. As it turned out, there wasn't one. No gold and, soon, no natives."

"I'd say the man's methodology was flawed."

"True enough. But it was the implementation that made him famous."

They stopped at an open storefront for *helados*, melon and mint, served in paper cones. When Andrew showed the address Mercedes had given him to the girl behind the counter she giggled and whispered in the ear of her older sister.

"*Más adelante*," she told them, pointing vigorously in the direction they'd been going anyway.

"Maybe we should have brought the car," said Edith, when they were back on the street. "I mean, those girls definitely could not read." She twirled the umbrella on her shoulder as if she were a nineteenth-century lady out for a stroll, or a chorus girl recalling one.

The *zona turística*, whose offerings had been growing distinctly seedier the farther they got from the Río Bravo, petered out completely two blocks later. White dirt, nearly sand, began to obscure, then cover, the asphalt roadway, and as their route continued uphill into residential Juárez, Andrew and Edith failed to notice when the pavement itself fell away.

At first the houses they passed were small but normal-looking structures with roofs, glazed windows, sometimes a concrete porch or a screen of ornamental block work. Parked outside most of them were worn but pragmatically maintained American sedans from the golden age of gas consumption. All the houses had TV antennae; most were attended in orderly fashion by phone and electrical line. The effect, optimistically considered, was of a scrappy working-class community fallen on hard times.

"I remember now," said Andrew as they pressed on into the desert. "Mercedes described this to me. We're almost there."

As the road had segued without ado from asphalt to dirt, so the houses now by degrees became shanties, huts improvised out of corrugated steel, unmortared cinder block, flattened car bodies and tires, cardboard and plastic. Windows were voids, doors were unattached to their jambs, roofs were low and sometimes incomplete. The landscaping medium of choice appeared to be truck tires, whether painted in pastels and buried to their diameters in rows to form a kind of yard trim, or set unadorned into the sides of storm washes as steps.

Ahead, a dusty blue bus filled to capacity with men in cowboy hats and white tee shirts—all facing forward, none of them speaking—hesitated at the intersection. When it rumbled off again, the single passenger it had discharged removed his hat to look at the sky, then put it on again and set out down the road.

"I'm asking myself why this doesn't feel more depressing," said Edith.

"Strange, isn't it? These people are bone-poor, obviously, but as a neighborhood the place seems to function. There's a coherence."

"Or maybe it's just us. In our giddiness."

Andrew shook his head. "See those shade trees?"

Here and there a crippled-looking cottonwood, paloverde, or tamarisk struggled for life in the white dirt. One house constructed entirely of cinder block and wooden warehouse pallets had two traumatized Lombardy poplars flanking its entry.

"I don't call that shade," said Edith.

"Maybe not, but somebody planted them and somebody waters them. Those two are at least twenty years old. Some of the others are older."

Chastened, Edith took his arm. "You're saying these places aren't as temporary as they look."

"In desert terms, they're vintage housing stock."

At the next intersection they made a right onto what seemed to be the main drag, and even as he saw the two men behind them do likewise, Andrew realized they must have been following him and Edith from the outset. Two men: one fat, one thin.

"Anyone we know?" asked Edith, who'd seen him looking.

"Them? Nah." Tightening his grip on her arm, he consulted his watch. "But we'd better step it up a little. We don't want to be late."

"I thought we were almost there." She stopped to inspect him more closely, a glint of caution in her eye. "What is it?"

"Nothing. A touch of *turista.*"

"Do you want to stop somewhere?"

"No, I can wait," he said, steering her across the street. "There's got to be a toilet where we're going."

From the corner of his eye Andrew could see that their pursuers were content for the moment to remain on the other side of the street, though they, too, had quickened their pace and were now almost even with them.

"I wonder what happened to Marisa and James," said Edith.

"They'll get here. Marisa will see to it."

"Poor James, though. She's a heartless one."

"Maybe," he replied. They stepped over a rusted-out automobile muffler, still attached to its pipe. "But valentines are not the theme, I think. She wants her pictures, he wants to sell them. A heart might be a drawback."

Despite himself, Andrew could not resist a quick glance across the street. He looked away again immediately. The heavier of the *dos amigos* now held a gun in his left hand and was waving it carelessly around as he spoke to the other guy. He seemed to be telling an elaborate shaggy-dog story or complaining about somebody not present.

"Funny," offered Edith, "but we've never actually said what we think about her as a photographer."

"Marisa? I kind of like her work. Don't you?"

Edith gave him no answer. "You know what she told me on the plane? She said she had an artistic primum mobile, one basic belief from which all her work flows, now and always—to wit, 'We're all skulls.' "

Even in his growing anxiety, Andrew was amused. " 'We're all skulls,' " he repeated. "Catchy. Myself, I'm pretty sure I didn't know that at twenty-eight, but good for Marisa. Surely you can't have any quarrel with that?"

"No," she agreed amiably. "I kind of like her work, too."

A small traffic drama had momentarily blocked Andrew's view of the two men from the *mercado.* Hitched to a two-wheeled

U-Haul van filled with aluminum window frames, a swaybacked mare was being led placidly down the street by her owner, himself a relic. Directly behind, two pickups circa 1955 and '60 were vying for the honor of passing this processional.

"Andrew, I'm just going to run in here and check our directions." She stood at the threshold of a turquoise concrete box with a rust stain running down the front. Over the door was a hand-lettered sign announcing *"Estilistas Unisex Laura."*

"Good idea." He looked quickly over his shoulder at the street derby, still in progress. "Let's both go," he added, pushing her firmly ahead of him through the door.

"Hey! What are you doing?"

"Sorry."

The proprietress, presumably Laura, poured a pitcher of hot water through the lustrous black hair of her only customer, a lanky girl still in her teens. *"Momentito,"* she told Edith and Andrew, as if she had expected them all afternoon.

"Ask her if there's a back way out."

Edith tilted her head, seeming to debate the merits of his request. "But who are we hiding from?"

"Just make something up."

While Edith engaged *la señora* in a lengthy discussion, twice submitting her own sun-damaged hair for the lady's inspection, Andrew stood well back in the shadows. Fat and Thin were still across the street, looking vexedly in either direction. Finally, Fat shoved Thin a couple of steps farther down the street, and they set off that way at a fast walk.

"I told her my husband was after us," said Edith as they tumbled out the back door and into the light. "It struck a chord with her."

"Those guys," Andrew began, "they followed us from the *mercado.*"

"Did they? Because of our quiet moment of affection?"

He caught her eye, then she held his until he found himself nodding.

"Do you feel like worrying about it?" she asked.

"No, actually. I don't. Do you?"

She smiled. "To tell you the truth, Andrew, I couldn't even if I had to. I haven't been this happy ever."

"It's true." He laughed, feeling foolish. "I mean me either."

A dust-colored dog with the ruling party's initials painted on its sides in green trotted purposefully past them, turned a corner, and was gone.

"Besides," Edith added, tucking her hand down the back of his pants, "we're all skulls anyway."

The meeting hall, immediately recognizable by the late-model cars parked outside, had already received Arévalo and his people. Unsmiling *paisanos* with automatic rifles flanked the door, a handful of others patrolled the perimeter with radios. There was no sign of Santiago. There was no sign, either, of Fat and Thin.

"What now?" said Edith, spinning her umbrella.

"We find some shade and wait. In the national manner."

She studied the meeting house unhappily. "They must have some part of that place set aside for Santiago. I suppose we could see if they'll let us in."

"Arévalo does not completely love us, remember?"

Across the street, looking at once profligate and decrepit to the point of collapse, was the first two-story building they had seen since leaving *el centro*. It was made of hot pink concrete—not concrete painted that color, though that too, but concrete into which so much pigment had been mixed that in places the structure had disintegrated. The balcony in front had mostly fallen away, weather had enlarged the second-story windows into blind man's eyes, and alarming craters had developed in the walls. Where the door had been, there now leaned a steel plate on which someone had painted the life-sized portrait of a young beauty (halter top, cutoffs, heels) whose cascading blond curls he had lovingly haloed with the name Dalila. And outside the right-most upper window, suspended by ropes and pulleys as if it might perform some structural function there, was an upright piano, folklorically painted with a sunset, cactuses, and a treble clef.

"Maybe," said Andrew, "we ought to look around a little more."

"What for? This seems like just our kind of place. Besides, I'm thirsty."

Andrew squinted. "You do know the rule about cantinas?"

"What? No women? That's not true here. Maybe in the boonies." Edith checked her watch. "Besides, don't you have to call that guy in Brazil? I see phone line running into that place."

"An international call from a no-name cantina?"

"Why not?"

As they stared at the sign scrawled in paint across the facade—*Todo Elemento Pasar X la Otra Puerta*—two Mexican girls cruising by in tailored jeans did just that, chatting happily, their shoulder bags bouncing in sync at their hips.

Edith bit her lip and looked at him, trying not to laugh.

"I give up," said Andrew. "Why not."

The *cantinero*, a man of middle age and bulldog build, was trying to replace an overhead light when Andrew and Edith stepped through the door. There was a makeshift bar to their right, some tables and chairs, maybe eight or ten of them occupied, to their left. The room felt large.

"*¡Chinche!*" called an adolescent boy's voice from somewhere in back. "*¿Me quieres conectarlos ahora?*"

"*¡Pendejo!*" shouted Chinche by way of answer. "*¡No me quiebres el culo!*"

The clientele laughed, and the lights came on.

Running in rows across the pitted ceiling and around its edges, red and blue fluorescent tube lights were set in pairs. Mixed, the two colors bathed the room in a soft white light.

"*Buenas tardes,*" Andrew said when he realized that people were staring openly at them. He put his arm around Edith and addressed himself in Spanish to the *cantinero*. "My *prometida* and I could not help noticing your splendid establishment, and we thought—with your permission, *caballeros*"—he bowed infinitesimally in the direction of the customers—"that we might impose upon your hospitality for a couple of beers while we wait for our friends."

Chinche nodded curtly and headed for the bar. The customers looked away and resumed conversation.

"You're overdoing it a bit," Edith whispered.

"It's okay," answered Andrew. "The less mystery, the less chance of getting swept up in a three-day *borrachera* with everybody and his cousin."

They sat at the bar, a small but solid affair topped with a cracked sheet of Formica in a scrambled egg motif. When Chinche produced the beers, Andrew gave him thirty pesos. The *cantinero* pocketed the money without comment.

"Big doings across the street," Andrew offered in a Spanish that he hoped was not overhearty. He felt the need to communicate.

"*Que caguenlos,*" replied Chinche with a shrug. "*No allá me.*" Let them shit all over themselves. It's not my concern.

Edith giggled, then blushed charmingly.

"Yes, it's the same on *el otro lado,*" said Andrew. "Too many politicians." At the same instant, at the end of the bar, he sighted the phone, a battered red desk model secured with hasp and padlock. "In the end," he ventured, "we have only our friends and ourselves."

"In the end," agreed Chinche.

A teenage girl with her hair skunked blond on one side glided in from outdoors and stood beside Andrew and Edith, waiting for her eyes to adjust.

"*Hola, Chinche. ¿Qué onda?*"

He directed her with a toss of his chin to a ratty sofa pushed up against the stairwell, midway back. Already seated there were the two girls Andrew and Edith had seen outside. A third walked back and forth smoking.

"*Por favor,*" Edith began. "Could you tell us what the occasion is? We saw the other two young ladies outside."

Chinche affected not to hear, though he made no move to leave them alone, either.

"What's with the girls?" asked Andrew.

Nodding gravely, Chinche seemed to imply that Andrew had, by sheerest intelligence, touched upon the very matter with which he himself had been struggling, possibly for years. Then a slow smile broke across his features, and he spoke a few sentences so rapidly that they passed Andrew by completely.

"*Exactamente,*" Andrew said anyway, hoping for the best.

When Chinche left his post a moment later, cursing his bar boy beneath his breath, Edith looked brightly at Andrew. "So you were right," she said.

"*Exactamente.*"

She laughed, and, watching her, Andrew realized it was true: he had never been this happy, ever. He had never been at ease.

"You're really good. You actually had me fooled for a minute there." She straightened a shoulder strap that her laughter had knocked into the crook of her arm. "He said that last night one of the *bailarinas*—I guess meaning exotic dancer, stripper, whatever—shot her pimp of a boyfriend dead, right here in the cantina. So she's in hiding, probably forever, and *those* girls are here to try out for her job."

"Neat," he said. "That probably makes this place the biggest employer in the area, after the *maquiladoras.*"

She eyed him shrewdly. "You're not going moralistic on me, are you?"

"Certainly not. I'm a friend to working girls everywhere."

"*Bailarinas,*" she corrected him.

They watched together for a while, sipping their beers, as the two standing girls conversed, one speaking in a high, deliberately pinched voice, as if mimicking someone, while the other flipped her hair around importantly and listened.

"Think maybe I'll go mingle," said Edith. Before Andrew could object she quickly added, "While you make your phone call," and sauntered off toward the four girls.

Watching her go, Andrew felt a pang of loneliness. He saw how much he dreaded calling Brad Lowell, and the impulse to put it off shamed him.

"*Por favor, Señor,*" he said to Chinche, who had finally finished upbraiding his bar boy. "Is it possible to use your telephone? I will pay you in dollars."

The *cantinero* inspected the phone as if he had never thought to look at it before. "My bar boy—it is a pity. I would send him to get the key, but he is as stupid as two stones."

At the corner of his sight, Andrew observed Edith speaking rapidly to the four would-be *bailarinas*, who bobbed their heads simultaneously in sympathy or agreement.

"The thing of the women," said Chinche, following Andrew's gaze, "is that they need the man to control them. It is a law of nature. Last night, without doubt, a tragedy occurred in this place. Not for her pimp of a boyfriend, although he is dead and stinking, but for Dalila, who shot him. She has lost everything. Our most popular *bailarina*, and who knows if she will ever be seen again?"

"Well," said Andrew, "why not?"

Chinche shot him an offended look. "She must hide now!"

"Yes. I see what you mean." Taking out his wallet, Andrew counted out five ten-dollar bills and, across the bar, pressed them into Chinche's hand. "Tell me, '*mano*, is there no other way of handling the matter of the telephone?"

Without looking at the money, Chinche put it in his pocket. "What I am telling you is that a man who does not control his woman is going against the laws of nature. Disorder arises." He reached absentmindedly beneath the bar and produced a second phone, baby blue and held together with surgical tape. Without ceremony, he placed it in front of Andrew. "But in Mexico these things correct themselves."

Andrew searched Chinche's watery brown eyes for signs of menace or mockery. He found none. "*Exactamente,*" he said.

Against all probability, the phone produced a dial tone and, shortly after, an operator who took Andrew's credit card number and told him to wait. He looked at his watch: five o'clock, exactly as he had promised Lowell the week before.

Watching Edith and the girls, Andrew allowed himself a moment of self-congratulation. What trials the day had so far laid out he and Edith had engaged without hesitation, and where they had triumphed, they had done it honestly and without undue self-regard. There was a civic element to the whole train of events, from the *maquila* to the *mercado*, that Andrew found invigorating. So much of what one did, he reflected, one did, in the end, for company of some sort or another.

A feline man in black jeans and a black-mesh shirt walked into the cantina. He continued without pause toward the back of the place, turning his head to scrutinize the women as he passed, but otherwise acknowledging no one.

"*Está*," muttered the phone, which had been ringing so long at the other end that Andrew had half-forgotten about it.

Stopping his free ear with a finger, he hunched over the bar in concentration. "*Alô, aqui fala Andrew Caldwell. Senhor Lowell é lá?*"

A long pause ensued. "*Momento.*"

While Andrew tried to construct his wishes in Portuguese, Edith caught his eye. She pointed repeatedly to the back of the cantina, then to herself, finally nodding and adding an encouraging smile to indicate how fine and fundamentally congenial was the company they had happened into. Then she and her new female friends swept off together in the direction she'd announced.

"Caldwell, is that you?"

"Hi, Mr. Lowell. You've been trying to reach me, I take it."

"Goddamn, man! Where you been? We've got serious difficulties here, serious!"

"I'm in Mexico. What's going on?"

"Mexico? Okay, okay. You're ahead of me, I'm going to hope. Now listen. They like titles down here, so I've named you chief financial officer of the reserve, assuming power of attorney in the event of my et cetera. Agreeable?"

Andrew's eyes came to rest on a line of *piñatas* strung along one wall. For some reason, looking at them made him sleepy. "But what's your situation right now, Mr. Lowell? And what does it have to do with Mexico?"

"Okay. I've just hired a dozen locals, good men, who've agreed to take their first month's wage as credits. That gives you time to clear the estate. The bad news is that the logging company is ready to move on us. The only thing stopping them is they don't know what to do about me."

"I remember."

"This is an unusually dirty company, even for here. Forced labor, imprisonment, beatings, and so on. They also move part of their funds through Mexico, even though they're not incorporated there."

"I must have missed a transition. Why can't they take their money wherever they want?"

"Well, that's just it, see. Mexico has a—" He paused. "Hang on one sec, will you?"

There ensued a series of noises that suggested the phone being dropped down an incline of corrugated metal. It was followed by a silence. Andrew had time to notice that the patrons at a nearby table had all turned to look his way. Grinning, they lifted their glasses and seemed to drink a toast to him. He nodded cautiously.

The next voice on the phone was Brazilian. "With whom am I speaking, please?" The man said it in English.

"I'm Andrew Caldwell, Mr. Lowell's attorney. Who are you, and where is my client?"

"Please call me Dom Gilberto. Your client, Mr. Caldwell, is in quite a deal of trouble."

"I'm sure it's a mistake, then," Andrew replied. "Is my client under arrest?"

"In a manner of speaking. You see, we're in the jungle here, Mr. Caldwell. So a different—I wouldn't like to say fairer, but certainly different—set of laws applies."

"I bet. But I also happen to know that Mr. Lowell's primate reserve enjoys the special favor of several highly placed, short-tempered people in your government and elsewhere. Strict enforcement, wicked penalties—as I'm sure you're aware." Andrew hesitated, uncertain how far to push it. "C'mon, Gilberto. Quit the bullshit and put my client back on the line."

The voice on the other end seemed to sigh. "I enjoy a good primate display as much as the next man, Mr. Caldwell. But put him back on the line? No, that I cannot do. And I doubt very much whether anyone else can, either."

His stomach constricting, Andrew recalled the square of paper Leticia had handed him while he was talking to Lowell from New York. "You're military, are you, Gilberto?"

He laughed. "No, I'm just a foot soldier in the march of progress, like you. A primate in clothes." In the background, two male voices contended in rapid Portuguese. "Now I must go, Mr. Caldwell. Good-bye, and try not to brood over things you can't help."

The line went dead. Andrew had been on the phone less than ten minutes.

He drank the rest of his beer slowly, thinking through what had just happened. Then he picked up the phone again and asked the operator to get him the American Embassy in Brazil.

"YOU CAN'T pay attention to Chinche," one of the girls told Edith in Spanish. "He's a good guy, but sometimes he's, like, superstrict."

The five of them were in a black-painted room in the back of the cantina. At the room's center was a small circular stage whose circumference was stepped down to form a counter, a kind of bar, around which maybe twenty chairs were pulled up. A steel pole ran from the center of the stage to the ceiling, and Beatriz, the girl with the skunked hair, swung from it tentatively, working up her routine. She had removed her jeans, but in her tee shirt and underwear she still looked quite dressed.

"Chinche's just all screwed up today," Beatriz offered as she practiced a kick, "because it was his gun Dalila used, and now he can't find it."

"Well, for sure she didn't take it *with* her," said Mela, the ample blond next to Edith.

"Of course not. She left it behind so Chinche could put a couple of slugs in, too."

They all laughed, a little guiltily.

"I guess nobody liked the boyfriend," Edith hazarded.

"That shitball son of an insect? He used to beat her, really so bad. And then he'd get pissed all over again because she couldn't work looking like that."

"It's better he's dead," agreed Mayté, the youngest-looking of them. "In hell there are vacancies."

Scanning the present company, Edith decided it was even money that she was not the only one pregnant. She glanced at her watch.

"Hey, is that your husband out there, *güera?*" The woman asking, much the most attractive of the four by *gringo* standards, had long, straight hair, black enough and obviously enough prized to add a hint of challenge to her use of the familiar "blondie." She had already removed her shirt and bra, and now, watching Edith, she lowered her jeans and panties in a bunch and stepped out of them.

"Almost," said Edith. "We're getting married as soon as we get back home."

"Ai yai yai, he's a handsome one," said Mela. "But you'd better watch out. I think Elvira has her eye on him. Look, she's already got her favorite wedding dress on!"

The black-haired girl and Edith exchanged a tepid smile while the others laughed.

"I didn't mean to interfere," Edith told Elvira. "My boyfriend and I are just waiting for some friends."

Elvira looked her up and down with the frankness conferred on her by her own lack of clothing. "You are not interfering. Is your boyfriend going to let you try out for the job?"

"We didn't discuss it. And anyway, I already have a job."

"Too bad. Tuercas would like you."

"Hey, cut it out, Elvira," called Mela as she took the stage for a few practice turns of her own. "We don't need no more competition, okay?" She was naked now and definitely looked it.

" 'Screws?' " asked Edith. "What kind of name is that?"

Elvira shrugged. "He's an auto mechanic, like half the guys in Juárez, but he wants people to think he runs some super-ultra carjack gang. That was him who walked by us out there, all in black. Anyway, he's Chinche's talent manager. He hires the girls and tries to fuck them."

"In which order?"

The girls were amused.

"Sure you don't want to give it a try, *chica*?" called Beatriz. "You don't have to tell your boyfriend everything."

Edith watched Mayté draw a green-, white-, and red-spangled outfit from her shoulder bag and shake it out.

"But I don't have a costume," said Edith, checking her watch again.

"It doesn't matter for a tryout," Elvira told her. "On the job there are millions of rules, but for a tryout the only one he cares about is no eye contact."

"No eye contact? Why not?"

Elvira stared expressionlessly at her, then shrugged. "It's the eyes that make them fight each other."

The collective pronoun, used with such casual certainty, stunned Edith. It hinted of a world, an existence, in which such things could be routinely known. The eyes of a dancing woman have the power to make men fight.

"But don't you do it anyway sometimes?" Edith asked.

Ignoring this gaucherie, Elvira reached out to feel the fabric of Edith's dress. "Ai, this is really beautiful. Did your boyfriend give it to you?"

"No, I got it before." She felt herself blush. "Would you like to try it on?"

Although Elvira, who was beginning to seem more and more like the leader of this band of unlikelies, said nothing, her eyes brightened, and a smile settled across her face. Edith turned around so Elvira could undo the buttons, then she pulled the green cotton dress over her head and handed it to her.

"Oooo, *chica*," said Beatriz. "You should get that man of yours to buy you some underwear. It's not safe to travel like that."

"She has nice tits though," observed Mela, leaving the stage to get a closer look. "For a *gringa*, anyway."

"Don't be rude, Fatty." Elvira stood still while Edith buttoned her up. "Not everybody can be like you with your great mother mangoes."

"Turn around," said Edith.

A cracked mirror was bolted to one wall where it could reflect the stage, and Elvira walked slowly to it, as if fearful of breaking something she had not till then been aware she carried. The others gathered behind her.

Watching this half-hardened desert beauty frown as she examined herself in the fractured mirror, first from one side, then the other, Edith felt something quite like joy rise up in her. Against the ruin of a million circumstances, whose certain sum was disappointment, still, if unpredictably, there was this: the pleasure of being flesh, of being drawn to flesh and drawing it, of giving birth to it, of knowing it was only lent to you. *There's your mind-body problem solved*, thought Edith. Q.E.D.: we're all skulls.

"You look fantastic," said Mayté quietly. "Really ultra."

"Don't put thoughts in her head. She already thinks she's too good for us." But Mela also was impressed. "The local beauty," she added, not unkindly.

A tiny lopsided smile had found its way to Elvira's face. "Do you think maybe I could make it on *el otro lado*?" she asked Edith. "Not Texas, but someplace liberal. Like California, maybe?"

But before anyone could answer, Tuercas made his entrance, clapping his hands with the ironic zest of a crew boss trying to rally his hopelessly lazy workers. "*Chicas, chicas, chicas!* Look at you! Standing there in front of the mirror like hypnotized chickens! Do you think that's the way you're going to learn to lay an egg?"

Elvira gave a short, urgent hiss to Edith and presented her back. Fumbling a little, Edith began unbuttoning.

"This is your lucky day, chickens. One of you is going to get a job, and all of you are going to have a chance to dance for me." His wraparound black shades obliged Tuercas to take a slo-mo approach to movement, and it sorted oddly with his high-strung style. Pulling a table and chair away from the wall, he set up his viewing stand a couple of paces from the stage.

"Every woman, in her dreams, wants to be a *bailarina*, whether she says so or not. To dance before an audience of men who can appreciate her, to make them think only of her—what better thing can life offer for a woman?" He paused, apparently inviting them to consider this insight. "But, my chickens, to be a *bailarina* is not a job for everyone."

When Edith finished unbuttoning the dress, Elvira hurriedly stepped out of it and handed it back to her. Edith draped it over a chair. They exchanged a look.

"You have to be strong. You have to be clean. You have to use your brains." Tuercas pored over the modest light-board setup in one corner, fiddling with the switches. "Most women have their brains in their pussies."

The stage lights came on, three beams of shaky wattage.

"So remember, while the *bailarina* is onstage, her job is to make love to all the customers, but never to just one. That's why we have the mirror, that's why the stage is round. And that's why my number-one rule is no eye contact."

Edith found herself nodding dutifully, along with the others.

"Okay. Now I know some of you probably brought your own music or costumes, but today we forget about that shit." Tuercas, who had so far barely glanced at his prospective talent, lugged an industrial-sized boom box over to his table and set it up facing the stage. "You each get one song from the tape, whatever comes up. Give me some basic moves on the pole, a little floor work, and finish up with something nice. No costumes, no clothes. And I don't want no shaved pussies, so if you shaved you can go home now. Anybody? Good."

He sat down at his table. *"La güera.* You first."

Edith looked at Mela, but everybody else looked at Edith. Tossing her hair huffily, Mela started up the walkway to the stage. For all her fleshiness, she had the musculature and agility of an athlete, with the mind-set to match. As she approached the pole, though, Tuercas put up a hand to stop her.

"Did I say bottle blond? Sit back down. I want the natural blond, the *gringa.*" He nodded to Edith. "You first, sweetheart."

Mela was beside herself with righteous indignation. "Are you stupid, man? She's not here for the job! Can't you see she's a fucking tourist?"

Tuercas leveled an index finger at Mela and wordlessly indicated the way down from the stage. With a snort of contempt she went.

"Don't worry," Elvira whispered into Edith's ear. "Inside he's just a little baby. Mexican men, they're all afraid of their mothers. Big secret, right?"

Not knowing quite how far she intended to take this exercise in foreign relations encouraged Edith to let it continue. This was the kind of situation in which a great deal could be learned very quickly if one avoided the morbid thought or self-centered perspective. And on this of all days, the beginning of her new life with Andrew and Kevin and her unborn child, she could not afford to refuse a challenge.

"So, what's your name?" Tuercas asked when she stood before

him onstage, her hands clasped loosely before her in an approximation of modesty.

"Edith."

"That's too weird, girl. No good." He had yet to remove his sunglasses. "You got to get a stage name."

"What would you suggest, Tuercas?" she deadpanned.

The girls, settling in for the spectacle, tittered.

"I won't know that until I get to know you better," he answered. "Turn around slowly. Slowly! Yeah . . . okay. All the way around. That's right."

As she turned, Edith put one hand on her waist and affected to inspect the nails of the other. For some reason, a couplet from Auden ran through her head: *Each language pours its vain / Competitive excuse.* Of course, for a United Nations translator like herself, both the sentiment and the occasion for those lines hovered always a little nearer to hand than was comfortable.

"Really good," Tuercas allowed. "You got a beautiful body."

She mimed a curtsy.

"Pinch your nipples for me."

She did as he asked, moistening them for good measure with saliva until they stood prominently out.

"You really trying out for this job?"

"No."

"Wow. You're some crazy bitch, you know that?" He shook his head in feigned wonder.

She saw she had rattled him.

"But you want to dance anyway, huh?" he asked.

"Sure, why not? I want to dance anyway."

Peculiar though it was, the undertaking had acquired a momentum of its own. Edith took hold of the steel pole, planted one foot at its base, and swung once around, testing her strength. *All I have is a voice / To undo the folded lie.*

"Remember," said Tuercas. "No eye contact."

There you go, thought Edith, *it's an authority thing.* She was with Auden on that one, though she couldn't quite remember the relevant line. *Authority / Whose buildings* something *the sky*. Poke? Stroke?

She took another spin around the pole. It seemed to her that her new friends, who had gathered off to one side, wished her well: *solidaridad* in the field. Fleetingly, she regretted Andrew's not being there to see.

As Tuercas leaned over the boom box to cue the cassette, Edith saw that he wore a tiny gold ring through one ear—a rarity among heterosexual Mexican men. *Grope*, she recalled. *Whose buildings grope the sky*. Then he hit the play button and she was on.

The song was "Louie, Louie," rendered *norteña*-style with horns, guitars, and skeezy organ. Taking her cue from the bass line, Edith did a cha-cha-esque circuit of the little stage, putting as much hip into it as she could without feeling ridiculous. Not until her eyes met those of the girls, all lined up together at the side, did she realize she had almost forgotten rule *numero uno*. When she got to Tuercas, her gaze was demurely lowered. She had the sense, though, that he had removed his sunglasses.

As the vocalist came in, a scratchy Mexican tenor attempting to render the lyrics in their original incomprehensible English, Edith began to enjoy herself. She took a running leap at the pole and slid slowly down it, scissoring open her legs. Not quite able to manage a split at the bottom, she got back to her feet and began another, much slower circuit of the stage—all tits and pelvis this time.

The eyes-averted business, she now realized, was not just to keep the customers at bay.

"Go, *chica*! Burn it up like that!" Elvira's voice, suddenly sounding much younger, made Edith smile.

Not looking, not meeting your audience's eyes, in a way made you more aware of them, she thought, working out a new move with her shoulders. Sight was such a preemptive sense. Sometimes you just had to close your eyes.

Lest we should see where we are, / Lost in a haunted wood. But Edith's high spirits had room for melancholy, and she put the Auden poem there. *There's no such thing as the State / And no one exists alone.* In a proper world, she thought, those words would be inscribed over the entrance to the UN. Maybe her daughter-to-be would live to see it happen.

Remembering she was pregnant made her breast-conscious, so she gave hers a little emphasis, cupping one in either hand and pinching the nipples as she had before. Not that she needed to, by now. What a sweet and fundamentally innocent activity this was, she thought. Timeless and sweet.

She strutted once around the stage like that, then backed herself up against the pole in front of Tuercas and slowly sank down on her haunches, knees spreading naturally to support her weight until she had laid herself quite open to him. It was a bit more than she had intended.

His sunglasses were now definitely off: they lay on the table beside a scattering of glass ampules—amyl nitrate, she thought. For a moment, propped as she was against the pole, Edith struggled to command her center of gravity. *There's more to this* bailarina *gig than meets the eye*, she thought, reaching behind her for the pole. When she heard Tuercas snap open a popper, she raised her own eyes instinctively.

His face was flushed red with the drug as he held the ampule to his nose, but his eyes, large and intelligent seeming, remained very clear. Looking into them reminded Edith with surprising force of just where she was—not simply onstage, or in the cantina, or in Mexico, but in some larger scheme of things, where one's responsibilities were both more and less exacting. *We must love one another or die:* Auden, for one, had been clear enough about it, even if the line had become so famous that it was now almost senseless.

"Let's give it to them right now," recited the singer on the tape, reproducing with comic precision the drunken slur of the original.

Watching Tuercas inhale deeply a second time from the popper, Edith pulled herself upright into the guitar solo and let her weight carry her once more around the pole.

How strange we are, she thought as she spun off for a final jaunt around the stage, working just a bit behind the beat. So tenacious as a species, but so prone to self-injury and detour. You had to wonder whether consciousness, as an evolutionary gambit, wouldn't itself prove to be a detour, a brief wrong turn, soon enough corrected. But that, of course, was where the love came in.

She performed a slouchy pirouette and bend that pleased her. *Not half bad*, she thought, repeating the figure.

But at that exact moment, Tuercas leapt to his feet. Grinning furiously, he hurled the ampule to the floor, where it shattered with a medicinal tinkle. "Ai-*yai*! Great-Grandmother of God!" he shouted.

Edith saw that her audition was over.

She allowed her momentum to carry her lightly to the walkway, down it, and off the stage at a stroll. The song lurched into its last chorus, and, led by Elvira, the girls began to applaud. As Edith passed by Tuercas, he attempted a little dance of vasodilation that turned into a stagger.

"I will fuck you crazy," he offered. "No?"

"No," she told him.

He made a grab for her that she easily sidestepped. Nothing could spoil her high spirits.

She had decided to give her dress to Elvira and take the jeans and tee shirt in exchange, but as she headed over to effect this transaction, she was brought up short. Standing in the doorway, each apparently watching a different movie, were James, Andrew, Mercedes with Kevin in her arms, and Marisa.

"*There* you guys are." Edith was both delighted and somehow surprised to see them. "I guess Santiago's already in the meeting hall?"

Mercedes was laughing. "He'll be very disappointed to have missed you. You were brilliant." She had her hand over Kevin's eyes. Protesting, he struggled to free himself.

"The Queen of Sheba," added James.

"Not me, I was just passing the time. Strictly amateur, as my friends here will tell you." She peered at Andrew, who looked shaken, pale, his hair awry. "Andrew?"

She approached him slowly, hoping she had it wrong. He was bright with distress. "Andrew, what's happened?"

STANDING before the unglassed window, Santiago watched two of Arévalo's men prime their roosters for a fight. Three, four, five times they held the birds up beak to beak, an explosion of feathers, so that briefly the creatures seemed to become a single tormented life; then, each time, the men swung them apart again at arm's length. Santiago was reminded, by the gravity and dolor of the men's gestures, of cello players.

"I didn't appreciate your taking Vendajes," he said, as he turned back to face Luis Arévalo, "but on reflection I think you deserve him."

His former aide raised his eyebrows and opened his palms in a shrug. "I was lonely. Anyway, he was more or less mine from the start."

Arévalo sat with his boots up on a battered steel desk that served as the meeting hall's podium. Along the facing wall, scavenged car seats had been lined up side by side to form a long banquette, and above them was a partly torn-down poster of Gutiérrez. Someone had painted a black bar over the candidate's eyes, along with the words "*¡La justicia no es ciega! ¡Viva la lucha!*"

"I'm tempted to ask," said Santiago, "how long you planned your departure."

"I didn't plan it. It accumulated." Arévalo smiled hospitably, as if recalling a youthful intemperance. "We never made a secret of our differences, you and I. We just overlooked them, to avoid personal discomfort. And so these differences evolved."

Santiago studied his friend. The jeans, boots, guayabera gave him an authority that he had never been able to extract from business suits. They also made him harder to read.

"I had hoped to talk it over with you before I left," Arévalo continued. "In a luckier world we would have had another of our back-room conversations, perhaps refreshed our thinking."

"In a luckier world," replied Santiago, "we would not be in politics at all."

Arévalo shot him a measuring look.

"So tell me," said Santiago, beginning to pace. "How much shit have the *gringos* given you? They must really want to shove it down your throat."

"Not so much, old friend. On the one hand, of course, they don't believe in me. On the other, and in memory of their dead consciences, they are frightened. This is amusing, no?"

"In theory."

"What theory? You were at that *maquila* today. That was praxis of the purest, most irrefutable kind. It was the force of history. And do you know what? We had one of our men videotape it. As you and I speak, television stations all over North America are preparing that footage for tonight's prime-time news. A tasty lifestyle segment for the *gringo* palate. And there will be much more to come, I assure you."

Santiago grimaced. While he knew Arévalo was partly play-acting, trying to goad him into tipping his own hand first, the truth was probably bad enough.

"Are you in contact with the rebels in the South?"

"With all respect, I must tell you they are not confined to the South. Some of them, for example, are standing outside on sentry duty."

Stopping in front of the desk, Santiago stared into Arévalo's black Mayan eyes, stubborn revenants of the continent's first blood. It was possible, he decided. Likely.

"I begin to wonder why you called me here," said Santiago.

"You came to Juárez on your own, don't forget. I followed you."

A jolt of anger surged through Santiago. To conceal it he walked behind Arévalo to the window. "The rebels will never make any headway at the border. You know yourself that this is a haven for the conservatives, who depend on the slop-over from the U.S."

"The border is effectively a denationalized zone for sixty kilometers on either side. Federal law, except for immigration, counts for rat piss around here, even on the *yanqui* side." Arévalo's voice took on an edge of irritation. "They have three train robberies a month in El Paso." He waited. "Are you going to tell me I'm wrong?"

Behind the hall the cockfight was already over. The loser's owner held his dead bird by the feet as he counted money out into the other man's palm.

"No," replied Santiago at length. "But I will say that if you are planning a revolution we must hope that you hire a tactician less romantic than yourself."

The smell of wood smoke drifted in through the window, incense burnt to a spirit both paltry and surpassingly indifferent. The spirit was Mexico, and Santiago, not for the first time, chilled at the harshness of its beauty. A lone man walking in silence down a desert road; a highlands woman in a roaring factory, her baby strapped to her belly; a cooking fire made from the table at which the meal might have been eaten. He himself had loved Mexico with a sense of fatality that only now revealed itself for what it was. It was possible, Santiago considered, to be overfond of life.

"A revolution," said Arévalo. "Fitting, don't you think, that Trotsky, the great believer in continual revolution, spent his years of exile here in Mexico with us? We who have made our revolution perpetual by never actually carrying it out?"

Recalling his own thoughts about Trotsky, the previous afternoon at the Zócalo, Santiago could not suppress a rueful smirk. "Of course. And now we have Trotsky as farce in the Partido Revolucionario Institucional."

"Exactly," said Arévalo.

It had long been a running joke between them that the ruling party's absurdly apt name, rightly understood, was its most vicious critique.

"But let's get to business, Luis." Santiago left the window to resume pacing before Arévalo, who was still seated with his feet on the desk like a comfortably louche *funcionario*. "Can you possibly imagine that if the *gringos* or the glorious Institutional Revolutionary Party, or even a few Japanese businessmen over lunch wanted to bring you down, it could not be done in less time than it takes to spit out your name?"

"Perhaps. But the climate is changing. Even the *gringos* can no longer afford to be seen to dictate Mexico's internal affairs directly."

"That, old friend, is a great stinking ball of shit that you have rolled for yourself. If the *gringos* really were afraid of you, believe it: I'd gladly vote for you myself."

A crooked smile had begun to spread across Arévalo's blunt features. "The markets are steady, the *gringos* are silent. A few soldiers at the *maquilas*, I admit, but after that tape is broadcast, you will see that nothing could be more useful to us."

"Us!" Santiago stopped abruptly in front of him. "Tell me about us. What do your polls say?"

"The same as yours, assuredly. I've taken half your vote and added a sizable portion from the committed left, mainly students and campesinos. Also *maquila* workers, needless to say."

"And Gutiérrez?"

"Even allowing for the opportunists who will eventually defect to hedge their bets, he wins by ten percent." Leaning back in his chair, Arévalo tapped his fingertips together thoughtfully. "These days polling is a science, but, of course, a speculative one. Things could go differently."

The two men stared at each other. "Well," said Santiago at last. "We can't undo the past."

It was an infuriating performance, pure Luis. Whatever bravado and mock-childishness lacked as negotiating maneuvers, they more than made up for in sheer blunt force. The trouble was, thought Santiago, that if you acted like a donkey, and boasted to people that you were a donkey, they'd be apt to think that's exactly what you were.

He had brought two Cuban Montecristos, and he gave one now to his friend and adversary. They fired them up, using Arévalo's gold Tiffany lighter.

"Please, Santiago, pull up a chair. I'm worthless as a host today."

Waving off the apology, Santiago dragged a straight-backed chair away from the wall and sat down astride it. Outside, the sunlight was starting to yellow with afternoon's end.

They smoked for a while in silence.

"Poor old Fidel," said Santiago, studying his cigar as he exhaled a long blue plume into the space between them. "Is that what you want? 'Within the revolution, everything; outside it, nothing'?"

"An attractive option on many scores. Not least because it would give the *gringos* a massive shit fit." Arévalo laughed darkly to himself. "But for now we must work with what's already in place."

"Good. So we still agree on this."

Arévalo gave no sign that he had heard. "Mexico is a nation that has never been young. I realized this just a few days ago. Maybe that's why the condition of waiting is so totally built into our national character. Born of two death-obsessed peoples, we have the patience of the dead." He looked hard at Santiago. "Even I, who despise mysticism, must acknowledge this."

"Of course. It is only simple truth."

"Only simple truth," agreed Arévalo. "And since revolution is not one of those good things said to come to those who wait, we must adopt an intermediate posture. A posture, shall we say, somewhere between supine and rampant." Taking a long pull on his cigar, Arévalo sent a stream of smoke rings gently to wrack against the fiberboard ceiling. "That's what I want to discuss with you."

Santiago shook his head wearily. "Ah, Luis. I don't know what you're talking about, and, God help us both, neither do you. Has it never occurred to you that the ruling party has given the *gringos* and big business a *guarantee* of your failure in exchange for a few weeks' grace?"

"What an idea!" Arévalo positively twinkled. "Why would I think it? Although tactics, as you said not too politely, will certainly be my undoing."

The door to the street had only a curtain of wooden beads for closure; just beyond it, well within earshot, two of Arévalo's men stood guard. He stared thoughtfully in their direction, then excused himself and, twirling his sunglasses by one temple, stepped outside.

Santiago's first thought was that he was about to be detained. Over Carlos's objections, he had left the larger part of his own security detail back at the gas station, with the disabled car. Of course, he had Oiticica, and Carlos was somewhere out back, chatting up the opposition, but the truth was—and he realized it with a relief bordering on reverence—he wanted this one for himself.

When Arévalo swept aside the beads again, the sentries were gone. "These *indígenos* are fearsomely loyal," he said, "but they haven't fully grasped the difference between security and imprisonment. Something you used to complain of in regard to me, as I recall."

"Now I have Carlos to berate."

"And Oiticica! A first-class goatfucker, that one." Arévalo tilted his head to one side indulgently. "Where did you get him?"

"From Hell's sacred shithouse. Who cares!" Santiago got up and walked to the back window. Behind the meeting hall, where the cockfight had taken place, two dogs and the owner of the vanquished bird were fighting over its corpse.

"Luis, I was mistaken about the *maquilas*. Whatever is to be done about them, they are an outrage. Every degradation we have suffered at the hands of the *gringos* and their dollar is embodied in those factories. I knew this, but I had forgotten."

He had his back to Arévalo, but he understood that it was to make such an admission possible that Arévalo had dismissed his guards.

"I am fascinated, of course," Arévalo said. "Tell me more."

"The border question is always with us, as you used to say. True, certainly. But I hadn't understood how complete a truth this is. With your permission, how elemental."

Arévalo's silence, though skeptical, was not, it seemed to Santiago, without sympathy.

"A man's first border is his skin. A laughably porous border—you can violate it with a toothpick, a bullet, the noonday sun. And on the other side of this border is the world."

Outside, the victorious dog gnawed and gagged on the rooster carcass, while the man watched, smoking thoughtfully.

"I think we never get over our disappointment at being stuck with this boundary," Santiago continued. "Maybe everything we do is in denial of it. In despite."

"A world founded on disappointment," said Arévalo, quietly amused. "I don't think that doctrine can be described as within anyone's revolution."

"On the contrary," said Santiago. "It is the one thing common to them all. Out of disappointment comes yearning, out of yearning, hope, and, in the best case, action."

"Yes, Santiago, I see what you mean." Arévalo tugged impatiently at his mustache. "But tell me, what would *you* do about the *maquilas*?"

Santiago turned to face his friend.

For a moment, ordinary time seemed to drain away like the life of the rooster he had been watching outside. Mexico was a solitude, an expanse of cruelty and fateful silences, where the bones of life were always on display. It was a literal place, a place for literalists like himself. Seeing it so, Santiago felt both exhilarated and sickened, fearful and indifferent. He had experienced this same mix of sentiment once before, during his voluntary captivity with the terrorists. That he had afterwards misremembered it as boredom now seemed a suitable mercy. There were, as it turned out, surprisingly few practical applications for a sense of eternity.

"The *maquilas*," repeated Santiago. "I think nationalizing them is a good idea as far as it goes, but we have to frame it properly. We don't want to end up embargoed like Cuba." Plunging his hands in his pockets, he started a slow walk around the room's perimeter.

"It would be better if, simultaneous with nationalization, we could announce that we were leasing the factories back to their previous owners at prices that in fact we had already secretly negotiated." He looked fiercely at Arévalo. "It is only simple justice that they pay for the use of what is ours."

Arévalo nodded solemnly. "Only simple justice."

"That way we keep the border open. In Mexico's case, an essential precondition to any domestic overhaul. Revolution or not." Santiago flicked his cigar ash into a diesel drum half filled with sand. "Now. As to the funds received."

"It is crucial," said Arévalo, "that such funds remain in plain view of the people. They will be skeptical, to put it mildly."

"Who can blame them?" Santiago smiled. "With the lease-back funds we set up a national workers' council. This will be the executive body to a newly independent labor union, maybe with government ties at first, but preferably not. Later we do the same thing in the South with the campesinos."

"A more difficult case," Arévalo pointed out. "We have no *gringo* factories to seize in the South, only the agribusiness lands and those of our own *latifundistas.*"

"But the campesinos have been radicalized since Zapata. Their readiness is axiomatic, even if some of them will have to be reawakened to it." Santiago shrugged. "For them we form a second council. When necessary it will act in concert with labor to counterbalance capital, but otherwise I think we can expect some salutary friction between the two. Enough to keep the fatter cats from leaving the country with their dollars that we so admire." He pointed his cigar at Arévalo. "Enough to make it work."

Arévalo's own cigar had gone out, and, as he drew out the business of relighting it, he furrowed his brow as if absorbed in difficult mental calculations. He sat back down at the desk, though without the studied informality of before. "Vendajes tells me that the *yanqui chiflada* and her friends are traveling with you. As part of your entourage."

"Now that you mention it, yes, they are."

"She's a bad element, Santiago."

"What do you know about it?" he replied irritably. "Just because you found some dirty picture she posed for, you want to think she's Mata Hari. Why are you so interested in her?"

"Your interests are my interests," Arévalo explained reasonably. He seemed at the point of elaborating, then changed his mind. "Tell me, Santiago. How much of your business support do you expect to keep, with the plan you just sketched out to me?"

"Against you on the one hand and Gutiérrez on the other? Certainly all of it."

"You don't think the *perfumados* would have preferred 'conspicuous consumption' as a campaign slogan?"

"No doubt, but they have little choice now. Gutiérrez belongs to the Jurassics; he's antihistorical." Santiago wiped a trickle of sweat from his brow. "And you—it's hardly a secret that they piss their pants at the very thought of you."

Arévalo smiled. "I enjoy that, of course. May they get pneumonia from the chill that follows."

"Luis, look. Nobody begrudges you a little sport at their expense, but we need the *perfumados* too. We need their capital, and we need their international aspirations." Santiago sighed. "Life is stupid. But it's also a compromise. We'll do what we can to keep the *perfumados* entertained."

Arévalo's merriment, though genuine, did not quite conceal a deeper emotion that now caused Santiago to approach the desk. From its bottom drawer, Arévalo drew a half-full bottle and two shot glasses, which he placed on the steel surface between them. He stood and poured them each a drink.

"My answer, Santiago, is yes."

"Yes?"

"Yes, I will accept your offer to join your revised campaign. I will bring as many of my own supporters as possible, and of course that means we must stick to the objectives we have just discussed. In return, I ask to oversee with full authority the formation of the two councils, one for the workers, one for the campesinos. Without that, my supporters would be right in thinking themselves betrayed. Is it agreeable?"

Imperfectly concealing his astonishment, Santiago nodded. "It's agreeable."

They raised their glasses together.

"*Tierra y Libertad*," proposed Santiago.

"*Tierra y Libertad*."

As he poured them another, Arévalo said, "Actually, so as not to appear antihistorical, I thought we might amend those noble words just a bit."

"Excellent idea." Santiago was lightheaded with surprise and release. "But how?"

"Well, given my success in naming your first campaign after *La Conspicua*, Edith Emerson, my thoughts returned to her. I toyed with '*Desnudez*,' but 'Land, Liberty, and Nakedness' does not quite capture what I had in mind."

Santiago laughed. "Evocative, though, and very inspiring. So what did you choose instead?"

"With your permission, and in the forward-looking spirit of the Revolution: *La Transparencia*." Reclaiming his cigar from the edge of the desk, Arévalo confided, "We must stand for a government without secrets, without silences or disappearances. One into which the people may look at any time and see their collective will unfolding according to their wishes. It must, in short, be a government of Transparency."

Santiago stared in amazement at his childhood companion. "Luis, you are a poet and a genius."

"Thank you, old friend."

They raised their glasses. *"Tierra, Libertad, y Transparencia."*

The thing had come together. Santiago had surprised himself, but Arévalo had surprised him more. Bound now and sworn to the long emergency of Mexico, the two of them had fallen back on prior graces—the goalie and the forward, at the outset of the game, connected to each other by an invisible current.

Arévalo came around the desk and put a hand on Santiago's shoulder. "All right, you dog of five legs. Now I must know the truth: did you fuck her?"

Santiago smiled and shook his head. "What about you and Fifi the other night?"

Flushing dark, Arévalo waved the idea away, then seemed to think better of it. "I am told that her pathetic prick of a husband locked her up in the wine cellar afterwards. He is a cretin."

"But certainly it was for his own protection," offered Santiago.

They laughed a little over their misalliances.

"Now," said Arévalo. "I know you haven't been talking to Freddy González, because he's in Washington and he's been talking to me." He produced a cell phone from his pocket and punched in a number. "But he has some unpleasant news regarding Edith Emerson and her friends."

He handed Santiago the ringing phone.

"I'd rather you hear it from him."

A C R O S S the street, upstairs at the cantina, Marisa set up her camera. A good deal of the roof had fallen in, so the second floor was a place of pink walls, redundant windows, and sunlight falling blatantly into once private space.

"But there's no way he can know that yet," said James, reaching through the window. His fingertips hovered over the keyboard of the piano that dangled outside, slung from ropes and pulleys. "You send an official-type American back there into the jungle, and I guarantee things will straighten out in no time."

"Not if the guy's already dead," said Edith.

"If he's dead there's nothing Andrew could have done." James hit a few chords, then withdrew his hands and inspected them as if they were close but unreliable relatives of his. "Anyway, I guess you've had your own experience in that area."

Edith pulled at her jeans, tight in the hips, glared at him, and walked away.

"James, I want your help," Marisa leaned over the Deardorff, peering through it at the back wall, awash in westerly light. "Pull that sofa forward about two meters. No, away from the shadow. That's good. Nice. Now sit down."

Stretching his arms out along the sofa's back as he settled, James sighed. "Did you hear that? Andrew thinks his primatologist just got whacked or something. That's not possible, is it?"

Marisa came toward him with the light meter. She held it against his cheekbone, scanning his face clinically. "James, can we just attend to the business at hand, please?"

Her black eyes seemed dilated; looking into them caused James a stab of loneliness. "I wonder how it's going," he said, meaning the conversation across the street.

She put a hand on his head and tilted it right, then left, considering the play of light. "So do I."

"There's a personal side to their rivalry that cuts both ways. It makes them hard to figure, don't you think?"

"You know I detest politics, James."

"But what about your brother? How closely does he really track these things? I mean, he can't know about this meeting, right? It was totally unplanned."

"Jojo always allows for a percentage of signal loss, as he calls it. Anyway, he doesn't think like you and me. He's more a philosopher or scientist. A visionary, really."

"Like your father."

"No, not at all like my father. Drop your chin, please."

Across the room, beside the stairs, a small shrine to the Madonna was built right into the wall, and Andrew lifted Kevin up to see it.

"What are those little silver things, Daddy?" The boy pointed to the hem of the Madonna's robe, which was actual and made of blue velvet.

"*Milagros,*" Andrew said. "That means 'miracles.' " He leaned close to inspect the tiny silver effigies—a heart, a lung, a leg, an eye—pinned to the fabric. "Each one is the prayer of someone who needs God's help. See that one there that's shaped like a leg? It was put there by someone whose leg hurts or maybe doesn't work right. The person is asking God to make him well."

Kevin cautiously reached out and touched the pin. "Do we need God's help?"

"Of course. Everybody does."

The ambassador had referred Andrew to the American consulate in Rio, where they seemed to take his story about Lowell very seriously indeed. Rather than risk a miscue with the military, they had promised immediately to dispatch a team of their own to the reserve, a hundred kilometers northwest of Rio. And although nothing had been volunteered, Andrew had received the distinct impression that the consulate knew all about Gilberto.

"No help from James," said Edith, coming up behind them. In Elvira's jeans and tee shirt, Edith looked like a volunteer for some vast and probably hopeless campaign of national improvement, like roadside cleanup or universal vaccination. "Hey, Kevin. Are you ready to have your picture taken with us?"

He scowled at her. "Mercedes didn't let me see you *dance.*"

"It was a grown-up dance," she said, smiling.

"I don't care!" He threw one little fist open to the ground as if disposing of something deadly to him. "I'm *big* now."

Andrew set him back down on the floor. "Go sit over there on the sofa with your uncle James."

"Don't blame yourself," Edith said when they were alone.

Instead of answering, Andrew squinted into the declining light. "This Gilberto, he wasn't what you'd think. He had a worldview, and he didn't fail to communicate it. Maybe that's what threw me."

"What worldview?"

"Nothing that he said directly. A hint here, a jape there. He was witty, actually. A fundamentalist Darwinian with a sense of humor."

She lay a hand gently over his cheek and temple where she had hit him, blood-black bruise shading now to blue and yellow. "Andrew, you're reading too much into it."

"No," he said, "I'm not. The terms he laid out included me. 'Foot soldiers in the march of progress' is what he called us. 'Primates in clothes.' I knew immediately what he meant. He was right."

"Any high school textbook says the same."

"Of course. It's just that he got through to me. And worse, he knew it."

The burnished light splashed down all around them—mesmerizing, golden, impersonal, empty.

The turquoise chair pushed up against the wall. The bag of nails half-spilled across the floor. The roof rubble in piles, hot pink. The dust.

"Andrew, we can leave tonight, you know. We've done what we came to do."

"Almost, anyway."

"And Kevin has to be back for Susannah."

"Right." He put his arm around her. "Hey, you know the one about the talking pig?"

She shook her head.

"A farmer discovers one of his pigs has learned to talk. At first he can't believe his ears, but it's true, so he rounds up all his neighbors to act as witnesses. He brings the pig before them and tries to start a conversation with it, but the pig says not word one. He acts just like an ordinary pig. The neighbors are enraged, of course, and in their fury at the deception they end up beating the farmer to death. When they're done, the pig trots over to the body, shakes his head, and says, 'Poor fuck. I told him not to let on he could talk.'"

She thought about it for a while. "I don't get it. What's the moral?"

He laughed. "I don't know. Maybe it doesn't have one."

Mercedes approached them, a lit cigarette in her hand. She wore a black dress polka-dotted white, and dark sunglasses in a harlequin design.

"Well," she said, assaying a smile. "Here we all are."

BEHIND the camera, at her best, Marisa always disappeared. She had learned to remain silent and be patient. Occasionally she would emerge to gently rearrange a limb or tilt a face. She never interrupted.

It was befitting and morally essential that her subjects find their own specific gravity.

"When I was a child," said Mercedes, "I was a daydreamer of orgiastic proportions." She sat at the middle of the dilapidated sofa, whose sun-rotten upholstery, pink and purple, was interestingly at war with her dress. "I could spend hours, days even, following my imaginary fates. Visionary nun, loyal girlfriend to imprisoned drug lord, nurse of the battlefield." She laughed. "One of the sisters at convent school sent my parents a note saying I was an 'unusually passionate child.' My father thought she meant I was a nymphomaniac. He kept me locked up at home for two weeks."

"I don't suppose it helped," said Andrew. He was seated on her right, half-turned to her.

"Quite the opposite," she said. "It launched me."

Edith handed round slices of the mango she'd bought downstairs. She sat forward on the sofa's edge, to the left of Mercedes. She opened the *mercado* umbrella to loose a fall of purple shade into which she and Mercedes leaned.

"Has anyone asked about that piano?" she inquired. "And is it coming or going, I wonder."

"Coming," said James. He sat to the front and left of her,

slouched in the turquoise chair he had dragged over. He was still wearing the beige suit, the panama hat. "That Chinche guy said he's turning this floor into a music and dance club. Tangos under the pitiless midnight sky."

"Tangos," said Andrew. "The gravest of dances."

"Like birds prepping for battle or love," James agreed.

"Not Mexican, of course," added Edith, trying to catch the mood.

Kevin sat at their feet, building a fort of rubble. His presence there seemed to hold them to a certain standard of contemplation and commentary. He seemed the one for whose benefit they spoke.

"Exactly," said James, warming to his subject. "Not Mexican. Because when it comes to death the Mexicans are blunt. So down to earth it's eerie, if that's possible. They're students of the pointless outcome, pieceworkers of teleology and death. Am I right, Mercedes?"

"Alas, quite right."

Marisa released the shutter, withdrew the negative holder, and put the exposed film in a canvas bag at their feet. She reloaded.

"I didn't realize you'd given it such thought, James." Without knowing exactly why, Andrew felt he wanted to extend this line of inquiry. "Let's have some field data. We need your help to understand these startling insights."

Edith sighed and, handing the umbrella to Mercedes, got up from the sofa. She strolled to the window overlooking the street.

Marisa released the shutter, reloaded.

"Consider," said James, "the Mexican relationship to appointments and invitations of all kinds. To refuse an invitation, no matter how real the reasons for refusal, is considered rudeness of the grossest sort. You must say yes, and say so graciously."

"Extravagantly is preferred," added Mercedes, determined to conceal her misgivings at what might or might not be transpiring between her husband and Luis Arévalo.

"There you go," said James. "Extravagantly."

Edith rested her fingertips gently on the keyboard of the piano. Across the street, the men who been guarding the meeting hall's entrance had retired to the shade of an attached *ramada*, where they were playing dominoes.

"But once you have accepted the invitation, your obligations cease. Whether you actually show up or not is an entirely different matter, one in which you're free to make a merely personal choice." James's voice had taken on an animation independent of its subject. "No one expects you to show up, but if you do, you're welcomed."

"What's that got to do," asked Andrew, "with bluntness and death?"

The hand that had painted the piano displayed a fondness for stylized detail that made Edith wonder if the same person hadn't painted the portrait of Dalila outside. Five nearly animate cactuses, each with its thorns painstakingly delineated in silver, adorned the piano's front panel to the left and right. At its center, rendered in multiple shades of yellow, white, and blue, a cool crescent moon shed its light upon the keyboard.

"No, no," James was saying. "That's just the point."

Softly, Edith tried a few chords.

"What is the one appointment you can't refuse?"

Discovering that the treblemost keys were jammed, she opened the top of the piano and looked in. *Of course*, she thought. *Exactly what I would have done myself.*

"The big nap," said James. "What else? And when you think of it that way, all other arrangements are, shall we say, tentative."

"Not bad, James." Andrew was losing patience. "You've just made incomprehensible something I've till now managed to take completely for granted."

Below, Santiago emerged from the meeting hall and was immediately joined by Carlos. As they conferred, crossing the street, Santiago caught sight of Edith at the window. They stared at each other.

It's the frame that makes the picture, she thought for the second time that day. When she gave a little wave, he raised a fist. The fist became a hand that waved. The expression on his face, it seemed to Edith, was not quite a smile.

"Here he comes now," she told the others.

MARISA had made twelve exposures when Oiticica came upstairs and whispered in her ear for a moment. She released the shutter and thanked him. He went back downstairs.

Santiago and Mercedes were sitting side by side at the sofa's middle, with Edith and Andrew flanking them and James in the chair. Santiago had explained the substance of his agreement with Arévalo, and the mood was one of celebration. Carlos had brought beer.

"So I guess Arévalo really had your number after all," said Andrew.

"He is an excellent friend," agreed Santiago. "A man of principle and, as he likes to say, a goatfucker."

Having reloaded and focused the camera, Marisa slung her canvas film bag over one shoulder. "I have to run downstairs for just two seconds," she said. "Don't anybody move. I'll be right back."

Mercedes, with a hand tucked around her husband's biceps, was radiant. "Though I dislike admitting it, Luis is the one person who may possibly know Santiago better than I do."

"Only in those areas you have ceded to him," said Santiago.

"Because they are not for a woman to know," she added.

Watching the two of them from her end of the sofa, Edith was struck by the odd sense of these words and by the tremor she observed at Santiago's jaw. As she considered it, the tremor caught and hardened into the shadow smile she had seen from the window, a rictus of suppressed expectancy. She had the impression that he held his body in the posture of relaxation only by the sheerest force of will. Mercedes, smoldering with pride and triumph, did not appear to notice.

"When will you and Arévalo go public with this?" asked Andrew.

Edith tried to catch his eye, but he was busy helping Kevin adjust the buckles of his tiny overalls.

"Tomorrow," said Santiago. "Why wait? As you can appreciate, we need all the time we can get between now and the election to make our case."

Below, Oiticica's radio issued a squawk, abruptly cut off.

"It's a brilliant move," said James. "Risky but brilliant."

"Thank you." Santiago directed a strained smile at James. "You can be sure that even Gutiérrez will be surprised."

Outside, a car pulled up, brakes squealing.

"And that itself is no mean feat," advised Mercedes. "The ruling party is like God—everywhere present but nowhere visible. What Santiago and Luis are proposing is an act more of theology than of politics."

"I like that, *alma mía.*" Santiago put his arm around her. "Perhaps I can persuade you to join my speechwriting team."

"Make me an offer."

The driver of the unseen car idled, raced the engine a couple of times, and engaged the clutch again. Edith got up to take a look.

"But Mercedes is quite right. We must expect a great deal of interference: from the ruling party, from the U.S., from independent interests."

Leaning out the window, one hand propped on the piano, Edith saw the departing vehicle, still visible through the dust it had stirred. It was an open-top military jeep; Oiticica was at the wheel. Beside him, in the suicide seat, was Marisa. When Edith called after them, Marisa turned around and waved a languid good-bye. She used her whole arm, as if signaling at sea. Then she settled back again, and the dust swallowed them.

"How do you like that?" Edith said, turning to face the others. "Oiticica and Marisa—they took off together."

"They *what*?" James was on his feet.

"In a jeep," she said, as if that were the answer he needed.

They all watched James curiously, waiting for him to set this situation to rights, but only Santiago seemed unsurprised. That, Edith, realized, had been the meaning of his smile.

"She was in with Oiticica?" James, his glance careening from face to face, fought visibly to replace fear with outrage, but it was not much of a contest. He opened his mouth to say more, then thought better of it and made a dash for the staircase.

"James!" Edith called after him. "Where are you going?"

Everyone but Santiago now stood, as if to demonstrate a readiness to be of assistance.

"What's this all about?" asked Edith evenly. "Andrew, go get him. He's not in his right mind."

Andrew glanced doubtfully at Santiago, who shook his head and gestured for Andrew to sit down. "I'm afraid it's too late," Santiago said.

Cars were converging on the cantina from four directions, the sound of their engines tearing through the air like jagged ropes racing to a knot.

"Isn't anybody going to—"

Out of the engine roar, sirens bloomed—first one, then three more.

Edith hurried to the window.

James emerged from the cantina's side entrance doing a fair imitation of a brisk walk. Glancing over his shoulder, he buttoned his jacket and headed down the middle of the street like a man losing himself in a crowd. But of course there was no crowd.

The police vehicles came at him from four directions. When James tried to slip through on the diagonal, one of the cars doubled back, brakes screeching, to cut him off. In the end, it drove him right onto the hood of another cruiser, nearly colliding with it.

"Jesus Christ, it's all cops down there," said Edith as the *federales* poured from their vehicles. "They got him."

"I'm going down," said Andrew, starting for the stairs.

"No!" Mercedes grabbed his arm. "You can't."

"Oh shit. Oh shit." Edith pulled at her tee shirt in anguish. One of the *federales* had James by the hair and was methodically pounding his face into the hood of the cruiser.

"I'm sorry about it, Andrew," said Santiago, still seated on the sofa. "Your friend and his girl had an arrangement with Gutiérrez, who now wants to be seen to close it down. She was tipped off at the last minute, so your friend must take the fall for both of them."

"What kind of arrangement?"

"Isn't anyone going to do anything about this?" Edith fingered the piano keys nervously. They had James kneeling in the road while they cuffed him. The same officer who had been dashing him against the car now kicked him full in the groin. It occurred to Edith that the man was angry at James for climbing onto his vehicle.

"Money laundering, more or less. Marisa's father was skimming from the logging operation in Brazil. Gutiérrez got the usual ruling party cut, but the money went largely through your friend's gallery."

"James? James was involved with this?"

"They're going to kill him, Andrew!" Edith had caught a glimpse of James's face, a slurry of blood and dirt.

"Come away from the window!"

A shot, then two more in rapid succession made Edith briefly think that kill him was exactly what they had done. But none of the *federales* had drawn a weapon.

Two men—one fat, one thin—emerged from the meeting house, surveyed the *federales* situation, and, sauntering around it, crossed the street.

"Andrew, it's those guys! The ones who were following us."

James, about to be thrown in the back of the police car, blundered into eye contact with Edith and raised an entreating arm. It seemed to her that he said the word "stop."

"Those were shots!" said Mercedes. "Didn't you hear?"

Santiago was on his feet, heading for the window.

"No!" shouted Mercedes, letting go of Andrew. "Stay away from there!"

"I think they might be coming over here," said Edith, more quietly than she had thought she could.

Carlos, who had been standing frozen in front of Santiago, took hold of his arm. "As your acting security officer, I must tell you to take cover."

"Let me go. They've killed Luis."

"No, they haven't," advised Edith. "Here he comes."

Arévalo had appeared in the doorway of the meeting house. He was bleeding quite a lot from the upper arm. His face twisted in disgust and anger, he looked up and down the street, then, seeing his bodyguards approaching, waved them off with his good arm and crossed. The *federales*, returning to their vehicles, ignored him completely.

"I don't get it," said Andrew. "If they were in it with Gutiérrez, why is James being busted?"

"The story will be in the papers tomorrow. They needed someone to feed to the press." Santiago sighed. "Carlos, could you take your hand off me, please?"

Below, the doors to the police cars shut in rapid succession, and the engines started up again.

"Wait a minute, Santiago." Andrew grimaced. "What's her father's name?"

"Gilberto de Borba. The brother, Jovãozinha, acted as liaison in the D.F. Whether they planned from the first to shop your friend, I don't know. Maybe it just became convenient."

"You are saying Oiticica was a plant?" asked Mercedes in a whisper. "A spy?"

"Friend of the family, it seems." Santiago succeeded in freeing himself from Carlos. "Luis told me all this. Where is he? He probably saved my life."

"James knew!" Andrew stared stupidly at Edith. "He knew!"

"Old friend!" called Arévalo as he climbed the stairs. "You have the better accommodations! As always. So I thought I'd drop in for a drink. We will watch the sunset together!" He looked surprisingly vigorous, considering the amount of blood he had lost. In the crook of his good arm he carried a bottle of mescal he had appropriated from downstairs.

"Who shot you?"

Arévalo shook his head in revulsion. "Incompetents. Fleas. Gutiérristas."

"Bring him over to the sofa." Mercedes, all efficiency and sober good works, tore a strip from the hem of her dress. "We must get the bullet out."

"Let the doctor do it," said Santiago. "It's time for us to leave."

"Sit here with me, Santiago, and have a drink. A toast to our plans."

The light fell in slant shafts the color of brass.

When she heard the two men arguing on the staircase, Edith lifted her chin at Carlos to signal that these were the guys. The fat one reached the top first, took a long pull from the bottle he carried, then staggered sideways and dropped it to the floor, where it shattered. In his other hand he held a long-barreled revolver loosely around the trigger housing.

"¡Pendejo!" his partner shouted up after him. "¡Fregado cabrón! ¡Ni un ciego podria errar dos veces!" Not even a blind man could miss twice.

Kevin began to cry, and at the sound of his sobs, the fat man turned in surprise to discover he was not at all alone. At the same moment Carlos drew a snub-nosed police revolver from beneath his shirt and, grabbing the man by the belt, pressed the mouth of the weapon to his neck.

The thin man was on Carlos at once, pulling with both hands at the arm holding the gun.

Edith was variously aware, as she reached into the piano, of Mercedes struggling to restrain Santiago, of Arévalo trying to get to his feet, of Andrew sweeping Kevin up in his arms and calling her name. It was all curiously quiet and restrained. Decorous. Like a folk pantomime recounting the history of nations.

She didn't have time to think about it.

Coming up matter-of-factly from behind, as if to administer a dose of bug spray, Edith drove the muzzle of Dalila's pistol hard into the thin man's back. "*¡Hela!*" she said testily. "*¡Hela! ¡Hela!*" He froze even before she finished telling him to. "*¡Abajo!* On the floor! *¡Pronto! ¡No me friegues!*"

With Thin off him, Carlos was quickly able to subdue the other man, who proved drunker than he looked. He pushed him to the floor beside his partner.

"Where did you get *that*?" Andrew asked Edith, careful to approach from within her field of vision.

She held the antiquated revolver in both hands, arms fully extended. It was square and blockish, an instrument of rudimentary but timeless passions. It suggested days of waiting, of staking out. Nights passed in arroyos mulling over inevitable things. Desert solitudes. It was a vulgarization of the idea of pistol—and so all the more satisfactory. A harbinger. An intimation. A glyph.

She aimed it alternately at Fat and Thin.

SANTIAGO drove them to the border. Sitting up front with him were Kevin, quiet and alert, and Arévalo, his arm bandaged with the fabric Mercedes had torn from her dress. Edith, Andrew, and Mercedes sat in back.

There was a small stand of cottonwood beside the river, a public park around which taxi drivers waited for sundown and with it the influx of *gringos* looking for the entertainments of poverty. Day workers trickling back over the bridge from Texas passed like shades among the half-strangled trees.

No one had followed them from the cantina, and they had not been recognized.

"What's going to happen to him?" Edith asked.

Santiago shook his head. "It will be difficult to do anything.

Gutiérrez won't want him talking to anyone, since he's the only one who could contradict the official account. A lot will depend on how much the press is able to find out on its own. Unless they get something solid, all Gutiérrez has to do is wait them out."

"You mean they're just going to let James rot in jail?"

"Unfortunately, that might be his best hope. They'd be much happier to see him dead."

A panel truck with a loudspeaker mounted on its roof passed slowly by, broadcasting a few uplifting thoughts on the subject of *continuidad.*

Santiago eased the car to the curb along the park's south side and switched off the engine.

Fat and Thin had presented Santiago and Arévalo with something of a problem. Handing them over to the authorities had not been an option, since it was the authorities who had set them in motion in the first place. Killing them offered the obvious moral satisfactions but finally would have been more trouble than it was worth. In the end they had used the leftover rope from beside the piano to tie the two men up. Gagged and bound together at full length on the floor, the two *caballeros* would have an opportunity to think about how unwelcome they might now be in the sight of their former employers. Maybe, if all went well, Carlos could send round a couple of his more convivial men tomorrow to talk them up over a few tequilas.

"It's a shame we have to part in such disarray," said Santiago, scanning the rearview mirror. "But you are not safe here. The dogs smell blood, and we'll have a night of it now."

"Are you sure you don't want to come with us?" asked Andrew. "Luis could have his arm looked at in El Paso."

"Thank you, no. There are things we must do."

The sun dipped below the horizon line. In the east: Venus rising, chilly white.

They exchanged embraces there beside the car, words of thanks, words of caution, promises to talk soon and often. Care was taken not to make too much of it, this leave-taking. Mercedes bent to tie Kevin's shoelace, whispering to him. *Ranchera* music drifted from the open window of a nearby cab. A freight train clattered past.

Setting out across the concrete esplanade that fed the bridge, Andrew, Edith, and Kevin fell naturally into the hypnotic all-night trudge of migrants and pilgrims. This seemed to involve a bodily memory of some kind, an ancestral knowledge. It was the walk one saw in TV news clips of war and famine.

People changing realms at last light, in cars, on foot, in silence. Slight men selling *refrescos* or *helados*, wading amid the slow-motion traffic like fishermen, expertly working its eddies and backwaters. Ahead, a conspicuously fit American boy in shorts and tank top amused himself by flipping quarters to the vendors. Edith watched one man follow a coin's trajectory with such concentration that he leapt partway onto a car's roof to catch it. The American applauded him grimly and threw another.

When Edith saw that Kevin was tired, she picked him up and carried him. He fell asleep. Andrew paid their toll, and the three of them passed onto the bridge.

"You okay?" Andrew asked her.

She said that she was.

Below, the river was sleeved in concrete, its course fixed, so that the imaginary meridian it marked would not wander like a thing of nature when it was an invention of man.

Borders were everywhere permeable, Edith reflected, and nothing about them was as moving as their ultimate failure to hold. They were a convention best observed in the breach—artifice and emblem of the force that everywhere drove men to set up barriers to the free movement of their kind. That force, she now saw plainly, was fear. Cosmic in scope and origin, prehuman in its genetic vigor, it was terror of the unbounded, the unpartitioned, the possibly infinite. An elemental cringing no different, finally, from the one that had led the Aztecs to discern in the night sky's vastness a race of mortal gods thirsting for the blood of innocents. Sooner or later, the boundless reminded everyone of death.

Half a kilometer to the west a helicopter hovered over the river, its floodlight trained on a dozen men and women who flailed about waist deep in the muddy water. They tried to scatter and escape the light, but the helicopter simply rose a few meters, enlarging the circle of illumination until it caught them again. Two Border Patrol vans waited on the far side.

This was the pageantry of disappointed hope. It had a logic of its own, unfolding with a stateliness that seemed to lift it beyond the lives of those enacting it.

A photo flash fired three times in quick succession behind them.

"Marisa hung James out," Edith said. "She hung him out."

In the course of fifteen minutes the sky had grown fully dark.

"He was in it too," Andrew said.

Edith took his arm.

Nearing the checkpoint, they passed a rust-colored sedan that had been pulled over by customs agents who now shone their flashlights solemnly into its open trunk. One by one, three Mexican boys emerged and lay down prone on the pavement, hands behind their heads. Both parties in this exchange seemed to be following a protocol so familiar to them that their own participation was beside the point.

There were two lines at customs, one for U.S. citizens, the other for everyone else. Andrew went ahead of Edith, and when he cleared, she found herself face to face with the customs official, a crew-cut man in an attitude of jaded alert. He had just asked her a question.

She nodded and started through the turnstile, but the official stayed her with the flat of his hand.

"Of what country are you a citizen?"

Edith looked to Andrew in confusion.

"He wants you to say the actual words, Edie."

"Really?" she said. "That's what he wants?"

For a moment she dared not take her eyes from Andrew's, fearful that she had somehow misunderstood her situation.

In sleep, Kevin put his arms around her neck. She recalled that there was nothing at all, now, she had to fear from thresholds.

She turned back to face the man and tell him what he needed to know.